HARD TO RESIST

Every other man who had ever held her was erased from her memory. No one else had ever come close to Slade's strength and mastery—the very things she resented about him. But she knew in her soul that she had to have both. She couldn't help a shiver of physical regret when he dragged his mouth from hers.

"Mmm. You've got the magic—very sexy magic, Lisa. You put a spell on me."

"I wish," she said softly. If she could do that, Lisa wasn't sure whether she would want to make him disappear or keep him by her side forever. It was hard to resist kisses this good. He could easily seduce her right now—if not right here—and she wouldn't be able to stop.

He kissed her again and took his sweet time about it. *Damn him,* Lisa thought, when he finally stopped to take a breath. Slade was the one who possessed the magic, trapping her inside the charmed circle of his arms with such sensual skill that she didn't even want to struggle free.

from "Low Country Liar"

BOOK YOUR PLACE ON OUR WEBSITE AND MAKE THE READING CONNECTION!

We've created a customized website just for our very special readers, where you can get the inside scoop on everything that's going on with Zebra, Pinnacle and Kensington books.

When you come online, you'll have the exciting opportunity to:

- View covers of upcoming books
- Read sample chapters
- Learn about our future publishing schedule (listed by publication month *and author*)
- Find out when your favorite authors will be visiting a city near you
- Search for and order backlist books from our online catalog
- Check out author bios and background information
- Send e-mail to your favorite authors
- Meet the Kensington staff online
- Join us in weekly chats with authors, readers and other guests
- Get writing guidelines
- AND MUCH MORE!

**Visit our website at
http://www.kensingtonbooks.com**

JANET DAILEY

It Takes Two

ZEBRA BOOKS
KENSINGTON PUBLISHING CORP.
http://www.kensingtonbooks.com

ZEBRA BOOKS are published by

Kensington Publishing Corp.
850 Third Avenue
New York, NY 10022

All Kensington titles, imprints and distributed lines are available at special quantity discounts for bulk purchases for sales promotion, premiums, fund-raising, educational or institutional use.

Special book excerpts or customized printings can also be created to fit specific needs. For details, write or phone the office of the Kensington Special Sales Manager: Kensington Publishing Corp., 850 Third Avenue, New York, NY 10022. Attn. Special Sales Department. Phone: 1-800-221-2647.

Zebra and the Z logo Reg. U.S. Pat. & TM Off.

First Printing: July 2005
10 9 8 7 6 5 4 3 2 1

Printed in the United States of America

CONTENTS

NIGHT OF THE COTILLION

CHAPTER ONE

"Thanks for the ride, Tobe," said Amanda, bending down to peer in the car window, her red hair shining in the rays of the late afternoon sun.

"Be sure to have Brad call me tonight." He nodded as he revved the engine and backed up the car.

"Will do," she promised. "See you!"

With a wave of her hand, she watched him roar down the street and then she turned toward the house, smiling a little as she imagined the face her mother would make at the racket. No matter how many times her mother reprimanded Tobe for driving so carelessly, he still did it—mostly, Amanda thought, to annoy her mother, who treated him like one of her own sons.

Amanda was convinced that was the reason he spent so much of his time at their house, because he felt like part of the family. Tobe and her brother Brad had been inseparable friends ever since their first day of kindergarten.

The Petersons had made a lot of money developing land once used to raise cotton, amassing a family fortune exceeded only by the Colbys, of Colby Enterprises, but Tobe's supposedly superior status in the community didn't interest him one bit. All of the Bennetts, including Amanda, tended to forget who his family was. His clothes and car were more expensive than theirs, and that seemed to be the only difference.

She took the porch steps two at a time, swinging open the screen door of the large two-story house and letting it slam behind her. "Mom! I'm home!"

"Ssh!" Her mother appeared in the dining room archway. "Your grandfather is taking a nap."

"I was," came a grumpy voice, "until that young fool blasted out of the driveway."

"That was Tobe," Amanda announced unnecessarily. "He gave me a ride home. Don't let me forget—he wants Brad to call him tonight." She walked swiftly to the elderly man who appeared in the doorway, his broad shoulders stooped with the weight of his years. "Hello, Grandpa." She planted a kiss on his leathery cheek. "How are you today?"

"Ah, my hip is acting up on me again," he grumbled, but his eyes were twinkling as he looked at his granddaughter. "Must be going to have a change in the weather."

"There's lemonade in the refrigerator," her mother spoke up.

"Does anyone else want a glass?" Amanda called over her shoulder as she walked toward the kitchen.

"Not me." Her grandfather shook his head.

"I'll have one." Her mother followed her out to the kitchen. "How did it go today?"

"Hectic." Amanda sighed, removing two glasses from the cupboard and filling them from the refrigerator ice-maker. "For a while this afternoon I was almost wishing the term wasn't over and I was still taking finals."

"Please don't wish that on me." Her mother laughed, shaking her dark auburn head, which was just beginning to be streaked with gray. "With all three of your brothers and you in college, and Bonnie in high school, and all your final tests falling in the same week, I don't know if your dad and I could live through that again."

"It was pretty wild around here, wasn't it?" Amanda smiled, a tiny dimple appearing in each cheek. "All of us staying up too late and fighting over the leftovers."

"At least you each had your own computer. Remember when you used to share one? That was not fun."

Amanda nodded. "At least working at Oak Run let me pay for my own. And now I'm teaching three new girls the ropes."

"I'm proud of you, honey. Usually Mrs. Matthews insists on doing the training herself."

Amanda poured the lemonade. "I've been a guide there since I was seventeen. I know as much about that ol' plantation as she does. Besides, she's all wrapped up in the plans for the cotillion. Which was another reason things got out of hand today. She was there with the florist trying to decide which flowers should go where, etcetera."

"Talking about the cotillion," Mrs. Bennett said, "you should try on your dress. I basted it together this morning. We can see how it fits and get the hem. Leave your lemonade here," she added quickly as Amanda started to walk out of the kitchen with the glass in her hand. "Don't bring it into the sewing room. I don't want to spill anything on that taffeta."

"Are they having that dance at Oak Run?" her grandfather mumbled as they passed through the dining room on their way to the small room that Bernice Bennett used as a sewing room.

"They do every year, Grandpa," Amanda answered, exchanging a knowing look with her mother.

"Jefferson Davis would turn over in his grave if he knew," the old man declared angrily. "It's an outright crime to celebrate the birthday of a Confederate general in that damn Yankee's house!"

"It's a tradition," her mother replied soothingly. "And Oak Run belonged to a fine old Southern family long before Colonel Colby bought it."

"That makes no difference! A Yankee owns it now. They should find somewhere else to hold their cotillion."

"Oh, Grandpa," Amanda scolded teasingly, waving away his dislike of anyone born north of the Mason–Dixon Line. "If it weren't for Mrs. Matthews and the Colby money, there wouldn't be any cotillion. Try to forget who owns the plantation and just figure that Jeff Davis is too dead to care. The way you carry on sometimes about Yankees, a person would think you'd fought in the Civil War yourself."

"My great-grandpappy did," he answered testily.

"That was more than a hundred and forty years ago," Mrs. Bennett said.

"But not forgotten," said the old man. "Not here in Georgia, leastways. If they had, you wouldn't be having any cotillion to celebrate Jeff Davis's birthday," he retorted smugly.

Mrs. Bennett lifted her shoulders in an expressive shrug and Amanda smiled. There wasn't any reasoning with her grandfather. There was the North and the South, and if he had his way, never the twain would meet.

"Come on, Amanda," her mother gestured to her, "let's try that dress on."

Amanda followed her into the sewing room while her grandfather began whistling "Dixie" as loud as he could. "Stubborn old cuss," she said fondly under her breath, shutting the door with a faint click. Then she saw the gown on the dressmaker's dummy. "Mom, it's beautiful!"

"You'll have to put the hoops on so I can make sure it hangs right. I don't think it will matter if you do without the petticoats for now."

Eagerly Amanda stripped down to her underwear and stepped into the wide-hooped underskirt while her mother carefully removed the old-fashioned ball gown from the dummy and placed it over her daughter's head. She stood impatiently while her mother stuck a few pins in strategic places here and there. Then she dashed to the full-length mirror.

"You're a genius, Mom," Amanda vowed. But while she was admiring her reflection, Bernice Bennett was frowning as she took in excess material with a tuck or two.

"With six children to clothe and feed and send to college, I'd better know how to sew," she said. "I made every party dress, prom gown and Halloween costume you girls needed. Of course the boys didn't much care. One flannel shirt was the same as another to them and it wasn't as if I could sew jeans." She adjusted the shoulder straps, which had been designed to look like cap sleeves. "We couldn't afford to buy a gown like this."

"It's just plain gorgeous," Amanda answered fervently. "I look like a genuine Southern belle."

The material was a rich green that shimmered from emerald brilliance to a deeper forest shade where the many folds draped over the hoops to her small waist. The bodice artfully molded her breasts and set off her creamy skin and the red-gold of her hair.

"The neckline is a bit too low," her mother declared.

"No, it's not," Amanda protested, her liquid brown eyes dancing with mirth. "It's daring, that's all."

"Just don't lean forward too much," her mother said, laughing. The front screen door slammed. "Is that you, Brad?" Mrs. Bennett called, turning briefly away. "I'm in the sewing room."

"Is Amanda there?" her brother answered, his voice coming nearer. "Cheryl is with me."

"I'm in here, Cheryl," Amanda answered. "Trying on my gown for the cotillion."

A dark-haired girl opened the door and peered around it. "Are you decent?"

"Not according to Mom, but come on in," Amanda replied.

"Oh, Mrs. Bennett, you didn't make that, did you?" Cheryl exclaimed. "It's gorgeous! With that beautiful red hair of yours fixed back in ringlets, you'll look fantastic, Amanda! What a shame you don't have green eyes."

"Amanda wouldn't want to trade in her spaniel eyes," her brother teased. "She enjoys having men drown in those liquid pools of brown."

"I wish I could drown you, brother dear!"

"Hush, you two," their mother intervened. "And hold still, Amanda, so I can pin this neckline."

Amanda cast a look of pretend sorrow at Cheryl. "Mom thinks the neckline is too low."

"Oh, no, Mrs. Bennett, don't raise it," the dark-haired girl protested. "Those old gowns always had some cleavage showing."

"Well, this new gown is going to show a quarter-inch less," Amanda's mother said emphatically. "That's all I can add without ruining the line."

"I wish I didn't have a tan." Cheryl sighed. "I have white streaks where my straps were."

"I tried to pull them down but you wouldn't let me," said Brad.

"Ha, ha," said Cheryl. "You shouldn't talk like that in front of your mother."

"Believe it or not," Mrs. Bennett said with a patient sigh, "I am aware that many men, including my son, do try to remove as much clothing as possible from women from time to time."

"Try covering the white marks with makeup," Amanda said.

"It might look blotchy," Cheryl fretted. "I can't dance if I look blotchy."

"I'll keep my hands on your shoulders," Brad said.

Amanda and her mother exchanged an amused look. "All done," Mrs. Bennett announced. "Brad, why don't you and Cheryl run out to the kitchen while Amanda changes? There's lemonade in the refrigerator and cookies in the jar."

"Hurry, Mandy," Cheryl urged. "I just found out the most fantastic thing. I'm dying to—"

"I'll be right there."

"Careful," her mother admonished. "It's only tacked and basted."

Once the gown was safely off and on the dummy again, Amanda put on her jeans and top. "I love it, Mom. Maybe when Tobe sees me in that, it'll make up for the fact that his parents are making him go to the cotillion."

"I think it was sweet of him to ask you to go."

"Heaven knows, I've talked about it enough." Amanda grinned. "It's been my dream to go. Guess I can consider myself lucky that Tobe is between girlfriends right now."

"He certainly plays the field," her mother agreed with a wide smile. "You'd better hurry out to the kitchen before Cheryl forgets what it is that she's dying to tell you."

Amanda winked at her mother before hurrying out to the kitchen. Cheryl did tend to exaggerate and overreact, but they had always been close friends and had become even closer since Cheryl had started dating Brad. For all the comments everyone made about her talkativeness, Cheryl could keep a secret to her dying day, as she liked to say. And there were many secrets shared between them.

"Here I am," Amanda said, walking into the kitchen where Cheryl and Brad were sitting at the table. "What were you going to tell me?"

"Sit down, sit down." Cheryl motioned at the chair beside her, which Amanda took. "Well, you know that Colby Enterprises transferred their computer and data-processing operations to Atlanta last year, and their electronics plant here in Oak Springs will be completed in June—next month."

"Yep. But everybody knows that." Amanda gave the brunette an inquiring look. "Everybody knows everything in this little town, come to think of it."

"Here's something new—" Cheryl paused to ratchet up the suspense a little. "Rumor has it that Jarod Colby is moving to Georgia. And he's going to live in Oak Springs, at the Winter House."

"Are you sure?" Amanda's heart gave a funny little leap. She hoped that the fleeting twinge of excitement she felt didn't show.

"Positive." Cheryl made the motion of crossing her heart. "And I even heard that he resigned as CEO from that steel company in Pennsylvania. He's centralizing all his companies here in Georgia. And—are you ready for this?" Cheryl leaned closer. "He's going to be the official host at the cotillion this year!"

"Now I find that hard to believe," Amanda said dryly.

"Supposedly he's going to announce his decision to live here permanently."

"He might as well," Brad said with a cynical laugh. "He practically owns the whole town. I suppose when we're introduced to him at the dance, we'll be required to bow in his royal presence."

"Who's that?" old Mr. Bennett demanded as he limped into the kitchen to catch the last of Brad's statement.

"Jarod Colby, who else?" he replied.

"Why would you be introduced to that Yankee carpetbagger?"

"He's going to be at the cotillion," Cheryl explained, darting a sparkling glance at Amanda. "Isn't it exciting?"

"Humph!" her grandfather snorted. "If it was me meeting him, I'd spit in his eye."

"Considering the fact that Dad manages some of the Colby real-estate holdings, it's a good thing you don't meet him, Granddad," Brad chided.

"And if I was your dad, I'd find me a better job and not work for no Yankee." The old man took a handful of cookies from the jar and ambled out.

"The South will rise again," Brad murmured, watching him go. "So long as Grandpa has enough chocolate-chip cookies." He went to the jar and scrabbled through the remaining cookies—looking for the biggest one, Amanda knew.

"Just think, Amanda," said Cheryl, lowering her voice to a whisper, "you're finally going to get to meet him!"

Once Amanda would have been thrilled by that idea, but that was a long time ago.

"No biggie," she said.

Cheryl drew in a breath before a knowing smile appeared on her face. "You don't mean that."

"Actually, I do," Amanda replied.

Brad returned his attention to them. "What are you two talking about?"

"We're talking about the dance," Cheryl said quickly. "Trying to decide what jewelry Mandy should wear with her gown."

"A diamond and emerald choker would do nicely," Amanda said. "Of course, I don't happen to have a million dollars to buy one."

"Oh, I know you have something nice," Cheryl said. Amanda knew her friend wanted to get her alone. "Let's go upstairs to your room and look through your jewelry box. Brad, you stay here and keep an eye on those cookies."

"Yes, ma'am," Brad said with his mouth full.

"Now, tell the truth, Amanda," Cheryl said as they went up the stairs to the second floor where the bedrooms were. "Aren't you excited about meeting Jarod Colby?"

"No, I'm not. I haven't given that man a thought in over three years. He doesn't mean anything to me anymore." Amanda walked into her room and crossed over to sit on the blue gingham bedspread.

"I know that isn't true. Nobody ever forgets her first love, especially if he got away. You end up comparing every man you meet with him. Even if you marry someone else, you'd always wonder what it would be like with that one special man."

"And how did you get to be such an authority?" Amanda teased, smoothing back her shoulder-length hair.

"It's common sense."

"Don't let Brad hear you talking that way!"

"Oh, Amanda, you of all people should know I've had a crush on your brother for years." Cheryl laughed. "I imagine I'm speaking partly from experience."

"You can hardly compare Brad with Jarod Colby," Amanda replied dryly.

"Not as individuals," Cheryl agreed. "But mark my words, no one ever gets over her first love."

"Cheryl!" Mrs. Bennett's voice called from downstairs. "Your mother's on the phone. She wants to know if you put the meat loaf in the oven. Says she's leaving work in about an hour."

"Tell her I'm on my way home right now!" Cheryl called, walking to the door.

Amanda grinned at her. "I'm not sure I want to get married anyway."

"Why ever not?" Her friend gave her a wide-eyed look.

"You start with true love and stars in your eyes, and you end up with meat loaf."

"Very funny. See you later, Mandy."

"Oh, do me a favor. Tell Brad that Tobe wants him to call tonight—I plumb forgot to mention it."

"Do you know"—Cheryl paused in the doorway—"my main competition for Brad's attention is that Tobe Peterson. I could deal with another girl."

"I wouldn't worry about it." Amanda laughed.

But her smile faded when Cheryl disappeared from sight. Amanda walked over to the small dressing table, skirted with fabric to match her bedspread. Before it was a small bench covered in blue. Sitting on it, she stared into the oval mirror.

There was no dreamy-eyed girl staring back. She was twenty-one. An adult, supposedly. Not that anyone took that concept very seriously where she was concerned, especially since she still lived with her parents. Amanda wondered if people ever really finished growing up, and when you knew. No doubt the cutoff date was different for men and women.

According to her mother, who had a wry sense of humor and tended to speak her mind whenever and however she felt like it, a lot of men never grew up at all.

Maybe for women it was when they stopped thinking every handsome man was really Prince Charming. Amanda smiled ruefully. In that case, she officially qualified as a grown-up.

She cast her mind back to the day six years ago when she had been traipsing through the piney woods not far from the Bennett home. That was when she had seen Jarod Colby for the first time. She'd known there were actual Colbys, of course, but the family hadn't seemed really real. Just impossibly rich and from somewhere else.

Jarod Colby had cantered his horse across the meadow, passing not more than ten feet from where Amanda had stood in the shadow of the trees. The Colby insignia had been embroidered on the saddle blanket or she might never have connected the dark rider with his family. He'd ridden past without seeing her.

Although she had watched him until he disappeared, she'd only caught a glimpse of his face. Thick black hair caught the sunlight as it fell at a rakish angle over his tanned forehead. His profile was pretty much perfect: straight nose, strong cheekbones and chin. Dressed all in black, too.

How romantic, she thought now. And how young she had been, and how easily impressed.

Amanda remembered hanging around that spot in the woods for almost three hours, hoping to see him again. It became imperative that she find out who he was. The only one who knew anything about the Colby company was her father. He'd worked in their cotton mill before he and her mother were married, before it shut down and cotton production was outsourced abroad; and he'd worked for the Colbys ever since, mostly in their real-estate holdings.

Too shy to reveal then the true reason she'd wanted to find out about the man on the horse, she'd asked once she was home on the pretext that the horse had been beautiful.

"That must have been Jarod Colby, the son," her father had answered. "He's the only one that rides. Waste of money to maintain the stable and those horses just for him, but it's none of my business."

"The Colbys have money to burn," her mother had said. "Someone at church mentioned that they were going to Gstaad after Christmas."

"What's a Gstaad?" Amanda asked.

"A ski resort in Switzerland, honey. Very swanky."

"I met young Colby the other day." Her father had been puffing on his pipe and paused to tamp down the tobacco. Amanda had waited breathlessly for him to continue, eager to hear anything about the man she'd seen. "He stopped in at the office of Colby Holdings. Struck me as being pretty sharp."

"How old is he?" Amanda had murmured.

"Must be around twenty-six."

Her mother had changed the subject to something more everyday than a sighting of an actual Colby, and life had gone on.

With one important exception: Amanda knew she'd fallen in love. The spot where she'd first seen him had become somehow special, and she revisited it on the sly more than once.

It had been a typical teenage obsession with an unattainable man, she realized now—but she hadn't realized it then. The times she saw him had been very few and always at a distance. His parents had been killed in a plane crash and his visits to Georgia became less and less frequent.

One year went by, then two. The fantasies and
dreams dimmed somewhat, but they were always
there in the background. Amanda hung out with
her friends, even dated a few guys, but no one
seemed as handsome, sexy, and above all, as tempt-
ingly out of reach as Jarod Colby.

In her silly teenaged way, she'd fantasized about
him much too much, and confided in Cheryl, who
adored anything in the least romantic. Amanda's
daydreams usually began with an oh-so-casual instant message—*hey, Jarod, just thinking about u*—and
ended with engraved invitations being sent for
their wedding, the wedding of the year in Oak
Springs.

But she'd never dared to contact him, of course.
When she turned seventeen, she'd decided to get
a job as a tour guide to the plantation home owned
by the Colbys—Oak Run. She'd cherished a secret
hope of meeting him there, even though she knew
perfectly well that the Colbys hadn't lived in Oak
Run for more than thirty years.

A rambling, ranch-style home had been built
some distance from the plantation. It was called
the Winter House by the locals, since that was the
only time the Colbys were there.

Mrs. Matthews, who was Jarod's aunt, had asked
Amanda to pick up an order of brochures that the
printer had had delivered to the Winter House by
mistake. No sooner had she parked the car in the
driveway than Jarod Colby came striding out. Her
heart had raced.

This was her big moment—or so she had thought
as she'd stepped out of the car.

"What are you doing here? Don't you know this
is private property?" His tone had been distinctly
unfriendly. He'd scowled. Even glared. She'd stood
frozen to the spot, without saying a word.

Not even when she was able to speak and could explain that she had a legitimate reason for being there did his attitude change. By the time she had received the stupid brochures and left, she was sick to her stomach.

Jarod Colby in the flesh turned out to be nothing like the Jarod Colby of her dreams. So much for Prince Charming.

The memory still stung.

Blinking out of her reverie, Amanda turned from the mirror. When Cheryl had mentioned his name, it suddenly brought back a lot of her hurt feelings—and a little of the thrill of having a secret crush on Jarod Colby.

She reminded herself of how arrogant he had been. No doubt he hadn't changed a bit. As her mother would say, no man was worth that much aggravation. Maybe, per her grandfather's recommendation, she would meet him at the cotillion and spit in his eye. Amanda chuckled at the thought of Jarod's outraged reaction if she did, and suddenly felt a whole lot better.

CHAPTER TWO

A set of knuckles rapped impatiently against her bedroom door. "Amanda, will you hurry up?" Brad asked. "You're holding up everything."

"She'll be there in just a minute," her mother answered for her. "Now, hold still, Amanda, so I can fix your hair."

Amanda obeyed, her brown eyes dancing with excitement as she watched her mother insert the rhinestone-studded hairpin into her hair. Red-gold ringlets tickled the back of her neck while shimmering waves framed her face. Her long, gold-tipped lashes hid the faint shadow of green on her eyelids, and her lips were glossed with a subtle pink.

"I'm so nervous," Amanda confided, slipping on the long, pale green gloves her mother handed her. "I feel like I'm going to my first dance."

"It's the social event of the year. You'll be rubbing elbows with the elite," Mrs. Bennett said, nodding. She stepped back to look at her daughter, a gleam of love in her eyes. "And they'll all be staring at you, saying, 'Who is that beautiful redhead in green?' "

"You're doing wonders for my ego," Amanda said. "I'd better go down." She smoothed the sleek taffeta skirt that billowed out from her waist. "If Tobe waits much longer, he's liable to back out and not take me at all."

The hoopskirt gave the effect that Amanda was gliding down the stairs and across the living room where her brother and Cheryl and Tobe were waiting.

"You're a little overdressed for a pizza parlor," Tobe teased, producing a corsage that he'd been holding behind his back.

"After all the work I put into that gown, Tobias Peterson, you'd better not take her anywhere except to Oak Run!" her mother said, joining them all in the living room.

"If we went anywhere in these clothes, they'd put us in the loony bin." Tobe glanced at Amanda and smiled. "You look gorgeous. I might not mind being locked up with you."

"Look on the bright side, Tobe," Brad spoke up. "Be grateful it's Jeff Davis's birthday we're celebrating and not George Washington's. The men wore wigs in his day."

"Both of you boys look very elegant in those suits," Mrs. Bennett said.

"I don't know why they couldn't just have a dance," Tobe grumbled, but everyone knew he was teasing. "Leave it to old lady Matthews to come up with the idea of antebellum costumes!"

"I think it's fun," Cheryl declared. "Don't you, Amanda?"

"I sure do feel feminine," Amanda agreed. "This great big skirt makes my waist look tiny." She pirouetted and the hoopskirt swayed a little from side to side.

"How do you get through doors?" Tobe asked.

"Sideways," her mother said.

Amanda took the corsage from Tobe and pinned it to the snugly fitted waistband of her gown. The pale yellow petals of the orchid were perfectly set off by the vivid green of the gown.

"I should have borrowed the truck," said Tobe.

"The truck? Whatever for?" Cheryl asked, tilting her head curiously.

"I don't know if you girls will fit in my car," he replied. "Those skirts will take up the whole seat."

"I think we can manage." Amanda grinned.

"I keep worrying that I'm going to forget about these hoops, sit down, and have the skirt fly up in my face," Cheryl murmured. "You're used to it, Amanda, having to wear these gowns all the time at Oak Run."

"That's why they don't have too many chairs at the cotillion, except for the older ladies," Amanda said. "They figure that girls who mostly wear jeans won't adjust their hoops correctly when they sit down."

"Do you mean we have to stand all night?" Brad moaned.

"When you aren't dancing with me," Cheryl said pertly.

"All they do is waltz," he complained, then smiled at the pout on Cheryl's face. "That won't be so bad, I guess."

Mollified, Cheryl turned a beaming smile on Tobe. "I don't know if I ever thanked you for arranging things so Brad and I could go to the cotillion, too."

"You didn't think I was going to go and be bored by myself, did you?" He chuckled, a mischievous look in his blue eyes.

"If you stand there talking much longer,"

Amanda's father declared, walking into the living room with his pipe and a newspaper in his hand, tall and lanky like all his sons, "you're going to miss the dance altogether. You're already late."

"Nobody arrives on time, Mr. Bennett," Cheryl said politely.

"Here, Amanda, take this with you. It might be a little cool tonight." Her mother handed her a three-cornered shawl made of the same material as her gown.

"Do you suppose we're late enough now?" Brad teased.

"The sooner we go, the sooner we can leave," Tobe added, winking at Mrs. Bennett, who wore an expression of pseudo-exasperation.

There was a chorus of good-byes mingled with "enjoy yourselves" as the two couples made their way out of the house to Tobe's car. Her parents waved from the porch, standing the way Amanda always thought of them, with one of her father's long arms draped over the shoulder of his slightly plump wife. They were more than husband and wife. They were friends and it was impossible to think of one without the other.

When they arrived at Oak Run, the brick mansion was ablaze with lights shining from every window. Spotlights had been discreetly placed among the ancient oaks and hidden in bushes edging the portico. Their glow illuminated the six towering white columns, each five feet in diameter, that graced the front entrance.

"I feel like a pixie in grown-up clothes next to you," Cheryl said in a nervous whisper as she and Amanda mounted the portico steps ahead of Tobe and Brad. "I should have worn a wig." Her hand self-consciously touched the short brunette curls that softened her angular face.

"You look great," Amanda insisted, glancing at the pink gown that emphasized Cheryl's petite femininity.

"Remember that time we hid in the bushes to peep through the windows at the cotillion?" she whispered.

"And nearly got caught," Amanda reminded her.

The gleaming, white-enameled double doors swung open into the main hall, three times the size of the Bennetts' living room. A gracious staircase dominated the hall, accented by a brass and crystal chandelier hanging above the center landing. Amanda noticed that the scrolled antique table had been removed from the hall, replaced by one less valuable, but the portrait of Colonel Colby still hung above it. Her grandfather would be outraged if he knew a painting of a Yankee officer was displayed in this antebellum home.

A gentle melody from a string quartet floated through the open doors on the right where the ballroom was located. After the girls had passed their shawls to one of the several uniformed attendants, the four moved toward the sound of the music. Cheryl still walked beside Amanda, her expression showing the bubbling eagerness that consumed her. Amanda, too, felt a rush of excitement as they approached the ballroom.

They reached the doors to enter at the same moment as two men were going out, and a wave of giddiness washed over Amanda as she stared into Jarod Colby's face. All four stopped, including Tobe and Brad, who were walking behind the girls. A purely masculine energy radiated from the man in front of Amanda. His features were more strongly drawn now, without the softness of youth, though his hair was still as ebony black as his eyes. She wished he didn't look so damned . . . arrogant. There was no other word for it.

As her mind instantaneously registered all this, Amanda was aware of his gaze on her, sweeping over her gown and the nipped waistline, lingering for seconds on the shadowy hollow between her breasts that the low-cut gown revealed. Then his eyes moved to her face, again in obvious appraisal.

The boldness of his gaze made her feel stripped and naked. In these old-fashioned costumes, he seemed to be playing the part of a rich rogue and she, a blushing belle. Amanda was suddenly conscious of a pain in her left arm. It took her a moment to realize that Cheryl was gripping it too tightly.

"Ladies." Jarod Colby's low-pitched voice was accompanied by an imperious nod while he and the man with him, whom Amanda hadn't even looked at, moved aside to allow them to enter.

Her feet automatically carried her into the ballroom, although she wasn't quite aware of ordering them to do so. Through sheer force of will she calmed the wild beating of her foolish heart and resisted the impulse to turn and see if Jarod was watching her.

"Did you see the way he looked at you?" Cheryl whispered. "I could have been King Kong for all the notice he took of me. I knew something like this was going to happen! I just knew it!"

"Nothing happened," Amanda said firmly, more to convince herself than her friend. "In five minutes he won't even remember he saw me."

"Honey, you were imprinted in his mind with indelible ink," Cheryl declared with a laugh.

At that moment, Tobe moved forward to

Amanda's side, preventing her from commenting on Cheryl's last remark. "You were right—there isn't an empty chair anywhere."

A glance around the room with its polished oak woodwork and cream-yellow walls showed that the few chairs scattered around the edge had been commandeered by the older guests.

To prevent her gaze from straying toward the door they'd entered by, Amanda looked at the French doors leading into the garden. The gold damask curtains were drawn back and flickering torchlight filtered through the white sheers on the doors. Only a dozen couples were gliding over the highly polished floor, waltzing to the strains of the inevitable "Blue Danube." All the interior light came from two enormous crystal chandeliers, one at each end of the room.

A waiter approached, carrying a tray of drinks. Cheryl touched Amanda's arm and leaned forward. "Are you supposed to drink with gloves on?" she murmured self-consciously.

"I think eating is the only thing that's taboo with gloves," Amanda replied.

"I'm so afraid I'm going to do some terribly gauche thing," Cheryl declared, pressing a hand against her stomach.

Amanda took two drinks from the tray and handed one to Cheryl. "Drink this," she ordered. "It might settle your nerves."

The truth was she felt in need of it herself. She had truly not believed that seeing Jarod Colby again would affect her very much, but her teenaged self seemed to be suddenly in charge at the moment.

Taking a sip of her drink, Amanda ordered her mind to concentrate on the conversation between her brother and Tobe. Whether it was due to the strength of her determination not to allow her thoughts to dwell on Jarod Colby, or the fact she didn't see him, nearly an hour later Amanda found she was enjoying herself, laughing and joking with her friends and meeting acquaintances of Tobe's family.

An attorney named Carl Grierson who had just joined them said to Tobe, "I haven't seen you dancing with this beautiful young lady tonight."

A smile quirked one corner of Tobe's mouth. "This isn't music I like to dance to, Carl. These damn hoopskirts don't allow a man to enjoy the advantages of dancing slowly with a girl."

Actually, Tobe had danced with Amanda once with an expertise that surprised her. Yet he had seemed embarrassed, as if he would rather clomp around like her brother did, in a stilted one-two-three, one-two-three rhythm.

"With a lady this pretty"—the attorney winked at her—"it's an honor just to be her partner. May I claim this dance?"

A nod from Tobe, and Amanda accepted the invitation with a curtsy. A faint smile of pleasure dimpled her cheeks as her partner led her to the dance floor. She enjoyed dancing to any kind of music, but the swishing material of her gown was made for the stately melodies of the past.

The middle-aged attorney guided her sedately around the floor. The height of her heels put her nearly eye level with him, but at five feet five in stockinged feet, she was hardly short.

"You sure do look lovely tonight," he commented. "And you dance well." His head dipped slightly as he made a turn to promenade position, enabling her to see the reason his hair was combed forward—to hide a receding hairline.

"You make it easy for me," Amanda replied, feeling suddenly very much like a Southern belle, artfully turning compliments back on the giver.

"If you had a dance card and I were ten years younger, I'd claim every dance with you. Unfortunately my wife might have some objections to that." He smiled, his pale blue eyes crinkling at the corners.

She tipped her head back and laughed as they turned—and found herself staring over the attorney's shoulder into the dark eyes of Jarod Colby. He was standing on the sidelines, chatting with a group of men, but his gaze was on her, with that same look of analytical appraisal as before. Nothing on his face revealed that he liked what he saw. There was no provocative gleam or message of appreciation in his eyes. Yet the very fact that he was watching her caused her heart to beat faster.

Forcing herself to look away, Amanda returned her attention to her partner. "You're very good for a girl's ego," she said flirtatiously.

"Believe me, it isn't difficult to compliment you. You look like my mental picture of Scarlett O'Hara. If she'd had red hair, of course."

"Well, thank you."

"Don't guess I look much like Rhett Butler." He smiled wryly. "But then they're fictional characters."

"Not to a lot of Southerners, they're not."

Carl Grierson laughed. "I know what you mean. So, do you live around here?"

The rest of the dance was occupied with questions and answers about Amanda's family. Her gaze didn't stray to Jarod Colby, although she felt sure he was watching her. There was a feeling of exultation in her heart that she couldn't ignore, no matter how much she tried to convince herself that his apparent interest in her didn't mean a thing.

But when Carl returned her to Tobe with a laughing comment about his wife's supposed jealousy, Amanda found it impossible to forget Jarod's presence in the room. Just because he had been rude to her once—and that had been six whole years ago—didn't mean she ought to condemn him forever.

Still, she couldn't exactly throw herself at him. Amanda contented herself with discussing the other women's dresses with Cheryl, until her friend stifled a gasp. "He's coming this way!" Her voice lowered to a squeaking whisper of excitement.

Amanda didn't need to turn around to find out who Cheryl meant. Without wasting a guess, she knew it would be Jarod Colby. She took a deep breath that didn't do much to calm her, considering that the nipped-in waist of her ball gown wasn't exactly made for breathing. She noted his unhurried approach and envied his confidence. He nodded and spoke to other guests while he made his way to their group.

When he was only two steps away from them, Amanda allowed herself a longer look at him. But his eyes lighted on Tobe, ignoring the two girls completely, much to her chagrin.

Very smoothly, he extended a hand to Tobe. "Jarod Colby," he introduced himself. "You're John Peterson's son, aren't you?"

"Yes. Tobe Peterson," Tobe supplied. Then he turned to Brad, who was standing beside him. "This is my friend, Brad Bennett. His girl, Cheryl Weston. His sister and my date, Amanda Bennett."

She had to admire the ease with which Tobe made the introductions while she watched Jarod Colby shake hands with her brother, nodding politely and with equal interest to her and Cheryl in turn. She was too conscious of Jarod standing between her and Tobe to pay attention to the polite small talk they were exchanging. Her senses were dominated by his potent presence and his rugged handsomeness.

Jarod turned to her and she looked up into his compelling dark eyes with a slight start. "May I have this dance, Amanda? With your escort's permission, of course." His tone implied that he expected no opposition from her or Tobe.

Tobe simply nodded, a curious smile on his face when he looked at Amanda.

Just on principle, she ought to refuse, she thought—then chided herself silently for dwelling on the imagined hurt of the past. After all, he was only asking her to dance, just as she heard the bandleader announce that it would be a "change partners" dance. She wondered if Jarod had known that when he asked her and decided that he had.

"I would be delighted, Mr. Colby," she answered coolly, offering him her hand.

She felt his gaze move lazily over her, and blushed. There was an amused gleam in his eyes when he brought her into his arms and moved with her to the dance floor. For lingering seconds he held her eyes with the compelling blackness of his own before they took their first steps together in time to the music. The firm pressure of his hand on her back left her in no doubt as to who was leading whom.

"Amanda . . . I like that name," he mused. "Sounds soft and gentle, but with a hint of spirit. Very traditional. And very Southern."

"That's true," Amanda replied with a nod, prickling a little as she wondered if she had heard a hint of mockery in his voice. "And you Yankees always seem to have such hard, uncompromising names, like Jarod."

"The way you drawl, it doesn't sound hard at all." The lines deepened around his mouth but without humor, and she knew he hadn't missed the edge in her tone. "Do you live here in Oak Springs?"

"All my life," she answered, gazing over his shoulder in waltz position, but not without noticing the expensive material of his black suit and the silver gray waistcoat and fine linen shirt—and the muscular chest beneath.

"Strange that we've never met."

"Oh, but we have." Her lips tightened just a little.

"When was that?" His eyes searched her face as though seeking something that would remind him of that forgotten occasion.

"About four or five years ago, when I first came to work here at Oak Run," she answered, discovering a candor she didn't know she possessed. "Your aunt sent me to the Winter House to fetch some tourist brochures that had been delivered there by mistake. You ordered me off the property."

"I'm ashamed to say I don't remember meeting you." But he didn't look ashamed and made no effort to apologize for his actions. "Did you get your brochures?"

"Yes, after you'd stopped insulting me long enough to hear my explanation for why I was there."

His expression was guarded and thoughtful as he met the slightly defiant look in her eyes. "And you still have a bad opinion of me."

"Yes." Her answer was simple and direct.

"Then I'll have to do something about that."

The pressure of his hand against the back of her waist increased as he whirled her into a fast series of spins while keeping to the gliding tempo of the melody. Feeling a little giddy, Amanda noticed the dancers separating and seeking new partners, and realized the signal must have been given.

"We're supposed to change partners now," she informed him.

He shot her an unreadable look. "One of the advantages of being Jarod Colby of Colby Enterprises is doing what I want to do."

"Oh, really?" she began, annoyed by his tone and noticing the interested glances from others as they still stood close together. He had not released her from the circle of his arms.

"I thought you wanted to dance with me," Jarod chided.

"I do." Then she wished she hadn't replied so quickly.

"Everyone is watching us. Just ignore them," he murmured. He made another cool appraisal of her appearance and smiled in a devilish way. "There are quite a few men who haven't been able to take their eyes off you all evening. That green gown and your red hair are a striking combination. And your face and your figure—oh, sorry. Am I embarrassing you?"

"Not at all," Amanda whispered, trying to sound nonchalant, as if she were used to male attention at this level of intensity. "But people are looking at me now because I'm dancing with you. We're supposed to—"

"I don't care what I'm supposed to do," he interrupted smoothly. "And I'm not going to let go of you. Not just yet. I usually get what I want, Amanda."

"Is that a fact?" She blurted out the rhetorical question before she could think. But being a Southern belle didn't mean she had to put up with Yankee obnoxiousness.

He grinned. "Aren't you going to ask me what I want?" His deep, husky voice vibrated over her.

"Oh, let me guess," she tried to force a lightness into her tone, "you want me to change my mind about you—that's one thing."

There was another signal to change partners, which Jarod also ignored. "Won't be too difficult."

It rankled her that he was so sure of himself. "Oh, no?" Amanda challenged him, raising one eyebrow. She caught a glimpse of herself doing it in a wall mirror as they revolved in front of it. Wonder of wonders, she did look a tad like Scarlett O'Hara.

"You mean my irresistible charm isn't working yet? You sure? You're still dancing with me."

Was he mocking himself or her? It was hard to tell. "You haven't let me go," she retorted. "And you just about ordered me to dance with you in the first place. Kind of like you were issuing a royal summons."

The amused look in his eyes told her that he didn't believe one word she was saying. "I believe it was a case of you knowing that I was attracted to you—and wanting a chance to score off on me for that incident a long time ago."

Attracted to you. Holy hell. There was no longer any reason to speculate about why he was dancing with her. In spite of all her efforts to remain poised, inside Amanda was quivering like a schoolgirl. Her knees went wobbly, and it was with relief that she heard the last notes of the dance fading away. She needed to sit down.

When he bowed slightly to her, looking more than ever like a rogue, she only nodded and forgot to curtsy. He took her elbow, gently guiding her off the dance floor. She looked at the side of the room where Cheryl, Brad, and Tobe had been standing, only to see that they weren't there.

"Would you like some punch?" Jarod asked.

He had brought her to the buffet table, where an immense, undoubtedly old punch bowl held a shimmering red liquid, surrounded by ornate cut-glass cups. Platters of artistically prepared hors d'oeuvres had been set to either side.

"Yes, please," said Amanda, glancing around the ballroom for some sign of her friends.

In what seemed like mere seconds he was holding out a cup to her, his gaze noting her search of the room. She took the cup from him and held it nervously in both hands.

"How about something to eat?"

"No," Amanda refused politely, looking at the tempting morsels on the platters and then at her gloved hands.

"I forgot," Jarod murmured. "Not proper to eat with gloves on, is it? We can remedy that." She watched him curiously as he eyed the trays, wondering if she should remove her gloves. "This pâté looks very tasty," he said. He picked up a bite-sized piece *en croute* and turned to Amanda. "Open wide."

Self-consciously she drew back, realizing that he intended to pop it in her mouth and noticing the glitter in his obsidian eyes. She had the feeling he would hold it in front of her mouth until she gave in.

He looked into her eyes with a very sexy smile on his lips. Almost unconsciously she opened hers—and he popped the tidbit in. His fingers brushed her lips when he did and the sensation of his touch remained, the incredibly intimate contact making her tingle all over.

"Your friends seem to have deserted you," Jarod murmured after Amanda had managed to swallow the hors d'oeuvre.

"I don't know where they could've gone," she said anxiously, looking this way and that.

"Maybe they stepped out onto the veranda for a breath of fresh air," he suggested.

"Yes, they may have."

"Shall we go look for them?"

CHAPTER THREE

Amanda hesitated, feeling ridiculously awkward and out of her depth. She felt uncomfortable standing beside Jarod in a room full of people, and to be alone with him on the veranda would make her even more nervous. But she managed to give the appearance of calm—or so she hoped.

There were several knowing looks cast their way as she and Jarod walked through the French doors onto the veranda outside. Very few people were outdoors, mostly the diehards who had come out for a cigarette. Amanda was conscious of Jarod waving away the secondhand smoke while she tried to peer through the shadows cast by the flickering torchlights.

"Are you going to college or working?" Jarod was the first to break the silence. He led her without touching her along the darkened path into the garden walk extending out from the veranda.

"Both," she answered, catching a glimpse of three people standing beneath an oak tree and holding her breath, only to discover that all three were men. "This fall will be the start of my last year in college."

"What are you studying?"

"English Lit. Minor in Journalism."

"Where are you working?"

"Here at Oak Run. I'm still a tour guide," she answered with an expressive lift of her shoulders.

"No wonder you look so natural in that gown. You wear them all the time." His steps ceased. "I haven't been paying enough attention to this place, obviously. I didn't realize the guides were so gorgeous."

"I'm not the only one—" she said and stopped. She found herself thinking of the other guides at Oak Run and wondering which ones might appeal to Jarod. She felt a twinge of irrational jealousy.

"You're the only one that interests me at the moment." He looked down at her, his superior height putting her at a disadvantage. The way his gaze moved over her face and shoulders made her all too aware that she and Jarod were relatively alone.

"Thank you," she breathed, unable to think of a comeback. She made a half turn to escape his scrutiny.

The night was languid and still, with a roof of stars above the thick foliage of the giant oaks. Distantly the strains of another waltz floated on the night air, while crickets chirped loudly in competition.

All of a sudden, his fingers brushed her neck . . . and blazed a trail to her shoulders. "Your skin is so creamy." It was more of a comment than a compliment, though his boldness in touching her almost took her breath away. Still, she didn't tell him to stop.

It occurred to her that he'd undoubtedly had too much of the punch, though it hadn't been all that strong. Maybe he had added a shot of moonshine just to give the sweet mixture some kick. No, she thought. That wasn't something rich men drank. Probably designer vodka.

Amanda turned her back to him, wanting and not wanting him to touch her, simultaneously. "Did you know crickets chirp until they ... fi ... find their mate?" What began as a bright attempt to change the conversation ended in a breathless whisper as his fingers moved down her shoulder, following the neckline of her dress over the swell of her breasts to the opposite shoulder.

"No, I didn't know that," Jarod remarked dryly. His eyes, dark and unreadable, held hers, making her look at him while his fingers caressed the hollow of her throat. "I want to take you home." The significance of his statement jolted through her.

"That's impossible," she replied without any conviction in her voice.

"Nothing is impossible." A smile played over his lips.

"I always make it a rule to leave a party with the man who brought me," Amanda said more positively.

"Rules are made to be broken." His gaze strayed to her mouth, and lingered there.

"Would you feel the same way if you'd been the one to bring me?" she asked, resisting the almost overwhelming temptation to agree.

He gave her a humorless smile. "If you were my date, I wouldn't have brought you to this charade. I would've taken you to a place where we could be alone."

"Well, that doesn't happen to be the case, since I did come here with Tobe," Amanda stated. "And

I'm going to leave with him. As a matter of fact"—
she swallowed, fighting the chill that shivered over
her skin as his hand fell back to his side— "he
must be wondering where I've gone."

"Maybe by now he's back inside," Jarod suggested.

He didn't look at all disappointed that he hadn't
been able to change her mind. Ironically, Amanda
was the one who felt disappointed that he hadn't
persisted, but she successfully hid it as they re-
traced their steps through the garden and into the
ballroom. Brad, Cheryl, and Tobe were waiting just
inside, and with a nod Jarod left her with them.

Amanda was convinced that she had seen the
last of Jarod Colby. The instant he left her, she saw
him walk over to an attractive blonde and escort
her onto the dance floor. She scolded herself for
feeling so let down. He had only been flirting with
her, more than likely expecting her to fall at his
feet because he deigned to pay attention to her.
But those moments she had been with him, sub-
jected to his unmistakable magnetism, had left a
strong impression.

Unwillingly she had to admit that it hurt to
watch him dancing with another woman, knowing
he was probably saying the same things to his new
partner. When Tobe asked Amanda to dance, she
accepted eagerly, determined to show Jarod Colby
that his indifference didn't bother her at all.

"What did you think of the local lord?" Tobe
asked.

"Kinda arrogant," she answered with a shrug,
keeping her brittle smile in place.

"He knows what he wants and he usually gets it.
Has he decided that he wants you?"

"I'm a little country girl. I think his taste runs
more to sophisticated blondes." Amanda knew Tobe

had seen Jarod with his new partner and her pride insisted that she be the first one to comment on it. "I expect he's a tyrant to work for."

"Well, you oughta know. You and your daddy work for him—indirectly, at least," Tobe reminded her. "At least he's more interested in making money than spending it, from what I hear."

Amanda didn't want to hear about the supposedly good qualities of Jarod Colby. Right now she needed to banish him from her mind, if that was possible. She was not going to allow herself to fantasize about him like she was still fifteen.

"When are your parents coming back?" she asked, changing the subject.

"Who cares?" he said, scowling.

"Tobe, you don't really feel that way," she scolded, the way her mother always did.

He sighed heavily. "I don't think any of you Bennetts realize how lucky you are. Your parents are always there when you need them. I remember when my dog was killed by a car on the highway. I was about nine at the time and I ran crying home to my father. He didn't say much at all, besides that I could always buy another damned dog just like it."

"That's awful, Tobe," Amanda said softly.

"It was your dad who went out there with me and got the body," Tobe went on. "He was the one who built the box and dug the hole so we could bury him." He gave a hard shake of his head. "If I had my way, I'd never go home again. I think it's your mother who makes me. The Bennetts are my family."

"We feel that way, too," Amanda murmured, thinking that Tobe Peterson fit the definition of a poor rich kid.

But Tobe wasn't one to feel sorry for himself for

long. "Let's change the subject," he said cheerfully enough.

At that moment a hand tapped Tobe on the shoulder and a voice said, "Shall we change partners?"

Both Tobe and Amanda glanced in surprise at the couple dancing beside them. It was Jarod and the blonde. Amanda's feet wouldn't move and Tobe interpreted her stopping as agreement. Not until Jarod's arm circled her waist did her heart start beating again. Her brown eyes searched the unfathomable expression on his face.

"Did you think you'd seen the last of me?" Jarod said softly.

His astute perception brought a rush of color to her cheeks. Amanda glanced at the sexy blonde now flirting openly with Tobe.

"She's really pretty," she murmured.

"I believe your date thinks so," Jarod replied complacently. "Lots of men think my cousin is pretty hot."

"Your cousin?" she repeated, casting a startled glance at his face. The amusement she saw there told her he had guessed that she hadn't known the girl.

"Judith will keep him occupied for the rest of the evening," he said, "and that should eliminate your objections to my taking you home."

"No." There was an infinitesimal shake of her head. "No, I won't go home with you."

His fingers tightened around her gloved hand. "You sure?" he asked. "You said before that I couldn't take you home because of your date. He's out of the picture now."

"How can you be so sure?" Amanda protested.

"Because—there's no really polite way to put this—Judith likes to have fun. And I can tell she thinks Tobe is a whole lot of fun." His gaze swept over Amanda's face. "Do you want me to take you home or not? Just say yes or no."

A strange feeling constricted her breathing, It would be so easy to say yes, to be swept along by the magnetism that surrounded him. Yet Amanda was just as conscious that he was treating her with the same arrogance he'd shown years ago when he'd ordered her off his property.

She raised her chin slightly. "The answer is no."

He arched a dark brow momentarily, reflecting his surprise at her answer. Amanda guessed it was rare that he didn't get his way, especially with women.

"I see," Jarod murmured coldly.

"I doubt very much that you do." The answering chill in her voice surprised even her. "I don't think you care at all what other people think. I don't think anything matters much to you—besides yourself, that is." The music ended and they stood facing one another. "Thanks for the dance. Good night." She hoped the whirl of her skirt signaled her disgust with him. What else could she do—slap him with her gloved hand, like a Southern belle of yesteryear?

Tobe was on the opposite side of the dance floor, talking to the blond Judith. Amanda sent her brother over to get him, pleading a headache as the reason she wanted to leave. The excuse didn't fool Cheryl, but she seemed to guess that Amanda had a valid reason and didn't bug her with a million giddy questions on the way home.

A girl dressed in an old-fashioned organdy gown in lavender and a large floppy hat came scurrying toward Amanda. "People are standing outside waiting to go on the tour," she declared worriedly. "They're getting impatient. We were supposed to open up fifteen minutes ago."

"I realize that, Pam," Amanda answered calmly. "The cleaning crew are finishing now. It'll only be a few minutes more."

"With the cotillion last night, they should have closed this place today," the girl pointed out. "Or else they should've had the cleaning crew come in earlier."

"Unfortunately, there wasn't anyone here to let them in earlier, but that's not our concern." Amanda found the situation irksome enough without having to listen to so much fretting and fussing, but she forced herself to stay cool. "Has Susan arrived yet?"

"She called," Pam said, adding sarcastically, "she claimed her car wouldn't start. More than likely she overslept. She said she'd be here in an hour."

"All right," Amanda sighed, massaging her temples, which were beginning to ache. "I'll give her tour through the first floor of the house. You can guide them through the second floor and Linda will show them the gardens." She glanced around. "Where is Linda?"

As if on cue, the other guide hurried into the hall, her pale pink gown identical to Pam and Amanda's, except for the color.

"The cleaning crew's finished," she said breathlessly. "Shall I open the doors now?"

"Yes," Amanda nodded, smoothing the ruffles of her mint green dress. "And be sure to explain the reason for the delay. Tourists don't know about our cotillion and most of them won't know that it was Jefferson Davis's birthday yesterday."

Except for a few grumbles, the visitors to the historic old plantation took the delay in stride.

Amanda was glad she was doing the first part of the tour. She had more experience than the other girls and was able to keep them entertained with an endless supply of anecdotes connected with the house. Once she was able to coax smiles or glimmers of interest from most of them, she knew they would forget that they'd had to wait.

As the group walked down a side hallway, one of the women asked, "How did the South acquire the name of Dixie? Was it taken from the Mason–Dixon Line?"

"No. The Mason-Dixon Line marked the boundary between the states of Maryland and Pennsylvania at first, although it was eventually regarded as the demarcation line of the North and the South," Amanda explained. "The name Dixie originated in Louisiana, which was settled predominantly by the French. Before the Civil War, a ten-dollar banknote was issued by the State of Louisiana with the French word for ten, *dix*, spelled d-i-x but pronounced dee, printed on it. Americans pronounced it as dix and later referred to Louisiana as the land of the dixie, the place where such money was found. Gradually the term came to mean all of the South."

She took a deep breath. Someone always asked that question and its answer was one of the longest speeches of the tour. Amanda led the visitors into the large study with its rich pecan woodwork.

"This last room," she continued, "was where all the business and agricultural matters of the plantation were seen to. When the Union Army commandeered this house during the Civil War, this room served as the private office of Colonel Bartholomew Colby. His staff was quartered here in the house and the rest of the company bivouacked in the grounds."

"What did they do with the owners of the plantation?" one of the women asked.

"At that time, only a Mrs. Reagan and her daughter were here. Her husband, Sean Reagan, was a cavalry officer under Robert E. Lee," Amanda explained. "Colonel Colby allowed Mrs. Reagan and her daughter to occupy the master bedroom upstairs."

"How long were the colonel and his soldiers here?" a man inquired.

"Only a few weeks. General Sherman had given orders that no private homes were to be destroyed during his march to the sea after the city of Atlanta was burned to the ground. It was an order that was eventually ignored, bringing about the destruction of almost all of the beautiful plantation houses that lay in the path of his march, which was some eighty miles wide at various points. However, Colonel Colby evidently appreciated the beauty and grandeur of Oak Run and refused to let his soldiers put it to the torch."

"I don't believe that was his reason."

The voice came from the back of the room. Everyone, including Amanda, turned toward the speaker. Her composure was shaken as she saw Jarod Colby make his way slowly through the small group. His bland gaze was focused on her in a way that caused her breath to catch.

"Ladies and gentlemen," she said, turning her attention to them and forcing a bright smile to appear on her face, "this is a rare treat. I'd like you to meet Jarod Colby, a direct descendant of Colonel Colby and the present owner of Oak Run."

He gave an oh-so-gracious nod of his black head at the scattered applause that ensued, much to Amanda's annoyance. The whispers rose to a buzz, but he talked over it. "I do hope you're enjoying the tour," he said, turning to stand beside Amanda.

A man's voice raised itself above the various assertions that they were all enjoying the tour. "You were about to tell us why the colonel didn't allow his men to burn the plantation."

"I have no doubt that the colonel found this home very beautiful, as Ms. Bennett pointed out," Jarod replied. "But the true reason he left it standing was the same one that led him to purchase the property after the war was over. He was infatuated with Mrs. Reagan." Jarod's dark gaze slid down to Amanda, dwelling on the startled roundness of her eyes. "You might call it the family secret. At the time that the Union troops occupied the house, Mrs. Reagan had been told that her husband was missing and presumed dead. As far as my ancestor was concerned, she was a widow. When the war ended and the prisoners were released, Mrs. Reagan and Colonel Colby discovered that her husband was very much alive but an invalid. To persuade Sean Reagan to divorce his wife, the colonel paid him twice what the plantation was worth in its day. But Mrs. Reagan had a last-minute attack of conscience and refused to leave her husband. The colonel was left with the plantation and his lady fair left with her money and her husband."

An uncomfortable hush settled over the small group. They followed Amanda a little slowly as she led them into the main hall where Pamela would take them through the second floor. Jarod was standing in the doorway of the study, obviously waiting for her when she had seen the last of the group follow Pam up the grand staircase.

"May I have a few minutes of your time, Ms. Bennett?" Jarod asked mockingly. When Amanda looked hesitantly toward the front where a new group of tourists was gathering, he reached in his pocket and took out a stub. "The young lady wouldn't allow me in without purchasing a ticket, so I believe that entitles me to speak to you."

"You've never been here before and the girl is new. It's understandable that she didn't know who you were, especially if you didn't identify yourself," Amanda replied with cool dignity.

"I'm sorry I'm late, Amanda." Someone came rushing up behind her. "The darned car wouldn't start." Susan glanced curiously at Jarod and Amanda wondered how much she had heard before she joined them. "Do you want me to take the next tour on the first floor?"

"Yes." She nodded. "There's a group at the front ready to leave now."

"Okay," Susan said. "It won't happen again—my being late, I mean."

"Now can I talk to you?" Jarod repeated as the other girl walked hurriedly to the front of the hall.

"I really don't know what we have to discuss," Amanda said.

"My aunt uses the old cloakroom as an office, I believe." Before she could protest, he was taking her by the arm and leading her there.

Once inside, Jarod closed the door behind them and leaned against it as if he expected Amanda to try and leave. He folded his arms over his chest and stared at her, and she shifted uncomfortably. The room seemed much smaller with him in it.

"Okay," she said. "Talk." She didn't sound particularly polite, but she didn't like the way he seemed to assume she had nothing better to do.

"I want you to have dinner with me." The expression on his face was completely unreadable.

"When?" she asked, trying not to let him guess that his question had taken her by surprise.

"Tonight."

"That's very short notice." Her stomach was doing somersaults. Last night she'd told herself that if Jarod was truly interested in her, he would have asked her out. Now he was doing just that.

"Do you have other plans?" Jarod demanded, straightening away from the door.

"If I did, you'd probably ask me to break them," Amanda retorted, more sharply than she had intended.

"Then you are free tonight."

Score one for Jarod. He'd figured that out easily enough. But that was what she'd implied and he'd simply seized on an opening.

"That doesn't necessarily mean that I accept," she said, tilting her chin at a defiant angle as she met his complacent gaze.

"What's bothering you?" Amusement lurked in his eyes. "Are you ticked off because I asked?"

"Should I be grateful that you can fit me into your schedule?" she demanded.

He chuckled softly and moved across the small room but didn't touch her this time. There was a fiery warmth in his eyes as they swept over her face. His expression became serious and compelling.

"The truth is I have to fly to Pennsylvania tomorrow morning. I won't be back until the end of the week," Jarod murmured, his husky voice caressing her with an unexpected softness. "If it will soothe your injured pride, I'll ask you to keep next Saturday open, too." He raised his hands as if he were going to stroke her shoulders the way he had the night of the cotillion but dropped them back. "I don't want to wait an entire week before I see you."

The declaration took her breath away. She could

only gaze at him in disbelief, her heart hammering against her ribs while a shimmering happiness made her brown eyes glow.

"Really?" It was a barely audible whisper that begged for his confirmation.

Jarod stood motionless and stared into her eyes. His gaze moved to her trembling lips.

"I want to see you tonight." The urgency in his voice was very clear.

"I'll be through here at six," Amanda said, wondering why she'd agreed so readily but not really able to resist this particular temptation. "I can be ready at seven—seven-thirty at the latest."

"I'll send a car for you."

"A car?" There was confusion in the look she gave him. "Aren't you coming to pick me up?"

Jarod smiled and it was the first time she noticed a smile reaching his eyes. For what it was worth, she told herself. She seemed to be able to set her natural caution aside when it came to this man.

"Doesn't that meet with your approval either?" he asked.

"It's all right," Amanda assured him quickly. "It's just that my parents . . . well, they're used to meeting my dates. Not that they would object if they didn't meet you. They do know who you are."

"I'll be there at quarter past seven. How's that?"

Her red-gold hair was loose, tumbling in soft curls over her shoulders. Jarod couldn't seem to stop himself from twining a lock around his fingers, but he let go as if it were scorching hot. Then he looked into her face for an answer.

"Fine." Amanda gulped, wondering where the adult she was supposed to be had gone. She felt more than ever like a moonstruck teenager.

"Okay. You'll be ready?" He seemed to breathe in deeply as the words hovered in the air, half command and half question.

"Yes."

His gaze moved caressingly over her face and bare shoulders one last time, then Jarod turned and left the room.

Amanda remained where she stood. She resisted the impulse to pinch herself to make sure she wasn't dreaming and gave herself a mental shake. She had to stop reacting to him in this infatuated way if they were going to go out. At the moment she was so rattled that she didn't know if it was his potent attraction that was drawing her, or an image of the past. She had to stop confusing the two.

CHAPTER FOUR

The rest of the day continued at the same frantic pace of the morning. The sunny June weather brought scores of people parading through Oak Run. It was half-past six before the last visitors left the grounds and Amanda could go home.

"You're late, honey," her mother commented as Amanda walked in the door.

"You wouldn't believe the chaos today," Amanda declared, turning her back to her mother so she could begin unhooking her dress. "I didn't stick around to change before I got in the car. Have you ever had to drive home wearing ankle-length organdy ruffles?"

"Come to think of it, no." Her mother laughed.

"Where is everybody?"

"Your father and brothers went fishing. There's cold chicken and potato salad in the refrigerator. You can help yourself."

"I'm going out to dinner and I only have about half an hour to get ready," Amanda replied, holding the gown up with one hand as she started to hurry down the hallway to the stairs.

"You didn't mention that this morning." Her mother followed at a more sedate pace.

"I didn't know this morning," Amanda said over her shoulder. "Mom, would you please run me a hot bath while I lay out my clothes? Pretty please?"

"Now who has you in such a dither?"

"I'm not in a dither. I'm just late," she protested. She held the long folds of her ruffled gown in her hand as she galloped up the stairs, then added, a little self-consciously, "Jarod Colby asked me out."

"Jarod Colby? *The* Jarod Colby?" Amanda's reply stopped Mrs. Bennett halfway up the steps.

"What about Jarod Colby?" Her younger sister, Bonnie, appeared in the doorway of her bedroom.

"I'm going out with him tonight," Amanda answered, trying to make it sound like the most ordinary thing in the world.

"You're kidding!" Bonnie squealed.

"I didn't even know you knew him." Her mother had regained control after her initial start of surprise.

"I met him at the cotillion last night and he stopped in at Oak Run this morning to ask me out." Inside her room, Amanda stepped quickly out of her gown and began rummaging through her closet.

"He doesn't waste any time," her mother said quietly, a frown on her face.

"I think it's terrific!" Bonnie sighed as she sank onto the blue gingham bedspread. "He meets you one night and the next day he comes looking for you because he can't get you out of his mind." Bonnie turned to her sister, her spiky hair bouncing a little. "What are you going to wear?"

"This black dress, I think." It was short, classy, and sexy. A triple threat.

"You look so sophisticated in that," Bonnie said dreamily.

"It is summer, though . . ." Amanda hesitated, looking back into her closet. "Maybe I shouldn't wear black. What do you think, Momma?"

"Black is never wrong," was her mother's answer. "What time will he be here?"

"Seven-fifteen."

"I'd better get that bathwater started," Mrs. Bennett declared.

By some miracle, Amanda was walking down the stairs when she heard the car pulling up out front. Bonnie had been keeping a vigil at the kitchen window and she came racing into the hallway.

"He's here, Mandy!" She tried to suppress the excitement in her voice and her words came out in a stifled shriek. "He's totally hot!"

"Who's here? Who's hot?" Her grandfather came shuffling from the living room. "Where are you going?"

"I have a date tonight," Amanda answered, deliberately ignoring his first questions. She brushed a kiss on the old man's cheek as the doorbell sounded. "I'll get it, Momma," she called.

"So she has a date. What's all the fuss about?" her grandfather demanded as his daughter-in-law walked into the hall.

Their voices followed Amanda as she hurried toward the front door. Her heart seemed to be in her throat at the knowledge that Jarod Colby was standing on the other side.

"Her date is Jarod Colby," Bonnie informed her grandfather. "My sister is going out with Jarod Colby."

"Jarod Colby," he repeated. "And are you allowing her to go, Bernice?"

Amanda heard her mother attempt to shush her grandfather as she opened the door. She stared into the strikingly masculine face with its chiseled features. *Oh, my.*

"Hello," said Jarod quietly.

"Come in." Amanda moved back, suddenly overcome by shyness.

With embarrassing clarity, her grandfather's voice pierced the air. "Do you mean to tell me that you intend to let Mandy go out with that carpet-bagging Yankee?"

"Keep your voice down!" her mother admonished.

Amanda glanced apologetically at Jarod, but he only seemed amused by the old man's outburst.

"My grandfather," she explained. "The Civil War only ended a few years ago as far as he's concerned."

"That's all right, I understand," Jarod replied.

Her mother moved swiftly toward them, her cheeks tinged with scarlet color. Her hand was extended in greeting to Jarod, which he accepted.

"I must apologize for my father-in-law's rudeness," Mrs. Bennett said quietly. "Discretion has never been one of his virtues."

"An apology isn't necessary," said Jarod, bestowing a rare smile on the older woman. "I've been called worse things than a Yankee carpetbagger."

Her grandfather was still mumbling in the distance and Amanda turned to her mother. "We'll leave now," she said. "Don't wait up for me."

"Have a good time," Mrs. Bennett called after them as Amanda and Jarod walked through the door onto the porch.

"Is your father averse to Yankees, too?" Jarod asked, his dark eyes twinkling with laughter as he helped her into the car.

"No, thank heaven." Amanda smiled. "He's off fishing with my brothers anyway."

"You have more than one brother?" The politeness of the question was underscored by the look he flashed at her, which seemed to say that he was interested in anything that had to do with her.

"Actually, there are six Bennett kids, but we're pretty much grown. My oldest sister, Marybeth, is married and she has two daughters. She and her husband live in Athens—Athens, Georgia, that is."

Jarod's nod said that he figured as much.

"Brian is a medical student, so he isn't home now," she continued. "Teddy is studying law and Brad, the one you met last night, is going to be an architect. The baby of the family is my sister Bonnie. Thank goodness she's still in high school."

"Why thank goodness?"

"It's a strain on my parents financially to have four of their children in college. Strain is probably an understatement." Amanda smiled. "We all work and contribute everything we can but the brunt of the tuition costs fall to Momma and Daddy."

"What's Plan A? What are you going to do when you graduate?"

"Probably get a teaching job. I want to start paying back my parents right away."

"You could marry a wealthy man and not have to worry about it," Jarod suggested dryly.

"Oh, right. Plan B. Don't you know that only happens in the movies?" She didn't want him to think she was after him, although the prospect of having his arms around her again was an increasingly irresistible thought. "Anyway, having a lot of money isn't high on my priority list."

He glanced at her thoughtfully and with a look of skepticism. Amanda could understand why.

He'd probably met a lot of people whose only interest in him was his money.

"It's a lovely evening." She sighed, wanting to change the subject.

"Yes, I thought we'd have dinner on the veranda."

"The veranda?" she repeated. "Is that a new restaurant? Being away at college most of the year, I'm not too familiar with all the new places."

A soft chuckle rolled from his parted lips. "I told you last night that I would take you someplace where we could be alone." His gaze seemed to caress her before it returned to the road. "I was referring to the veranda at my house, not a restaurant."

"Oh," she said in a very small voice. He had dressed for an occasion. Jacket. Tie. Really nice shirt, even if it was white. The whole nine.

"Do you still want to have dinner with me?"

Her hands were folded in her lap, feeling suddenly clammy and cold. At the same time, she felt hot and light-headed. It had never occurred to her that he would be taking her to the Winter House. If she refused to go, he might just think she was being all prim and proper for no particular reason. But the idea of sharing an intimate dinner with him, alone in his house, was a bit much.

Nonetheless, the smile she gave him was bright and confident, not exactly a true reflection of the way she felt inside. "I do hope you have a good cook. I'm ravenous!"

His gaze slid over her, lingering for brief seconds on her mouth. "So am I," Jarod said. The wry note in his voice made Amanda believe that he wasn't talking about food. The air in the car suddenly seemed a whole lot hotter. She reached out and turned the air-conditioning dial on the dash to High Cool.

* * *

"That was delicious." Amanda sighed, leaning back a little in her chair. "I do love strawberries."

"And whipped cream," Jarod added, watching a faint wisp of smoke from the pillar candle on the table swirl upward. "I always thought Southern girls ate before going out so their dates would think they had very small appetites."

"That was true in the olden days, but not anymore," she said with a smile.

"You can clear everything away, Hannah," he told the older woman as she walked through the open door into the screened patio. "I won't need anything else tonight."

Not wanting to interfere with the housekeeper's work, Amanda rose from the table and wandered idly to the mesh wall, wondering if Jarod was following her. The sun had dipped below the horizon, leaving a glow of pink and gold behind.

The fragrance of an expensive and subtle masculine cologne let her know that Jarod was approaching. The housekeeper could not prevent the clatter of dishes on the serving trolley she was taking back to the distant kitchen and Amanda hadn't heard his footsteps on the patio tile.

She heard him dismiss the housekeeper for the evening, presumably when she had finished with the washing up and putting away.

As the clatter faded away, Amanda was suddenly very conscious of the fact that they were alone at last. With the sun down, the twilight turned to a deeper blue that seemed to grow darker with every passing second. She didn't want to just stare out into nothingness. She turned and found herself even closer to him than she had thought, looking straight up into his unfathomable eyes.

The corners of her mouth turned up in a faint—

very faint—smile. She couldn't think of anything to say.

"It's getting dark. Would you like to go inside?" he asked, a hint of something sexual in his tone.

"Yes," Amanda agreed hesitantly as he stepped to one side.

The screened patio led into the living room. A single light was on, making a path of white across the carpet. It was a large room with masculine, clean-lined decor, done in warm earth tones.

"How about some music?" he said, walking over to an expensive sound system.

"Sure." She hoped he wouldn't choose some seductive crooner with a get-her-in-the-mood voice.

Immediately a soft, languid melody she didn't recognize permeated the room through unseen speakers. Unsure of where she should sit, Amanda wandered around the room and fixed her interest on an abstract painting that hung on the wall.

With all the swirls and drips and globs, it wasn't clear which end was up. Kind of how she felt at the moment.

"Like the painting?"

"Sure," she said again. Actually, she didn't, but she hadn't come here to criticize his art collection. Amanda turned to face him, her hands clutched tightly in front of her. His gaze was dark and brooding as it traveled the length of her body and stopped at her face.

"Are you nervous?"

"A little," she admitted, spreading her fingers and rubbing them together in an effort to relax.

Jarod Colby watched the movement with indifference, subtly making her aware of the breadth of his shoulders and his intimidating height. The soft music in the background didn't soften his physical impact on her senses any. The silence between them was getting to her.

"Will you be leaving early in the morning?" Amanda asked, trying to make her voice sound natural. He had said he was going to Pennsylvania. Now that seemed like a safe, unsexy subject. They could talk about Pennsylvania until the cows came home.

His eyes flicked back to her face. "Early enough."

"It must be a pain to commute back and forth."

"Not really. I use a corporate charter jet service."

"I bet that saves a lot of time, what with security checks and all."

"Yes."

His clipped reply made her rack her brains for something else to say. How could she pursue a conversation that he wasn't willing to take part in? She broke away from his compelling gaze.

"You have a beautiful home," Amanda said. Trite . . . but true enough. The Winter House looked like something out of an architecture magazine.

The comment passed unnoticed as he held out his hand to her. For a minute she blinked at it uncertainly, then hesitantly extended her own. His strong hand closed warmly around her fingers, pulling her to him as his arm moved around her waist. He carried her fingers to his lips while he guided her to the slow tempo of the music. The brooding expression in his eyes didn't change as he looked at her face.

Last night when they had danced, her hoopskirt had kept some distance between them. Now Amanda was held tightly against him, her legs burning with each brush of his thighs while the softness of her breasts felt the imprint of the buttons of his shirt. She hadn't been prepared for the contact of his body, hard and muscular and very male. Her head was tilted back, revealing the bareness of her throat as she watched his lips move over her hand in a caress that had her whole arm tingling.

There was an unreal quality about the moment, a dreamlike magic that sent her senses spinning. The hand resting near her shoulders could feel the taut muscles in the arm that circled her waist. The nibbling of her fingers ceased as he turned her hand to expose her sensitive palm and pressed a warm kiss in its hollow. The sensual touch of his tongue against her skin released an avalanche of sensation inside her. Exhaling slowly in surrender, Amanda rested her head against his chest, all resistance flowing from her body.

Leaving her hand against the shaven smoothness of his face, Jarod trailed his fingers firmly down her arm and up to her shoulder, caressing her flesh with controlled firmness. Of its own volition, her hand stayed where it was, her fingertips exploring the jutting line of his jaw and the prominent cheekbones.

There was no urgency in the languid passion between them, even though the slow-burning flame kept growing hotter as his mouth trailed across her flushed cheek to her earlobe.

After a minute his mouth sought hers, not in a gentle probing caress but in a demanding, hungry kiss. Her hands were locked around his neck as she stood on tiptoe, instinctively arching her back to be closer to the lean hardness of his body. In sweet ecstasy, Amanda knew she had been kissed with passion before, but she couldn't recall returning more than a small part of it until now.

Then something made her stop, pulling her out of the whirling ache of desire.

"Jarod, please . . ." Her lips moved in protest against his mouth. Her senses felt drugged by his kiss, unable to perceive anything more than the pleasure he was giving her.

He let her move a little ways out of his arms, the smoldering fire in his eyes nearly sending her back into them. "What is it?" he demanded.

His voice was hoarse and his breathing uneven. Amanda could feel the iron control that he had over his emotions. Oddly, that hurt. She wanted him to be as stirred by her touch as she was by his.

"The music's stopped," she murmured, suddenly at a loss to admit how deeply affected she was by his embrace and his caresses.

A scowl of annoyance flashed across his face, quickly replaced by an enigmatic look that Amanda couldn't fathom. His hands dropped to his sides and he turned away, leaving her standing on wobbly legs.

"Go and change it, then," Jarod ordered smoothly. "Pick something you like."

She nodded and went over to a rack of CDs. His taste seemed to lean toward slow, bluesy jazz and other sexy stuff. There were no safe choices. She picked one at random and slid open the drawer of the CD player, watching the digital readout on the little screen. Track 1. A low, throbbing sax solo throbbed through the hidden speakers.

Amanda turned to ask Jarod if he approved of the selection, but he was filling a glass from a bottle of something that looked unbelievably expensive, probably cognac or single malt. His eyes met hers across the room.

"Would you like a drink?" he asked.

Amanda shook her head.

He took a hefty swallow of liquor, then refilled the partially empty glass and walked to a large chair, where he sat down. She stood beside the sound system, wishing she could act that nonchalant. His eyes studied her with a penetrating thoroughness that made her feel hot all over.

"Come here," he ordered crisply.

Swallowing, she walked toward him, stopping beside his chair and gazing down at him. Her long hair fell across her face and she nervously tucked the red-gold locks behind her ears. Amanda watched him impatiently remove his tie, tossing it on the table on the other side of him. He unbuttoned the top buttons of his shirt.

The sight of the dark hairs curling on his chest made her heart skip a beat or two. She started to turn away, but his hand caught her wrist.

"Your pulse is racing," he said.

"I know."

"Do I do that to you?"

With him watching her so closely, she couldn't answer that question. To admit that he did would make her too vulnerable; to lie that he didn't was impossible.

His hand slid across the lower part of her body and rested on her hip. "You don't need to answer that question," Jarod said softly. "I can feel the way you almost melt when I touch you."

Her startled eyes swept his face, but he was looking at the agitated movement of her breasts and the way the material covering them strained at the narrow straps of her dress.

"Jarod, please—" she began.

"Please what?" he growled. His eyes blazed upward to her face. "For twenty-four damn hours, I've been remembering everything about you. Your face. Your lips. The way you move is enough to—"

"Don't say that," she protested.

"Why not?" He pulled her down into his lap and she didn't struggle. "Why shouldn't we go for it?" His hand moved roughly over her hip to her back while she felt the thudding of his heart beneath her own hands. "I wanted to hold you like this last night. Don't tell me that you didn't want it, too."

"I did," Amanda whispered.

"I couldn't forget how you looked after I'd danced with you. Walking down that garden path. You let me touch you."

She had let him, that much was true. But she pressed her face into his chest rather than reply.

"I couldn't forget the scent of your perfume or how soft your skin was," he murmured, threading the fingers of one hand through her hair. "This morning was even worse. Being in a room with you alone and not touching you, that was torture. And just now, watching you eat strawberries and cream for dessert—hell, Amanda, I'm not made of stone. I've been aching with the need to see and touch every inch of you."

A whimpering moan slipped from Amanda's lips at the passion in his voice. His fingers moved to her mouth and he parted her lips, readying her for his kiss.

His arms crushed her against him as he possessively demanded her complete response. The masterful caress of his hands over her thighs and hips, across her back and shoulders, aroused her to a fever pitch of longing.

A sudden release of all inhibitions seemed to enclose her in a velvet mist. Her head was tilted back over his arm while Jarod ran his mouth over her collarbone, pushing aside the strap in his way and sliding it down her arm. Amanda felt his fingertips brush her breasts but stiffened instinctively when the material of her dress slipped down.

Instantly alert, no longer possessed by her drowning senses, she felt his hand sliding along her back, down her bare spine. With sickening swiftness she realized that the sensation of release she had experienced before had been the expert movements of Jarod's hands when he had unzipped her dress.

The suddenness of her lunge away from him was unexpected. She stumbled shakily to her feet, clutching the bodice tightly to her, her eyes shimmering with tears of shame and uncertainty. Desire still blazed in his gaze, but it was quickly replaced by a confused anger as she backed away from him.

Nice going. The town tramp couldn't have done it better, Amanda told herself bitterly. She swallowed back her tears.

CHAPTER FIVE

"I want to go home." Her voice was jerky with emotion.

Jarod rose to his feet, a black scowl on his face. Amanda would have fled then if she had believed that her legs would carry her.

"Did I miss something?" he demanded, looking at the tears that clung to her lashes. "I don't think you said no. Or told me to stop. I made it clear that I wanted you. You sure didn't seem to mind at first."

No, she hadn't minded. But she had been too inexperienced and blindsided by his overwhelming desire for her to say yes—at least a yes that meant a full understanding of how far they would go.

His anger was justified to that extent and she found she couldn't meet his eyes.

"I'm sorry," she said softly. "Would you laugh if I said I wasn't that kind of girl?"

"Maybe. If I wasn't so damn frustrated. Amanda . . . don't tell me you're a virgin. I don't believe that I'm the first man to touch you that way."

"It doesn't matter whether you believe me or not." Her throat was working convulsively.

Jarod moved with such striking swiftness that she wasn't able to avoid his grip on her shoulders.

"I don't give a damn," he growled. "I don't have to be the first man. There's no need to play the innocent."

"I'm not playing!" Amanda cried out bitterly. "It's the truth! Now let me go!"

He let fly a string of angry curses as he released her. "From now on," Jarod muttered under his breath, turning his back to her, "you'd better stick to the shallow water until you learn to swim."

Amanda was too embarrassed to reply as she struggled to slip the strap over her shoulder and make her shaking hands zip up her dress. But she was just too clumsy. In the next minute, Jarod was turning her around and pushing her hands away.

"I've had more practice at this than you have." He closed the zipper with one fluid movement.

His fingers clasped her waist, firmly pivoting her around to face him. For one crazy moment, she thought he was going to take her in his arms. As she brushed the tears from her cheeks, she realized that she wanted him to hold her and ease the ache in her heart.

"We'll forget about next Saturday night," he said tautly. "The less I see of you, the better."

"Of course," Amanda murmured, wondering if a breaking heart made a noise.

"Come on, I'll take you home." Jarod was striding away from her toward the door and she followed, scraping together what little dignity and self-respect she had left.

Jarod said not a word as he held the car door

open for her, not even when he slid behind the wheel a few seconds later. The sky was black with lingering clouds blocking out most of the stars and allowing the moon to peep out occasionally. As soon as Jarod reached the main road, he accelerated until the telephone poles were only a blur. Amanda knew he could hardly wait to get her home. When he finally pulled up, the Bennett house was ablaze with lights.

"What time is it?" she asked nervously.

"Nearly ten." He hadn't switched the engine off.

Her family would be up, no doubt waiting to hear all about her evening. Amanda began patting and smoothing her tousled hair and tried to wipe away all traces of tears from her face. With an angry sigh, Jarod turned off the motor and flipped down the visor in front of her, revealing a mirror on the other side.

"You're a mess," he muttered. Rummaging through the glove compartment, he paused to hand her a comb.

The reflection in the mirror confirmed his statement. Even in the dim glow of the light coming from the house, Amanda could see the smudged streaks on her face where her mascara had run. Her hair was so messed up it looked like she had just climbed out of bed. As she remedied that with the comb, she saw Jarod tear open a tiny packet that held a commercially packaged moist towelette.

"Turn around." His fingers touched her chin and made her do as he requested.

"Why are you doing this?" Amanda whispered. The pungent scent of citrus facial cleanser revived her to something like alertness as he carefully wiped the traces of mascara from her cheeks. "Why do you care what my family will think?"

"You have three grown brothers and a big, strong

daddy. This is the South. I don't want a backside full of buckshot for something I didn't do."

"You know who my father is?" she breathed. "There are several families named Bennett in Oak Springs."

"But only one Bennett works at my real estate company," he said.

"Then you ought to know that he doesn't go around waving shotguns and making threats."

He grinned. "No, I've never met your dad. Guess your grandfather gave me that idea."

"Well, he's a little nuts," Amanda said defensively. "But the Bennetts aren't hillbillies."

Jarod sighed and sat back. "Still and all, I can't let you walk in that door looking like I did something to you that you didn't want me to do. They'd come after me first and ask questions later. It's a guy thing, Amanda. Obviously you have a lot to learn on that subject."

She sniffled and rubbed her nose.

"Don't start the waterworks again. Please. That's the only towelette I have."

Amanda contented herself with giving him a woebegone look. Her lower lip trembled, but she couldn't help that. He leaned over and kissed her for a long, comforting minute. Then, suddenly, the interior of the car was flooded with light. She heard the laughing voices of her parents, followed by shocked silence. They had come into the driveway and turned on the outside lights for some reason. She and Jarod had been fully illuminated for several seconds. Even Bonnie must have glimpsed their clinch. Her younger sister was peeking out from behind her mother.

"Oh, no," Amanda said miserably. "Just my luck."

Jarod moved back into his seat, and opened his door. He got out, keeping himself somewhat in back of the open door and waved to Amanda's father.

"Hello, Mr. Bennett," Jarod greeted him calmly.

"Mr. Colby." Her father returned the greeting with a nod, recovering as quickly as Jarod had. "I apologize for the, ah, lights. I didn't know this was your car. That is, not until Bernice informed me of that fact about three seconds ago. Amanda hasn't been home from a date at this hour since she was sixteen."

"Daddy," she hissed at him, "now I'm twenty-one."

"I know that, pumpkin," he said patiently. "Well, thanks for bringing her home before bedtime—"

"Call me Jarod, please."

"Jarod it is."

"I have an early flight to Pennsylvania tomorrow morning," Jarod went on, as if that were the explanation. "It was nice meeting you, Mr. Bennett. Good night, Mrs. Bennett." He nodded briefly in her mother's direction before turning his face to Amanda. His features were expressionless. She had to hand it to him. Jarod Colby was the essence of cool.

"Good night, Amanda," he murmured with patronizing politeness.

"Good night." She forced the words from her throat.

She used the precious moments that it took for him to get in his car and drive away to gather her wits, pretending to search for something in her handbag before climbing the porch steps to the porch where her family was waiting.

Her grandfather was grumbling under his breath about Yankees while he rocked in his favorite chair as Amanda joined them. No one spoke.

"Um, well, hello again, everybody. I think I'll

turn in." She knew that no one was fooled, but her parents let her go inside.

Her younger sister Bonnie was not so easily put off. She trailed after her as Amanda walked into the house. "Where did you go? What did you do?" Bonnie whispered excitedly. "If he kissed me like that, I'd totally melt on the spot. When will he be back? Do you suppose he'll call while he's gone?"

Amanda pressed her fingers against her forehead, feeling like she was about to snap in two. "Bonnie, please," she protested with an agonized whisper, "I have an awful headache. I don't feel like talking tonight."

A stunned look crossed her sister's face. They always got together for an hour of girl talk after either came home from a date. Now Amanda was shutting her out.

"I'm sorry," Amanda murmured and raced up the stairs to her room.

With the door securely closed behind her, she wished her memory had a delete button that would obliterate the evening forever. If only she could forget what a complete fool she'd made of herself. She wound her arms tightly around her middle, trying to forget the thrilling sensation of Jarod's expert kisses. But she had only to close her eyes to imagine the sensual pressure of his lips on hers and the awesome maleness of his body.

There was a light rap on her door in warning before her mother walked into the room, enabling Amanda to start unzipping her dress as though she had been in the act of changing her clothes.

"Hello, Momma," she said, striving for a casual tone.

"Bonnie said you had a headache. Is there anything wrong?"

"It's only tension," Amanda answered with a shrug, reaching into the closet for a hanger.

"I hope we didn't embarrass you tonight. We honestly didn't know you were out there."

"I know." She yawned. "No biggie. Don't worry about it."

"Your Jarod seems like a very nice man."

"He's not my Jarod!" Amanda snapped and immediately covered her mouth as she turned her rounded brown eyes on her mother. "Sorry—I didn't mean to shout at you."

A tiny frown made worried lines on her mother's face. "Will you be seeing him again, Mandy?"

It all became too much for her. Amanda couldn't keep up the pretense that nothing was wrong, not for one more second. Her shoulders hunched forward as she wrapped her arms around her churning middle one more time.

"No, Momma," she said, shaking her head. "I won't be seeing him again."

She felt the touch of her mother's hands on her shoulders and turned instinctively for the comfort they promised. She suddenly didn't feel like an adult.

"Do you want to, Mandy?" her mother asked softly, cradling her silent daughter against her breast, feeling the pain that was transmitted.

"Yes." Then, "No, I don't." Amanda straightened and breathed in deeply. She wasn't going to let herself cry. Not again.

"Tonight . . ." Mrs. Bennett began hesitantly, picking up the vibrations of conflicting emotions warring inside her daughter.

"Tonight was a mistake that neither Jarod nor I want to repeat." Amanda sighed. "I really am tired, Momma."

"All right, honey. No more questions," The older woman smiled and brushed her cheek with a fleeting kiss before leaving the room.

"Which one of you girls is going to pick up your father?" Mrs. Bennett called from the back door of the house.

Amanda glanced at Bonnie. "Don't look at me," her sister said. "As soon as I finish watering the garden, I'm going in the house to water myself. You go and get Daddy."

"Okay," Amanda agreed, rubbing the sore muscles of her lower back. "Hose my legs off, but for heaven's sake don't get my shorts wet because I don't want to change my clothes."

Bonnie obligingly turned the nozzle toward her sister, letting the water spray over the lower part of Amanda's legs while avoiding the red material of her shorts. Water squished in Amanda's canvas shoes, but it felt refreshingly cool after two hours in the hot afternoon sun.

"The last of the snap beans are inside the back door, Momma," Amanda called. "Where are the car keys?"

"They're still in the car," her mother answered. "Come back soon!"

Waving to Bonnie, Amanda backed the car out of the driveway and headed to the office of Colby Holdings. The man her father usually rode to work with was down with the flu. Rather than leave his wife without transportation—Bernice refused to drive the rattletrap car that Amanda had bought to get her to Oak Run and to do her own errands—her father decided to have one of them drive him to work in the morning and pick him up at night.

After Amanda had parked the car in front of the office building, situated on landscaped grounds that had once been a Colby cotton field, she glanced in the rearview mirror to make sure there weren't any smudges of dirt on her face from working in the garden. Spending five days a week in a long ruffled dress, it was nice on Monday and Tuesday, the days Oak Run was closed to tourists, to kick around in shorts and tank tops, especially in this hot June weather.

She slipped the car keys into the side pocket of her shorts and walked to the door just inside the entrance marked PRIVATE. One hand lightly rapped on it while the other turned the knob and opened the door.

"Hi, Daddy. You ready to go?"

Three steps inside the office, Amanda came to an abrupt halt as she stared at Jarod Colby standing beside her father's desk. She knew her face had grown pale, although there was practically no reaction on his. Her father was sitting in his chair, taking in the look of stunned surprise on his daughter's face.

"Have a chair. I'll only be a couple of minutes," he told her.

After one brief glance at her when she had walked in the door, Jarod had merely nodded so as not to totally ignore her in front of her father, then turned his attention to the papers spread in front of him on the desk. Since he had chosen not to greet her, Amanda ignored him as well. Her legs numbly folded into the support of the chair behind her.

For the last three weeks, she had attempted to block out the memory of what had happened the night of their dinner date—and what had almost happened. Now here they were, together again, and only a few feet away from each other. It didn't matter much that he was wearing a suit at the moment. He had been fully clothed on that disastrous night and it hadn't mattered much then. Her imagination seemed fully capable of visualizing the man beneath whatever he had on. She knew she would never be able to forget what that muscular hardness had felt like pressed against her own body.

The two men were discussing the contents of the papers Jarod was studying, but Amanda was in too much of a daze to hear what they were saying. Someone knocked at the office door and she nearly jumped out of her chair.

"Can I see you a minute, Mr. Bennett?" a man requested, opening the door but not entering the room.

"Is it important, Joe?" her father asked.

"Yes, sir."

Her father darted a look at Amanda, then brought his gaze back to Jarod, who was concentrating on one of the papers. "Excuse me for a minute."

"I'm in no hurry, Sam," Jarod replied, glancing up briefly from the sheet of paper that seemed to interest him so much.

When the door closed behind her father, the room became uncomfortably still. Amanda sat hesitantly on the edge of her chair, afraid to breathe and draw those dark eyes her way. Then she told herself not to be such a wuss. She had every right to be there and she had no real reason to be scared of Jarod Colby.

Then he thrust his hands into his pockets and walked around to the front of the desk, where he leaned against it and let his gaze wander calmly over her bare legs to her face.

"Hello, Amanda," he said.

"Hi, Jarod," she said, pretending a casualness that was so fake it ought to annoy him. But he seemed as imperturbable as ever.

"So how are you?"

"Fine."

"You look great in shorts."

"Shut up, Jarod." Her cheeks flushed.

"I believe the polite answer would be 'Thank you.' But never mind," he said affably. "It's nice to see you again, my sweet little Georgia peach."

Her eyes grew round. "What did you just call me?"

"I apologize. You're not that sweet. But I have to hand it to you. You really do know how to drive a man crazy. Quite an act, Amanda."

"Is that what you think it was? An . . . an act? For your benefit or mine?"

He shook his head. "You tell me what it was."

"Well, maybe I got a little carried away," she said primly, feeling ridiculous but not willing to give him an inch. "Now if you'll excuse me, I'll wait for my father in the car."

"No, stay here," he commanded.

"Look," she began nervously, "I didn't know you were going to be here."

"I know," Jarod replied with the same blandness as before. "I came in just when your father was phoning home for a ride. I gathered you would be coming, so I stuck around."

She really wanted to smack him. But not if she had to explain it to her father. "Why did you do that?"

"I wanted to see you. Didn't seem like you were going to pick up the phone and call me anytime soon, and I already took the guided tour of Oak Run." He shrugged. "So here I am."

She rose from her chair and drew herself up to her full height. Her wet canvas shoes made a squishing sound, which didn't add anything to her dignity. "You know something, Jarod? You were exactly right when you said the less we saw of each other, the better."

He looked her up and down in a truly wicked way. "Doesn't apply now. At the moment. I'm seeing more of you, not less."

She tugged at her shorts. Try as she might, they weren't going to cover her knees or even much of her thighs. "This thing is getting blown out of proportion."

"Is it?" he inquired. "I find that I'm incredibly attracted to you."

"Okay, whatever. I could see how you could get the wrong impression about that night. I ate dinner with you. I listened to your Barry White Seduce-O-Matic CDs. I let you kiss me—"

"Seemed to me like you were a very active participant in those kisses," he observed, moving closer to her.

Just one whiff of his hard-to-define but pleasantly male scent and she could feel herself melt. She took a step to the right. Too late. His lips just touched her cheek before he whispered into her ear. "Friday night, we'll drive to Atlanta. Go to a dance club where they never even heard of the waltz and really get down. What do you say?"

"No."

He didn't seem bothered by her refusal. The width of an angel's hair was all that separated her from his next kiss. She lacked the strength to push him away as his mouth continued on a tantalizing path down the side of her neck. "On Saturday we'll drive to the coast. Spend the day on the beach."

It was becoming increasingly impossible not to

make that one tiny movement that would give him possession of her lips. "I have to work on Saturday and Sunday," Amanda declared breathlessly, fighting to cling to her sanity.

His soft laughter tickled her ear. "I own Oak Run, remember? I can close it for a weekend if I want to and give everyone two paid days off. Say yes, Amanda."

"No," she said again.

"We'll swim in the ocean and sunbathe on the beach. Fully dressed, of course. Wouldn't want to ruin your reputation."

A sigh escaped her lips at the same moment that footsteps sounded outside the office door, followed immediately by the rattle of the knob. Just before it opened, Jarod moved away from her, nodding casually at Sam Bennett.

Amanda's darting glance at her father caught the quizzical expression in his gaze. She turned as red as the material of her shorts.

"I'll . . . I'll wait for you in the car, Dad," Amanda stammered, eluding Jarod's eyes as she hurried out the door.

When she reached the car, her breath was coming in jerky gulps. Another minute, another second, and she would have given in. She bit hard into her lips to make them stop trembling. He was playing a game of which he was master. And it didn't matter if he thought she was incredibly attractive. She didn't possess the power to demolish his self-control, but he could take away hers with a few sweet nothings and a hot kiss. It wasn't fair.

Her breathing had regained a degree of normalcy when the two men walked out of the office. Without a glance in her direction, Jarod walked by the Bennett car to his own. Involuntarily, she watched as he drove away before she became aware of her father sitting behind the wheel of the car, his hand outstretched for the ignition keys.

She snapped out of it. "You look tired, Daddy," she said affectionately as she handed him the keys from her pocket. "Did you have a rough day?"

He smiled with wry amusement. "I didn't think you'd noticed me at all, but yes, it was a long day."

Amanda shifted uncomfortably, her eyes straying toward the dust cloud left by Jarod's car. "That's not true," she said. "About not noticing you, I mean."

"Isn't it? I had the distinct impression that I was creating an unwanted crowd of three."

"Did Jarod say that?"

"No, but he did say I had a strong-willed and beautiful daughter."

That statement did nothing to calm her nerves. Her gaze shifted self-consciously to the slowly passing scenery outside the window of the now moving car.

"What do you think of him, Daddy?" she asked quietly.

There was a pause before her father answered, and then it was with deliberation. "You're an adult, Amanda. What do you think of him?"

"That he's out of my class."

"How so? He's a man like any other. Puts on his pants one leg at a time."

"Oh, Daddy." She sighed. "You know as well as I do that the Colbys live in a different world. Hell, they could probably afford to buy their own planet. They make their own rules, that's for damn sure."

"Amanda, they're no better than we are and no worse."

She shook her head. "They have a lot more money."

"That doesn't matter as much as you think it does, honey."

She nodded. "Okay. Maybe you're right. I hope so."

"Thanks. Do I get to be right for the whole rest of the day? Tell your mother that."

"You mean you get to be right about everything?"

"Absolutely everything," he said firmly. "Until midnight."

"It's okay with me. But I can't speak for Momma."

He laughed his goofy dad laugh that she'd always loved and they dropped the subject of the Colbys.

CHAPTER SIX

Her decision was tested later that evening when the phone rang and Bonnie announced that it was for her. Before she reached the receiver, Amanda guessed that it would be Jarod.

"Is seven o'clock too early for Friday night?" his voice asked the minute she said hello.

"I'm not going out with you," she answered in a low voice.

"Saturday?"

"No."

"Then . . . when?"

She could hear the exasperation in his voice. "Never. The answer will always be no. Tomorrow. Next week. Next month. No!"

"I just don't accept that. And I don't think that's what you want."

He was too accustomed to overcoming a woman's objections, that was clear. Very slowly Amanda replaced the receiver on the hook, afraid that if she talked to him any longer, he would somehow still succeed.

"That was Jarod Colby, wasn't it?" The sound of

her sister's voice brought Amanda round. "And you just turned him down? You're either insane or really ingenious."

Amanda lips tightened fractionally. "I don't want to get on board a fast train going nowhere, Bonnie."

"What's that supposed to mean?"

"Never mind, brat. If he calls back, tell him I'm not here."

Bonnie shrugged and disappeared into her room. Amanda heard the Dixie Chicks turned up good and loud, singing about just what was going to happen to someone named Earl.

Jarod didn't call back. With each day that passed, Amanda became more convinced that he had taken her answer as final. Yet her second meeting with him stayed in her mind.

Her father's take on the situation—that Jarod was a man like any other—didn't quite allow for the fact that Amanda had never felt so strongly about any other man. She found herself wishing that she hadn't been so adamant in her refusal. He had only wanted to see her again, and honestly, she wanted to see him.

There was nothing wrong with just having some fun with him, was there? So long as he understood where she drew the line and why, Amanda thought she could handle Jarod.

She was inexperienced, true, but she was also realistic. If marriage figured anywhere in his plans for the future, it wouldn't be to a small-town nobody like her.

He would have to understand that she really didn't want to be his girlfriend. Amanda had a feeling there was too much competition in that department and its subcategories: Significant Other, Friend With Benefits, To Have But Don't Hold.

Forget that, she thought. Amanda just wasn't interested in investing a lot of emotional energy in part-time, half-hearted romance, even though some of her best buddies seemed happy enough with what they'd settled for.

So she was still a virgin. So what? That was nobody's business but her own.

Still, the idea of having a fling with Jarod Colby was downright tempting. Yet Amanda wondered how deeply she cared for him. She wasn't willing to risk a commitment of any kind to a guy who could have any woman he wanted. She had to admit it; they really didn't know each other and the attraction could be just physical. Meaning it wouldn't last.

The thought was depressing. She looked out a window of the Oak Run house, trailing a raindrop rolling down the outside with a fingertip on the inside. It was a gray, dreary day with a slow drizzle falling steadily. Few tourists would be tramping around this afternoon in such dismal weather.

"Pam." Amanda turned from the window to the trio of girls chattering in the corner. "Why don't you and Susan go on home? Linda and I will stay until closing. I don't expect a sudden deluge of visitors to appear."

"Okay!" Pam replied as she and Susan rose eagerly to their feet. "I have a million things to do at home—I don't mind one bit."

"A car is pulling up out front," Linda announced with a sigh. "Just our luck."

Amanda sighed, too, but in relief. She didn't like having so much time to think. Everyone in town knew she'd gone out with Jarod Colby, including her three coworkers. Each time Amanda had tried to join in their endless banter about clothes or music or men, they shifted the subject to Jarod, showing curiosity, envy, and even a touch of malice over the fact that she hadn't been out with him again.

Not even for the sake of pride would she confide that she had turned him down. It wasn't something they would understand or believe.

"How many people are there?" Amanda asked, nodding to the departing girls moving down the hall as she sifted through the brochures that were given to each visitor.

"Two. A man and a woman," Linda answered, peering through the sheer folds of the curtain. Then she gasped loudly. "Amanda! I think it's Jarod Colby!"

Amanda stiffened, not really noticing that the other two girls had stopped and turned around to see her reaction. She could feel herself blush as the front door opened.

Jarod wasn't the first one to walk in. A gorgeous brunette preceded him, wearing clothes Amanda knew she could never afford if she saved a whole year. It hardly seemed fair that the woman had sapphire blue eyes and perfect features. She looked like a model, with a big-city sophistication that made Amanda feel awfully dowdy.

Jarod was right behind his friend—if the woman was a friend, Amanda thought resentfully. The intimate way the brunette turned and spoke to him made it clear that she was very well acquainted with Jarod Colby.

"Hello, Amanda," he said easily. "This is Vanessa Scott."

"Good afternoon, Mr. Colby. Ms. Scott. What a surprise to see you here." There. That was frosty enough to keep him at a safe distance. But she didn't need to look around to see that the other guides were interested in the exchange between her and Jarod.

His gaze turned to the brunette securely attached to his arm. "Vanessa has never been through Oak Run. I thought this would be a perfect day for her to take a leisurely tour of the plantation house, considering that you don't have any other visitors. Ours was the only car in the parking lot," he added.

"The weather is keeping them away," Amanda murmured defensively, "You and—" She stopped and gathered her wits. "The two of you will have the place to yourselves. I hope you enjoy your tour." The last comment was directed at the brunette, who was regarding her with barely concealed amusement.

There was a sardonic glint in Jarod's eyes. "Sorry, Amanda. I guess I didn't make myself clear. I'll be using the office to make a few phone calls. Rather than have Vanessa get bored waiting for me—"

"Not a chance, honey." The woman smiled provocatively.

"I thought she could go through Oak Run." He returned Vanessa's smile.

"Of course," Amanda agreed tightly. Her fingernails were making marks in her palms. Every nerve in her body screamed with jealousy. The woman was just too much. Those sparkling blue eyes gazing so rapturously at Jarod. The parted, glossy lips that breathed the word *honey* at him.

Amanda turned quickly to Linda, keeping her tone cool and professional. "Linda, would you—"

Jarod broke in. "As you're the senior guide, I would prefer that you show Vanessa around, Amanda."

She glared at him, indignant anger blazing in her eyes. "Is that an order?"

Amanda didn't need to hear the sudden intake of breath from her fellow guides to know that she had crossed a line that they never would, not in a million years.

"Yes, it is," he snapped.

Fighting off the desire to run from the house rather than escort his mistress, or whatever she was, through the building, Amanda nodded and stepped forward. The long skirt of her ruffled gown gave a regal grace to her posture and added to the proudly defiant way she held her head.

"Please come this way, Ms. Scott," she said in a polite but icy voice, not waiting for the other woman as she started down the hall.

Her overwhelming need to escape Jarod prompted Amanda to change the course of the tour, which usually began with the rooms on the first floor, by leading the woman to the grand staircase. She began her recitation.

"As we go up the stairs to the second floor, you'll notice indentations and scars on the original oak steps. These disfiguring marks are believed to have been caused by Union soldiers riding their horses through the house when it was first taken."

The tour of the second floor took very little time, with Vanessa Scott showing only desultory interest in the valuable furniture and the ornate canopy beds. She even stifled a yawn of indifference as Amanda led her back down the stairs.

"Which room is the ballroom?" she inquired, glancing idly around at the various doors that led off the main hall. "I'd like to see that."

Usually that was one of the last rooms shown before a tour group was taken upstairs, but since

Amanda had already changed the route to suit herself, she saw no point in not doing it again.

"It's through these doors," she said, walking ahead of Vanessa to open them. She began describing some of the antiques in the room when she was interrupted.

"Is this where the cotillion is held?"

"Yes," Amanda answered politely. "Since the early nineteen hundreds, there's been a dance, or cotillion as we call it, in celebration of Jefferson Davis's birthday."

"Have you ever been to one?" For the first time since the confrontation in the hall, Vanessa's blue eyes turned their speculative gleam away from her surroundings to study Amanda.

"Yes, I have. It's quite a festive occasion. A string quartet provides the music and all the guests are required to wear costumed dress of the Old South days." Amanda artfully used the personal question to describe the atmosphere of the ball, hoping to sidetrack any other nosy inquiries. "The style of the gowns is quite similar to the ones that tour guides wear, only much more elaborate."

"With your red hair, you must have worn green," Vanessa commented.

So much for sidetracking her, Amanda thought ruefully. The truly nosy could never be stopped or made to feel ashamed. "Yes, I did," she replied evenly. "Now, if you notice the chandeliers on each end of the room, they were imported—"

"Did you meet Jarod's cousin Judith?"

Amanda stopped her speech and turned slowly around to face the brunette. "No, I didn't." She waited for the next question. As sure as God made little green apples, there was going to be a next question. Jarod's friend was a royal pain in the—

Vanessa interrupted her silent fuming. "How well do you know Jarod?"

"I barely know him at all, Ms. Scott," Amanda replied coldly and truthfully. "I'm employed by his corporation as a guide here."

"And that's all?" The blue gaze flicked over Amanda's face. The other woman was being deliberately annoying, she just knew it. But she said nothing as Vanessa continued. "I understood from Judith, who's a very good friend of mine, that Jarod caused quite a sensation the night of the cotillion with the attention he paid to a certain redhead in an emerald green gown. Was that you?"

"As I recall, I did dance one dance with Mr. Colby." Amanda's voice was icy.

"Not something you're likely to forget," Vanessa said dryly. "Did he ask you out?"

Amanda pressed her lips together for a second, but replied through clenched teeth. "That is none of your business."

"It seems to be the whole town's business. And everything that has to do with Jarod I make my business." She directed a sickeningly sweet smile at Amanda. "You see, Jarod has his little flings from time to time."

"Really."

"Yes, but they never seem to last."

"If that's true," Amanda murmured sarcastically, "what's the point or purpose of this discussion?"

"None, really." Vanessa shrugged her elegant shoulders. "I was merely curious to see who the little country charmer was."

"You've seen me. Guess there isn't any reason to continue the tour." Under normal circumstances, Amanda never allowed even the most irritating visitor to Oak Run to get under her skin, but she was going to have to make an exception for Vanessa. "You must want to get back to Jarod and make sure he's still there. He could be talking to one of the country charmers, to use your phrase."

Vanessa's glossy mouth opened in a shocked *O*.

"That's enough, Amanda!"

Amanda whirled around at the rough sound of Jarod's voice. Black fire blazed in his eyes. She would have to disagree with that statement. In her opinion, she hadn't been rude enough. But she kept her mouth shut, watching Vanessa put a caressing hand on his arm and say something soothing but inaudible into Jarod's ear.

"Would you wait for me in the car, please?" was his cold reply. "I want to talk to Amanda."

"Of course," Vanessa murmured, flashing a triumphant look at Amanda before sauntering out the ballroom door.

Amanda glared at her back. If there were any justice in the world, she thought, someone that glamorous ought to slip in the mud. There was plenty of it outside and she hoped Vanessa Scott would sink in it up to her neck.

She turned to face Jarod. "I'll save you the trouble of firing me. I quit," she snapped.

"I don't give a damn whether you quit or not! I want an explanation for your rudeness to Vanessa!"

"I lost my temper!" she shouted back.

"That's an excuse, not an explanation." He lowered his voice, but it still vibrated loudly in her ears. "I'm waiting."

"What do you want me to say?" she demanded. "How did you expect me to react to—whoever she was. Was I supposed to smile and nod as if she was just another stranger?"

"Why should it matter to you?" His dark head was thrown back and he was looking arrogantly down at her. "You made it clear the last time we talked that you wouldn't go out with me. Didn't you mean it?"

"Yes, I meant it," Amanda said, suddenly regretting her jealous outburst.

His hands closed around her waist. "Really?"

"Yes," she answered in a tiny voice.

"I don't think you did." He arched one thick black brow. "I believe you would like to go out with me again."

Amanda gazed helplessly into his face. The magic of his touch was beginning to work on her again. Damn him. And double damn the magic.

"I won't beg you," Jarod went on. "I'll ask you one last time. Let's keep it simple. The answer has to be yes or no."

It was an ultimatum. Amanda knew instinctively that he would never ask again. It was a second chance if she wanted it. She did . . . and yet . . .

"I would like to, but—" she began nervously.

"Then you name the day, the place, and the time."

"Monday." She breathed in deeply, braving the darkness in his gaze. "At one o'clock. We can spend the afternoon at Stone Mountain."

He didn't look exactly thrilled. Jarod took his hands from her waist and started to turn away. She caught one of his hands and held it between her own, unconsciously caressing the curling hairs on the back of it.

"Jarod, I . . . I do want to see you." Amanda swallowed to ease the tightness in her throat. "But let's go where there are other people around. A lot of other people."

"Right. So I can't take advantage of you. Little Miss Innocent Amanda." He sighed.

She could understand his frustration—she was

feeling something like it herself. But there was no reason to rush things.

"Okay. Stone Mountain it is. I'll pick you up Monday at one." He slipped his hand from her unresisting hold and walked to the door.

"Jarod?"

He paused on the threshold to look back at her. "What?"

"Do I still have a job?"

"Of course. Do you really think—never mind. I don't want to know what you really think of me." He slammed his hand against the doorjamb, hard. "Ouch."

She studied him for a long moment. "Sorry, but I had to ask. I have to work to help with my college expenses this fall."

"Damn!" he said under his breath. "Amanda, I don't interfere in the management of Oak Run. This place is my aunt's pet project, and she does the hiring and firing. Ask her if you don't believe me."

That was the last thing Amanda wanted to do. His offhand reassurance would have to be enough. But his tone only reinforced the fact that he had never had to worry about mundane things like money and didn't really get it.

"Hey, I need this job, okay? There isn't a whole hell of a lot of work available around here. Even for a little country charmer like me."

"Uh-oh. That sounds like something Vanessa would say. So that's why you told her off." He shot her a knowing look. "Thanks for the explanation. See you Monday."

This time Jarod didn't linger at the door. He left without another word, striding down the hall to the front door and going out. Amanda stayed in the ballroom for a moment or two, trying to collect herself before she had to face the other girls.

"Did he fire you?" Linda asked in wide-eyed wonder. "I couldn't help overhearing some of it."

"No." Amanda sighed. By the end of the week, she knew the story would be all over town, with a few embellishments added for good measure. There was more than one price to pay for seeing Jarod Colby, she realized.

CHAPTER SEVEN

Rising above the Georgia pines was a dome-shaped monolith, five hundred and eighty-three acres of solid granite, which looked a lot like a gigantic gray whale from a distance. But not once Amanda and Jarod got closer.

Into its side was carved a monumental sculpture in relief of Jefferson Davis, president of the Confederacy; Stonewall Jackson, a general in the rebel army; and Robert E. Lee, a general and commander of all the Confederate armies. But the entire work, the size of a city block, didn't look much bigger than a postage stamp when compared with the immense dimensions of Stone Mountain.

Amanda leaned back against Jarod's arm, his hand resting near her waist. As many times as she had seen the sculpture, she was still awed by it.

"Isn't it ironic," she said, glancing into his face, "that Gutzon Borglum did great portraits of Lee and Lincoln?"

Jarod nodded and let her talk.

"He was first commissioned to do this carving in the 1920s, but he left in frustration after roughing in the figure of Lee and became famous later, for his work at Mount Rushmore in South Dakota. Here he was supposed to depict the heroes of the Confederacy and there he completed the faces of four U.S. presidents, including Abraham Lincoln."

"Once a tour guide, always a tour guide," Jarod murmured into her ear. "Next you're going to hand me a brochure and say 'Right this way, please.' "

Amanda blushed. "Okay, guilty as charged."

"Have you seen Mount Rushmore?" Jarod asked.

"No," she answered as a woman bumped into her and quickly apologized.

"It's getting crowded here. Let's go somewhere else," he suggested, moving her away from the viewing area below the sculpture. "Where to now? Do you want to visit the game farm where you can feed the animals? Go on a train ride or tour a plantation?"

There was a slight impatience in his tone. The crowds of tourists seemed to make him restless. Amanda marveled at her own audacity in asking him to bring her here.

"We could go over to the carillon," she suggested.

"Do you think it's safer to walk or drive?"

"I'd rather walk." They skirted Memorial Hall, sometimes following the wake of other sightseers and other times going against the flow of those arriving. "I'm sorry, Jarod. It wasn't a very good idea to come here, was it?"

"If you think there's safety in numbers, then it was an excellent idea," he said. "I'm surprised you even allow me to hold your hand."

"Stop making me feel more miserable than I am," she said unhappily.

"This was your idea," Jarod reminded her. "What were we supposed to accomplish today?"

"I wanted to get to know you better, to find out

more about you than the fact that you own Colby Enterprises." Her voice was uneven.

"I can think of better places than this to get to know someone," he said.

"Let's forget the carillon. Just take me home, okay?"

He shrugged. "Okay. I guess you did learn something about me today."

"That you don't like crowds."

"That, and the fact that I'm willing to put up with them in order to persuade you to meet me halfway." He winked at her and Amanda felt a little better. "But, as beautiful as this park is, I can't say I'm sorry to leave."

"Is that why you came here today?" She gave him a disbelieving look.

"I know you're a little afraid of me. I can see it in your eyes sometimes. But guess what? I'm really not a big, bad wolf." He opened the car door for her.

Amanda leaned back in her seat, thinking that casual statement over quite seriously while he got in, turned the ignition key, and fiddled with the dashboard controls.

The truth? She knew the answer to that question. She was afraid of herself. And it didn't help matters that she still didn't know Jarod very well.

"We don't have very much in common," she said at last.

"I have to breathe, eat and sleep the same as you. The only difference is I may have steak more often than you do." He grinned at her. "Having money doesn't set a man apart or make him better than others who don't have as much. Don't look so surprised."

"I never expected to hear Jarod Colby say such a thing."

"Well, I have been accused of certain flaws in my character from time to time. By you. And a few other people."

Amanda folded her arms across her chest. She didn't want to know who the other people, undoubtedly female, were.

"I am accustomed to getting what I want," Jarod admitted wryly. "Mostly because I won't take no for an answer."

"Once you get something, do you still want it?"

"What are you asking?" Dark eyes glanced her way. "Do you want to know how long I'll keep you around after I know you better? That's a question I don't have the answer for yet."

"At least you're honest about it." Amanda breathed out slowly.

"I try to be honest about everything. I told you in the beginning that I wanted you. I wouldn't be here today if it weren't still true." His comment was made almost indifferently and Amanda found herself annoyed by his candor. "How do you feel about me?"

"I don't know if I like you." She spoke hesitantly, staring straight ahead as he drove easily through the heavy traffic. "I mean, physically, yeah, I do. But I can't make up my mind about you otherwise."

"Don't take too long." Beneath the teasing note in his voice, she sensed a warning.

The traffic stayed heavy all the way back to Oak Springs. There wasn't much more for them to talk about, and they were silent for the most part until Jarod stopped the car in front of the Bennett house. Shifting his weight, he stretched his arm along the back of the seat and looked at her.

"Now that you're a little less nervous, will you have dinner with me tomorrow night? In public.

At a restaurant," he added, with a wicked gleam in his eye.

"I'd like to, yes," Amanda agreed. The movement of her mouth brought dimples into play. "Thank you for today."

"Don't let my patience go unrewarded, Amanda." His fingers closed over her shoulder and slowly drew her to him. He gave her a lingering but tender kiss, then gently pushed her back to her own side of the car.

Her hand closed over the door handle.

"What time will you be here tomorrow?"

"Six-thirty."

"I'll be ready," Amanda responded with a smile, suddenly feeling very happy as she got out of the car.

The next twenty-four hours winged by unbelievably fast. Before Amanda realized it, she was dashing down the stairs to meet Jarod. This time there was no tension in the conversation. They talked easily on varied subjects during the drive to the restaurant.

He turned on the charm, but in a realistic way that made her feel genuinely flattered. He got her giggling time and again. Just her luck—he had a great sense of humor, something she hadn't seen much of until then. By the time dinner was over, she knew her feelings for him now were a lot stronger than her teenaged infatuation.

"Where are we going now?" she asked as they left the restaurant.

"You," he said lightly, "are going home."

Amanda glanced at her watch. It was barely nine o'clock. As if he'd read her mind, Jarod added, "I'm leaving early in the morning and I have work to do before then."

"Oh, I see," she said uncertainly. A question

rushed out before she could stop it. "When will you be back?"

"Saturday, I hope. Why? Will you miss me?"

"Don't tease, Jarod. You know I will."

"Why do you think I would know that if you don't tell me?" They were still inside the car and he switched on the interior light so he could see her face.

"You always seem so sure of yourself."

"Not when it comes to you," he said after a moment. "Maybe that's why I find you so interesting, Amanda. If that's the right word."

Interesting—was that how he thought of her? Not the most exciting or romantic way to describe someone, she thought crossly. "Are you going to Pennsylvania again?" was all she said.

"Yes. I'll try to be back by Saturday night. We may yet have our date on a Saturday." His fingers closed over her hand. "Do you have to huddle against the door?"

"I'm not huddling," she protested.

"You're an awfully long way from me."

"The car has bucket seats. I can't climb over the gearshift," she pointed out.

"True." He put the car into reverse, looked over his shoulder to move it back, and gave her a fast, brushing kiss on the cheek before she knew what was happening. "Sorry. It's been a while. The last time was in your father's office."

A warm glow spread over her. "Right. You were trying to get me to go out with you."

He nodded and drove out of the restaurant parking lot onto the street. "Not easy. I must use my superpowers of persuasion with you, Ice Girl."

"Wow, I didn't know I was dating a comic book hero," she teased. "What's your secret identity, Jarod?"

He thought about it. "Smooch Man. I just can't get enough."

"Oh? Am I the only one who gets the super smooches?"

Jarod grinned. "Do you want to be, Amanda?"

"Yes. No. I mean, I don't know."

He groaned. "I'm changing your name. You can be Indecision Girl."

She punched him in the shoulder.

"Ow!"

"Don't tell me that hurt, Jarod."

"Not really. Okay, here we are." He pulled up in front of her house. "Did you enjoy yourself tonight?"

"Yes." Her affirmation was a soft whisper.

"What are you going to do while I'm gone?"

"Why?"

He ignored her query. "If I have any problems, I may not be back by Saturday. I'll call you if so. All right?"

"Of course," Amanda agreed. It wasn't as if she had a choice. She turned to him and felt her lips being immediately possessed by his kiss. She closed her eyes in bliss and just enjoyed his sensual skill. Smooch Man was a damn good name for him.

"Saturday is so far away," he murmured, breaking the kiss at last. His mouth moved against the side of her cheek, intensifying her feverish glow.

"Too far," she moaned softly. "Do you have to go?"

He nipped her earlobe, evoking still another small thrill. "I've been asking myself that and I keep coming up with the same answer. Yes, I do."

She sighed and nuzzled into him, wanting nothing more than another kiss. And another.

"I don't want to let you go into that house," Jarod muttered. "But you'd better go while I can still take my hands off you."

"Not yet," she pleaded, stroking his neck and

running her fingers through his hair. He felt so good—so warm and strong.

"Sorry, Amanda," he said almost fiercely. "But I have to ask you to stop that. You're getting me a little too hot."

"All right." Her voice was uncertain, quivering just like her body was, thanks to his touch. She noticed that his breathing was as uneven as hers. "I'll be waiting for you Saturday—whatever time you come back."

He leaned back in his seat and took a deep breath. "Yeah. Whatever." He raked a hand roughly through his black hair, as if he wanted to cancel the sensation of her tender touch.

"Are you angry about something?" she asked.

"No." He made a low sound in his throat, almost a growl. "Well, maybe at myself. I guess I get to go home and take a cold shower," he concluded dryly. "If you would get out of the car, I could calm down enough to drive home. You don't know what you do to me, Amanda."

She sat forward, feeling the truth of his words deep within her own body. A few more minutes under the arousing caress of his mouth and hands, and she might have begged for the satisfaction he promised.

Yet he was, more than ever, still an unknown quantity. She couldn't begin to understand why Jarod, who admittedly was used to having his way, should allow her to deny him.

"You will call if you won't be back by Saturday?" Amanda couldn't hide her aching need for him.

He drew her briefly to him while he pressed a last, fierce kiss on her mouth, then moved back.

"I told you I would, honey. I don't say what I don't mean. Now will you please get out of this car? Don't make me touch you again."

She swung the door open and got out at last. "Hurry back," she whispered and turned away as she shut the door.

Before she reached the porch, he was driving away. After the comparative silence outside, the house seemed alive with noise as she entered. The muted thump of a boom box came from upstairs and mingled with voices coming from the living room TV. Not quite ready to let go of the private ecstasy of her moments in Jarod's arms, Amanda slipped into the empty kitchen. As she absently poured a glass of milk, she heard footsteps coming into the room. She glanced up to see her father appear in the doorway.

"Well, hello." There was surprise in his greeting. "You're home early again tonight. Anything wrong?"

"No." Amanda felt awfully self-conscious, but her father had no way of knowing what she had been doing in Jarod's car. "But Jarod has to leave early in the morning again. He'll be back Saturday."

"Will you be seeing him then?"

"Yeah." A wide smile spread across her face. She couldn't help but look idiotically happy.

"So you two are getting along okay, I see."

"Oh, yeah." She took a big gulp of her milk and licked her lips. "You were right about him, Daddy. He really is pretty down to earth."

"It's easy to see. Convincing you was the hard part."

She drank the rest of her milk and set down the glass. "Consider me convinced."

Something in his daughter's tone made Sam Bennett look at her a little more closely. "Are you falling in love with him, girl?"

A wry smile lifted the corners of her mouth. "I think I already have."

"You've heard all the gossip about the women in his life, I guess." He took the glass of milk and put it under the faucet to rinse it out. "Or have you?"

Amanda laughed lightly. "Are you giving me a warning?"

"I suppose I am." He smiled and put an arm around her shoulders. "If he weren't seriously interested in you, I know he wouldn't be seeing you. I don't want you to get hurt, though."

"I know." She planted a milky kiss on his cheek and rubbed it off with a fond swipe. She understood that Jarod had the power to hurt her, like any other man, but she didn't want to look any farther ahead than Saturday. "Tomorrow is another workday, Daddy. I think I'll call it a night."

"I imagine I'd be wasting my breath to wish you pleasant dreams." He chuckled.

"That's right!" Her brown eyes sparkled as she walked lightly out of the kitchen. "I don't have any other kind these days," she called from the hallway.

The black telephone seem to stare back at her. Amanda readjusted the book she'd propped on her knee and looked away, telling herself again that Jarod would be back on Saturday as he had promised and there would be no need for him to call.

But the closer it got to Saturday, the more apprehensive she became that something would happen to detain Jarod in Pennsylvania.

"We're going out to get Cokes, Amanda." Her brother Brad slapped playfully at her leg, Cheryl Weston standing beside him. "Quit moping around beside the telephone and come with us."

"Tobe's coming, too," Cheryl urged. Amanda knew her friend wanted her to make it a foursome so Cheryl wouldn't have to compete with Tobe for Brad's attention.

At that moment, Tobe walked into the living room. Brad waved him over. "Tobe, take over. Use your influence with Amanda," he ordered. "She won't budge."

"I don't feel like going out tonight," Amanda declared with a shrug.

Tobe took the book from her unresisting hands and tossed it on the table beside the phone, then joined her on the couch. His arm encircled her shoulders.

"How's this for influence?" he asked Brad.

"Not bad."

"Take your big brother's advice," Tobe said with a wink. "You can grow old sitting around waiting for the mighty Jarod Colby—you said yourself he wouldn't call until tomorrow. It's Friday night. Who wants to stay home on a Friday?"

"I do," Amanda insisted with a laugh.

"We're only going to go out for a couple of hours," Brad urged.

"Maybe he'll find out you were with me," Tobe teased. "It might make him jealous."

"I'm not interested in making him jealous," she said, taking the hand that was resting on her shoulder and raising it over her head so Tobe's arm was back at his side.

"We'll go somewhere and dance." Tobe didn't give up. "You like to dance. It'll be fun. Then maybe Cheryl will stop looking daggers at me."

Cheryl threw him another angry glance before looking guiltily at Brad. "I am not," she defended herself, then added her plea to Tobe's. "Come on, Amanda. We won't get back late."

"Amanda!" her mother's voice called. "You have a visitor."

All heads turned in unison. Amanda's heart skipped a beat . . . and stopped. Jarod was standing there. She sprang up from the couch, moving to him with unconcealed happiness.

"I didn't expect you tonight," she said softly, gazing into his face.

"Obviously," he replied, casting a stern look at Tobe. "I finished sooner than I thought I would."

"Another fifteen minutes and you would have been out of luck," Tobe said breezily. "Good thing you got here in time. She would've killed me if she'd found out you'd come while she was gone and I'm too young to die."

"Right."

"What's the matter, Jarod?" Amanda asked softly.

"Just tired, I guess." He sighed and looked around at the group, and then back at her. "Would it really have bothered you that much if you'd missed seeing me tonight, Amanda?"

Her mouth opened immediately to assure him of that, but her brother broke in before she could speak.

"Is that an understatement! She hasn't set foot out of the house since Tuesday night except to go to work. Nobody was allowed to stay on the telephone longer than five minutes in case you called."

"Bradley Bennett!" Amanda cried in embarrassed protest, her gaze sliding self-consciously to Jarod. She noticed that her parents had come into the living room and took him by the arm to hustle him out before they said something tactless, too. "Let's go out on the porch."

Jarod nodded politely to the older Bennetts and followed her down the hall to the front door. Once outside, Amanda walked quickly to the railing.

"I hope you didn't get the wrong impression in there," she said nervously, smoothing back her hair. "My stupid brother is always teasing me about my dates."

"You mean you didn't miss me?" Jarod asked.

Amanda turned sharply. "Oh, yes, I did." At his soft chuckle, she realized he had been teasing her and she colored.

"For just a second, I thought you didn't when I walked into the room and saw you sitting on the couch with that Peterson guy," he said.

"Tobe? He's like another brother to me."

"He'd better be." There was just enough underlying emotion in his voice to let her know he meant it. In the glow of the summer moon, she watched him lean back against the outside wall. It was actually enjoyable being just a little distance away from him so she could look her fill.

"Momma didn't give me any warning of your arrival," she said.

"Did she need to?" He gave her an odd look. "What does your family think of me, anyway?"

"My younger sister thinks you're awesome. My brothers don't seem too impressed. But then they're guys. Being impressed would be uncool."

"I've only met Brad."

"Like I said, Tobe is just another brother."

He nodded. "What about your parents?"

She crossed her arms over her chest and walked up and down on the porch, wondering what he was getting at. "My dad likes you. I think he even admires you. He's said some really nice things about you. And my momma—well, I guess she likes you, too. Everybody knows who the Colbys are."

As she looked at his enigmatic expression, she realized that wasn't quite true. It would be a while longer before she got to know this particular Colby really well, but she was looking forward to doing just that.

"Sometimes I wish I wasn't a Colby," he said wearily. "It's just too damn much responsibility and too much work."

"Jarod," she breathed. "Something is the matter. Why don't you tell me?"

He groaned and let his head rest against the siding. "I've gone thirty-six hours without sleep and crammed four days of work into three. I left a team of attorneys to tie up the loose ends, caught a plane back to Atlanta and drove straight here because I couldn't stand being away from you another minute."

Amanda stayed a few feet away, rooted to the spot. He made no move toward her, didn't seem to want to hold her.

"Damn it all." He sighed again. "I don't know why I'm snapping at you. But I am bone-tired. And frustrated. Nothing went the way I planned it. I hoped to find you alone."

"I was waiting for you," she said quietly.

"Not by yourself."

"Let's not go over that again. You have absolutely no reason to be jealous."

He shook his head. "I guess I don't. Look, let's get out of here and go for a ride somewhere, okay?" He straightened up and caught her hand, holding it as if her warmth were a lifeline.

"Yes," she murmured, as if she needed to say it when she was already moving toward the car.

"Better tell someone," he said.

"You mean, where we're going? But you haven't told me."

He just smiled and shook his head. "Then tell

your parents not to wait up. They don't need to know everything. Any reasonable excuse will do."

She turned back and went into the house to explain.

CHAPTER EIGHT

The moon shone silver above the pine trees, and a smattering of stars winked in the darkening sky. Amanda had no idea where they were going, but she didn't care. Her parents had only said to call if she was going to be very late, and they didn't seem inclined to breathe down her neck.

Her brother, Tobe, and Cheryl had even refrained from teasing her. Another miracle. But Amanda supposed her friend would demand the details later.

Jarod slowed the car and turned onto a well-maintained dirt road. "This is a secret road to a place I know. Okay with you?"

"Sure," she said. He had come back and she was happy. That was all she needed to know right now. Three days of separation from him had only intensified her feelings for him.

If he had missed her that much—and worked so hard to return a day sooner—then things were going her way. He drove the car several more miles until they were at the edge of a small clearing and stopped. "This is it."

She looked around at the open expanse of land and then up at the starry sky arching above. "Where are we?"

"Technically, in the middle of nowhere. One of my favorite places. But you're on Colby land. It's posted. Maybe you didn't see the signs."

Amanda hadn't. She got out of the car when Jarod did and looked around. It was a beautiful summer night, alive with the whispery rustling of the pines. The familiar sound came to her on the warm, pine-scented breeze.

So far, so good. She was up for adventure. It sure beat sitting on the couch staring at a telephone that never rang, and it beat going out for Cokes with people she'd known all her life.

She wasn't even nervous. In fact, at the moment she felt like nothing could go wrong with Jarod by her side.

Which was exactly where he was. He had grabbed a blanket from somewhere, probably the backseat, and held it under his arm. "Let's go lie down and count stars."

"That'll take all night."

"I have time." He looked at the luminous face of his watch. "Maybe you don't. When will your folks expect you back?"

Amanda shrugged. "I'm with you. They won't worry until sometime after midnight."

"Then we've got a few hours. Come on."

He took her by the hand again and walked with her to the center of the clearing, where he shook out the blanket and spread it on the grass.

Amanda kicked off her sneakers and lay down on one side of it. Jarod did the same. For the better part of an hour, they looked up at the night sky. She scarcely knew what she was seeing, but he pointed out a few constellations, and then they lay in silence, close enough to kiss but not touching. She had the wonderful feeling that they had gone off the edge of the world together, into a private little Eden of their own, lost in the woods.

Of course, Jarod owned these woods, so he couldn't get kicked out like poor old Adam. The thought made her laugh a little, and he laughed, too, after she explained.

Then Jarod put an arm around her body and drew her close. Amanda didn't stiffen. She melted into him with all the pent-up longing of their time apart. Three days had felt more like three months. It might have been three years, as far as she was concerned. The mere touch of his hand was enough to unlock the passion she could no longer hold back.

Her mouth was soft with longing, her lips parting in anticipation of his kiss. He buried his face in the hair that tumbled over her shoulders, then plundered the softness of her throat, making her arch her head back.

He moved back to her face, raining kisses on her eyes, cheeks, and ears until Amanda was turning her head to find his wandering mouth and take her own pleasure.

The kindled fire he had sparked burst into searing flames of demanding passion when he finally allowed her lips to touch his. She whimpered softly, craving his deeply sensual caresses and not wanting—not even thinking—to say no.

He allowed her to caress him in return and her hands explored his body, unbuttoning his shirt with fumbling eagerness and letting her hands run over his chest. He was almost hot to the touch, radiating a sexual warmth that melted the rest of her inhibitions.

Resistance was impossible. It never even crossed her mind to protest when his fingers undid her blouse and unhooked the front clasp of her bra, and she felt his fiery touch against her naked skin. She was molded in his hands, submissive to his gentle mastery, willing to become whatever he wanted.

Slowly Jarod moved over her, the sensual pressure of his body holding her still and ready. As his legs slid intimately between hers, a shudder of mindless ecstasy quivered through her.

His mouth moved across her cheek, the warmth of his breath, uneven like hers, ruffling her hair that was now tumbled over the blanket. "Do you want me?" he whispered. "I won't hurt you, angel, I promise."

The sound of his husky voice opened the last gate and released the torrent of love behind it. Her hands lovingly cupped his face to allow her lips to move over his.

"I love you, Jarod," she whispered, aching certainty in her voice. "I love you completely. I love you. I love you."

It took a full minute before Amanda felt the stiffness with which he held himself. Then her caressing fingers felt the tight muscles of his jaw. In the next instant, he pushed himself away from her, unmindful of the hands that tried to hold him. Hurt, she rose halfway, propping herself up on one arm and trying to recover her wits.

"Jarod?" Her voice was questioning and puzzled.

He drew her against the comfort of his body, but the intimacy they had just shared was gone. Amanda could feel the tension in his muscles, the sudden rigidity in the way he held her.

"What did I do?" She studied his face in the moonlight, unable to believe that his desire could disappear so quickly.

"I want you." The skin of her throat burned where his fingers touched it even as his cold voice struck her like a blow. "I want you, but I'm not going to lie, Amanda. I don't love you."

She gulped back a cry of pain and looked blindly away from his face. Hot waves of humiliation and shame engulfed her. She tried to pull free of his arms, but he kept her there. In a strange way, she was too stunned to protest.

"You don't care for me—at all?" she asked with agonizing softness.

"I want you," he repeated bitterly, and then he went on. "The same way I've wanted dozens of other women."

Her heart clenched with pain. "So I'm nothing special. Not different in any way, huh?"

"What difference could there be?" Jarod said, rolling back onto the blanket.

"Love."

"There's no such thing."

For a while, the only sound was the chirping of crickets and the rustling of the pines. Amanda rolled onto her back, too, and started buttoning up her blouse. At least no one had seen them—or heard her foolish avowals of love. She shivered, feeling a chill that had nothing to do with the warm summer night.

She sat up, looking around the edge of the blanket for her sneakers.

"That was lust, in case you were wondering." His low voice startled her.

"Thanks for the explanation. I get it."

"Love is a joke."

"Maybe to you it is. I believe it's real. It's just not real to you."

Amanda found one sneaker but not the other.

She held it in her hand and untied the knotted laces she hadn't bothered with when she'd kicked them off to join him on the blanket.

"There's two divorces for every marriage."

"Jarod, we're sitting on a blanket under the stars. We almost made love, passionate love. And you want to talk statistics. Here's one for you: My momma and my daddy have been married for I don't know how many years, and raised six kids, and they still love each other."

"They're lucky," he said. "And so are you, to have parents like that. My mother and father weren't exactly an example of a happy marriage. They drove each other crazy."

"I see. And what about you? Are you crazy?" She contemplated whapping some sense into him with the sneaker but thought better of it and set it quietly aside.

"No. Well, maybe a little. I've been thinking about you—about us—too much, I guess. Losing sleep. That's not good for my thought process."

Amanda nodded, watching him sit up and button up his shirt. So much for passion under the stars. So much for love without end. Jarod Colby wasn't going to change his stripes—make that pinstripes, she thought wryly—to suit her emotional needs.

"You said that you love me." His tone was flat.

"Sorry. Me and my big mouth—" she began.

"It won't last," Jarod interrupted her. "The newness will wear off and so will the excitement. Trust me on that, Amanda."

"A few months?" she asked, appalled by the cynicism in his voice. "Is that how long most of your affairs last?"

There was a pause. "Yes."

"Even Vanessa?" Her lips trembled as she said the name.

"Vanessa Scott didn't even last that long. She wants to marry money. Believe it or not, I don't have enough for her. Or I wasn't willing to spend it all on her. Same difference. She's a bitch."

"I could have told you that," Amanda said.

He only shrugged. "She looked good. Arm candy, if you know what I mean. Always welcome at corporate functions."

"I can't believe I'm hearing this." Her hands moved to cup her ears. "And I was so determined not to seem clutchy or needy or weird that I didn't even ask you about her until now. I assumed that—"

"You don't have to assume anything. She's out of my life."

Amanda picked up the sneaker again, wondering where the other one was. She wanted to get out of here as soon as possible—and yes, out of Jarod Colby's life, just like Vanessa. She turned to look at his brooding profile and her stupid heart skipped a beat. It couldn't be true. He wasn't that cold. *Oh, yes, he is,* said a little voice inside her head.

"I wish I hadn't told you that I loved you," she said very softly.

"Amanda, I don't know how to explain this in a way that's going to make sense to you."

"Try," she said miserably.

He leaned back on his elbows and looked up at the stars. Their positions had changed. The moon had reached the tops of the pines and seemed to be settling into them.

"You let yourself get carried away by your emotions."

Amanda snorted. "You got me pretty stirred up."

"But I never asked you to believe in something that doesn't exist."

"You're talking about love again, right?"

"Right."

"Just wanted to make sure. Go on."

He gave a harsh sigh. "You want me and I want you, but don't mistake the desire you feel for love. You're young, Amanda. Romantic dreams must seem very real to you."

"I love you, Jarod," she said very softly. "The way I feel is no dream that's going to fade in the morning. But if all you want from me is sex, then the answer is no. I'm not really interested in an affair. And if the only thing you feel for me is lust, I don't ever want you to touch me again."

He turned to face her at last, studying her closely by the fading light of the moon. His mouth tightened and he said nothing more for an interminable minute.

"Okay. I'll take you home."

They got to their feet, found their shoes, picked up the blanket and headed for the car. He opened the door for her, tossing the blanket in the backseat first.

"I feel sorry for you, Jarod," Amanda said numbly as she started to get in the car. "To not believe in love must make you the loneliest man in the world."

He only shrugged, as if he felt sorry for her. The cold look in his dark eyes froze her. Each slow beat of her heart seemed to widen the crack that was slowly appearing in its walls.

Jarod slammed her door and she stared out the window with unseeing eyes. There wasn't much to see. The clearing where they had lain together fell into shadow as the moon slipped behind the trees at last. The dirt road that led to it, the highway that took them home, were lost in a blur of tears.

* * *

It was days before her numbed shock wore off. And after them came a succession of more days when Amanda desperately tried to hate Jarod. If he had deceived her, she might have succeeded. Instead she found her love for him laced with compassion. Even pity. She wouldn't want to be him, not for a minute, but she loved him all the same.

The searing heat of August at least held a promise that the cooler days of September were not far away. Amanda held on to her sanity by convincing herself that when September came, she would leave behind the memories of her summer love, and chalk it up to experience.

Might work, if the man you loved was a little less memorable, she thought wistfully. Jarod's burning kisses, his dark good looks, his warmly sensual lovemaking—all of that made for tempestuous dreams.

At first her family had teased her about Jarod's sudden absence after all the attention he had been paying her. Then they began to read between the lines of her stoic replies and see the strain behind her smile. His name was avoided. The unasked questions in her parents' eyes were the hardest to ignore. Only once did her mother asked what had happened. Amanda had merely shrugged and said they'd quarreled, adding, to stave off more questions, that it was personal.

Her parents thought the world of him as an employer and as a person, unfortunately. Somehow she couldn't bring herself to destroy that, no matter how much he had hurt her. Vengeance just wasn't something that gave her a thrill.

Beads of perspiration had collected on her forehead and upper lip as Amanda turned to wave her thanks to Linda, who'd given her a ride home from Oak Run. Her clunker was up on the hoist in Bubba's Garage at the moment, and her father had failed to come for her. A smile flitted across her face as she noticed the family car still parked in the driveway. He'd probably gotten all wrapped up in a baseball game and forgotten the time.

As she mounted the porch steps, she listened for the blare of the radio or TV but heard nothing. She swung open the screen door and noticed the faint whirr of an oscillating fan in the living room. There was no rattle of dishes or silverware, no aroma of food being cooked for Saturday-night dinner, no voices, only the lonely whirr of the fan.

"Mom! Dad!" A puzzled frown wrinkled her brow as she walked down the hall glancing into each empty room. "Grandpa! Where is everybody?" Her path carried to the stairwell. "Bonnie, are you home?" Only her own voice echoed back.

A car door slammed in front of the house and Amanda hurried back to the door. She reached the screen door at the same instant that a tall, dark figure strode onto the porch. Amanda paled.

"What are you doing here?" she whispered as Jarod opened the door and walked in.

"I went to Oak Run to pick you up, but you'd already left," he said, as if that terse reply answered her question.

Her eyes scanned his face, memorizing each ruggedly handsome line of it just in case they got into another fight and he walked right out again.

"What do you want?" she demanded as she turned away before the temptation to melt into his arms would become irresistible.

"Amanda . . ." he began.

His hand reached out to grasp the soft flesh of her arm, left bare by the ruffled gown that was her uniform, but she wrenched free of his light hold, crying out. "Don't touch me! Don't even come near me!"

"Stop it!" This time his fingers held her shoulders in an iron grip from which she couldn't shake free. "Your father is in the hospital. I promised your mother I would bring you there as soon as I could."

Her struggles ceased. "That's not true! You're saying that to . . . to . . ." Fear clouded her eyes as she stared into the unchanging, harsh expression on his face.

"It is true, Amanda. The doctors are pretty sure your father had a stroke," he answered grimly.

"I don't believe you." Her red-gold hair tumbled free of its pins as she shook her head vigorously. "How would you know what happened to my father?"

Jarod breathed in deeply as if to control his anger. "I'm a director on the hospital board. We were touring the hospital this afternoon to make recommendations on updating the facilities. I was there when the ambulance brought your father in."

"No!" Her protest was a horrified gasp, but this time Amanda believed him.

"Don't get hysterical on me," Jarod ordered. He must have seen the panic in her eyes. "He's alive but in critical condition. Your brother and grandfather are at the hospital now, but I think your mother needs you there, too. Go upstairs and change out of that gown. Where's your little sister?"

"Bonnie?" she asked blankly, trying to gather her scattered wits and react with the calmness he possessed. "She's, er, she's working, I think . . . She's a waitress at Shorty's Café. I . . . I can't remember what time her shift ends."

There was a frantic sob in her last statement and the pressure of his hold increased slightly in a silent command not to panic. "I'll call and find out while you change," he said firmly. He turned her around and pointed her in the general direction of the stairs.

After the first few faltering steps that Amanda took, tears began streaming down her face. She gathered the long folds of her gown in her hands and ran the rest of the way to her room. Her parents had always seemed indestructible, growing older without ever aging. She couldn't even remember them ever being sick. Now her father was lying in critical condition in the hospital. Her fingers were trembling so badly she couldn't unhook the back of her gown. Sobs of despair tore at her throat as she attacked the metal fasteners again.

"Amanda?" Jarod's voice came from the upstairs hall.

"I'm . . . I'm in here," she called weakly.

The door to her room opened immediately. "Bonnie left the restaurant about five minutes ago. She'll be here any minute," he told her.

"I can't undo these hooks," she murmured. The sight of his composure forced back the sobs as she quickly scrubbed the tears from her face.

Under any other circumstances, Amanda would have been conscious of the swift, sure touch of his fingers as they unhooked her gown. Right now she was only grateful for their steadiness. The need for haste pushed aside her modesty as she stepped out of the ruffled gown, letting it fall in a heap on the floor. Somewhat aware that her scanty undergarments didn't cover much, Amanda accepted the clothes that Jarod took at random from her closet and thrust at her, not looking at him or them.

"Hello! Where is everybody?"

With her clothes in her hand, Amanda ran to the door. "I'm upstairs, Bonnie!" she called. "Come up here!"

Then she turned, not listening to the sound of her sister's footsteps on the stairs. Her frightened eyes searched Jarod's face, needing the assurance of his self-possession to break the news about their father.

"Get your clothes on," he said quietly. His calm tone helped Amanda to calm down, too, but her heart suddenly accelerated when Bonnie burst into the room.

"Where's everybody gone?" she demanded. She stopped short at the sight of Jarod standing in the center of the room and Amanda just slipping on a pair of cargo pants. Bonnie immediately took a hasty step backward, her face turning crimson with embarrassment.

"Bonnie, wait!" Amanda called out, glancing guiltily at Jarod as she realized how intimate the scene must look. "Jarod is here because—" She walked over quickly to take her younger sister's hands. "Daddy is . . . Daddy's in the hospital."

Bonnie looked from one to the other in disbelief. "No!"

"I couldn't believe it either, but it's true." Amanda stared down at the hands she held in her own.

"Your father has had a stroke." Jarod walked up behind them and handed Amanda the top he'd pulled off a hanger, a gentle reminder to finish dressing. "As soon as Amanda is ready, I'll take you both to the hospital so you can be with your mother."

"But Daddy's never been sick," Bonnie protested. "You must be wrong!"

As her younger sister seemed about to give in to her own rising hysteria, Jarod stepped between

them, his soft, husky voice gently admonishing
Bonnie to stay calm, and telling her that her mother
would need the strength of all her children. All
the while his dark gaze kept track of Amanda, so
that when she was ready to leave, he was already
guiding Bonnie out of the room and to the stairs.

At the hospital the two girls were shocked by the
ravages of the fear and grief that seemed to age
their mother as they watched. A numbed sense of
disbelief hung like a cloud over everyone, including their grandfather, who sat hunched in a corner in a chair that was too small for him, unable to
accept that somewhere in the hospital his son was
fighting for his life.

"How is he, Momma?" Amanda asked, extracting herself from her mother's tender hug and
helping her to another chair.

"I don't know," was the mumbled reply.

"The doctors are still with him." Brad was standing beside the chair, his eyes bright with unshed
tears. "The neurologist is examining him now."

Her mother turned an imploring look to Jarod.
"Perhaps you could find out," she said anxiously.
"But I shouldn't ask you. You've done so much al-
ready."

"We've been over that, Bernice." Jarod smiled,
ignoring Amanda's look of surprise that he should
address her mother so familiarly. "I'll see what I
can find out for you."

Then he was striding away without waiting to
hear the fervent thank-you from her mother. They
all remained in huddled silence for long minutes
before Amanda rose and walked to her brother.

"Have you phoned Marybeth and Brian? Where's

Teddy?" she asked in a low voice so her mother couldn't overhear.

"Jarod's already contacted everyone," Brad told her, shaking his head as if he couldn't believe it himself. "Mandy, I don't . . . I don't know what we would've done if he hadn't been here at the hospital. Momma just sort of went to pieces and Grandpa—he hasn't said a word since we got here."

He cast a glance at the old man and shook his head.

"I'll get him some coffee in a minute," Amanda said. "There must be a vending machine around here somewhere."

Brad nodded. "It's down the hall. Anyway, I did what I could, but it's not like I could get doctors to talk to me the way Jarod can. Momma kept crying and crying because she didn't know what was going on. But soon as he took charge, things didn't seem so damn crazy. He and Momma went off in a corner until she finally stopped crying. I don't know what you and Jarod had a fight about, but whatever it was, he more than made up for it today."

Her brother's words made Amanda's love for Jarod grow a little more. No . . . a lot more. Knowing how his common sense in a crisis had kept her from falling apart and the way he had calmed Bonnie down, she understood how his quiet authority had benefited her mother. She felt a glow of pride in him when he returned a few minutes later, bearing the news that the doctors believed her father's condition had stabilized.

"It will be a while before you're allowed to see him," Jarod told her mother, "but I think the worst may be over. It might even be okay to shed a few tears of happiness now, even if he isn't completely out of the woods."

Weak, laughing sighs of relief echoed through the room as they all said silent prayers of thanks. Yet none wanted to voice their jubilation aloud. As Jarod had said, he wasn't out of danger yet. Amanda touched Jarod's arm, wanting to express her gratitude for all he had done. She smiled tentatively as his dark gaze moved thoughtfully over her face.

"May I see you alone?" she asked softly. He gave a slight nod and she turned to her mother. "We'll be back in a few minutes," Amanda assured her.

With a smile that was divided equally between them, her mother nodded her understanding and Jarod and Amanda walked from the small waiting room.

CHAPTER NINE

The hand resting on her back guided Amanda to the vacant sunroom. Now that she was alone with Jarod she felt self-conscious. She watched him walk to the glass window that overlooked a beautifully landscaped garden and gathered up the courage to speak.

"I want to thank you for all you've done," she said hesitantly, her eyes downcast.

"Maybe you should save your thanks until you've found out what it is that I have done." Before his voice had been persuasively soothing; now there was a brittle quality to it that got her full attention.

"What do you mean?"

"How familiar are you with your parents' financial situation?" he asked.

"What has that got to do with it?" Amanda frowned.

"Are you aware that the equity in your parents' house has been tapped out with second and third mortgages?"

"No," she whispered.

"They wouldn't make a dime if they sold it at this point."

She drew in her breath sharply and held it.

"Did you know their health insurance was canceled?" Jarod went on. "They've been buying low-cost college-issued insurance for you and your brothers, of course, and keeping up with Bonnie's premiums through a state-sponsored program. But they don't have any coverage."

"I didn't know that," Amanda murmured, her eyes wide. "Momma didn't tell me, and it's not like I would go snooping in her papers or Daddy's things."

Jarod shrugged. "Well, you must be aware that they have no savings, not with paying a hefty chunk of the tuition for four. Even with student loans, their contribution is breaking them."

Amanda hadn't know that either—but her parents had always sacrificed for their children's higher education, saying it was well worth it and that they were proud to be able to.

"At the moment, the only money they can count on is the sick leave pay your father is entitled to receive from my company. They can file for disability, of course, but that takes a while to come through and it isn't much." He paused to let the gravity of the situation sink in.

"Oh, my God." She put a hand to the side of her face in shock.

"In less than a month, there'll be no money to pay bills, provide food or shelter, nothing for the hospital costs, and no tuition money for you or your brothers."

Amanda reeled from the almost physical impact of his words. She would never have guessed, not in a million years, that there was so little—or how severe the effects of a catastrophic illness would be, in terms of their ability to care for their father and keep a roof over their heads. "Does Momma know all this?"

"She told me," he said simply. "And I convinced her that my company would take care of everything. I didn't mention that whether Colby Enterprises keeps that commitment largely depends on you."

"On me? Why does it depend on me?" she whispered.

"Well, you see . . . I still want you."

Her stomach lurched sickeningly. "So what are you asking?" She was surprised that her voice could sound so calm.

"That you come to me for the help you need."

She nodded to indicate that she'd heard, not to agree. "And what do you get out of it?"

He gave her a cold look. "What a cynical thing to say. Why do you assume I would get anything out of it?"

"Because you're Jarod Colby. Ruthless tycoon. Beautiful girls hanging on your arm, begging to be your mistress. You get what you want—at least that's what you said."

"Sounds like a bad soap opera. Something tells me you don't think very highly of me, Amanda."

She swallowed hard. "I did—because of the way you helped me and Bonnie and . . . and Momma. But you've got me all confused now. I think what you mean is that you want me to, uh, take care of you and in return you'll take care of my family. That can't be right."

"It isn't. You got some essential details wrong. And you jumped to a few conclusions."

He paced the room, not looking at her.

"And what details would those be?

Jarod smiled slightly. "I'm not looking for a mistress. No, we'd have to be legally married."

She stared at him incredulously. "What did you just say?"

"We'd have to be married to get the full tax benefit for a disabled family member. The IRS doesn't have a box marked *Mistress* on the 1040 form. Not yet anyway. You'd have to be my wife, and we'd have to file jointly."

Amanda got to her feet, felt awfully dizzy, and immediately sat down again. "You're rich. You don't need a picayune tax break like that."

"No, but there are others. I'll have my accountants look into it."

"Jarod Colby, you are a cold-blooded reptile."

He flashed her a burning look. "Am I? Do you hate me that much?"

"No, I don't hate you. In fact, I—" She was not, repeat not, going to tell him that she loved him. That emotion was not uppermost in her mind right at this red-hot moment. "I don't know what I think of you."

"You just said I was cold. Let's leave out the part about me being a reptile."

She nodded. "Okay."

"Want to meet some really cold people, Amanda? How about a sheriff with an eviction notice in one hand and a couple of do-right deputies at your door? They throw your stuff in the street, you know. Then the bank repossesses your car and forecloses on your house."

Amanda shook her head. In a small Southern town like Oak Springs, hard times could and did hit some unfortunate families fast. She had passed by a few forlorn-looking houses with foreclosure notices tacked on the side, but they hadn't been in her neighborhood. She was ashamed to think now that she hadn't given much thought to the people those sad houses once belonged to.

Now, in a very real way, her family stood to lose everything. And Jarod was offering to help. But on his terms, and very strange terms they were.

"I don't have to go back to college. I can work. Brad has enough saved for his first semester's tuition. Maybe Teddy does, too, and Brian," she said frantically.

"Even if all four of you worked, it wouldn't solve the problem of the bills and the loan payments and medical costs, not counting what it would take to live," he pointed out in a strangely reasonable voice that she found scary. Or was it the facts that he was outlining that were scary?

"Your father is going to need rehabilitative care, and neurological workups and a health aide when he comes home. The list is endless and the cost is appalling."

"Shut up, Jarod," she blurted out.

"What?"

"This is crazy. Just plain crazy. My father is fighting for his life and you're giving me a lecture and making a list and . . ."

"He's going to need every single thing on that list. Somebody has to think about this. I volunteered," he said dryly. "As they say, no good deed goes unpunished."

Amanda fell silent.

"Not even Tobe Peterson would be able to loan or give enough money to keep you all going, particularly since his rich parents don't think much of your family." There was a sardonic gleam in his eyes. "Tobe hangs out at your folks' house a lot, but he's not exactly in a financial position to reciprocate their kindness."

"He would if he could." Amanda defended him.

"Believe me, I thought of that. I've considered all the possibilities that might be open to you as alternatives to my offer. If you want your family to get through this, you'll have to come to me."

She shivered at the calculating coldness in his voice. "How can you expect me to agree to—what is it you want me to agree to again?"

"Let me explain."

"Please do."

"I've studied your family. You actually believe in that old motto, all for one and one for all. Sacrifice is second nature to you. With your father lying in a hospital bed, you and your brothers would rally round."

"Of course," she said indignantly.

Jarod nodded. "Exactly my point. And you would set aside your education and your future for a minimum wage job, and never think about the consequences."

"We'd get by. We always have."

He shook his head. "Not for long. Not with the economy in the shape it's in."

"Is everything a business transaction with you?" she burst out.

"You seem to think so."

Amanda rose, standing very straight, if only because she was angry. "So with the blessing of the IRS, you want to marry me. How romantic. Remind me to send an engraved invitation to your accountant."

"You're beautiful right now, do you know that?" he mused. "So proud. So pissed off."

"You got that last part right," she said evenly.

"Don't let your pride keep you from helping your family and your father, Amanda. Your father wouldn't want to hear that you and I were just fooling around. He's an old-fashioned guy, and he would worry about you. He doesn't need to worry; he needs to get well."

"True enough."

"But a husband . . . both your parents would approve. And they wouldn't think twice about letting me, as your husband, prove my love and devotion to you." The edge in his tone made her shiver.

"So you really are asking me to marry you." Amanda needed to hear the statement in order to believe it.

"Yes," Jarod answered without any show of emotion. "Aren't you in love with me anymore?"

For one charged second, she almost thought that he was going to admit he loved *her*. That he had found their separation unbearable. But he didn't say it.

He had once told her that he always got what he wanted. Evidently she was what he wanted at the moment. And at the moment, she was between a rock and a hard place—the biggest rock in the world and the hardest place a person could be in.

"All right," she suddenly said. "If you want me so damn much, you can have me. But I intend to pay you back someday."

He smiled slightly. "I wonder how."

She could take that statement two ways. Either he thought she was going to exact revenge someday for putting her in this position—a very tempting thought, even for someone like her who didn't hold grudges. Or he was actually just wondering.

Not as if she knew the answer to that. Their relationship would be temporary, of course. Getting a divorce or annulment shouldn't be too hard. But for now the Bennetts weren't going to be homeless and they weren't going to go hungry.

Whether or not she had ever loved him—right

now she sure as hell didn't—was irrelevant. Their passionate moonlight rendezvous weeks ago now seemed like no more than a bad dream. She was officially, painfully awake. And love had nothing to do with the arrangement he had in mind anyway.

"I think it's best if we stick to business, Jarod."

He raised an eyebrow. "All right. What are your terms?"

"You agree to help my family in every way you can. Everything gets put in writing. And I want a full accounting, down to the last penny, and I am included in every financial decision that concerns my father and my family." He nodded as she went on, "And I agree to . . . to marry you." She stumbled over the words.

"When?"

"I don't know. I guess we should do it before the end of the year, if you want the tax benefits."

"Spoken like a businesswoman," he said approvingly.

She shook her head. "I'm selling myself."

"Don't undervalue the goods."

Amanda hauled off and gave him a stinging slap. He rubbed his reddened cheek. "If nothing else, it's going to be an interesting wedding. The sooner, the better, I think. With just the immediate family. Since the marriage is a farce and you really don't have feelings for me, we can dispense with the sentimental stuff. All we have to do is get a license and stand up in front of a judge or a minister."

Amanda tensed. "How soon?"

"Next Saturday. Under the circumstances, no one will wonder why we want to keep it simple, and we can skip the honeymoon."

"Good."

"Nothing lasts forever, Amanda," he said bluntly,

not at all upset by the sting in her voice. "Don't worry. You'll come out ahead in the end."

"Marriage really doesn't mean a thing to you, does it?" she said wonderingly.

"No. That's the difference between you and me. A piece of paper or a vow in church aren't what keeps people together. Only love can—" He stopped himself. "What am I saying? You're the romantic. I'm the realist."

"One more thing," she said suddenly, not really hearing what he'd just said. "What about children? We're not making babies, right?"

An indefinable something flickered across his face. "No. I don't want children. Never did. Any more questions?"

"No, none," she said, shaking her head sadly.

"I saw the doctor go in to speak to your mother. Shall we join the others? We don't have to tell them we made a deal."

"Believe me, I won't."

The stroke, a severe one, had left her father partially paralyzed and deprived him temporarily of his speech. He regained consciousness that evening and the family was allowed to see him. Jarod, of course, was permitted to enter the restricted room, not questioned by the hospital staff, who seemed to assume he was part of the family.

Amanda's heart turned over at the sight of her father's lanky frame covered with a bedsheet and surrounded by various tubes and monitoring devices. The worst was trying to summon an encouraging smile as she stared into his brown eyes glazed with fear. The reality of his helplessness sank in, hard. Her throat constricted until the simplest greeting couldn't squeeze through. Jarod's arm moved around her waist as he almost physically carried her the last two feet to her father's side.

"Hello, Sam," Jarod said quietly. "Or maybe I should call you Dad. We have some good news."

Her mother's weariness lifted for a few seconds as she turned to look hopefully at him. But Amanda could barely suppress her start of surprise. Jarod had said in the corridor that they wouldn't tell the family until the next day. Then she saw her father's questioning eyes move to her face for confirmation.

He could hear. He did understand. Her heart almost shattered as she spoke slowly and distinctly. "It's true, Daddy."

"I don't want you to worry about a thing," Jarod said in that calm, authoritative tone. It grated on her now. "We're all family and I'll take care of everything until you're back on your feet."

The nurse on duty in the room blinked at the pair in surprise, but Amanda didn't notice. The frightened look in her father's eyes had dimmed as his eyelids fluttered down and a small breath of relief slipped from his pinched lips.

She knew then that his fear had been for his family and not his own welfare. There was satisfaction in knowing her action had relieved that burden. Instinctively, she raised her eyes to Jarod to thank him for easing her father's mind but thought better of it.

She saw no need to make him feel like a hero. He might enjoy playing that part, but it was only a part.

In the week that followed, Amanda was exposed to the many facets of Jarod's character. With her brothers he became the older brother, establishing a camaraderie even as he gave the impression he was consulting them. Her mother welcomed his wise counsel as he placated her fears on the one hand and smoothed the way on the other. Even her grandfather stopped making snide comments about Yankees and pulled himself together.

Where there was disorganization, Jarod organized. Indecision was swept away by his decisive action. He never explained, yet people were always left with the impression that he had. Charm, diplomacy, compassion, authority, loyalty—all came into play as they were needed.

Amanda had thought he would flaunt his generosity, and essentially buy his way into the family, but Jarod managed to handle the necessary financial transactions in such a businesslike way that no one saw a reason to question him.

She marveled at the ease with which he persuaded others to go along with his suggestions, never issuing ultimatums or reminding them in any way of the power he held as CEO and sole owner of Colby Enterprises.

True to his word, he provided her with a full accounting of every expense from the very first. She was learning a lot—and she vowed that she would never, ever live without a safety net that she planned to put in place once the Bennetts could manage and she was able to resume her own, interrupted life.

It was ironic that Jarod was also honest. If he hadn't been, she would have succumbed to his considerable magnetism in the belief that he loved her. She wondered which was the worst hell—having an affair with a man, then finding out he didn't love her, or marrying a man knowing he didn't love her?

The plain gold band on her finger caught the light. There was no longer any reason to make imaginary comparisons. She was Mrs. Jarod Colby, for better or worse. At the moment it felt worse. But it was fear Amanda felt.

Standing at the altar with Jarod at her side, she had repeated the marriage vows that to her had always been sacred. The quiet clarity of Jarod's voice had made her heart ache. He had sounded so sincere, yet when her hopeful gaze had turned to him, there was no expectant light of tenderness in his dark eyes, only a possessive look that seemed to brand her as his. Until the ceremony everything seemed to have been moving at triple time. Now it had suddenly ground down to half speed.

The filmy net curtain slipped from her fingers. The only thing visible was her own reflection staring back at her from the windowpane. The sleek satin sleeves of her robe felt as chilly as the apprehensions that enclosed her heart.

Knowing there was no bond of love between them was beginning to make her believe that the ceremony and the marriage license meant nothing, and knowing that any minute Jarod—correction, her husband—would walk into the bedroom didn't ease the emotional turmoil that brought wary shadows to her brown eyes.

Except for the coolly indifferent kiss Jarod had given her at the wedding, he had not touched her. That was another thing she couldn't understand. He professed to want her so much, yet he hadn't shown the slightest trace of emotion or desire.

Her hands rubbed her arms, trying to rid herself of the shivers that trembled over her skin. A flush of shame colored her cheeks as she wondered how she could possibly meet Jarod's eyes. In retrospect, Amanda could see he had bought and paid a high price for her. But that had been her choice and she knew it.

"Are you afraid of the dark, Amanda?"

The mocking voice spun her away from the window, her fingers automatically sliding up her pale green robe to clutch the front more tightly together. She had thought her hearing was attuned to the water running in the shower of the adjoining bathroom but, lost in reverie, she had not heard it stop. Every light in the muted gold bedroom was on, an attempt by Amanda to take away the dominance and luxurious intimacy of the turned-down bedding.

Jarod's question hung in the air. She stared, wide-eyed, at the short toweling robe wrapped around his middle. He was tanned all over, and his broad chest with its thick cloud of curling black hair tapered to narrow hips and a flat stomach. The sinewy muscles in his thighs and legs seemed coiled, waiting for the command to carry him across the room to her. Her gaze moved to his face, noting his faint smile of amusement at her inadvertent scrutiny of his body.

Amanda turned away and stared out the window once more, her face hot.

"What induced that becoming blush?"

The gold carpet didn't betray the sound of his movement, but the snapping sound of a light being switched off warned her that he had moved. There was another click and another light went off, leaving only the lamp beside the bed. Then her nose caught the clean scent of soap behind her and she stiffened.

"Not thinking about what Cheryl said, are you?"

Her head dipped slightly as she remembered the mortification she had felt when Cheryl blurted out the story of Amanda's schoolgirl crush on

Jarod at the small reception after the wedding. She would never forget the cynical smile on his face as he listened.

"Must you bring that up?" Her fingers nervously raked back the red-gold hair that had fallen forward.

"It's a funny story. And it explains a few things."

"Such as?"

"The way you resent me, for one."

She snorted. "I have a lot of reasons to do that."

"Well, maybe not. Your girlhood dream came true when you married me this afternoon. Now you have me right where you want me."

"I don't want you. Not like that." She turned around to face him, but she hadn't realized how very close he was to her. The few inches that separated them made the impact of his virility all the more potent. She couldn't catch her breath.

Amanda quickly averted her gaze, although she seemed to have lost the power to move away from him. She had a clear view of the bed behind him and she shut her eyes tightly for a second against the sudden vision of Jarod's raven black hair contrasting with the whiteness of the pillow.

"I can't go through with this," Amanda whispered. "I thought I could, but I can't."

"Why?" She had expected arrogance or anger, but not that note of amused curiosity in Jarod's voice. "We made a bargain."

"Yes, but—oh, don't you see?" Her eyes were round and pleading when she looked at him, her fingers once again tightening their hold on her robe. "You don't want *me*. I'm only something you paid for and you want your money's worth. That's different."

He didn't deny it. As he stood his ground, there

was an air of satisfaction in his expression, as if he were glad she had made the discovery.

"And how did your astute mind reach that conclusion?"

"Oh, Jarod." Just saying his name hurt. "In all the times we've been together this past week, you never once indicated that you ever wanted to touch me, let alone make love to me."

"Would you have preferred that I did?"

"Yes," she admitted softly. "It might have made tonight easier for me."

His hand moved under her chin and tilted her head back. "Did you want to kiss me? Do you want to be held in my arms?"

"Yes." She could not hold back the two tears that slipped from her lashes as his hand lightly rested on her shoulder.

"Why?"

"You know why," she answered in a tormented whisper. "I do love you. I wish I didn't, but I do."

Both of his hands moved over her shoulders, down her arms, to close over her wrists, gently tugging so that her fingers would release their hold on her robe before he drew her hands to his chest. His bare skin was fiery hot to the touch. Amanda didn't think she could have pulled her hands away from its irresistible warmth if she had tried. She felt his fingers deftly untying the sash that held her robe in place.

"Why didn't you even kiss me once?" Her words came out in an agonized moan as his hands slid around her waist, their touch burning through the thin fabric of the nightgown beneath her robe.

"Because I swore I would make you ache for me just the way I have ached for you all this time." She could see how tightly leashed his control still was as he pulled her roughly against him, his physical need for her very obvious. As always, the contact of his lean, muscular body dissolved all resistance.

"Jarod, please!" Her hands moved around his neck, though she hadn't wanted them to. He kissed the sensitive side of her neck first, ignoring her plea. "Just pretend that you love me, if only for tonight," she begged shamelessly. She brushed a soft kiss against his chest and murmured something more. "Pretend that our vows mean something to you, too."

With incredible ease, he swung her into his arms and carried her the few paces to the bed. As the weight of his body settled beside her, love and shame mingled in her heart and tore at her.

His mouth brushed the side of her face. "I don't have to pretend. There was one vow I will keep," Jarod declared huskily. "With my body I thee worship."

With a whimpering moan of surrender, Amanda turned her lips to him and surrendered to the spreading fire of his touch.

CHAPTER TEN

The happy trill of a bird singing its song to the rising sun drifted into the silent room. Amanda shifted slightly in protest at its wakeup call. Instantly the arm around her tightened to prevent further movement and she became conscious of the even rise and fall of the muscular chest beneath her head. A deliciously warm sensation filled her as she watched her hand slide intimately over the flat stomach to the dark hairs on the chest that was her pillow. "Jarod," she whispered lovingly to no one in particular, cherishing the sound of it. "Jarod, Jarod."

She could have repeated it a thousand times, but she didn't for fear that she might wake him. The languorous warmth of the strong arms that held her was too blissful to be ended by rousing him from his sleep. Carefully Amanda tipped her head back so she could look at his face. The desire to touch it, to let her fingertips explore the rugged planes and hollows, became almost too much and she lowered her gaze, closing her eyes to snuggle deeper into the crook of his arm.

Then the hand that had been resting on her shoulder slipped to her face. The lean fingers were so close to her mouth that she couldn't resist the slight movement required to brush her lips against them. But at the first gentle kiss, the fingers closed around her chin and Amanda was pulled upward in one swift movement until her head was resting on the pillow inches from Jarod's face. The bright gleam in his black eyes told her that he had been aware of every movement.

"Good morning." There was a faint shyness in her voice.

He smiled and leaned over to press a lingering, sweet kiss on her lips before he moved back to study her thoroughly.

"That's the way to say good morning," Jarod informed her, a smile tugging again at the corners of his mouth. "Or at least the prelude."

"I didn't mean to wake you," Amanda murmured.

"Didn't you? Then why did you keep repeating my name?" His hands were repeating their wayward caresses of last night, moving with tantalizing slowness over her back and hips.

"I like it," Amanda responded softly, feeling the flames of desire rekindling.

"And last night?" He arched her closer so he could nibble on her smooth shoulder. "Satisfied?"

"Yes," she breathed in deeply. "What about you?"

"No." At the hurt look in her eyes, Jarod chuckled and used the weight of his body to push her back against the mattress. "Last night I was satisfied but not this morning."

"I probably should be getting your breakfast," she said in a soft voice.

"Aw. My little wifey. Don't bother." His indifferent reply was muffled in the hollow of her throat.

Her fingers moved lightly over the bare skin of his shoulders. "Isn't that what newlyweds are supposed to do for each other?"

"Mmm. Until they get bored with playing house and Spouse A sends Spouse B off to work with a cup of coffee and a peck on the cheek," Jarod said cynically.

"Somehow I can't imagine you making coffee for me."

"I make excellent coffee. And I don't need a wife to wait on me." His head was raised, allowing him to look into her face, mockery in his black eyes. "I forgot. You're still wrapped up in those romantic notions about marriage and all that happily-ever-after crap."

"Don't make fun of it, Jarod," she insisted, her hand reaching out to stroke his stubbly cheek. "I believe that stuff. And I do love you. I can't help it if I never want to leave you, no matter how shameless and silly it sounds."

"You can keep your dreams, Amanda. I won't take them away from you," he muttered. "Hold on to them for as long as you can."

"What made you so bitter?" Her heart was aching, hurt by the certainty with which Jarod declared that nothing lasted.

"I'm not bitter. Just realistic. How about if we stop talking and do something else?" There was a hint of a smile before his mouth closed over hers.

"Did Jarod say what time he would be home tonight when he called, Hannah?" Amanda asked as the housekeeper walked into the dining room. Just for something to do, Amanda was polishing the silver.

"No, he only asked where you were and what

time I was expecting you home," the older woman replied, taking the pieces Amanda had finished and placing them in the buffet. "And I explained that you'd gone with your mother to the hospital and that your father was being released today. You were going to help her get him settled at their home, but you would be here by four o'clock."

"And he didn't give any other reason for calling?"

"No, he didn't, Mrs. Colby."

A thrill still went through Amanda every time the housekeeper addressed her as Jarod's wife. Amanda silently wondered if she would ever get tired of it, then decided she was acting like a silly bride in a sitcom. They had only been married three weeks. Such a short time when she thought about it, yet it seemed somehow as if she had always belonged to him.

She kept firmly at the back of her mind the secret fear that someday all this undeserved and unexpected happiness would end. Dwelling on it was pointless. She was convinced that heaven and hell were a state of mind and she was determined that the days, weeks, or months she spent with Jarod would be heaven. The hell would be living without him.

Her agonized doubts about him had vanished for the most part. She remembered only vaguely the desperation she'd felt when they'd struck their odd bargain and agreed to wed. The terrifying days spent running from the hospital to her parents' house and back again were not something she wanted to recall.

She was his wife. Everything she had ever wanted was hers. For however long it lasted, she suddenly reminded herself.

Jarod chided her occasionally for playing house,

but she had discovered that the best way to shut him up was with a kiss and then proceed from there. The wild ecstasy of their lovemaking had only intensified.

Since their marriage, she had even attempted a few dinner parties at home for his business colleagues, who were just as likely to be women as men. Amanda knew she was out of her depth when it came to sophisticated entertaining, but with Hannah's help and an eleventh-hour foray to the nearest gourmet supermarket within driving distance, they managed. Candlelight made up for a lot of things, Amanda had discovered. She put pillar candles everywhere and added fresh flowers in simple but striking arrangements.

She enjoyed the pleased look on Jarod's face when he came to inspect the preparations and stick a spoon in one of Hannah's simmering pots to taste. And Amanda hadn't missed the look he gave her somewhere between the last cup of coffee and getting everybody's coats: he appreciated what she'd done, he was having a great time, but he wanted to be alone with her.

A glance at her watch told her it was nearly four and she handed the last of the silver to the housekeeper. She began gathering up the rags and the polish and the papers.

"I'll take care of that," Hannah announced.

The housekeeper didn't object to Amanda taking on some of the extra tasks around the rambling house, but she drew the line at the simple chores of cleaning up, making beds, and doing dishes. Hannah had her routines and she didn't want them interrupted.

Amanda had been accustomed to doing those things all her life, but Jarod had made it clear that she wasn't there to replace his housekeeper. Which was fine with her. Even with the home healthcare aide they'd hired, her mother would need help caring for her father for months to come, until Amanda returned to college as she had planned.

The hands of the clock moved past four and the telephone remained silent. Amanda hadn't realized how much she had been expecting it to ring. Jarod had never called her during the day before, one of the many little things that indicated he really didn't regard her as his wife. She couldn't entirely fool herself on that subject. Their relationship had a significant flaw: the love was one-sided.

With a heavy sigh, Amanda gave up looking at the telephone and started toward their bedroom, deciding to shower and change before Jarod came home. The sound of the front door opening and his voice turned her around to the foyer, a smile of happiness lighting her face.

"You're early," she said, pleased to see Jarod standing there. Then she looked at the older, balding man, briefcase in hand, at his side and her face fell.

Jarod's hand reached out to draw Amanda forward, but he had reverted to that impersonal, corporate-friendly touch that she knew and disliked. At the moment it reminded her sharply that she was only one of many women he'd known, even if she was the only one he'd married.

"Amanda, I'd like you to meet my attorney, Frank Blaisdale," he said.

"Mrs. Colby, it's a pleasure. I've heard a lot of nice things about you." He smiled, but she didn't miss the shrewdness in his blue eyes. Amanda guessed that he hadn't come to chat with her over afternoon tea.

"Thank you," she said simply and let her gaze slide to Jarod. "Would you like coffee or drinks in the study while the two of you are working?"

"I won't be staying long, Mrs. Colby," the attorney said.

"Frank's brought some papers that you'll need to sign," Jarod added in explanation. He met her quizzical look with a bland smile.

"My signature?"

"Yes. Actually, we should've had an agreement drawn up before we were married, but Frank was out of town and he usually handles my personal legal work. I didn't want a junior partner doing it." He said it as if he was doing Amanda a great big favor.

She shook her head ever so slightly as he walked to the door of the walnut-paneled study, but she followed him inside.

"What agreement. What are you talking about?"

"You said you wanted everything in writing, Amanda," Jarod murmured in her ear when they were inside the study and he had shut the door. "Just doing what you asked me to do, that's all."

The attorney was busy unlocking his briefcase and pulling out a few overstuffed, legal-size manila folders. "It's really very simple, Mrs. Colby." He put three sets of documents on the desk, checked to make sure everything was in order, then handed one set to her, one to Jarod, and kept one for himself. "This is what could commonly be called a marriage contract. It outlines your husband's agreement to be responsible for the medical costs of your father's illness, the continuation of his salary as an absentee manager, and the tuition, etcetera, for your college education and your brothers'. There are also provisions here for a lump sum cash settlement in the event of a divorce. Read it over and see if you have any questions."

Amanda nodded.

"You should have your own attorney look it over before you sign, of course," Frank Blaisdale said affably. "You could say later in court, not that we want to go to court, that you signed under duress or that you didn't understand what you were signing. Judges don't like that."

The paper in Amanda's hand seemed to catch fire. Her brown eyes were wide with shock as she glanced at Jarod, seeing only coldness in his gaze.

"Do you have any questions?" His tone was just as cold, piercingly so.

"Is this what you want, Jarod?" she asked softly.

"Yes."

The hard indifference of his monosyllabic reply made Amanda cringe. "Well, I can't sign it right here and now. As Mr. Blaisdale says, I have to talk to my attorney. But I don't have one . . ." She didn't finish the sentence. She wasn't able to think straight.

"I can recommend someone not associated with our firm, if you'd like." The attorney's tone was pleasantly professional.

"Yes. Please do. Thank you, Mr. Blaisdale."

"Call me Frank."

She shook her head. "This is a business matter. Let's stick to business, Mr. Blaisdale." She clutched her set of documents in her hand and left the room.

Her wobbly legs carried her straight to the bedroom, where she hoped she could throw herself into the pillows for a really good cry. A flat-out, Kleenex-soaking kind of cry. She sat on the edge of the carefully made bed and looked at the document in her hand without really seeing it. She could—she would—read it later and memorize every word. But her eyes stayed dry. The tears just wouldn't come. As Jarod had pointed out, he had given her exactly what she asked for.

Crying just didn't seem like an intelligent thing to do under the circumstances, even though the thought of reading the papers in her hand was infinitely depressing.

She set them to one side and rose to look at herself in the mirror. There was a faint smudge of silver polish on her chin, which she rubbed off with the palm of her hand. Jarod was right. She had been playing house. But the document she'd just been handed would make it clear that the game had a few rules. "Are you ready for this?" she asked her reflection.

"Ready for what?" Jarod spoke as he opened the bedroom door and entered, and she turned around to face him.

Amanda took a deep breath and tried to think of what she wanted to say. "I can't say no to anything in this document and you know that."

"Basically, it outlines what you asked for and grants you that. With certain legal protections for me, of course. I'm not a fool, Amanda."

No, I am, she thought wildly. *I'm a fool for agreeing to it, and a fool for loving you in spite of it, and a fool for thinking that all I had to do to make things right was marry you and hope it would turn out for the best.*

She reminded herself that her father was still very weak and still unable to handle the most basic tasks by himself. He wouldn't be able to work for months. And Daddy couldn't ever know that she had taken such a drastic step.

No, she would just have to tough it out.

Her chin dipped in defeat. "What can I say? It's been a great three weeks? Please don't spoil it?"

"You know it won't last," Jarod insisted.

"What? My love or our marriage?" she said softly. She blinked the tears from her eyes. "I know I'll go on loving you after you stop wanting me."

"I told you I don't believe in love." His tightly controlled tone gave no hint of his emotions.

"Yeah, I remember you telling me that. Under the stars, by the light of the moon. What a night. It would have been very romantic—with some other man."

Jarod's jaw clenched. "Well, I'm the man you married all the same. So let's not talk about romance, all right?"

She stood up straight and looked him right in the eye, hating herself for crying. "All right. I've known from the start that it wouldn't last. You'll have to forgive me for enjoying myself. I actually liked sleeping in your bed in your arms, and I liked playing the role of your wife at a dinner party, and I even liked polishing your freakin' silver. Don't ask me why."

"Okay, I won't."

"I guess I convinced myself that I could be happy with what little affection you're capable of giving me. But you can be so passionate, Jarod . . . why do you . . ." She let her words trail off.

"Don't confuse the physical and emotional, Amanda."

She crossed her arms over her chest and threw him a stubborn look. "Is there a clause in the agreement that covers that? The undersigned agrees to keep her emotions to herself at all times, etcetera. There shall be no mention of the dreaded word love, and so forth."

"No." Jarod moved swiftly to where she stood and took her in his arms. She didn't pull away. But his inner coldness made Amanda huddle closer to the warmth his body generated, the shelter of his strong arms offering her the only apparent security that was left.

"Forget the agreement. It's just a piece of paper. I thought it was what you wanted, Amanda." He rested his cheek against the side of her head.

"I don't know what I want," she murmured.

But the agreement wasn't any easier to forget than their marriage license and vows. During the next three months, Amanda understood the subtle strain it placed on their relationship. Behind every smile there was a shadow, silently reminding her that life with him was on a day-to-day basis, never sure when she woke in the morning whether Jarod would decide that this was the day he didn't want her any longer.

She, unfortunately, was all too sure that she wanted him. But she wondered where the hell her pride and self-respect had gone. Her mother would say that Amanda lacked gumption, if her mother knew all the details, which she didn't, not by a long shot.

At least her father was doing better, that was one good thing. But some days were better than others. His doctors had made it clear that that pattern was typical of stroke patients, and reassured the Bennetts that his physical recovery was progressing. He could walk unaided now, but he still tired easily and his moodiness was very difficult for her mother.

Amanda was doing her damnedest to stay cheerful. Being out of her parents' house and in Jarod's did help. She went home several times a week, but she was glad to come back here. If nothing else, the physical comfort of his arms—and his lovemaking—kept her sane.

But he avoided emotional intimacy just as carefully as he had before. She knew perfectly well that he could just up and leave if and when he wanted to . . . husbands did it all the time. In the mornings it was difficult to keep from reaching out to him to reassure herself that he was lying in the bed beside her and reaffirm that he still welcomed her touch. At least that had been so every morning until recently. Now she lay quietly in the bed, watching him dress, and waiting for the moment when he would walk over to kiss her goodbye.

"Hey, lazybones." Jarod smiled into the mirror as he adjusted his tie, his dark gaze alighting on the contrast of her copper hair against the white pillow.

"There's no reason to get up yet." Amanda smiled faintly back, her eyes filling with love at the sight of his strong, bronzed features.

"No, I suppose not."

"There's a chance of showers today. Don't forget to take your raincoat."

He walked to the bed, a mocking glitter in his eyes. "You still enjoy playing the loving little wife, don't you?"

Amanda swallowed hard. "Don't make fun of me, Jarod."

"You used to laugh when I said that," he reminded her gently. He bent down to kiss her mouth, taking his sweet time about it. "Mmm."

She pushed him away, not feeling very well all of a sudden. He stood up and studied her for a long moment, "You look peaked this morning."

"No makeup. What time will you be home tonight?"

"I have to drive to Atlanta, so it'll probably be around seven," he said, brushing the tip of her nose with his finger before he turned to walk away.

"Be careful!" she called after him, and received a last look over his shoulder as he walked out the door.

Amanda lay in bed, visualizing the route that would take Jarod to his study where he would collect his briefcase and papers, then out to the living room where he would tell Hannah what time he would be home for dinner that evening, then finally out to his car. Only if the wind was in the right direction would she hear the purr of the engine signaling his departure.

This morning she heard nothing. Very slowly she swept back the covers and eased herself upright, swinging her feet to the floor. Her legs were shaking badly but she made it to the bathroom before the waves of nausea couldn't be held back any longer and she began retching.

When the last wave had passed, she clung to the sink, fighting the weakness that threatened to buckle her knees. Several deep breaths helped her regain some of her strength and she turned to reenter the bedroom, only to find Jarod blocking the door.

"Why didn't you tell me you were ill?" he demanded, covering the distance between them in one stride and sweeping her up in his arms to carry her into the bedroom.

"I . . . I didn't want to worry you," Amanda stammered.

"From now on," he growled as he placed her on the bed, "I'll make the decision as to whether you're going to worry me or not. Stay here and I'll go tell Hannah to fetch you some hot tea."

Her mouth opened to call him back, but her voice refused to cooperate until the door was closing behind him. By then it was too late. Turning her head into the pillow, she began to cry, using the softness of the pillow to muffle her sobs. Several minutes later Hannah walked into the room carrying a cup of hot tea, not saying a word, but the look in her eyes said it all when Amanda avoided her gaze to mumble a thank-you.

The teacup was drained and she was about to leave the warm luxury of the bed when she heard voices in the hall. Her gaze darted anxiously toward the door just as it opened and Jarod walked in, followed by a tall, thin man. Her heart somersaulted. Only someone with Jarod's wealth and status could get a doctor to make a house call, and this man was undoubtedly a doctor.

"This is Dr. Simon—my wife," Jarod introduced them.

"Good morning, Mrs. Colby. Your husband tells me you aren't feeling well today." The doctor walked briskly forward but Amanda shook her head at him and glared at Jarod.

"I don't need a doctor," she protested. "It's nothing. Probably a virus."

Dr. Simon looked from Jarod to her. "I can't examine her without her consent. You've put me in a very awkward position here, Colby. I stopped by as a favor to you, but if your wife doesn't want to talk to me, she doesn't have to."

"I'm not sick," Amanda insisted, almost fiercely.

"You gave an excellent impression of being sick," Jarod retorted. "Come on, Amanda. All you have to do is talk to Dr. Simon."

"Jarod, please, I want to talk to you—alone. I don't need a doctor."

Her oh-so-concerned husband scowled at her and she fought the urge to slap him. He had a lot of nerve, dragging a stranger into their bedroom. She was still in her nightgown, for heaven's sake, and feeling like road kill. But Jarod spoke before she could do or say anything more.

"Stop acting like a child," he snapped.

"Okay." Amanda took a deep breath, then looked him right in the eyes before she continued in a calmer and quieter voice. "I'm not acting like a child. I'm acting like a woman *with* child."

"What?"

"Nice, old-fashioned phrase, isn't it? It means I'm pregnant."

The silence after her announcement threatened to continue as Jarod stared at her with an unfathomable look in his eyes.

"Happens a lot when a man and a woman have unprotected sex," she added. "But you don't have to take my word for it. Ask the doctor."

Dr. Simon, looking a little foolish, merely nodded at Jarod, then turned to her. "Have you seen a gynecologist yet?"

Amanda shook her head. "Nope. But I will. Just so you know, Jarod, I bought five pregnancy tests at the drugstore last week and did one a day. Every one was positive."

"Well, then . . . congratulations," Dr. Simon said hesitantly. "I'll, er, leave you two alone."

CHAPTER ELEVEN

At the soft click of the closing door, Amanda hesitated. "So now you know."

He only shrugged. Was he pretending that her pregnancy meant nothing to him? She had expected something more typical of him: a flash of fiery anger, followed by a carefully controlled lecture about letting things get out of control, or something like that. But not silence.

It wasn't as if she had gotten pregnant all by herself. He couldn't argue that. He had not asked about birth control. She hadn't said anything. When it came right down it, they had let it happen.

"Why didn't you tell me as soon as you knew?"

"I wasn't sure how you would feel about it."

He gave her a wry look. "And how do you feel about it?"

"Jarod," she snapped, "we're not going to bounce the same question back and forth until I'm ready to scream. I'm too tired to scream. And I just might throw up again. Don't you have to get to work?"

"Yes," he said.

"Then go. Buy a few companies, fire a few CEOs. Cheer yourself up."

He sighed. "You still have a high opinion of me, I see."

"Look, you told me you didn't want children. But we never even talked about birth control and we had lots and lots of sex. Like I said, it happens."

"Can't argue that point," he said slowly.

She looked at his handsome, stubborn face and felt the tears well up in her eyes. The salty taste in her mouth made her want to gag. This was *so* not fun. But the first trimester usually wasn't. She had peeked into a what-to-expect book on pregnancy in the drugstore after she'd bought the tests. What with the nausea, hormonal moodiness, and the emotional and physical changes, she could expect to be fairly miserable for a little while longer.

And then, according to the book, in the second trimester she got to glow . . . and experience surges of energy and enjoy nest-building activity, like picking out a paint color for the nursery and buying a layette. When she was not doing all those wonderful things, she could bask in the radiance of her husband's love. Yeah, right, Amanda thought, feeling even more queasy. That wasn't going to happen.

"Jarod, I want this baby. I know I'll never be able to have you, but this baby will be a part of you and it will be mine. That might not make sense to you but I can't explain it any better than that. When it comes right down to it, I get to make the choice. And I choose to keep this baby."

He scowled. "What you're really saying is that you have me just where you want me."

"Excuse me, Mr. Wizard. Do you not know how that magic wand of yours works? You are just as responsible for this baby's existence as I am. Put that in your agreement, not that I ever signed it, and shove it."

"Wow, you are romantic."

She grabbed a tissue and blew her nose, not caring how she looked or what he might think of what she said. "Guess what. You're not the center of the universe. Not even your own little universe. We just made a baby. Your baby. My baby. In about six months, you get to see what it looks like."

"Me, I hope," he said dryly. "And do you expect my help in bringing up this child?"

"Help would be nice. Yes, I do expect that."

He shook his head. "You'll get what the law requires. We are legally married and there's nothing I can do about that."

"Oh, but we can get a divorce. You can walk out on every promise you made to me and us Bennetts will manage somehow. We always do."

Jarod raked a hand through his dark hair as if he was ready to pull it out. "Maybe so. But what about when you get bored with motherhood? That happens, too, you know."

"Really. Tell me more."

"You'll find some other man when we split up, who won't want the responsibility. What will you do then? Ship the kid to boarding schools? Conveniently forget that you have one, except at holidays, if you remember to send a present?"

"No, his childhood won't be like yours. That I promise you."

"What do you know of my childhood?" he snapped.

"Only the bits and pieces I've picked up from Hannah." Amanda couldn't meet the coldness of his gaze and looked down. It wouldn't be much use to tell him how many parallels she'd noticed between Jarod's childhood and Tobe's. Having a ton of money didn't automatically make people into good parents.

"Isn't that nice. I'm glad she confides in you," Jarod said sarcastically.

"She cares about you. And she's known you forever."

"Most of my life," he amended, giving her a long look. "What else did she tell you about me?"

"Nothing much. I didn't ask for a list of girlfriends, if that's what you mean."

He shrugged. "But I have only one wife."

"So far."

"Amanda, sometimes you really don't know when to stop, do you?"

She went to the closet and took some clothes from various hangers without really looking at her choices until she'd flung them on the bed. None of it matched. She didn't care.

"What are you doing? Packing?"

"No, I'm getting dressed. If you don't mind." She picked up the pants and slid them on under her nightgown, tugging at the waistband, which pinched when she buttoned it. Next thing she had to look forward to, she thought with fury, was not being able to see her toes. And wearing really weird bras.

"Listen to me," he began.

"I don't feel like listening to you," she retorted. "I'm going to see my parents. My loving, kind, generous parents who raised six kids and considered themselves blessed, even if they didn't have a dime to spare while they did it. We all turned out pretty well, if I do say so myself. And I'm going to tell them that I'm pregnant. They'll be thrilled. *You* can tell them that you don't want—"

"No," he cut in sharply. "And be careful what

you say about me. I think I have the right to speak for myself, when I'm ready. There's nothing I haven't done for your family."

She hung her head. That was true. The thought of upsetting her father in any way just seemed wrong. She would have to wait to tell them absolutely everything—and she would have to play this damned game Jarod's way.

"Let's get one thing straight, Amanda. We're staying together until after the baby is born. Then we'll see."

She didn't answer right away, just pulled her nightgown over her head, threw it on the bed, and grabbed her mismatched top. His eyes moved automatically to her bare breasts, which were full and high—one nice effect of being pregnant, she thought wryly.

"Do you agree to that?" he said softly.

He was always in control—she had to hand it to him. Jarod wouldn't change. "Yes," she said. "You know I can't go back home. Not just yet. You have me just where you want me, not the other way around."

He came around to the side of the bed where she stood and captured her in his arms. The hard contact of his body triggered her seemingly insatiable desire for his possession of her.

"I do want you, Amanda." He kissed her with passionate abandon, running his hands over her breasts with sensual gentleness. "More than you know." They fell backwards on the bed and her fingers curled into the thickness of his raven hair as he buried his mouth in her neck.

But in the months that followed, Jarod avoided any mention of the baby, even when her stomach thickened to a proportion that couldn't be ignored. More of his evenings were spent away from the house, drawing questioning comments and looks from the housekeeper. And he was often away on business trips, leaving her to wait and wonder.

Amanda couldn't bring herself to ask if he still wanted her. His standoffishness made the answer all too obvious. But there was comfort in the life kicking vigorously inside her, although it would never replace the blissful sensation of Jarod's arms around her, a feeling that she didn't get to enjoy as her time grew nearer.

The click of her knitting needles competed with the tick of the clock. Amanda had decided to learn to knit. It was supposed to be soothing. So far it was driving her crazy. She cast on a nice neat row and began another, which looped unevenly. Tugging on the yarn only made it worse. She began to wonder if she had the patience for the craft—at the rate she was going, the baby sweater would be finished in about, oh, eighteen years.

She set her needles and yarn aside, and leafed through the course catalog that had come from her college. The students in the glossy pictures seemed awfully young all of a sudden, though most of them were her age. It was difficult to imagine ever being that carefree again—and she wouldn't be, once she had the baby. But she was determined to go back to school. Her mother would set aside time to care for her new grandchild and Amanda knew that Bonnie would, too.

She wasn't about to ask Jarod for permission to continue her education. She wondered whether he would be home for dinner or if he would call at the last minute to say he was delayed and that she should eat without him.

The front door opened. She put the course catalog down, picked up her needles and cast another row onto the loopy one, trying to look busy. If she screwed it up, she could always unravel it later and start again.

Amanda glanced up as he appeared, a closed, emotionless expression on his face as he ignored her greeting to walk to the bar and pour himself a drink.

"How are you today?" His clipped question betrayed his lack of interest.

"Fine," she answered, swallowing the lump in her throat and knitting furiously. She could feel his brooding gaze on her.

"You don't have to do that, you know," Jarod said suddenly. "If you want money for baby clothes, just ask for it."

She concentrated on the sweater. So far she had two inches of one sleeve. "I enjoy knitting. It gives me something to do." An uneasy silence followed her statement. The baby kicked as if to remind Amanda of its presence. "By the way . . . I've been thinking about names for the baby," she said hesitantly. "Michele if it's a girl and David if it's a boy."

"What am I supposed to say?"

"I thought you might . . . want to make a suggestion," she ended lamely, unable to read anything good or bad into his flat tone of voice.

"It's up to you," he said, rising from the leather stool at the bar. He didn't come to her as she had hoped but just stood there, looking at her with an expression she couldn't read either.

Call it indifference—but it hurt. And as big as she was, she couldn't get up from the couch with ease to walk out. She resumed her knitting until the yarn was hopelessly snarled, then threw it all to the floor.

"Damn!" he muttered. "I'm sorry, Amanda. Sometimes I wish I was someone else. Or somewhere else—"

She struggled to sit up. "That makes two of us. Or should I say three of us?"

He came toward her, as if he was about to help her up. She waved him away and stayed where she was.

"Look, Amanda, I haven't been around much but it's for the best—"

"What do you mean?" she snapped.

He merely shrugged. "It's one way to avoid fighting."

"I suppose you're right," she said, feeling the baby kick again. She put a hand over the spot and gave it an answering pat. She already loved this baby, and she intended to keep right on loving this baby. Even if loving the baby's father turned out to be the biggest mistake she'd ever made, her life was still going to go on and she was going to find a way to be happy. With or without Jarod.

He stood there, drink in hand, and watched her. "By the way, I'll be leaving in the morning for Philadelphia," he said finally.

"Oh," she said. "Another business trip?"

"Yes."

"Have fun," she said icily. It had occurred to her that he was seeing someone else—how many business trips could a guy take?—and she guessed by the look he gave her that she was right.

"I'll be gone about a week." He went to the hallway that led to their bedroom. "You can tell Hannah that while she's packing my clothes, she might as well move the rest of my things into the guest bedroom. I'll sleep there from now on."

Her mouth opened to protest but she closed it quickly, thinking better of it before she said something that would sound totally pathetic. Something like *I still love you, you know* or *you really don't want this baby, do you?* She was just glad that his back was to her so he couldn't see the pain in her eyes.

"Mandy, honey, how are you feeling?"

Amanda blinked her eyes open and stared into the beaming face of her mother. A small sigh slipped from her throat.

"Exhausted," she murmured in return, levering herself into a sitting position in the hospital bed. "Have you seen the baby yet? Isn't he adorable?"

"All five pounds and two ounces of him," her mother answered, patting her on the arm. "The pediatric nurse said that's big for a preemie. She reassured us that he's perfectly healthy. He's beautiful, honey. And so are you."

She pressed a kiss to her daughter's forehead. Amanda smiled wearily. It was about the only part of her body that didn't feel strange and achy and sore. Exactly what the what-to-expect book had said to expect.

"He may be three weeks premature," her father said, his speech still a little slurred from his stroke, "but he has enough hair to pass out to the other babies in the nursery. The bald ones, I mean."

"Amanda was completely bald, remember?"

Her father nodded. "And a screamer. You could hear her all the way down the hall to the hospital nursery."

Shivering a little, Amanda drew her robe tightly around her. "Ever wonder why you kept me?"

"You were our pride and joy, honey. Still are. Don't ever forget that."

Her parents stood together, beaming at her, and Amanda noticed how unobtrusively her mother put a steadying hand upon her father's waist, instinctively making sure that he had her support if he needed it. They truly did love each other after all these years and all those kids, Amanda thought wistfully. If only that were true of her and Jarod . . .

She wiped away a tear, and then another. "Hormonal fluctuations," she said brightly to her mother. "The book said to expect them in the days and weeks right after the birth. Nothing I can do about it."

Her mother nodded. "Honey, we reached Jarod about an hour ago. He's flying in from Philadelphia. I know you must be sorry he wasn't here with you when David was born but—"

"Everything happened so fast," Amanda finished for her.

"Yes."

Her father left his wife's side and took the few steps to the bed with ease. Amanda watched him, silently reminding herself that her father had wanted for nothing during his recovery and daily physical therapy seemed to have done him the most good. Her husband—the concept still seemed unreal—had kept his promise to help her family, even though she had never signed that stupid agreement. That was something, she thought miserably. Could be a start. If he learned to love his son, they might have a chance.

A few more tears rolled down her face as her father reached out to give her a clumsy hug. "We're just glad you're all right."

Her mother fussed with the bedding and made sure Amanda was tucked in. "Get some sleep, Mandy. The nurse asked us not to stay long so you could get some rest. We'll be back to see you later today."

Amanda's eyes fluttered shut almost the instant

her parents left the room. It seemed as though only a few minutes had passed before she heard the gentle voice of a nurse telling her that they would be bringing her baby in to her.

As the small bundle was placed in her arms, Amanda knew a joy that was beyond expression. A whole new world opened up at the sight of those tiny little hands wrapped in puny fists, flailing the air while the baby sucked vigorously on the nipple of his bottle.

Once his hunger was satisfied, he slept contentedly in her arms while Amanda gently pushed the silky fine black hair that covered his head into a semblance of order.

"My beautiful David," she crooned softly, lightly touching the button nose of the still red face. "I love you more than anyone else. Do you know that?"

Her newborn son, his eyes scrunched tightly shut, only yawned. She sang him a lullaby, very softly, his first on this earth. She couldn't remember the words but the blissful baby didn't seem to care.

The door to her private room opened but Amanda barely noticed, assuming it was the nurse come to bring David back to the nursery. But she didn't hear the wheels of the Plexiglas bassinette, just footsteps. She glanced up.

It was Jarod. She couldn't help smiling, she was much too happy. Her soft brown eyes looked down again at the newborn sleeping in her arms. "Isn't David the most beautiful baby you've ever seen?"

Jarod studied the two of them for a long moment, then came a little closer. Amanda tried to gauge his reaction to his son in the black steel of his eyes.

"Yes," was all Jarod said at first. He looked at them as if he were drinking in the sight, his face transformed by emotion. "And so is his mother," he added softly.

"Oh, Jarod . . ." She scarcely knew what to say to him. "Where were you?"

He gave her a remorseful look. "In a corporate boardroom. With a bunch of people I don't care about and am never going to see again. When the message came that you'd been rushed to the hospital, I got here as fast as I could."

He reached down to touch the baby's cheek, his fingertip tracing the chubby contours with infinite tenderness. "I sat next to a nice grandma on the plane, Amanda. She'd been bumped up to first class and she was thrilled. She was even more thrilled when I told her I was about to become a father." He paused, fighting back tears. "She gave me some good advice, too."

Amanda just stared at him, dumbstruck. Jarod—*crying?* Then she found her voice. "What did she say?"

"She said that all we had to do was love each other—truly love each other—no matter what, and the rest would take care of itself."

The baby stirred in her arms and whimpered a little in his sleep.

"And she said that babies were a lot of hard work. But pure joy on the good days. I'm ready for some of that . . . at least I think I'm ready." He took a deep breath. "I'll do the best I can."

"Pure joy, huh?" Amanda whispered, looking from their son to him. "I'm ready for that, too."

Jarod sat beside her on the bed, taking great care not to jostle her and the baby. "I am so unbelievably sorry that you had to go through that without me. I should have been here."

"I managed," she said weakly. "Us Bennetts always do."

"I have a feeling I have a lot to learn from you, Amanda."

She had to smile. "Maybe. Right now I'm too damn tired to do anything but love up this little guy in my arms. But I can recommend a few good books if you're interested in babies."

"I am."

"Good. You have one."

Jarod stretched out his arms to encompass them both, awkwardly but gently. He kissed her on the cheek, then on the lips. "I have you. I love you, Amanda. And I love our son. Now and forever."

"That sounds a lot like a promise."

"It is. To cherish."

They were stretched out on the bed, Amanda partially under the covers and Jarod atop them, locked in a loose embrace with the sleeping baby between them by the time the nurse came back with the bassinette. "Don't you know enough to take your shoes off before you get into a bed, sir?" the woman laughed.

Jarod grinned at her sheepishly and kicked them off one by one, letting them fall to the floor with a clunk.

"That's better," the nurse said approvingly, preparing the bassinet for its little passenger. She beamed at them. "And that's what we like to see. A happy family."

Amanda looked up and nodded. "That's what we are."

LOW COUNTRY
LIAR

CHAPTER ONE

With a relaxed sigh, Lisa Talmadge leaned against the curved back of the chair. It was a beautifully restored antique, reupholstered in a patterned brocade that picked up the color of the chair her Aunt Mitzi sat in.

Lisa felt she had been talking nonstop since she arrived, bringing Mitzi up to date on the latest family happenings. Soon it would be time to get down to the true reason for her visit, which was more than just a wish to see her favorite aunt. In any case, Lisa knew that her aunt could find out everything she wanted to know in a matter of seconds.

"Now then," Mitzi began. "I know you had a safe trip from Baltimore, and both your parents are fine, and your brother is dating a girl who drives him crazy. But what brought you to Charleston? Can't be just my scintillatin' company, I know that." She gave Lisa a mischievous wink.

At fifty-two, Mitzi Talmadge looked much younger and her brunette beauty hadn't faded. She was warm, vivacious, and she loved to talk, true to the traditions of her upbringing in the Low Country of South Carolina.

Lisa knew her aunt would get the reason out of her sooner or later. She might as well tell the truth. "Believe it or not, Mitzi, you brought me to Charleston."

"Me? Goodness, why ever for?" A wry smile deepened the corners of her mobile mouth. "Are you having problems with a man? I may not be the right one to ask for advice, considering the mess I made of my marriage."

"You can't claim sole responsibility for that. Uncle Simon had a part in it somewhere." Lisa dismissed her aunt's self-deprecating statement with a shake of her silver-blond hair, a gold hoop earring glittering through the long silken strands.

"That's what Slade says too," Mitzi Talmadge sighed.

Lisa's smile tightened. Her aunt had just put a name to the reason Lisa had come. For the time being, however, that was Lisa's secret until she could find out what was really going on.

"Well, that's nice of him, but people still talk," Mitzi continued, "especially around here and especially the older folks. Lisa, when I was growing up, divorce was still considered a scandal. My momma always said that a woman was supposed to make a marriage last no matter what."

"Things have changed. Even in the South," Lisa murmured.

"Yes, that's true," Mitzi sighed. "But you can understand why I feel so guilty that my marriage failed, even though I know that Simon and I just weren't suited at all." There was a reflective look in her dark eyes as she smiled, her cheeks dimpling.

"I married him because he was so quiet. And I divorced him because he was so quiet," she laughed.

"Which proves I am an eternal romantic. I was all caught up in the idea of the strong, silent type when that wasn't what I really wanted or needed. Poor Simon didn't get any bargain with me, either."

"Don't blame yourself, Mitzi," Lisa said.

"Oh, hush. I was so disorganized when it came to anything outside of my writing that it drove him to distraction. I spent most of my days in front of my computer. I used to tell Simon that my true love's name was Dell."

Lisa had to smile.

"He wanted a happy little homemaker and he got someone who couldn't boil water. Thank God for microwave ovens or the poor man would have starved to death."

Lisa supposed there were still men of her aunt's generation who couldn't fend for themselves in a kitchen. She was glad that things had changed.

"Ours was a very sad mismatch. But at least he had a few happy years with his second wife before he died. She could cook. All that gravy probably killed him."

"Oh, Mitzi. By now you could've met somebody new." Lisa's tone was nonchalant, but there was a sharp edge to the look in her eyes. "Don't you want to? Tell me about the men in your life."

"Men in the plural? You make me sound like a femme fatale. I love it." Mitzi shook her head laughingly, a bright twinkle in her eyes. "You're going to be awfully good for my morale, Lisa. And exactly how did the subject get changed to my love life when I asked about yours?"

"And I thought I'd dodged the question." Lisa smiled broadly. "The fact is that I don't have a love life at the moment."

"I find that hard to believe. You've grown into a beautiful woman, Lisa Talmadge. You have your mother's cheekbones and her blond hair. Those green eyes are definitely from the Talmadge side, though. Do you know, your dark lashes look just like Simon's, not that he's any relation to you, of course. But they are striking."

Lisa blushed.

"But you're sidetracking me again," Mitzi went on. "Now why have you come? Did you break up with some special man?"

"No. There isn't anyone special." Lisa raised her hands as if to ward off more questions. "I'm escaping from nothing but work," she insisted.

"Oh, really? What happened to that young man you were engaged to?" Mitzi prompted.

Lisa reminded herself that her aunt hadn't seen her in person for several years. Without new information, Southerners were apt to recycle old gossip, just to have something to talk about.

"Michael? That was over, hmm, about three years ago. When I graduated from college." Lisa picked up her drink, a delicious, homemade lime rickey. She touched a fingertip to the lime wedge floating on top and watched it bob in the liquid.

"What really happened between you two?"

"Ambition, I guess. I wanted to do something with my degree and focus on a career. He wanted a stay-at-home wife and babies. He was a very traditional kind of guy."

Mitzi made a face. "At least he didn't expect you to do everything. Now women are supposed to have careers and raise perfect kids and keep house all at once. Least that's what I read in *Newsweek*. Probably have that issue around here somewhere." She glanced at the huge, messy stack of magazines on the end table, an expensive antique. "I could find it for you, but if I pull out one the rest will fall and someone'll get hurt."

Zebra Contemporary

Whatever your taste in contemporary romance – Romantic Suspense … Character-Driven … Light and Whimsical … Heartwarming … Humorous – we have it at Zebra!

And now Zebra has created a Book Club for readers like yourself who enjoy fine Contemporary Romance written by today's best-selling authors.

Authors like Lori Foster… Janet Dailey… Fern Michaels… Janelle Taylor… Kasey Michaels… Lisa Jackson… Shannon Drake… Kat Martin… to name but a few!

These are the finest contemporary romances available anywhere today!

But don't take our word for it! Accept our gift of 3 FREE Zebra Contemporary Romances – and see for yourself. You only pay $1.99 for shipping and handling.

Once you've read them, we're sure you'll want to continue receiving the newest Zebra Contemporaries as soon as they're published each month! And you can by becoming a member of the Zebra Contemporary Romance Book Club!

As a member of Zebra Contemporary Romance Book Club,

- You'll receive four books every month. Each book will be by one of Zebra's best selling authors.

- You'll have variety – you'll never receive two of the same kind of story in one month.

- You'll get your books hot off the press, usually before they appear in bookstores.

- You'll ALWAYS save up to 30% off the cover price.

SEND FOR YOUR FREE BOOKS TODAY!

To start your membership, simply complete and return the Free Book Certificate. You'll receive your Introductory Shipment of 3 FREE Zebra Contemporary Romances, you only pay $1.99 for shipping and handling. Then, each month you will receive the 4 newest Zebra Contemporary Romances. Each shipment will be yours to examine FREE for 10 days. If you decide to keep the books, you'll pay the preferred subscriber price (a savings of up to 30% off the cover price), plus shipping and handling. If you want us to stop sending books, just say the word… it's that simple.

FREE BOOK CERTIFICATE

Yes!

Please send me 3 FREE Zebra Contemporary romance novels. I only pay $1.99 for shipping and handling. I understand that each month thereafter I will be able to preview 4 brand-new Contemporary Romances FREE for 10 days. Then, if I should decide to keep them, I will pay the money-saving preferred subscriber's price (that's a savings of up to 30% off the retail price), plus shipping and handling. I understand I am under no obligation to purchase any books, as explained on this card.

Name _____

Address _____ Apt._____

City _____ State _____ Zip _____

Telephone ( ) _____

Signature _____

(If under 18, parent or guardian must sign)

Thank You!

Offer limited to one per household and not to current subscribers. Terms, offer and prices subject to change. Orders subject to acceptance by Zebra Contemporary Book Club. Offer Valid in the U.S. only.

CN124A

THE BENEFITS
OF BOOK CLUB
MEMBERSHIP

- You'll get your books hot off the press, usually before they appear in bookstores.

- You'll ALWAYS save up to 30% off the cover price.

- You'll get our FREE monthly newsletter filled with author interviews, book previews, special offers and MORE!

- There's no obligation — you can cancel at any time and you have no minimum number of books to buy.

- And—if you decide you don't like the books you receive, you can return them. (You always have ten days to decide.)

llı..ı..lll..ı..ıllılı.ı.bı.ı.lı.ıll.ı.ılll.ı.l

Zebra Contemporary Romance Book Club
Zebra Home Subscription Service, Inc.
P.O. Box 5214
Clifton , NJ 07015-5214

"That's okay," Lisa laughed. "I read it too. Anyway, I didn't object to that as much as I objected to him telling me that was what I wanted. It's just as well, because it would've never worked between us."

"You're not sorry, then?" Mitzi asked.

"Not at all," Lisa replied without any regret. "Now I just steer clear of the strong, masterful types and their big egos."

"Smart girl." Mitzi took a sip of her drink and crossed her legs. "Now, you said you were escaping from your job. Every one of your last e-mails complained about staff and management. Hope you're using your home computer."

Lisa nodded. "Hell, yes. When I can. I went almost a year and a half without a vacation," she said. "Since the network brass gave the go-ahead to our local-news show a year ago, it's been hectic, to say the least."

Mitzi raised an eyebrow. "Working in television sounds fascinating to me."

"Well, yes, it is. And very rewarding in a lot of ways. I can't complain."

"See that you don't," Mitzi teased.

Lisa smiled. "I'd only worked as an assistant on other shows. This is the first one I've produced myself, so I put in a lot of hours to prove myself. I was sure the show would fall apart without me. Finally I realized I would fall apart if I didn't get away for a while."

"So you came here." Mitzi's curiosity over Lisa's choice to move out of the fast lane was still obvious.

"I couldn't think of a better place than Charleston. It seems so timeless—and the pace is so leisurely. And you're here," Lisa concluded. There was another reason that she had come, of course, but she was still keeping that to herself.

Mitzi nodded. "I sure am. Sometimes I think my rear end has grown roots right into this sofa." She patted the generous curve of her hip and grinned. "But I hope you don't find Charleston too boring after the exciting life you've been leading."

Before Lisa had a chance to reply, Mitzi Talmadge made one of her lightning-fast changes of subject. One thought often triggered another in Mitzi's mind; it was a trait that was characteristic of her personality. "Do you remember that e-mail you sent me after your first interview? You were so irate when they said they wanted to hire you as a weather girl."

"Yes, I remember. They don't call them weather girls anymore, Mitzi."

"Oh, sorry. It's meteorologists now, right?"

"You got it," Lisa said. "And a lot of guys do it. I guess because someone with a deep voice gets taken more seriously when he talks about rain and snow."

"Of course," her aunt laughed. "Never mind looking out of the window and seeing for yourself. If a man in a suit says it's raining, then it must be true."

Lisa nodded. "Anyway, I held out for a production assistant job. Seemed like a better way to move up."

"And you did," Mitzi said. "Quickly too. I'm proud of you, girl."

"Thanks, Aunt Mitzi. But no one knew how often I was bluffing when I first started. I found out that if you acted like you knew what you were doing, management assumed that you did. Good thing I was a fast learner. Sometimes I wonder why they hired me."

"That's what Slade said. I told him about all that when I heard you were coming for a visit."

The mention of his name set Lisa's teeth on

edge. She attempted a bright smile. "I'm dying to meet this paragon you call Slade Blackwell. You've mentioned him so many times—half a dozen." Lisa was being polite. A half a hundred would have been closer.

"Guess I spend too much time online," her aunt said. "I would've invited him to dinner this evening, but because it's your first night here, I thought it would be best with just the two of us. I promise that you'll meet him soon. Maybe tomorrow night," she suggested.

"I believe you said he was the son of an old family friend?" Lisa's inquiry was as casual as she could make it.

"Mm-hm, yes." Mitzi sipped her drink, replying absently. "I met him quite by accident shortly after I moved back here to Charleston when my divorce from Simon became final. If you remember, my mother died soon after my divorce, so I really had a very trying few months."

"I can imagine," Lisa murmured.

"But Slade was wonderful," Mitzi continued, not really hearing Lisa's soft comment. "I never had a head for business, and things got complicated with the divorce and the settlement of the family estate. Slade simply took over for me and handled everything down to the last itty-bitty detail. You know how I hate fussing over details, Lisa," Mitzi smiled. "Now that Slade is looking after everything I don't have to bother. He makes out all the checks and all I have to do is sign them."

With a sinking heart, Lisa felt as if her worst suspicions had been confirmed. How could her aunt be so gullible? Her communications this past year had been filled with "Slade said," "Slade suggested," or "Slade told me." He had been quoted as an authority on anything and everything.

It was Slade Blackwell's idea for Mitzi to reopen the old family home in Old Charleston. Lisa remembered that he had also recommended the interior decorator who had renovated the venerable mansion.

Her gaze swept the living room with its high ceiling and rich cypress woodwork. Lisa couldn't find fault with the décor, which was a smooth mix of antique and modern. It invited a guest to sit back and relax, instead of giving a museum effect that said FRAGILE—KEEP OFF.

Yet it grated, just as it grated to know that Slade Blackwell has suggested the landscape architect for the walled garden outside the colonnaded portico. In the waning hours of a March dusk, the garden was abloom with early spring shrubs—azaleas and camellias and budding magnolia trees, the scent of honeysuckle drifting in the air. Magnificent old oaks dominated it, with their elegant draping of silvery moss.

The same company that had designed the garden still maintained it. Lisa couldn't help wondering what kickback Slade Blackwell got out of the deal. Those two things were just the obvious ones; she guessed there had been many other deals made as well, with contractors and home-renovation suppliers and people like that.

Now that Mitzi had informed her that Slade Blackwell made out checks for her signature, Lisa was even more worried. Her absentminded aunt probably didn't even verify what she was signing. The man was probably stealing her blind.

"Does this Blackwell guy manage all your money?" There was a note of challenge in Lisa's question. She simply couldn't keep it out even though she tried.

"All except some I keep in an account of my

own. I call it my mad money. My momma always had a secret stash like that. Daddy never knew a thing about it."

Lisa sighed. She saw no point in being sentimental about money but she didn't want to openly criticize Mitzi until she'd found out more. God only knew how much was in that account. God or Slade Blackwell—Lisa didn't want to hazard a guess.

She did know that her aunt had received a considerable sum from Simon Talmadge when they had divorced. Lisa's father had also explained that Mitzi's wealthy mother had left her everything and Mitzi was an only child. With the income from the romance mysteries her aunt wrote factored in, Mitzi was worth a lot.

"Aren't you being a little too trusting, Mitzi?" Lisa set her glass on the coaster sitting atop a marble inlaid table, trying not to sound too nosy.

"Do you mean where Slade is concerned?" The other woman laughed lightly, a melodious sound. "No. A more honest, dependable man doesn't exist. You haven't met him yet, but when you do, I know you'll like him."

Lisa couldn't keep her doubt out of her expression, apparently. Mitzi hesitated, her gaze narrowing. "On second thought, maybe you won't."

"Oh?" Lisa was instantly alert. "Why?"

"You said you didn't like the strong, masterful type. That would be Slade. Of course, he can be very charming and gracious too."

When it suits him. Lisa added the qualification silently. An older woman probably seemed like an easy target to Slade Blackwell. Mitzi didn't have any close family—her parents dead, no aunts or uncles living, the husband she had divorced gone too. What money he didn't steal from her while she was alive he probably hoped to inherit on her death.

"What did he say when he learned I was coming for a visit?" Lisa asked.

"I don't recall that Slade said anything in particular except that he was glad Simon's family hadn't forgotten me."

"We didn't forget you," Lisa protested. Anger against this Blackwell guy slowly began to burn. No doubt he wanted Mitzi to be isolated and totally dependent on him,

"I didn't mean to imply that you had," her aunt said with an easy laugh. "But you must admit it was awkward when Simon was alive. After all, he was your father's brother and we were divorced. I couldn't very well be included as if nothing had changed. I wouldn't have wanted it that way if your parents had tried."

"Well, as far as I'm concerned, you're still part of my family," Lisa said emphatically, "regardless of any divorce."

"God love you, Lisa," Mitzi laughed. "I feel the same way. That's why I'm so glad you've come for a nice long visit." Just as quickly, she became thoughtful. "There's only one thing I regret in my life. Oh, not the years I spent with Simon," she assured Lisa hastily. "But the fact that we never had children. I couldn't and Simon didn't want to adopt. You seem like my own daughter, though, and Slade my son."

"Is Slade Blackwell related to you?" Lisa asked. It suddenly occurred to her that there might be a family connection she hadn't known about.

"No," Mitzi said somewhat ruefully. "His father once proposed to me, though, many years ago. Sometimes, when I'm in a really sentimental mood, I start thinking that if I'd married him instead of

Simon, Slade would be my son. But of course I didn't and he isn't and it's all water under the bridge." She dismissed the subject with a wave of her hand and a smile. "Now tell me what you would like to do while you're in Charleston."

"Don't worry about entertaining me." Lisa folded her hands in her lap, relaxing more fully in the cushioned chair. "I know you're in the middle of a book. You just keep right on writing and I'll wander around on my own. There are a couple of people I want to look up while I'm here."

"College friends?"

"More or less," she answered without lying.

But her true plans were just beginning to take shape. One of the first things she was going to do was meet this Slade Blackwell and find out what his game was. She was determined to accomplish this without her aunt present.

If there was one thing she'd learned producing a show on local news, it was how to handle people. And more importantly, how to ask the questions that revealed a person's real self and motivations, either by doing it herself or having a reporter do it for her. Slade Blackwell was going to have quite a few questions to answer.

Mitzi glanced at her wristwatch. "Goodness, it's past seven!" She frowned and looked toward the dining room with its teardrop chandelier suspended above a gleaming, white-clothed table. "Mildred usually serves promptly at seven. I wonder what's wrong."

As if on cue, the housekeeper-cook appeared. There was an exasperated thinness to the line of her mouth, and a grim set to her features that said she had put up with more than her share of domestic crises.

"As near as I can tell, dinner is going to be about

thirty minutes late tonight. That dang oven is on the blink again," she announced in a martyred tone.

"Oh, no!" Mitzi said. "And it cost a fortune too. Didn't Slade say that it was top-of-the-line?"

"I called him first thing, ma'am," the housekeeper replied.

Lisa suppressed a scowl. Was Slade in charge of everything? The thought was a little scary.

"He'll have the man out first thing in the morning. But in the meantime, dinner will be late."

Lisa waited until she returned to the kitchen. "Couldn't you or Mildred call the repairman, Mitzi?"

"I suppose so," was the answer, as though it hadn't occurred to her until Lisa suggested it. "But it's so much easier to call Slade. He seems to know the most capable people."

Yes, Lisa thought cynically. Capable of rewarding him for passing on business. A house as old as this one was costly to maintain. And Mitzi had expensive taste, for all that she didn't take very good care of things. It seemed to Lisa that her suspicions regarding Slade Blackwell would be all too easy to confirm.

"It isn't that difficult to find reliable repair people," Lisa insisted. "It would require a few phone calls and some checking, but you could do it and not have to rely on someone else."

"Oh, but I'm lazy," Mitzi said with a wave of her hand and an unconcerned smile.

"I find that hard to believe. Look at your writing schedule," Lisa argued.

"Ah, but that's something I enjoy doing. It isn't work. As far as anything else goes, I don't want to be bothered," she said with a shrug. "If I didn't have Slade to turn to, I'd probably see to these little things. But I do have him. He spoils me outrageously and I love it."

What could she say to that, Lisa wondered. Her aunt seemed to love acting the part of a traditional, coddled Southern belle, even though she was an intelligent woman. Why didn't she realize how vulnerable she was? Perhaps the word was gullible, Lisa thought.

Dinner was eventually served about a quarter of an hour later than Mildred had said. The evening passed quite pleasantly. The conversation was filled with reminiscences of old times and gossip about family. The only irritant Lisa found was the way Slade Blackwell's name kept cropping up. Mildred plodded into the living room to the low, marble-inlaid table in front of the sofa. She picked up the empty coffee service as if it weighed a ton and started to leave. At Mitzi's chair, she paused.

"Will you be wanting anything else tonight, Mitzi?" But she didn't give her employer a chance to answer. "If you don't I'll be turning in now."

Her lugubrious tone implied that she was on her last legs, and any further requests would be a severe strain on her health.

"I'm sure there's nothing else we'll need," Lisa's aunt responded with a sympathetic smile. "Have a good night, Mildred."

"I'll try," was the sighing reply as the housekeeper shuffled out of the room. She made it appear that it was too much of an effort to pick up her feet.

When the housekeeper was out of sight, Mitzi's twinkling gaze slid to Lisa. "Isn't she a character? She could do the work of an army, but she likes to act like the smallest chore is just too much. Bless her grumbling soul. I don't know what I'd do without her. Slade found her, of course."

"Of course," Lisa echoed dryly and tried to swallow a yawn, but she couldn't.

"You're tired, aren't you? I sometimes forget how exhausting it is to travel, because I don't. Bet you'd like to turn in too."

"Oh, no, really—" Lisa started to protest.

"Don't argue. You are tired. We'll have plenty of time to talk in the next two weeks. There isn't any need to use up all the conversation in one night," Mitzi said.

Lisa was tired and didn't object at all to having her arm twisted. "If you're sure you don't mind . . ."

"I don't mind. Do you remember which room you have?" Her aunt rose and Lisa did likewise.

"Yes, I remember. Turn right at the top of the stairs and it's the second room," she recalled.

"That's it. I'll be going up to bed myself in a few minutes. Now, I rise with the sun to write, but you sleep as late as you want," her aunt instructed. "Remember, you're on vacation."

"Which means not dashing out my door at six. What a treat." Lisa smiled. She started toward the foyer and the staircase leading to the second floor. Over her shoulder she added, "By the way, thanks for letting me spend my vacation here."

"Thanks aren't necessary. I can't tell you how happy I am that you came to Charleston to see me. Good night, honey."

"Good night, Mitzi." Lisa waved as she rounded the open double doors into the foyer.

The heavily carved cypress staircase rose in a lazy spiral to the second floor. Lisa climbed its carpeted steps, a hand sliding along the smooth wood of the banister to the top. The plaster walls of the upper hallway were painted a pearl white. The color gave light to the high-ceilinged but narrow corridor.

Turning right, Lisa entered the second room. Her previous inspection of the room had been brief, a hurried tour on her arrival, cut short by her desire to return downstairs to visit with her aunt. Now she let her gaze wander around the room.

Mitzi had said that she'd chosen this guest room for Lisa because it seemed to be "her." The walls were a rich jade green, accented by woodwork painted ivory. A small alcove held a sofa decorated in vivid greens and golds. The silk draperies were also ivory, and matched the bedspread on the canopied bed. The rug was oriental, patterned in colors that harmonized with the rest of the décor.

The sight of her suitcases standing at the foot of the bed reminded Lisa that she hadn't unpacked. She sighed, then noticed her nightgown and robe lying across the bed. She picked up one suitcase. It was obviously empty.

Setting it back down, Lisa walked to the closet. All her clothes were there, neatly hung up. The rest of her things were in the drawers of a Provençal-style dresser. The housekeeper had obviously unpacked her suitcases for her.

"Bless her grumbling soul." Lisa repeated her aunt's earlier comment about Mildred, murmuring it in all sincerity. Kicking off her shoes, she walked to a second ivory-painted door. It opened into a bathroom where her cosmetics were arranged on the counter in front of a well-lighted vanity mirror. There wasn't anything left for her to do.

Lisa glanced at the large porcelain bathtub with its gold fixtures and green-and-gold shower curtain, but the bed looked infinitely more inviting at the moment. Closing the bathroom door, she changed into her nightclothes.

Climbing between the clean-scented sheets, she switched off the light on the stand beside the bed. Lisa stared at the pale silk of the canopy above. Tomorrow she would be meeting Slade Blackwell.

She wanted to be well rested for that. She closed her eyes.

As Lisa followed the descending rail of the spiral staircase the next morning, she could hear the soft staccato of a computer keyboard coming from the downstairs study. Smiling to herself, she knew not to make any explanations to Mitzi. Her aunt was hard at work on her new novel.

At the bottom of the stairs, Lisa paused in front of the large oval mirror to make a last minute inspection of her appearance. Her clothes were chic, but not so much so as to stand out in a conservative city like Charleston. Her hat was the one really individual touch she'd permitted herself. A silky blond wisp escaped it, trailing the curve of her neck. Lisa tucked it beneath the hat and adjusted the large gold stud of her earring.

Satisfaction sparkled in her eyes, their color enhanced by the subtle green of her outfit. She liked the image of the woman looking back at her, professional yet definitely feminine. Her gaze slid to the handbag, seeing an edge of the downloaded city map she'd tucked inside it. Slade Blackwell's business address was marked with a small red star.

Lisa had no doubt that he would see her this morning, regardless of whether or not she had an appointment. He wouldn't turn away Mitzi Talmadge's niece. Once Lisa got inside the door, Slade wouldn't find it easy to be rid of her.

"Would you like breakfast now, miss?"

Glancing toward the sound of the voice, Lisa saw the long-suffering Mildred standing just inside the doorway and smiled. "No, thanks, Mildred. I function much better on an empty stomach."

"Beg pardon?"

"It doesn't matter." Lisa didn't bother with an explanation of her statement. "If Mitzi asks where I am, tell her I've gone to see an old friend."

As often as she'd heard Blackwell's name in the past twenty-four hours, it did feel as if she'd known him a long time—and disliked him for just as long.

"Will you be home for lunch, then?" Mildred asked.

Lisa hesitated. "No," she decided. "I'll be back sometime in the afternoon. What time does Mitzi usually stop writing for the day?"

"It depends, miss. It depends," was the answer, as if anything more definite was beyond her.

Concealing the smile that tugged at the corners of her mouth, Lisa wished Mildred a standard have-a-nice-day and walked out of the ornately carved front door. The air was balmy and the sun bright, without a hint of blustery March winds.

The lovely old mansion was narrow and long. The house didn't actually front the street in Old Charleston; its entrance door opened onto the portico running the length of one side. Lisa's heels clicked noisily on the smooth stone as she walked to the false house door opening onto the street from the portico.

Closing it behind her, she heard the rumble of carriage wheels and the steady clop of horses' hooves. Lisa paused to watch a horse-drawn surrey around the street corner, its fringe waving with the motion.

Tourists sat in the seats behind the guide, taking a carriage tour of Old Charleston. They had obviously seen her coming from the mansion, Lisa realized, and they stared openly. She smiled and waved, knowing that they believed she was a full-fledged Charlestonian instead of a tourist like themselves.

The carriage ride looked like a fun way to see Old Charleston, whose history encompassed the Southern manner of gracious living, the sad days of the Civil War, and before that, the era of colonial America. Lisa glanced around the immediate neighborhood. Magnolia trees and massive oaks draped with Spanish moss towered beside and above fine old homes. Colorful splashes of flowers ornamented every lawn and garden, creeping along fences and sprouting from stone urns.

Lisa squared her shoulders. There would be time enough to sightsee later on. For the time being, she couldn't be distracted by the beauty around her, not until after she'd had her confrontation with Slade Blackwell. The click of her heels made a purposeful sound as she started out.

It was a short walk along the stagecoach-width street to Meeting Street, where Lisa asked for directions to the law offices of Courtney Blackwell & Son. Slade Blackwell was, of course, the "son." The office, too, was located in Old Charleston, in a venerable merchant building with an elaborate cornice.

The instant Lisa entered the offices she knew the firm had a small but exclusive practice. Paneled walls, their wood gleaming with the patina of years, gave the place a distinguished air, while antiques and leather furniture added warmth to the overall atmosphere.

The receptionist was an older woman with sleekly coiffed gray hair. She wore glasses with half lenses over which she peered at Lisa. Yet she managed to give an impression of polite deference.

"May I help you?"

"I'm here to see Mr. Slade Blackwell." Lisa didn't bother to inform the woman that she didn't have an appointment or that he didn't know her.

Surprisingly, no questions were asked. The woman

nodded to a set of carved oak double doors. "His office is right that way."

That was easy, Lisa thought. No preliminary introductions. No explanations. Slade Blackwell was proving to be much more accessible than she had believed.

The doors opened to a small office, complete with desk, computer, and filing cabinets. Obviously it was supposed to be occupied by his private secretary, but there was no one in sight to greet Lisa. Closing the doors, she walked into the office, deciding it had once been partitioned from a larger room.

An overstuffed leather armchair took up a corner. There was a magazine rack placed beside it, but Lisa didn't want to sit. Instead she walked to the vacant desk and saw that it held an appointment book, left open.

She glanced cautiously toward the door leading to Slade Blackwell's inner office. There was no sound coming from it, but the walls of the old building were thick. Carefully she slid the appointment book around to peep at his day's agenda.

Without warning the inner door opened and Lisa nearly jumped out of her shoes. She quickly concealed her start of guilty surprise to inspect the man confronting her. His tall, leanly muscled build was clothed in an impeccably tailored suit of oyster gray, complete with vest.

There the lawyer image ended and the man began. And he made an immediate and very physical impression on Lisa, even if he scarcely seemed to look at her. The breath she had been holding she released slowly, then seemed unable to take another. Every nerve in her body quivered with the alertness of an animal scenting danger.

So this was Slade Blackwell. Lisa needed no introduction. If she had expected the suave image of a southern gentleman, chivalrous and courtly, charming a rich, lonely woman with his pearly smile, she would have needed to make an immediate reassessment. Somehow, though, Lisa hadn't gotten as far as picturing her opponent.

Strong and masterful, Mitzi had described him. Tame words, Lisa concluded silently. *Extremely male* was her take. Slade seemed as hard as a piece of granite that had somehow come to life. He exuded an air of masculine vitality that got to her, and a sensual power that was overwhelming.

Raven-black hair grew thickly away from his forehead, without too much thought given to styling it. His eyes were the color of his hair, an intense black.

His lean face and the slight hollows in his cheeks accented the angular slant of his jaw. There was an unyielding firmness to his mouth, but his dark, thick brows were finely drawn. One was arched slightly higher than the other now.

"It's about time you arrived." His voice was low-pitched. It might have been pleasant had his tone not been sharpened by impatience. "The agency assured me they would have someone here by nine-thirty. It is now half-past ten. I have some important letters that need to go out right away."

"But—" Lisa said.

He didn't let her finish as he waved the sheaf of papers in his hand. "I assume you're familiar with legal terminology and there are previous letters in document files you can review. I've done the rough drafts on my computer and sent them to that one." He indicated the computer on the secretary's desk with a nod. "So get started."

He turned and reentered his private office, closing the door with a sharp click.

CHAPTER TWO

Lisa's mouth opened. The words formed to call him back, her hand raised uselessly. Then she hesitated, her hand coming back to her mouth as she began to thoughtfully nibble a fingernail.

Why not? a mischievous little voice inside her demanded. Obviously Slade Blackwell had been expecting a temporary replacement for his legal secretary and had mistaken Lisa for her. Why should she bother to tell him differently? If she wanted proof to confirm or deny her suspicions, what better way than through his own records?

It was a heaven-sent opportunity. She would be a fool not to take advantage of it. With luck, she could bluff her way through the rest of it.

Decision made, Lisa stepped behind the desk. The first thing she had to do was cancel the request that had gone out to a temp agency. Fortunately, the agency's name and number was listed in the appointment book, scrawled in the margin of yesterday's page. She reasoned that if the phone number of Courtney Blackwell & Son came up on their caller ID, they would assume the cancellation was legit.

And if the real temp showed up, Lisa would send her away with a hundred-dollar bill, after extracting a promise not to tell. Temps made less than half that per day after taxes, she knew—Lisa had hired temps herself.

One more phone call to make. She checked the little address book in her purse and dialed her aunt's number.

"Talmadge residence," said Mildred in a grumpy voice.

"Mildred, this is Lisa." She hurried her words, speaking softly and quickly. "I'm just calling to let you know my . . . my friends and I are going to make an afternoon of it. Tell Mitzi I'll be back after five o'clock."

"Did she tell you?"

Lisa frowned at the receiver. "Tell me what?"

"That Sl"—the housekeeper corrected herself—"I mean, Mr. Blackwell, is coming for dinner tonight."

"Good Lord," Lisa muttered to herself, seeing all kinds of complications ahead. "When?"

"He usually comes for cocktails around six," was the reply.

"I'll be there by then." An irritated "damn" slipped out as Lisa replaced the receiver on the hook.

But there wasn't time to dwell on her eventual unmasking. She had to start working on the letters before Slade Blackwell became suspicious about the silence in his outer office.

She turned on the computer and clicked on the e-mail icon. There were the letters, sent as attachments from his computer. She opened the first one, then checked the document files for previous letters like it, as he'd suggested.

So far, so good. She polished his rough draft, saved it in a new file with today's date, and printed it out on letterhead. She cast a glance at the metal filing cabinets, which she was dying to get into. But she stayed where she was. She didn't want Slade Blackwell coming out to discover her going through the files when she should be typing.

Working on the fourth—and what she hoped was the last—letter, Lisa heard the connecting office door open and mentally tensed as Slade crossed the room to her desk. Her cool green eyes slid a brief glance in his direction as he picked up the letters she had finished. He concentrated on them and not her.

She had tried to increase her typing speed—a mistake, as she misspelled a word by reversing the letters. The spell-check function hadn't caught it, since it was still a word. Just not the right word in that context.

But Slade saw the error and marked it with a pen he picked up. "Redo this, please." He looked at another letter. "And this one. The word is 'guaranty,' not 'guarantee.' " He stopped talking for a moment but he was still focused on the letters. "I don't know your name, by the way. What is it?"

"Ann. Ann Eldridge." She altered her voice instinctively to say the false name. It came to her so quickly that Lisa was astounded.

"Okay, Ann. Make the corrections and print out a revised one. The word is repeated several times in the letter."

"I'll do it over," Lisa agreed with a deferential nod, but she was mad enough to spit. He seemed to be waiting for an explanation of her error, and

Lisa grudgingly gave him one, masking it in sweet politeness. "Actually, I'm not familiar with legal terminology, Mr. Blackwell."

"I specifically requested a legal secretary."

"The agency didn't have anyone with law-office experience available." She hated playing dumb, but there was nothing else she could do. "I'm sorry. I'm doing the best I can."

She didn't dare look him in the eye. Lisa knew her expression was anything but apologetic. She could feel his sharp gaze studying her and tried to ignore the uncomfortable sensation it aroused.

"I'm sure you are. Maybe if you took off that hat, you could see better."

Her hand lifted to her head in surprise. She had forgotten to take it off in her haste to get onto the computer. But maybe she could turn her gaffe to her advantage, she thought wildly. She sure as hell didn't want him to identify her if at all possible.

"Oh, gosh," she said. "I can't take it off. My hair is a mess."

"Really," he said dryly.

She looked up at him for a fraction of a second from under the brim. One side of his mouth quirked with amusement at her answer, but he made no further comment about the hat. He didn't seem to be really all that aware of her as a human being, period.

Maybe he thought of temps as robots. Interchangeable. If he did, then she was in luck.

"I have a lunch date. I'll be back around one o'clock," he told her and walked through the double doors leading to the reception area.

Waiting, Lisa listened for the opening and closing of the outside door before she darted from the desk to the metal filing cabinets. Alone at last, she had her first chance to investigate the files. She tried not to think about how unethical her search was, if not downright dishonest.

The drawers had been carefully labeled but not well maintained. Hundreds of files were jammed inside, some so dog-eared that the folder tabs were impossible to read. Frantically Lisa began looking for her aunt's last name. The door to the reception area opened and Lisa gave a start.

"Hello." A man walked in, shorter than Slade Blackwell, but of about the same age, in his late thirties. He wore glasses and his brown hair was combed across his forehead in an effort to conceal a receding hairline. "You must be Mary Lou's replacement."

"Yes, I am." Lisa heard the nervous tremor in her voice and tried to return the man's broad smile naturally. She glanced toward the connecting door to Slade Blackwell's office. "I'm sorry, but Mr. Blackwell has just left for lunch."

"Yes, I know. I saw him in the reception area before he left," was the answer, but the man made no move to leave.

Her fingers were resting on the handle of one drawer. The metal felt almost hot to the touch. It was so obvious that she was looking for something that she couldn't move away from the cabinets. She silently wished her guilt wouldn't give her away and reminded herself that she was doing this to protect her aunt from an unscrupulous lawyer.

"Was there something I could help you with?" she asked politely, praying that he would go.

Mr. Combover was staring at her, his expression making it plain that he liked what he saw. Her prodding question seemed to snap him out of it.

"Yes." He walked quickly toward her. "I came to get the Talmadge file."

"The what?" Lisa breathed weakly.

"Talmadge, Miriam L. Also known as Mitzi," he said, apparently not noticing the way the color drained from her face.

She straightened up, mentally searching for an out. "I'm sorry, but these are Mr. Blackwell's files. I couldn't possibly—"

"I'm sorry," he interrupted with a laugh. "I didn't introduce myself, did I? I'm Slade's assistant, consultant, whatever label you want to pin on me." He extended a hand to Lisa. "The name is Drew, as in Andrew Rutledge—unfortunately no relation to the Charleston Rutledges of yore. And you are?"

"Li—" She caught herself just in time. "Ann Eldridge."

When Lisa had first placed her hand in his, he seemed inclined to hold it. But he let go. Maybe working in a legal office had familiarized him with the term *sexual harassment,* Lisa thought.

"Well, welcome to the firm," Drew said affably. "Slade always picks a pretty one. You're his type."

Maybe he hadn't heard the term. Lisa gave him a frosty look.

It seemed to bounce right off him. "He has a reputation to uphold, of course. Man about town and all that. But Blackwell is single and proud of it. We've had a standing bet since college as to which of us gets married first, you know."

"That's fascinating," said Lisa, trying to look fascinated. Why was it that some of the least attractive men still thought of themselves as sexy? She'd bet anything this guy thought that combover was a magnet for chicks.

"We've both had our share of close calls," Drew went on.

"Haven't we all?" Lisa said. He looked at her curiously. "But once you meet the right person you don't want to settle for a close call."

"So I've heard," he smiled, the curiosity leaving his eyes at her reply. "Well, guess I'd better let you get back to work."

"Yes." She tried not to let her relief show. "I have a lot to do."

"I'll get out of your way, then," he said, "just as soon as you hand me the Talmadge file."

Her hope that Drew had forgotten the reason he had come in faded with his statement. She hesitated. "I really don't think I should—"

"You guard the files more than Mary Lou," he laughed.

Lisa seized on that. "Well, no one told me who you were or that I should give you files. I don't want to get in trouble."

"Right. You can check with the receptionist for my bona fides. But I need that file."

"Listen, I'm just a temp," Lisa said. "Maybe you should wait until after lunch when Mr. Blackwell comes back."

There weren't any more excuses left. She railed inwardly against the fate that had brought him in here for the Talmadge file and no other. Here she was with the ideal chance to do some undercover work, and the info she needed was about to be taken away. Maybe she could catch a glimpse of its contents before she had to give it to him. At the very least she could stall him a little longer.

"Do you know where it's filed? I don't know this system," she said.

"Our system is top secret," Drew replied. "But I'll tell you. The files are in alphabetical order."

"Oh," she said, feeling stupid.

"I'll find it," Drew offered. She stepped aside. He opened the drawer below the one she had been going through. "T is for Talmadge. How about that?"

Lisa had a fleeting glimpse of her aunt's name

on the tab before he tucked it under his arm and closed the drawer. It was frustrating to know how close she had been to it.

"Don't look so upset," Drew teased. "I'll bring it back first thing tomorrow. I hope," he tacked on.

"I'm not upset. Not really." Lisa composed herself. "I was just wondering if anyone else would be coming in looking for files." She latched on to the first excuse she thought of for her agitation.

"No need to worry," he assured her. "There's only me, Slade, and Ellen Tyler at the reception desk. Bob Tucker, the other assistant, consultant, whatever to Slade, isn't here. He should be back this weekend, although Mary Lou took a two-week leave of absence."

"Mary Lou? Mr. Blackwell's secretary, the one I'm replacing?"

"She's also Bob's wife. There was a death in her family," Drew explained. "After two weeks here, you'll know your way around the office and filing system like a pro."

"I may not be here for two weeks." Not when Slade Blackwell discovers who I really am, Lisa thought.

"Why not?" He shot her an inquisitive look.

"I'm not a trained legal secretary. The agency didn't have one available when Mr. Blackwell called. They'll be replacing me with someone more experienced."

Her gaze kept darting to the file under his arm. Lisa turned away to walk back to her desk before Drew noticed her preoccupation with the folder.

"I'll put in a word with Slade to keep you on until Mary Lou comes back. Experience doesn't count for all that much in this place. Slade likes things done his way, which is not necessarily according to the book."

Lisa could vouch for that, especially if she could find a little hard evidence.

"That's very nice of you," was all she said, "but Mr. Blackwell might not agree."

"I know what he'll say," Drew nodded. "He'll tell me the same thing his father always tells me—that I can't resist a pretty face. As if Slade can."

Wow. You're so suave, Lisa thought. "His father? The Courtney Blackwell of Courtney Blackwell and Son?"

"That's right, the old man himself."

"Has he retired? You didn't mention him when you ran down the list of people in the office."

"He retired the year after Slade got his law degree." Drew walked to Lisa's desk, leaning against the edge, hooking a knee over the corner so he was half sitting on the top. "He didn't like practicing law, said he was a gentleman farmer at heart, but there's been a Blackwell practicing law in Charleston for years. When Slade qualified, the tradition was carried on with him and Court moved out to the country."

"To farm." She imagined the senior Blackwell behind a plow, wearing a three-piece suit like his son's. Something was definitely wrong with that picture.

"Yes, he bought what had been the old Blackwell plantation that the family lost after the Civil War. The original house was still standing, but one wing was beyond repair, what with the termites and all, and had to be torn down. They've restored most of it, though. It's quite a place," he smiled. "You should see it. I could take you out."

"Sounds interesting." Lisa wondered if Slade Blackwell was contributing Mitzi's money to the restoration.

"So, uh, do you have a boyfriend?" Drew asked unexpectedly.

"You mean Burt?" She couldn't believe the way these lies and fake names were coming so easily. She just hoped she could keep them all straight.

"Uh-oh. He sounds like a big guy. Burt is a big name. Is he the jealous type?"

"Well, no," she said. "He's not particularly jealous. Or big." *He's a figment of my imagination, you idiot,* she wanted to yell. How did a man this clueless manage to work in a law office? She assumed he didn't handle any important clients—and then reminded herself that he was apparently handling her aunt's legal affairs. She would have to make nice and play along.

"I'd like to take you to lunch tomorrow. I'd make it for today, but I have this"—he looked at the folder he held—"to work on. Which means I'll have to settle for Ellen ordering me a sandwich from the deli." He noticed her hesitation and teased, "Come on, Ann. I'm harmless. Just look at me. I wear glasses, I'm short—shorter than Slade, anyway—and I'm losing my hair. But I have a great personality. Perfectly harmless, I promise."

"I'll bet you are," she laughed with mocking skepticism.

"What do you say? Is it a date?" Drew wasn't going to be put off.

"Ask me tomorrow." *If I'm here,* Lisa added to herself.

"I'll do that." He started to straighten from the desk, glancing at the watch on his wrist. "Speaking of lunch, if you want yours today, you'd better skedaddle. Things get pretty hectic around here in the afternoons."

Lisa looked at her own watch, realizing how fast the time had gone by since Slade Blackwell had left. It was nearly noon and her stomach was protesting. She opened the desk drawer where she had put her purse.

"That's a good idea," she told Drew. "See ya."

Later, sitting alone in a booth at a small nearby restaurant crowded with lunch-hour customers, Lisa stared at her empty plate and pleated her paper napkins into folds. She'd had time to think while she was eating and she was just beginning to realize what a very complicated and potentially embarrassing situation she'd got herself into with her lies.

She'd winced at the guilty look on her face when she'd glanced into the mirror of the restaurant's ladies' room, reminded of the who-me expression of a suspect doing a perp walk on the evening news. All that was missing was a burly cop at her side.

But Drew Rutledge had the file folder Lisa wanted and he wouldn't return it before tomorrow. Which was too late. That left her with two options.

The first was to go back to the office and tell Slade Blackwell who she really was before he discovered it for himself.

But how could she possibly explain? He wouldn't think it was funny. He'd probably take legal action.

The second alternative was to continue the deception until she could get her hands on her aunt's records and take the risk of being discovered. The only way she could do that was by avoiding meeting Slade Blackwell as herself, Lisa Talmadge.

Considering that her aunt had invited him to dinner tonight, that was already impossible. He might recognize her instantly. Then she would have to be the one who did all the explaining instead of the other way around.

Sighing, Lisa glanced out the restaurant window. The sunlight hit the glass at just the right angle to reflect her own image. She could hardly see her eyes under the hat.

She couldn't see her hair at all.

Lisa Talmadge had shoulder-length silver-blond hair. Ann Eldridge, whose hair had been concealed under the hat she'd happened to wear, would have—Lisa thought for an instant—red hair.

It would be a perfect foil for her fair skin and green eyes and such a startling contrast to the true color of her pale hair. With luck, Slade Blackwell—who seemed incredibly self-absorbed anyway and had barely looked at her, a mere temp—would never compare the two women.

Within seconds, Lisa had left enough money to cover the bill and a generous tip and skedaddled, as Drew would say, to the old-fashioned phone booth tucked away in the corridor that led to the ladies' room.

She had seen the Yellow Pages attached to a chain inside and now she leafed through it to find the number of the nearest wig shop. There had to be more than one in Charleston, she thought, with so many retirees. Now, if she could only find one within walking distance . . . there. She put her finger on an ad. She had seen that street name on her downloaded map, which she took from her purse.

Lisa ran out and down the street and then down another. The place turned out to have a pretty good selection. She picked a wig in flaming orange, cut in pixie style. She mumbled something about going to a costume party as the saleswoman helped her put it on.

"Are you going as Peter Pan?" the woman asked.

"Um, yeah," Lisa said. "But I think I'll wear it out. Just to see if it's comfortable."

"Good idea. You can exchange it if not."

"Right." Lisa gave the woman a credit card to complete the transaction and made a face at herself in the mirror. The wig wasn't enough. She scrabbled in her purse for the lipstick she hadn't bothered to put on this morning, and applied it thickly.

At ten minutes past one, she was rushing toward the Blackwell office, hat in hand, well aware that she had been gone too long. She crossed her fingers and hoped she could make it back before Slade Blackwell did.

After all this, she didn't want to give him a reason to fire her on the spot and have the agency send him someone else. Not when she hadn't accomplished her objective.

Unfortunately, she saw him coming. Slade Blackwell's long strides brought him to the door three seconds before Lisa reached it. He waited for her, his dark eyes making a sweeping appraisal and stopping at her hair.

"Sorry I'm late," Lisa murmured. Self-consciously she raised a hand to the red wig. "I stopped at the hair salon for a cut."

His gaze flicked to the hat in her hand. There was nothing in his serious expression that indicated he didn't believe her story. "Okay." He seemed not to care. No doubt he thought he had been sent the temp from hell and had resigned himself to it.

Lisa offered no further explanation but let him hold the door open for her.

"Holy cow!" said Drew as they entered. "So that's what was under that hat. Hey, how come you let Slade take you to lunch and not me?"

"I didn't take her to lunch, Drew," Slade said, shooting him a shut-the-hell-up look.

"She has a monster boyfriend, you know. His name is Burt. Better watch out, Slade."

Lisa only nodded and smirked at him. Funny how an imaginary boyfriend could seem so real to a guy who didn't know any better.

"Good," Slade said. "Drew likes redheads. But he'll have to find one on his own time." He addressed his next remark to his assistant, to Lisa's relief. "We don't need a lawsuit."

"Hey, you like blondes," the irrepressible Drew pointed out.

What happens when you have both in one? Lisa thought, her cheeks dimpling a little at her unspoken question. But that was her secret and she hoped it would stay that way. She had barely walked around the desk to sit in her chair when Slade Blackwell's curt voice wiped the trace of a smile from her face.

"Haven't you finished those letters yet?" As before, he concentrated on them and not her.

"Not yet," Lisa said. "After you left the office, Mr. Rutledge came in to ask for the Talmadge file."

"Right," he said, a thoughtful look in his eyes.

"He told me he was your assistant or consultant or something like that," she said quickly. She thought it was wisest to keep on playing dumb. "If you want, I'll go and get it and bring it back." Please say yes, she begged him mentally. Gladly, on winged feet, she would go after it.

"That's not necessary." Slade Blackwell dismissed the suggestion without hesitation. "Get Mrs. Talmadge on the phone for me. Look in the front of the appointment book. Most of my clients' numbers are in there."

"Yes, sir." Lisa hid her dismay and quickly flipped to the front of the book until she found her aunt's number. Not as if she had it memorized. Her pulse was hammering in her throat as she dialed and listened to the ring.

"Talmadge residence," Mildred answered on the fourth ring.

"One moment, please. Can you hold? Mr. Blackwell is calling for Mrs. Talmadge—" She couldn't disguise her voice much longer, not with Slade Blackwell standing beside her desk, even if he was leafing through a copy of the *South Carolina Law Review* at the moment. She punched the hold button when Mildred sighed a yes.

"Did you want to take the call here or in your office?"

"In my office." He started to turn, then stopped, his gaze narrowing on her. "By the way, Ann, I just wanted to say something."

She gulped. "What?"

"If Drew gets too friendly, come to me. You have work to do and so does he. But he and I were friends in college and sometimes he takes advantage of that."

"Yes, Mr. Blackwell. Thank you. He is, um, kind of a, um . . ." She trailed off, not sure how to finish that sentence without insulting one or both of them.

"He's a pain in the butt sometimes," Slade said flatly. "But he's a nice guy. A little desperate," he added.

Was that a ghost of a smile on his mouth? Lisa couldn't be sure. "Yes, sir," she said. "Anyway, I have a boyfriend."

"So he said."

He turned away and went into his office. "Go ahead. Transfer the call. But please don't make me talk to Mildred."

Lisa punched the hold button again and spoke to the housekeeper in high-pitched receptionese for a moment. She heard Mildred yell for Mitzi and another line being picked up. At her aunt's soft hello, Lisa transferred the call, knowing Slade would pick it up in his office when he saw the light flash on his call buttons.

She breathed a sigh of relief. This was getting truly weird. She fought the impulse to listen in and returned to working on the computer. When the light for his call to her aunt went out, a few more calls came in, which she transferred without mishap. She went back to the letters, wanting them corrected and printed out, ready for his signature when he asked for them, which she guessed would be soon.

Despite numerous interruptions—more phone calls, clients coming in, and instructions from Slade to note future appointments with various people—Lisa completed the letters he had given her that morning and several more from rough drafts he sent her from his computer. She checked and rechecked them all several times.

She sat back, taking a breather. The wig itched. She scratched it discreetly and quickly stopped when the door to his private office opened.

Slade walked out. "Did you finish those letters?"

"Yes. Here they are." Lisa wasn't able to keep the ring of triumphant satisfaction out of her fake voice as she fanned them out for his signature. Nancy Drew, girl sleuth, couldn't have pulled this off.

He looked them over and signed them with a flourish, using a very expensive fountain pen with a gold nib.

"Okay. Now for the legal briefs. You can use the

templates in our legal software for a lot of clauses but not all. And they are crawling with 'whereas-es' and 'to wits' and all that. Think you can handle it?"

The prospect of spending the rest of the afternoon staring into a computer screen was depressing, especially if she had to create legal documents. It brought her no closer to the purpose of her crazy masquerade. But she really had very little choice.

"I . . . can try." She smiled in an attempt to hide her lack of enthusiasm.

"Okay. I'll bring them in to you." The instant he disappeared inside his office, Lisa took a deep breath and exhaled it angrily in a sigh.

Almost as quickly, Slade came back and Lisa stared into the screen, trying to keep her face turned away from his as much as possible. He too looked into the screen, going over previous documents that were similar to the ones he wanted and explaining exactly how he wanted these done.

It was a good thing he was familiar with the legal software, because she didn't know one thing about it. But it did seem to do a lot of the work for whoever was using it.

And he wouldn't be arguing a case in front of the Supreme Court, she told herself. This seemed to be routine business law and nothing that would have a significant impact on anybody's life.

He was all business himself, very professional, yet patient with her ignorance. Lisa had to give him credit for that. She couldn't accuse him of being a tyrannical employer.

After he'd left so she could begin typing, Lisa wished she had not taken advantage of his mistake in taking her for a temp. It was proving to be a huge headache and a mountain of work she wasn't positive she could fake her way through. There must be an easier way, she thought gloomily.

But, short of tying Slade Blackwell to his desk chair while she ransacked the files, she couldn't think of one. She opened the Legal Eagle program and pulled down the Help menu. She was going to need it.

CHAPTER THREE

A block from her aunt's house, the street was empty of cars and strolling tourists. Even the horses had gone home for some hard-earned hay, she thought. Grateful for the darkness, Lisa paused to pull the itchy red wig from her head and free her blond hair from its confining pins. Stuffing the wig in her purse, she briskly ruffled her hair to take away the matted look.

Some vacation, she thought wearily. Her arms, neck, and shoulders ached from her long stint at the computer. If this was what it was like to work on a keyboard all day, she was going to recommend Donna, her production assistant, for a raise when she got back to the Baltimore TV station.

A car turned onto the street behind her, and Lisa cast a frightened look over her shoulder. Before leaving the office, she had heard Slade Blackwell mention to Drew that he was going straight from the office to Mitzi's house. She expected him to overtake her any minute. Not this time, though, as the car passed her and Lisa saw the driver was a much older man with white hair.

But the scare prodded her into walking faster. She had to get home before Slade and change her clothes.

The wrought-iron gates blocking the driveway entrance from the sidewalk were closed when Lisa reached the house. She didn't breathe easy until she was inside. Her plan to rush immediately to her room and change was thwarted by her aunt, who appeared almost the second Lisa closed the entrance door behind her.

"You made it back without getting lost, didn't you?" Mitzi's wide smile of greeting was swiftly replaced by a look of concern. "You look exhausted, Lisa."

"It's been a long day." The muscles in her arm protested as she tried to brush her hair away from her face.

"Goodness, whatever did you and your friends find so much excitement in sleepy ol' Charleston?" Mitzi asked. "If I'd known you were going to overdo it on your first day here, I would have waited till tomorrow to invite Slade for dinner. But it's too late to cancel. He'll be here any minute," her aunt said.

"I'd better run upstairs and change, then."

"There's no need," Mitzi insisted. "From the looks of you, you'd do better to sit down and put your feet up and maybe have a relaxing drink."

It sounded like a heavenly idea to Lisa, even though she knew she couldn't accept it. A drink might make her blurt out a clue or two—or just fall asleep with her tired face in her plate. She shook her head.

"Besides," Mitzi continued, "the outfit you're wearing is very cute. Why change it?"

But that was precisely the point. She did have to change it. Slade Blackwell had seen her in it practically all day. She'd really tried to keep him from getting a good look at her face, but he was likely to remember an identical outfit, even if he was a guy. Lisa couldn't tell her aunt that, of course.

"Oh, Mitzi, I got kinda sweaty running around all day. I really need a bath and fresh clothes." That was no lie, Lisa thought. In fact, it might be the first true thing she'd said for hours. Even though she was telling one whopper after another on her aunt's behalf, she still felt guilty about doing it.

"Well, do what you think is best," her aunt conceded.

Lisa started to hurry toward the stairs. "If Slade Blackwell arrives before I'm down, apologize for me, would you?" she said over her shoulder. Pausing on the first step, she added, "I noticed the driveway gates are closed."

"That's all right." Mitzi waved the comment aside. "Slade will probably walk, he usually does."

Suppressing a shudder at the thought that he might have been a block or two behind her all the way from the office, Lisa darted up the stairs. As she reached her room, she heard the entrance door open downstairs. Another minute and her deception would have been discovered before she'd had a chance to make it work.

Lisa hurried to the bathroom. She would have loved to take a quick shower but there wasn't time. So she settled for splashing lots of cold water on her face to rinse away the tiredness and wiped off the lipstick she'd put on in the wig shop.

From the closet, she chose a demure blue dress. Its style and subdued color made her look positively dainty, even shy, a definite contrast to the chic, look-at-me outfit she had chosen that morning.

Reapplying her makeup, Lisa was adding the

finishing touch of mascara to her lashes when she noticed the way the color of her dress brought out the green of her eyes. Only last night Mitzi had made the comment that Lisa's eyes were her most striking feature.

Two women with the same unusual shade of green eyes would definitely be noticed by Slade Blackwell. And Lisa had looked at him more than once—she'd had to.

Not that she happened to have any colored contacts with her to make a quick change, of course. Breathing in sharply, she dropped the mascara wand on the dressing table and raced into the bedroom. Her bag was on the bed where she had left it. Lisa opened it and dumped the contents, weird red wig and all, onto the bedspread, scattering everything around until she found her sunglasses.

They were Oakleys, bought in a shop in the mall, with a high-tech coating that lightened indoors. It would provide some coverage without being completely opaque. That demented-drug-addict-in-shades look wouldn't go over too big at a Charleston dinner table, no matter how eccentric Mitzi was.

She slipped on the wraparound sunglasses and dashed back to the mirror. The smoky tint did its job and hid what she wanted to hide. "Praise be," Lisa murmured with relief.

Dressed and with every potential problem countered, she had no more reason to linger in her room. At the top of the stairs, she hesitated, hearing the low voices coming from the living room. She pressed a hand against her stomach, trying to quiet the butterfly sensation.

Her palms were clammy from nervousness. She couldn't put off the moment of truth. Fighting her wobbly knees, she descended the stairs and entered the living room.

"There you are, Lisa. I—" Mitzi's bright exclamation ended abruptly as a frown creased her forehead.

Lisa was conscious of Slade Blackwell courteously rising to meet her but she kept her attention on her aunt.

"Honey, why are you wearing sunglasses at this hour?" Mitzi asked with astonishment.

"Oh, gosh. I bet I do look sort of strange. But the bright lights in the television studios really make me sensitive to light. After being in the sun all day, my eyes started to bother me." Lisa was certain she was a natural-born liar. "A specialist recommended that I wear dark glasses, even indoors, whenever that happened."

"You never mentioned it," her aunt said doubtfully.

"It isn't a serious problem. More of an inconvenience than anything," Lisa assured her and turned to meet Slade Blackwell.

He looked her over as she walked toward him, extending a hand in greeting. She had been covertly watching his face ever since she'd entered the room, but hadn't detected any glimmer of recognition of her as Ann Eldridge, the redheaded temp from hell.

"You must be Slade Blackwell." A full smile parted her lips as she spoke. "I'm Lisa Talmadge, Mitzi's niece."

"So I guessed." He returned her smile with one of his own.

The warmth it gave to his chiseled features was astounding. In fact, it slowly took her breath away. Lisa realized how very potent his charm could be when he turned it on, as he was doing now. Her hand was lost in the firm grip of his, being held longer than was necessary. The butterflies in her stomach did a few more loop-the-loops.

"Mitzi described you perfectly," he said.

"Oh, really? What did she say?"

"That you were a beautiful, intelligent blonde. But she didn't mention that you had cold hands," he mocked, the velvet quality of his voice taking the sting out of the comment.

"Cold hands, warm heart," her aunt said.

"I think it's a sign of poor circulation." Lisa withdrew her hand from his warm grasp.

She had felt herself beginning to warm to him. Seeing this side of him, she could well understand how her sentimental, romantic aunt had been taken in. The secret, Lisa figured, was to keep away from that magnetic force field emanating from him. His physical attraction was a little overwhelming at close range.

That was something she hadn't noticed about him at the office where Slade Blackwell had been aloof and impersonal, crisply professional except for his remark about her hat. Correction—Ann Eldridge's hat. She hoped she hadn't left it on the rack downstairs. She couldn't honestly remember.

"May I fix you a drink, Lisa?" Slade asked smoothly.

"Lisa drinks gin," Mitzi said, turning to Lisa to add, "Slade has a bartender's touch with mixed drinks."

"What'll it be?" Slade looked at her, waiting for an order.

"Oh, not gin. I'll just have some juice." As tired as she was, Lisa knew better than to have so much as a sip of alcohol.

"Are you sure?" He gave her a chance to change her mind.

"Yes," Lisa nodded.

He walked to a beautifully carved tea trolley that her aunt used as a bar. "There's tomato and orange juice here," he said. "Which would you prefer?"

"Tomato." Lisa watched him pour the tomato juice into a heavy crystal glass with a flat bottom, and add a dash of Tabasco and a wedge of lemon. He plunked in a few ice cubes and stirred the drink with a leafy little stalk of celery, presenting it to her with a smile. Never once did he stop to find what he needed.

"You know where everything is, don't you?" she commented, letting a little sarcasm creep into her voice.

"I drop in often." He shrugged, but his dark gaze probed hers. Maybe he was wondering why she'd used that tone.

"But not often enough to wear out your welcome." Her tongue seemed to be running away with her. Had he sneaked some gin into the tomato juice? Not possible. She'd watched him make it.

"I hope not." But this time his smile didn't reach his eyes.

"You couldn't possibly do that, Slade," Mitzi laughed, missing or overlooking the tiny barbs in Lisa's remarks. "Mildred and I love having you here. You couldn't come often enough. I would be delighted if you looked on this as your second home. You should. After all, you're responsible—directly and indirectly—for all that's been done here."

"Of course, how could I have forgotten?" The words were out before Lisa could check them. But she only knew that she had gone too far to turn back now. "Mitzi told me that you persuaded her to reopen the house and supervised the remodeling and redecorating. Naturally you would be familiar with everything, wouldn't you?"

"A house in this neighborhood of Charleston is an investment. Besides, it would have been a shame to let this beautiful home fall apart," Slade replied.

"I agree with you completely," said Mitzi. "In fact, I did the first time you suggested renovating, Slade, but I never would have attempted it on my own. Not that I couldn't have done it, but it's so time consuming and there are so many things that depend on other things—I couldn't keep track of it all. You know how I dislike details, Lisa," she laughed at herself. "If Slade hadn't taken charge of the project, I doubt if I would've bothered to fix the old place up, simply because I can't stand the hassle."

"Yes," Lisa agreed. "You were lucky to have Slade take care of all that." She turned to him, a saccharine smile curving her mouth. "Ever since Mitzi moved back to Charleston she's been singing your praises. You seem to be indispensable to her."

"Mitzi and I have become good friends. The purpose of friendship is to help each other when help is needed." There was a challenging set to his jaw although his voice remained calm. "Now that Mitzi's on her own, without a man to look after her, I try to do what I can to help."

"I'm sure you do," Lisa taunted softly, and his gaze narrowed with piercing thoughtfulness.

"Believe me, I appreciate it," Mitzi stated. "I have no head for business, and I don't want to be bothered with investment credits and capital gains and stock dividends. It's a relief to turn it all over to someone I trust totally. I'm afraid I've taken advantage of Slade's good nature, though."

"It must be wonderful to have someone you

trust so much," Lisa said, gritting her teeth. It wasn't the time or place to inform her aunt that she was risking everything with her lackadaisical attitude toward her finances. "It's an awesome responsibility for Slade, though, to have virtually sole control of someone else's money."

"Yes, it is," he agreed.

Lisa saw his mouth tighten but she didn't care if he didn't like what she was saying. She wanted him to know that she was aware of the degree to which he exercised that control. He could think what he wanted about that.

She really should be more subtle about it, though. But she was taking a fiendish delight in antagonizing him.

Her subconscious seemed to have come up with a daring battle plan. While Lisa Talmadge attacked him boldly head-on in her aunt's house, Ann Eldridge could sneak up on him in his office and screw up his paperwork, if nothing else.

"Lisa thinks I'm *too* trusting," Mitzi sighed with amusement. "But I'd rather be. And of course she doesn't know you as I do, Slade."

So the invisible darts she had been tossing hadn't escaped her aunt's attention. Neither did Mitzi seem upset by them. Yet her words seemed to hint at a truce between Lisa and Slade, however temporary.

"You are too trusting," Lisa said, but gently and with affection. "It would be too easy for someone you like to take advantage of you."

Her subtle accusation against Slade Blackwell had been made but not in such a way that he could openly take offense. But he didn't like it—Lisa could tell that by the hard look in his eyes.

"May I fix you another drink, Mitzi?" Slade rose from his chair, carrying his empty glass.

"I don't believe so." Mitzi swirled her drink, ice cubes clinking against the side. "I still have some left, but help yourself, by all means."

"I think I will," he said grimly, walking to the bar trolley. "In one way or another, it's been a really long day."

You can say that again, Lisa thought, remembering the chaos in the office that afternoon.

The phone had almost never stopped ringing, and clients kept stopping in, expecting to talk to Slade whether they had appointments or not. The letters had taken forever to finish, and the legal briefs weren't even half-completed.

"I never did have a chance to ask how your day was, Lisa." Mitzi turned to her, curious and interested. "You left a message with Mildred that you were going to visit some friends. Did they take you sightseeing?"

"We were going to go after lunch," Lisa lied again, "but we got to talking. One thing led to another and before I knew it the afternoon was gone."

"I didn't know you had friends living in Charleston," Slade commented.

"College chums," Mitzi said.

"Yes, Susan, Peg, and I were roommates in college." Lisa hoped that wherever they were, they didn't mind her using them in her story. "We're planning to make a day of it tomorrow since they're on vacation too," she said, establishing a reason in advance for her absence tomorrow.

"You must invite them over some time. I'd like to meet them," her aunt suggested.

"I'll do that," Lisa smiled. What else could she say?

From the archway came the sound of someone clearing their throat to get attention. Lisa glanced over her shoulder to see the unsmiling face of the housekeeper framed in the opening.

"If you all come into the dining room, I'll dish up the soup," she announced gruffly.

"We're coming," Mitzi said. Slade was at the older woman's side when she rose from her chair.

"Did you fix my favorite, Mildred?" There was a teasing lightness to Slade's question.

Lisa was surprised to see the housekeeper look flustered. There was a definite pink in her cheeks, which she tried to hide by turning away.

"It's she-crab soup, if that's what you're asking," she retorted.

Not only was her aunt under Slade's spell, Lisa realized, but the housekeeper was as well. Lisa had not thought anything or anyone could get past the armor of weary indifference that Mildred wore. The more she thought about it, as they followed the housekeeper into the dining room, the more logical it seemed that Slade would butter up the housekeeper as well.

He was the one who had hired Mildred in the first place, Lisa remembered. She would naturally be loyal to him and he would need an ally in the household to keep him informed. Lisa hoped her fatigue was not making her paranoid, but that was how things looked to her right now.

Mildred was being used by Slade as surely as her aunt was. The man was completely without scruples. But Lisa was determined to expose him for what he was.

She shot him a guarded look as they entered the dining room. He ignored it.

Lisa looked around. The dining room was a formal, yet comfortable space with three ways into it: a set of double doors that opened into the living room, another set opening into the hallway, and a third door to the kitchen. The luster of the woodwork and furniture was enhanced by the subtle pattern of the embossed wallpaper, a shade of peach. The crystal teardrops of the chandelier cast rays of refracted light on the high, beamed ceiling.

The leaves had been removed from the oak table to seat the three of them comfortably without a long stretch of white linen tablecloth to separate them. As Slade pulled out the chair at the head of the table for Mitzi, Lisa walked around them to sit on her aunt's right.

Reaching for the carved wood of the chair back, her hand instead touched the back of his. Lisa drew it back in surprise, as if encountering something unpleasant. Slade was directly behind her, his dark eyes wary. An inner alarm seemed to clang at his closeness.

Lisa stepped aside quickly. "Thank you," she murmured tightly as he pulled out the chair for her. Her shoulders felt the brush of his strong fingers through the silky material of her blue dress, her nerve endings quivering in reaction.

It was a purely physical response, and had nothing to do with the fact that she disliked him intensely. Or maybe it had everything to do with that fact. Whatever. Being around Slade Blackwell was confusing, no matter which way she looked at it. But she didn't intend to be distracted by his sensual good looks or his good manners.

He seated himself across the table from her, and she found herself staring at him. He looked her right in the eye with a wary alertness. For a panicky second, Lisa thought he'd figured out what she'd been thinking.

More than once, she'd been told how expressive her green eyes were. But that wasn't the case this time, she remembered. The tinted sunglasses were her salvation.

"You were saying you had a long day, Slade," Mitzi commented, "Did all hell break loose at the office?"

"No more so than usual," he replied. Lisa didn't think that boded well for tomorrow. "It's just that both Bob and Mary Lou are gone, which means a lot of extra work for the rest of us."

"Vacation?" Mitzi leaned back a little as Mildred began serving the aromatic, fragrant bowls of she-crab soup.

"Well, I hate to bring this up at the dinner table," Slade sighed, "but Mary Lou's parents were hit by a drunk driver. Her father was killed out-right and her mother is in the ICU. Needless to say, my problems don't mean a thing next to that but—"

"That's just awful," Mitzi interrupted him. "I didn't know that. I'm so sorry for Mary Lou. When did it happen?"

"The day before yesterday."

"Remind me to send flowers to the hospital, Lisa. What were you going to say, Slade? I didn't let you finish."

"I'm stuck with a temp as my secretary. The office routine is shot to hell."

"Is that her fault?" Lisa instinctively defended her own inadequacies in the position.

"I didn't say it was," he corrected with dry sharp-ness. "But it would have been considerably easier on all of us if I had trained help. The one the agency sent showed up late and she doesn't seem to know the first thing about legal documents."

"Trained help?" Lisa bridled a little. "You make it sound as if she's supposed to jump through hoops. You should give her credit for doing the best she can. Temp agencies send whoever they've got if they have to."

Slade's dark eyebrows raised high. "Are you always so quick to defend people you don't know?"

Lisa realized she had been too vocal in her defense of the supposedly unknown secretary. She quickly dipped her spoon in the soup and got busy stirring it.

"Let's just say that I always root for the underdog, especially if she's a woman." But the statement sounded just plain odd and she knew it.

"Now, now, you two. I guess it was just too much to hope that you wouldn't clash," Mitzi sighed, looking from one to the other. Her expression was a mixture of regret and amusement.

"We aren't clashing." Lisa wished she hadn't spoken so frankly in front of her aunt. "We just have different points of view."

"Perhaps not as different as you think." Slade's tone suggested some mysterious message that Lisa was supposed to understand, but she didn't.

And she said so. "I don't think that's true."

"You pretty much said that I haven't given this temp a chance. But that's not true. If she's willing to learn, then I'm willing to teach her. Mary Lou's going to be out for a while. But you can't fault me for saying that I'm overwhelmed—and frustrated. That's a fact," he concluded, so reasonably that it set Lisa's teeth on edge.

Lisa doubted that he meant what he said. He was preaching to the choir, as her aunt would say, and that choir was made of women who adored him, like Mitzi and Mildred.

"Tell me more," Mitzi said. "She can't be that bad if you're willing to teach her."

"She's young."

"Well, that's no sin, is it?" Mitzi asked.

Slade's gaze flicked briefly to Lisa and she held her breath, knowing that he was making a fleeting comparison between herself and her alter ego, Ann Eldridge. "In her early twenties—about Lisa's age, I'd guess. She has bright red hair, short and kind of spiky, and eyes the color of—"

"Isn't that typical?" Lisa rushed to interrupt him, afraid Mitzi would make a comment about her green eyes if Slade mentioned Ann's. "You ask a man to describe a woman and he immediately gives a physical description, judging a woman on looks instead of ability—"

"Lisa!" Her aunt shot her a warning look.

"Never mind, Mitzi," Slade said. "Lisa has a point, unfortunately. A lot of men do that. I had to warn Drew not to bother this girl. He saw her red hair and got all hot and bothered."

Mitzi shook her head. "That Drew Rutledge. He's such a hound."

Lisa had taken a spoonful of soup and did her best not to choke on it. She succeeded, wiping her mouth with a napkin and giving her aunt a blank look.

"Anyway," Slade continued, "I think this temp is actually pretty bright. But the reason I didn't mention her skills is because she doesn't have any. At least not legal secretary skills, which is what I need."

"Then why keep her on?" Lisa asked, changing her contentious tone to one of polite interest. She didn't want to plant the thought of firing Ann Eldridge in his mind.

"Because she has a remarkable ability to handle several things at once without getting distracted or flustered. That's a great trait," he said. "When Mary Lou does return, she'll have a backlog of correspondence to catch up on, but in the meantime, I don't have to be out there holding Ann's hand."

"If she's attractive," Mitzi teased, "maybe you're missing something."

"Don't think so," Slade said. "She has a boyfriend. Drew got that information out of her right away. I swear, he doesn't know when to shut up or what to say, let alone what constitutes professional behavior in a law office. But I'll fire him if he doesn't toe the line. I won't tolerate that crap."

"Language," Mitzi said automatically.

"Sorry, Mitzi." Slade cast a look at Lisa. *Okay, that's one in your favor,* she thought grudgingly.

"Well, too bad," Mitzi went on. "Sounds like that was one girl who might have kept up with your many and varied interests."

"I guess that's something I won't find out." He shrugged. "How's the new novel coming along?"

"Wonderfully!" Mitzi declared, and the topic of conversation was finally switched.

As far as Lisa was concerned, the dinner was awkward with Slade there. She took little part in the discussion, a fact that Mitzi didn't seem to notice as she warmed to the subject of her latest book. Slade pretended to concentrate on what her aunt was saying but Lisa was intensely conscious of how often his gaze focused on her.

"Mildred, we'll have our coffee in the living room," Mitzi informed the housekeeper when they had finished dessert. "That way Slade can add a little brandy to his." She laughed briefly and changed the subject again, hardly drawing a breath in the transition.

"Oh, I wanted to show you the review of my latest book. It's in my study."

"I'll get it for you," Lisa volunteered quickly, eager for a few minutes alone.

"Would you mind?" The absent question from Mitzi was answered by a shake of Lisa's head. "It's in the pile of papers on the right-hand side of my desk. Somewhere in the middle, I think."

"I'll find it," she assured her aunt, hastily retreating while Mitzi and Slade headed for the living room.

Study was a loose term for this room, Lisa decided. Nothing about it resembled a study except for the abundance of books. Yet the décor expressed the creative side of Mitzi's personality, despite the clutter of papers, notebooks, and magazines. It was definitely a feminine room, painted a bright, cheery yellow. A flowered sofa repeated the color. In a corner by a window sat a small, round table, painted white with a white, cane-backed chair beside it. It was where Mitzi had her coffee and, often, her lunch.

There were no bookshelves as such. But books were stacked in every corner and balanced on every piece of furniture, along with scraps of paper. A computer took up the center of a long, counter-style table. The table's surface was buried beneath papers, pencils, CDs, floppy disks, and more books. There was a desk in the room, but it seemed to be used mostly as a catchall for other miscellaneous stuff.

She saw three stacks of paper in all shapes and sizes on the right-hand side of the desk. Lisa searched through all three and finally found the newspaper clipping in the last one. Restoring the stack to its former ordered disorder, she checked her reflection in the beautiful old mirror on the wall above the desk, then turned to leave.

The study door opened as she made her turn and Slade walked in. For an instant, Lisa was too surprised to react. She stood in front of the desk, holding the clipping and staring.

The click of the door latch closing seemed to

suddenly isolate them from the rest of the house. Her throat tightened and she couldn't speak as he pinned her with his gaze.

"Did Mitzi send you in here?" She swallowed hard, not sure why she was afraid.

"No, I came on my own." There was hardly a crack in his granite-hard features as he spoke.

"You didn't have to." Lisa's chin tipped up defiantly, her shattered poise beginning to come back together. "I found the clipping. It was under a lot of other stuff."

"So I see," Slade nodded, his gaze darting indifferently to the paper clutched in her hand.

A nervous hesitation made her quiver. There was something about his being there that was getting to her.

"Okay. Guess I should give it to Mitzi." Lisa realized she was rattled and her voice betrayed it, but she couldn't help it.

Slade stood in front of the door, barring her way, but Lisa took a step forward anyway, expecting him to open the door for her. He didn't move.

"You aren't leaving yet," he said.

Lisa stopped short. "What do you mean?"

"You aren't leaving until you explain what's going on," he said simply.

CHAPTER FOUR

Lisa felt her confidence drain away as rapidly as the color faded out of her face. Slade Blackwell had obviously seen through her improvised ruse, not to mention her sunglasses. If only she had hung on to that file.

She would have something to back up her suspicions—something to take to her aunt. As it was, she had nothing with which to confront him. And how could she explain her deception? Her aunt would think she was crazy.

"So what's going on?" he repeated.

"I don't think I know what you mean," Lisa tried to stall.

"Don't you?" Slade hadn't moved since entering the study. Yet he seemed to fill the room, intimidating Lisa until she wanted to sink into the nearest chair and confess. But that would be too much like admitting guilt.

He was the unscrupulous one who should feel guilty.

"I—I'm confused." And suddenly unable to lie. What was up with that, she wondered. She'd been lying through her teeth all day and feeling more and more ashamed of it.

At his step forward. Lisa wanted to retreat but the large desk was right behind her. There wasn't anywhere to run even if she could make her legs move.

"So let's talk, Lisa."

"About what?"

"Why you're sneaking around, for starters."

She stared at the fluttering piece of paper in her hands. "Mitzi sent me in here for this. I wasn't sneaking around."

"You know damned well that's not what I mean."

"I just don't understand what you're talking about."

His gaze narrowed. "Then I'll have to make myself clearer. Mitzi may believe all that nonsense about clashing personalities but I don't."

Lisa breathed in sharply. He was talking about their silly squabble at the dinner table. Thank God he still hadn't realized that she was Ann Eldridge.

"Whatever. You're entitled to your opinion."

"Okay." He clasped his hands and stood his ground. "Here's another one. I don't believe in love at first sight or hate at first sight. But I'd have to say that your obvious dislike of me comes close to being the second one."

"So?"

"I want to know why you hate me. We just met." His mouth curved in an ironic smile.

"Hate. That's a strong word. I wouldn't say that I hate you."

Slade shook his head. "You've been sniping at me all evening. Why?"

Lisa took a deep breath and plunged in. "It's very simple. Unlike my aunt, I don't trust you."

"You made that clear."

"Did I?" Lisa said. "Good." A smile accompanied her honey-coated comment.

"What's your game?" His dark head tipped to the side, the angular planes of his face expressionless and cold.

She arched an eyebrow delicately, pushing up her sunglasses. "Back to square one. I don't know what you mean."

"Oh, yes, you do, Lisa."

He scowled at her and her temper suddenly flared. "Your apparent concern for Mitzi is just plain sickening," she said. "She must seem like easy prey to you. Divorced. Not too good about taking care of things. Alone. No close relatives. And let's not forget wealthy. You could even claim old family ties."

"The key word here seems to be wealthy," he mused.

Her anger didn't seem to worry him, she realized with dismay. Slade was closer now, looming in front of her. His height forced her head back to meet the black glitter of his gaze. She was all too conscious of his physical presence.

"Yes," she agreed. "That is key. You've gone to great lengths to make yourself indispensable to Mitzi. You must be thrilled by how gullible she is."

"Is that what you think?" he asked quietly.

"Yes. She trusts you and you're stealing from her. I know it."

"Can you prove it?"

"I will, Slade. Give me time," Lisa said softly. "She isn't quite as alone as you obviously thought. Even though she and my uncle divorced before he died, my parents and I still think of her as part of the family. And we sure as hell won't let some slick lawyer like you take advantage of her!"

"Oh." Slade seemed coldly amused by her vehemence. "What are you going to do about it?"

"I'm going to make her see the truth," she declared.

"Then what?" He eyed her steadily.

"What do you mean?" Lisa frowned, not seeing the relevance of his question.

"What are you going to get out of it?"

"The satisfaction of Mitzi seeing you for who you really are," she retorted.

"That's all? You seem intent on getting me out of Mitzi's life and her affairs. Would that be because once I'm gone, you can step in?"

Lisa tensed, picking up his implication. "What are you getting at? That's a leading question if I ever heard one."

"So you know what a leading question is. You must watch *Court TV.*"

"Actually, I don't," Lisa snapped.

"Here's what I'm getting at, then. You aren't a blood relation to Mitzi. She has none left." His sharp gaze never left her face. "Admittedly, you're her niece. Left over from a marriage that ended in a bitter divorce."

"That's a technicality."

"My profession deals in technicalities," Slade reminded her. "Here's another interesting fact. Mitzi's lived in Charleston for several years now, but this is the first time you've visited."

"It's the first chance I've had to come," Lisa said, wondering why she was arguing the point.

"Or the first time you thought there was reason?" he countered.

"Reason?" She stiffened. "What the hell are you saying? I probably shouldn't even talk to you without a lawyer present, you're such a weasel."

"You have a way with words, Lisa," he said with

an icy smile. "I was just trying to point out that your motive for being here may not be as pure as you pretend."

"What?" Lisa's tone was incredulous.

"It seems to me that you scheduled this visit after you became aware of how much and how often I was helping your aunt. Mitzi often told me that she wrote to you and e-mailed you and told you all about me. But I think you got the wrong idea. Even so, you were pretty sure of her affection for you. But you didn't bother visiting her until you got the idea that someone else was after her money. Someone whom you thought didn't deserve it. That's what brought you here—Mitzi's money," he concluded.

"Quite a speech, counselor," Lisa began in outraged anger. "Are you accusing me of—"

"All I'm saying is that you decided to dislike me because Mitzi turned to me for advice on how to manage her money and her property. And you see that as a threat not to your aunt but to yourself." Slade looked at her with contempt.

"That's ridiculous!" Her fury had reached the boiling point. Lisa hauled off and slapped him. Hard.

He barely blinked. "I have never hit a woman. And I'm not going to do it now."

She struck at him again, but this time he was prepared and caught her wrist in an iron grip. "Don't, Lisa. Assault is assault. There are laws against it, you know?"

"Would you stand up in front of a judge and say a woman beat you up?"

He shook his head. "I wouldn't say that. I don't think you could. But did you just hit me?"

"Yes! Twice! You had it coming."

He shook his head and didn't let go of her wrist.

"The law doesn't make exceptions because some-one had it coming. You're not in danger. We argued but I didn't threaten you in any way. Control yourself, Lisa."

He let go.

She began to tremble but kept her hands at her sides. The atmosphere in the room was so charged, his gaze was so intense, she scarcely knew what to think or what to do next. Slade just stood there. She took a step toward him.

And another. Before she could stop herself, she went into his arms. He looked down at her—and wonder of wonders, he kissed her tenderly.

Her lips throbbed, her smooth skin rasped by the faint stubble of his beard, barely noticeable by sight but definitely by touch. Her heart was beating double time, her cheeks flushed.

"What the hell are we doing?" she murmured.

"I was kissing you."

She let her head rest against his neck.

"Ready for another round?" he said softly, his lips against her hair. "I think you should take off those sunglasses."

"Oh, no," she said quickly. She pushed him away. "You just said a lot of really nasty things."

"So did you, Lisa."

She began to pace the cluttered room, kicking the books on the floor out of her way. "I don't know what to do next."

He sighed. "I think we'd better come to an understanding."

"I'm not going to bargain with you." No matter how good it had felt to be in his arms for that inexplicable kiss, she thought, she would not give in. Tough luck if he didn't like it. "And I don't understand you. Therefore, we can't come to an understanding, as you put it. Not that I know what you mean by that."

"I just—oh, hell." Slade didn't have a chance to finish what he was going to say. Three light raps sounded on the study door.

Mitzi opened it and peered around the room.

"You two have been in here so long I figured you were squabbling again. Need a referee?"

"No, Mitzi. Thanks, though," Lisa said slowly. There was no way she could explain what had happened to her aunt. She couldn't even explain it to herself.

The newspaper review had fallen to the floor, she noticed. Lisa stooped to pick it up. "Oops. Here's that clipping. Guess I dropped it."

Mitzi looked at her niece and Lisa wondered if her lipstick was smudged. She had scrubbed off most of it before coming down to dinner. But she could see a trace of dusty pink on Slade's mouth, a souvenir of that mind-blowing kiss.

Her aunt took the clipping from her hand. "Well, it's a little wrinkled but so am I. Ha, ha."

Lisa managed a wan smile. Slade was looking everywhere but at her.

"Okay. The coffee's still in the living room, if you two are still interested."

Slade pushed aside the cuff of his jacket to glance at his watch. "It's getting late for me. And I probably don't need any more stimulation."

Lisa gave him a sour look. *Very funny,* she thought. That argument had been upsetting, not stimulating. But the kiss—well, it could definitely be defined that way.

"Thanks anyway, Mitzi," Slade was saying. "But to show you how much I enjoyed the dinner and the company tonight, I'd like to take you and

Lisa out tomorrow night. If you're both free, that is."

Lisa decided to let Mitzi answer.

"Oh, yes!" the older woman said. "We would love to go. Wouldn't we, Lisa?"

"Sure," Lisa mumbled, not looking at Slade.

"Okay." Slade turned back to Mitzi. "Dinner tomorrow evening. I'll pick the two of you up at seven."

"Wait a minute. No," Lisa said. "I—I can't."

"Don't be silly," her aunt said. "Slade knows every good restaurant in Charleston."

"Some other time," Lisa said. "Mitzi, I'm going to be out all day with Peg and Susan. I'm not going to feel like going out tomorrow night."

"No problem. We could do it Thursday, the day after," Slade suggested.

Lisa thought it over. By then, she would have her hands on the Talmadge folder and he wouldn't be able to distract her with a kiss. She scolded herself silently for being stupid enough to go into his arms in the first place. *That mysterious magnetic force field got the better of me, Captain Kirk,* she thought. No, kissing Slade was not an experience she would willingly repeat. He was way too sexy. And she still didn't trust him—or herself.

"Lisa?" her aunt prompted.

"What?" She snapped out of her reverie.

"Is dinner Thursday night all right?"

"Ye-es, as far as I know," Lisa said slowly. Might as well leave herself an out. She might need it.

Slade gave her a maddeningly smug smile. "Looking forward to it," he said. "Good night, ladies. And thanks again, Mitzi. I know my way out."

"What an infuriating man," Lisa muttered as the study door closed behind him. "I don't know what you see in him, Aunt Mitzi."

"All interesting men are infuriating," her aunt said cheerfully. "That's just how it is. If you don't feel like smacking them now and then, they aren't worth knowing."

Lisa turned away to hide her guilty expression.

"Now if I were your age—" Mitzi began.

Lisa interrupted her without looking at her. "If you were my age, you'd be welcome to him." She caught a glimpse of herself in the antique mirror on the wall and touched a finger to her lips. They still tingled a little from his kiss. "He leaves me cold."

"Cold?" Mitzi sounded a little doubtful about that. "I think hot is more like it. Don't you want to have some fun while you're here?"

"Please, Mitzi." Lisa lifted a hand in protest. "Slade Blackwell wouldn't be my choice for that. And that's not why I came to Charleston."

"It's a romantic place, Lisa. Make the most of it."

"Could we talk about something else?"

With a heavy sigh, her aunt seemed to give in— or at least drop the subject. Lisa knew that Mitzi was puzzled by the animosity between two people she liked. But she reminded herself of her original goal: to find hard evidence that would prove Slade Blackwell had been mismanaging her aunt's finances and even stealing from her. Until then, Lisa really didn't want to heap lie upon lie by pretending that she liked the guy.

"Come have coffee with me, honey. I hate being alone after dinner." Lisa had to say yes. She went downstairs with her aunt. The first thing Mitzi did was turn the lights down low. "There. Now you can take off those sunglasses. I like to see someone's eyes when I talk to them, don't you?"

"Yes, Mitzi. Sorry. I didn't mean to be rude but I do have to wear them indoors sometimes."

"I understand. Now how do you take your coffee? I plumb forgot."

"Black. Thanks." Lisa accepted the cup of decaf that Mitzi poured and listened patiently to her aunt's amusing chatter.

By ten o'clock, mental and physical exhaustion set in. Lisa was grateful when Mitzi suggested it was time they went to bed. Upstairs in her room, Lisa ignored the bed in favor of the bathroom, where she took advantage of the massaging showerhead, letting the jets of water pound the aching muscles of her shoulders and neck.

Toweling off, she tumbled into bed and turned off the light. In the darkness, she wondered if her thoughts of Slade and what would happen next would keep her awake until the sun came up. That was the last thing Lisa remembered thinking.

The study door was open when Lisa came down the spiral staircase a little after seven the next morning. She didn't hear the soft clatter on the computer keyboard and assumed her aunt was elsewhere.

She was wrong. Mitzi appeared in the study doorway an instant later. "You're up early. And all dressed too."

"I just don't want to sleep my vacation away," Lisa said in the perkiest voice she could manage. But she secretly wished she could stay snuggled up in her canopy bed for at least another two hours.

"Come in and join me for coffee. Mildred just brought it in," Mitzi said.

"Thanks, but no." Lisa glanced at her watch. "I'm meeting Peg and Sue for breakfast." The minutes were ticking away. She needed the early start

to make the transformation into Ann Eldridge before reaching Slade's office. Her hands clutched
her purse, its sides bulging with the red wig she
had crammed inside.

"Oh, I see. How nice? Where are they staying?"
For once Lisa was grateful for her aunt's habit of
rattling on, because Mitzi didn't wait for an answer. "You know, there's a tour boat that takes you
to Fort Sumter where the first battle of the Civil
War took place. It's really quite fascinating to wander around the old battlements and listen to the
park ranger explain about the long siege of the
fort."

Lisa, engaged as she was in a battle of wits with
Slade Blackwell, could identify with the siege part.
She nodded. "I bet it is."

"Did you know," Mitzi said, "the South never lost
it to the Union. They ultimately abandoned it toward the close of the war, but it was never taken
from them."

"How about that," Lisa replied, thinking that
she would never let Slade take another kiss from
her. "I'll mention it, Mitzi. But I'm not sure where
they want to go today. They might have made
other plans."

Mitzi sighed. "All right then. Back to work for
me. I was actually in the middle of a very tricky
scene when I heard you come downstairs."

"I hope I didn't distract you."

"No, honey. I'm very good at distracting myself.
I don't need any help to do that. You go on and
have a great time, y'hear?"

"Thanks, Mitzi." She gave her aunt a hug and a
kiss, and dashed out the door.

Using the ladies' room of a different restaurant
to change, she donned the flame-colored wig and

outlined her lips with coral gloss. She looked at herself in the mirror. There was only one word for the way she looked and that word was *eek*.

She dashed out, wondering if anyone had noticed the blonde going in and the redhead coming out. But the place was busy with a crowd of morning regulars and no one even looked at her.

When Slade arrived at the office, she was hard at work on the legal briefs. Nodding an indifferent greeting, he picked up the few phone messages from her desk and a thick sheaf of letters and other mail. He went directly into his own office. Lisa hoped that he hibernated there. Now that he had met Lisa Talmadge, she didn't want him noticing the obvious similarities to Ann Eldridge. Especially since he had heard her real voice.

At each sound coming from the outer reception area, Lisa glanced expectantly toward the door. Drew was supposed to return her aunt's file this morning and she desperately needed to get her hands on it. She couldn't hope to fool Slade indefinitely. He wasn't stupid and this disguise wasn't exactly impenetrable. Having to talk like a dumb temp was driving her crazy.

Half the morning had passed before Drew appeared. Lisa was on the phone when he walked in. She smiled a greeting, her eyes lighting up when she saw the Talmadge folder in his hand.

Drew smiled back, in full suave-guy mode. While she transferred the call to Slade, Drew hovered near her desk, gazing at her silently.

"Burt's a lucky man," he said when she hung up.

"Who?"

"Burt. Your gigantic boyfriend."

"Oh, right. Yes, I guess he is," she said indifferently. "Hey, you brought the folder back just like you said."

"Do I get a gold star?" he asked playfully. Lisa wished he would knock it off.

"Is everything inside it?" What could she do but play along, she thought, already annoyed with Drew.

"Yup. It's all here," he said. "So how about lunch today?"

"No. Can't. Sorry." She knew exactly how she intended to spend her lunch hour: glued to the folder.

"Come on, have a heart," Drew coaxed. "Make a man happy for an hour."

He was really asking for trouble, Lisa mused. But she couldn't very well call Slade and have him rescue her. "Sorry," was all she said. "I have to do a whole bunch of letters. Actually, I was going to ask Ellen to order a sandwich for me and eat in."

"Okay," he capitulated unexpectedly. "If that's what you want, I'll buy the sandwich and we'll have a little picnic right here in the office."

"No," Lisa said, then tried to temper the sharpness of her refusal. "If you join me, then we'll talk and I won't get anything done, which would defeat my purpose for not going out to lunch. Let's just make it another day."

"Guess I'll have to console myself with knowing that you didn't turn me down flat." Drew gave an exaggerated sigh.

"Exactly." Lisa busily stacked and restacked the papers on her desk. Then she reached for the folder.

He gave it to her at last. She fought the impulse to clutch it to her chest.

"Tell Slade I said not to work you too hard," was Drew's last comment. He squinted one eye at her in an attempt at a debonair wink.

"Bye, Drew," she said. She watched him go and opened the folder. The very first document caught her attention. It seemed to be a power of attorney.

Before she had a chance to examine it, she heard the sound of a doorknob turning. She barely had time to close the folder when Slade walked in and she knew she'd jumped a little in her seat.

"Sorry, Ann. Didn't mean to startle you." His hard, handsome mouth softened slightly.

"I—I just didn't hear you." Her fingers tightened nervously on the edge of the folder. His dark gaze moved to it.

"What do you have there?"

"Oh, this?" She made a show of looking at the identifying tab but she didn't dare look up at him. "Um, it's the Talmadge file. Drew just returned it. I was going to put it back in the filing cabinet."

"No need." He held out his hand. "I'll take it. There's a couple of things in there I want to look over."

No, she cried inwardly. Aloud, she murmured a hopeful "Now?"

"Yes, now. Why do you ask?"

"I was hoping—that you'd go over these letters with me." She covered her gaffe as best she could.

"Later."

Reluctantly, Lisa handed over the folder, keeping her eyes down. "Will there be anything else?" she asked.

"No, nothing else." Just like the day before, he barely seemed to look at her. She watched him go back into his office.

Lisa sighed. Twice the file had been in her grasp and twice it had been taken from her. Frustration was beginning to set in.

Having told Drew that she was ordering in for lunch meant that she was trapped in her office for the noon hour. Although Slade had walked off with her aunt's file, she was determined not to waste time. Perhaps she could find some incriminating evidence in the files of the decorators, contractors, and landscapers that Slade used.

The trouble was that she didn't know their names and the files were organized by names and not types of business. And she had a few scruples left, even though she'd told enough lies to earn a free, one-way ticket to hell. She didn't want to randomly prowl through files that had nothing to do with her aunt. She would just have to wait for Slade to finish with the Talmadge file.

Before the lunch hour was over, Lisa knew how a spy felt. Bored. And frustrated. Every creaking floorboard in the old building made her jump. Voices filtering in from the street had her looking around in alarm. Snooping was an unpleasant occupation, especially when one came up with zero results.

The sound of Slade's voice in the outer reception area sent her scurrying to her desk. How had he gotten out? There must be a back door to his inner office that she didn't know about. She could have gone in there and peeked at the folder. Damn and double damn.

She was staring into the computer screen, her back to him, when he came through the connecting doors.

"Any calls for me, Ann?"

"No. Things have been slow." That was no lie.

"I'm expecting Clyde Sanders to stop by. When he arrives, send him in."

"Yes, sir." Lisa swiveled around only when she heard him walk by her desk. She scowled at his back when he went into his private office and shut the door.

CHAPTER FIVE

By the end of the day, Lisa was engulfed in frustration. She had been waiting and waiting for Slade to return her aunt's folder so it could be filed . . . after she had looked through it, of course.

Shortly after three that afternoon, Slade had left the office on an errand. Desperate, Lisa had sneaked into his office to see if he had left the folder behind. She couldn't find it among the papers on his desk. One drawer of his desk was locked and he'd taken his briefcase with him. She'd assumed it was in either of those two places.

This goofy deception was threatening to last much longer than she'd ever intended. The longer it continued, the greater the risk of being unmasked. Lisa knew she had to take advantage of every opportunity. If an opportunity didn't present itself, she would have to do a little scheming.

A few minutes after five, Lisa was still at the computer. She had the hang of the Legal Eagle software by now. Slade seemed satisfied with the legal documents she was completing—or at least he didn't complain.

Her plan was to keep working until after Slade left and hopefully find the folder in the briefcase he'd brought back with him. Slade was still in his office with a client. No matter how tired she was or how much her wrists ached, Lisa was determined to outwait him.

Her patience was rewarded several minutes later when she heard the connecting door to Slade's private office open and the voices of two men talking as they came out. Her fingers continued tapping at the keyboard.

Lisa faked total concentration on her task and hoped Slade would leave with the man. But he only walked him as far as the door to the reception area and said good-bye. When the client was gone, Slade turned. Lisa felt his gaze rest on her. Her skin prickled with the awareness of it, sensitive nerve endings reacting. But she tried to give no sign that she knew he was looking at her.

"It's after five, Ann," he spoke, not allowing Lisa to ignore him any longer. "You should have left twenty minutes ago."

Her fingers paused on the keys but she didn't look up. "I'll be leaving soon," she assured him with vague indifference.

"What about Burt?"

She stalled for time with a yawn but couldn't think of an answer before Slade spoke again. "Guess you two have been together for a while," he said wryly.

"Well, yeah. But I love him. The big brute."

"Isn't he expecting dinner?"

"He can cook," she said. "Good thing too because he's always hungry." *Tell him another, Lisa.* She was almost beginning to believe in Burt herself.

"What does he do?" Slade asked without much

curiosity. He was leafing through a legal periodical. He seemed to like to do that at her desk, Lisa noticed.

"He's in construction. Heavy lifting perks up his appetite."

Slade tore out an article he seemed interested in. "He sounds a little scary."

"No, not at all. He's a sweetheart," Lisa said quickly.

"Well, you'd better get on home to him, then."

"Ah—he's probably putting in a few hours of overtime. He does that in good weather. I'll be home before he is, even if I stay until six." Lisa shrugged her unconcern.

"Suit yourself. But there isn't any need for you to stay late."

"I want to finish this. You can go ahead and leave." The sooner the better, Lisa added to herself. "As soon as I'm through here, I'll leave, but I know how important it is—"

"Nothing is so important that it can't wait until tomorrow," Slade interrupted. "I appreciate your conscientiousness, Ann, but it isn't necessary."

"I really don't mind staying," Lisa protested.

He lifted a dark eyebrow. "I said it wasn't necessary."

She got the point. Lisa turned off her computer and started cleaning up her desk. That seemed to satisfy him. He returned to his private office.

Lisa took her time, using every excuse to linger, sharpening pencils and arranging the things on the desk with fussy precision. There was still a chance Slade might leave before she did. Ten minutes later, she was straightening the papers in her filing tray as Slade walked out of his office.

"Are you still here? I thought I told you to go home."

"I like everything to be ready for the next day." She aligned the corners of a stack of company letterhead and returned the stack to its slot in one of the desk drawers. "Just give me another minute."

His mouth thinned as he turned and walked to the filing cabinet. The hope that he might be on his way home died as he removed two folders and returned to his office. There was nothing Lisa could do but leave and hope for better luck the next day.

Walking the blocks to her aunt's house, Lisa tried to formulate another plan of action, but she was too tired and dispirited to think. She felt something brush her hand and looked down. The red wig seemed to be trying to crawl out of her purse. She stuffed it back in, thinking again how much she hated wearing the stupid, itchy thing. But she had to.

She had barely entered the house and not closed the door when Mitzi called to her.

"Lisa, is that you?" She came sweeping out of the living room into the foyer. "Gracious, I was about to send out a search party."

"Sorry I'm late," Lisa said, a faint sigh in her voice. "I didn't mean for you to worry."

"You look exhausted. Sightseeing all day must have worn you out." A sympathetic smile curved her aunt's mouth. "Did you and your friends try to see everything in one day?"

"Something like that," she hedged and arched her back to ease her cramped, sore muscles. "Right now the only thing I want to see is a tubful of hot water."

"A nice hot bath works wonders, I always say. You go soak for a while," Mitzi instructed. "Later you can come downstairs and join me for a drink before dinner."

"Sounds good," Lisa said. She climbed the spiral staircase to her room.

While the bathtub was filling with water, Lisa undressed. Halfway to the bathroom, she remembered the wig was still crammed in her purse. She took it out and hid it in the rear of a dresser drawer. She followed the scent of the fragrant bubble bath to the tub, turned off the faucets, and climbed in. Lisa had no idea how long she lay soaking in the bath but the water was cool when she climbed out to towel herself dry.

She sighed when she slipped on the brown silk kimono-style robe, running a finger over its pretty ivory embroidery. The long bubble bath had eased her stiffness but it had done nothing to wash away the troubled light in her green eyes.

Opening her closet door, she immediately turned away. She didn't feel like dressing even though she knew Mitzi was waiting downstairs for her. The silk robe swished softly about her ankles as she walked barefoot to her bedroom door.

Maybe her aunt wouldn't stand on ceremony. A quiet evening lounging around at home was what Lisa dearly wanted and needed. She seriously doubted if Mitzi would object.

Her hand reached for the carved banister of the staircase. Something—a sound, a voice—stopped her, her foot poised on the edge of the first step. At the bottom of the stairs stood Slade Blackwell, dark, arresting, and vital. The sight of him paralyzed Lisa, and her hand clutched the loose fold of her robe together at the waist.

His gaze traveled down the length of her. She reddened as she realized her action had drawn the clinging fabric more tightly over her curves, possibly revealing that she wore nothing beneath her.

Her skin felt hot under the appraising look in his eyes. She didn't miss the suggestive gleam in his gaze, and she released the robe immediately, spreading her fingers to try to relieve the sudden, elemental tension that claimed her.

"What are you doing here?" She finally broke the silence, her voice tinged with a challenge born of embarrassment.

"I don't think it's any of your business since I'm here to see Mitzi," he replied smoothly.

"Why?"

"I told you, it's none of your business." Slade continued to study her feminine shape with an arrogant unconcern that had to have been bred into him. The almost physical touch of his gaze was having a disturbing effect on her senses, but Lisa was determined not to reveal it. She was at enough of a disadvantage, being dressed—or barely dressed—as she was.

"Mitzi is my aunt and that makes your presence here my business," she retorted.

"Our lawyer-client relationship doesn't include you." He smiled cynically. "Sorry."

"Where's Mitzi?" Lisa demanded.

"Looking for her glasses. She misplaced them." He caught her gaze and held it. "Why don't you come down and entertain me?"

"I'm not dr—" The word "dressed" died on her lips when she heard him chuckle. She wasn't usually so slow on the uptake. She shook her head.

"Okay, don't." His dark head tipped slightly to one side, studying her with fresh interest, puzzled and curious. "There's something different about you," he drawled thoughtfully. "Maybe it's your eyes, minus the sunglasses."

Lisa stiffened. He couldn't see the color of her eyes at this distance, not looking up the length of the staircase. But his remark acted like a cold splash of ice water. "There's nothing different about you!" she flashed. "Tell Mitzi I'll be down when you leave."

Pivoting on her heel, she hurriedly returned to her bedroom, trembling with delayed shock. That had been close, much too close.

Slade's unexpected appearance changed Lisa's mind about lounging around the house in her robe. In her room, she slipped out of the robe and put on a pair of pale yellow pants, and a blouse in green and yellow. Might as well match. Everybody did below the Mason-Dixon line. She waited until she heard the front door close before venturing downstairs again. Mitzi was alone in the living room when Lisa entered it.

"You look better. How do you feel?" Mitzi walked to the bar trolley and fixed Lisa a drink.

"Much better." Especially now that Slade was gone. Lisa settled into the brocade chair. Slade's refusal to say why he'd come prompted Lisa to ask Mitzi what he'd wanted. Lisa said only that she'd seen him arrive but not that she had spoken to him.

"He stopped by with some legal papers that needed my signature," her aunt explained.

"Oh?" Lisa took the drink her aunt brought her and sipped at it, wishing she could've seen those papers. "What kind of document was it? You did read it before you signed it, didn't you?"

"Of course. I always do. And Slade always explains everything," Mitzi said calmly. "But I never remember the exact wording. Legal language isn't meant to be clear, dear. If I wrote my novels that way, my readers would never be able to figure out the plot."

"So what document did you sign?" Lisa knew

she was being nosy, but her aunt's lack of concern was alarming.

Mitzi lowered her voice to a conspiratorial whisper. "I'm setting up a retirement fund for Mildred. Nothing very large, mind you, but it will supplement her Social Security. She's been so loyal to me, and a good friend in her way, despite her crabbiness. She's a regular skinflint but I know she hasn't been able to put very much aside. This seemed like a good way to help her without making it look like charity. Slade agreed when I mentioned it to him."

"I see." It sounded harmless. Lisa hoped it was.

Mitzi leaned back in her chair. "Tell me, what all did you see today?"

Lisa dreaded having to come up with a bogus explanation. She racked her brain for anything that would sound plausible. "Well, after breakfast, we took a carriage ride." That was the one thing she'd promised herself she would do. "The driver took us all around. As a matter of fact, we came right by here."

"I wish you had stopped for coffee. I would like to meet your friends. You're welcome to invite them over anytime," Mitzi said.

"I thought about bringing them in," she lied, "but I knew you were busy with your new novel. By the way, how is it coming along?"

"Marvelously." Her aunt's face seemed to light up with excitement. "I'm getting to my favorite part, where the plot thickens, if you'll forgive the cliché." She began explaining the twists and turns of the plot, the element of suspense that was beginning to build, and the characters.

The rest of the evening Lisa adroitly maneuvered the conversation to focus on Mitzi's interest and avoided telling more lies about places she had supposedly seem. That night in bed, she asked herself silently how much longer she was going to be able to get away with this deception. It seemed that only time would tell.

Lisa peered into her computer screen when Slade walked out of his office, pretending to read over a partially typed letter, the last of several he'd asked her to do. He paused briefly beside her desk.

"I'm going to lunch, Ann. I'll be back after one," he informed her. After her close call last night, Lisa took pains to avoid looking directly at him just in case some expression or gesture would seem familiar to him. Even now, when he was talking to her, she kept her face turned slightly away, feigning concentration on her work.

"Yes, Mr. Blackwell," she replied in a deliberately absentminded manner.

When he walked away, she peeked at him through her downcast lashes. His day's calendar of appointments indicated a business lunch, but he wasn't carrying his briefcase.

She breathed in deeply, knowing that it was probably still in his office.

From the reception area, she could hear him speaking to Drew. Lisa clicked *Print* on the commands menu and removed the finished letters from the printer one by one as she heard the street door open and close. Slade was gone.

Taking the letters into his office to put them on his desk, ostensibly for his signature, she looked around. The expensive briefcase was on the floor beside the large swivel chair at his desk. Lisa put the unsigned letters on his blotter and bent to open the briefcase. Her hands shook badly as she opened the latch.

She felt like a thief and had to remind herself that Slade was the real thief. Still, her hearing was acutely tuned to any sound of invasion from the outer office.

Her aunt's file was not in the briefcase. Lisa rose, swearing under her breath, and looked at the stacks of papers and folders on his desk. She began riffling through them, making too much noise to hear that she had company.

"What are you doing?" Slade's cold voice demanded.

Lisa froze for a panicked second, not believing that he could have come in without her hearing him. There was a hard look in his black eyes that made her toes curl.

Nervously she moistened her lips and tried to smile. "I brought some letters in for your signature." But that didn't explain why she was going through the other papers on his desk and his silence reminded her of that fact. "Your desk was such a mess, I thought I'd straighten it for you."

"Thank you." Polite words without a trace of sincerity. "But I prefer the mess," he said icily. "Strange as it may seem to you, I know where everything is."

"I'm sorry." Lisa back away from the big desk, self-consciously aware of her foot bumping against his briefcase. Had he come in just a few moments earlier, she would have had to explain a great deal more.

"You can neaten up the outer office," Slade replied crisply, "but not this one." Apparently he accepted her explanation. "Would you hand me my briefcase?"

"Of course." To give it to him, Lisa had to walk around the desk, her nerves leaping in awareness.

"It's nearly noon. Since you have the letters done, you might as well take your lunch break now." Briefcase in hand, Slade courteously stepped to the side to let Lisa precede him.

"Okay," she agreed.

Any hope of going through his office at noon vanished as he waited expectantly in her outer office. Haphazardly she tidied her desk, gathered her purse and jacket, and led the way out of the building. In the street, they parted company. Slade gave her a curt nod but said nothing more.

Lisa worked late that day but Slade worked later. It was after six when she dashed into Mitzi's house. Her aunt was nowhere in sight and Lisa was grateful she didn't have to explain where she'd been all day.

She had less than an hour to get ready before Slade arrived to take her and Mitzi to dinner. After undressing and bathing in record time, she reapplied her makeup and hurried to the closet.

Her choice of clothes was limited to the blue dress she had worn before and a satiny pantsuit in an unusual champagne shade, very nearly the color of her hair. A touch of vanity made her pick the pantsuit rather than something Slade had already seen. Last, she set the tinted sunglasses on the bridge of her nose, disguising the green of her eyes.

At ten past seven, she hurried from her room to find Slade waiting at the base of the stairs. "Sorry I'm late." There was a hint of breathlessness in her voice.

"That's all right." He looked at her but not too closely. "My car's outside."

She assumed Mitzi was outside as well and nodded, which made her sunglasses slip down her nose. She pushed them back up. That got his attention, unfortunately.

"Sunglasses again, huh?"

"I did too much sightseeing today." The story she had rehearsed for Mitzi sprang immediately to her lips.

"You seem to have a tendency to overdo things," Slade commented dryly.

He could say that again, Lisa thought. What had begun as reasonable concern for her aunt had turned into an amateur spying mission. It would be funny, except that so far she had managed to trap only herself and not him. But that was the story of her whole life. Lisa had never done anything halfway.

The light fragrance of the azaleas scented the dusk, their vibrant pinks and purples muted by the waning light. The bearded oaks cast dark shadows on the luxury car parked in the driveway parallel to the portico entrance.

"I'll sit in the back. Mitzi can have the front seat," Lisa said as Slade stepped ahead of her to open the car door. She intended to be a mouse in the corner that evening, observing and saying as little as possible.

"Too late," he announced, more or less propelling her into the empty front seat and closing the door.

Turning in the seat with a hand on its midnight-blue leather upholstery, Lisa said, "Mitzi, I—" She didn't finish her sentence. There was no one in the backseat.

"Where's Mitzi?" she demanded as Slade slid behind the wheel.

"She's not coming." The key was in the ignition and being turned.

"What?" Lisa stared at his boldly defined profile. "Why not?"

"She said something about her heroine being in danger. She can't take a break from writing until she figures out a way for the hero to rescue the girl." He shifted the car into gear, not sparing a glance in Lisa's direction.

"You put Mitzi up to this!" she accused in an angry hiss.

"I know you think I have unlimited power over her." The look he shot her glinted with mockery. "But I don't. Nothing short of the end of the world would've dragged Mitzi away from her computer tonight."

"Am I supposed to believe that?"

"Ask her when you get back. You don't have to take my word for it."

Lisa thought it over. "I think I will. Turn the car around."

"No."

"I'll jump out at the next corner."

He looked in his rearview mirror. "Better not. There's an SUV right behind me. Looks like it's filled with frat boys getting an early start on spring break. They might run you over."

His tone suggested that he wouldn't be heartbroken if it happened. She twisted in her seat and saw the SUV. He was probably right. But the vehicle and the rowdy group of guys inside soon turned off onto a side street.

She noticed him look in the rearview mirror to watch it go. Then she heard all the locks go down when he touched a button on the driver's side. Lisa fumbled along the armrest, looking for the button that would unlock her door. "Let me out."

"Look, Lisa, I'm trying to do Mitzi a favor. And taking her spoiled niece out to a nice dinner is a pretty big favor, in my opinion. I could think of more pleasant ways to spend the evening."

"Then go right ahead and call a girlfriend. Let me out."

Slade was silent. Lisa was still fumbling without success to find the button that would unlock the door. He would probably be able to override it, anyway. The car he was driving was that new and that expensive.

She sat back against the seat with a whump. "Come to think of it, I don't think you should wine and dine some babe with my aunt's money. Maybe I will go out with you, just to keep you from doing that."

"Would you stop?" he said wearily.

"I'm looking out for my aunt. Too bad if you don't like it."

"You're overdoing the dramatics, Lisa." His tone was dry with indulgence.

The street didn't widen until they turned on to Battery. Slade pulled over and parked, unlocking the doors. She darted into White Point Gardens, hoping to lose herself in the dark shadows under the trees, but the pale, shiny material of her pantsuit was like a beacon in the darkness. He was at her side within seconds.

"Hello," he said pleasantly. "Nice evening, isn't it?"

"Not with you around," she retorted.

He shrugged. "You can walk back home if you want to. It's back that way." He pointed. "But I wasn't lying. Mitzi really didn't want to go out tonight and she really is writing."

Lisa hesitated. Maybe she had overreacted. It might be a more intelligent course of action to get to know Slade a little. Use her womanly wiles on him. She realized that she was thinking like Mitzi.

But she would have to admit that her charming aunt did know a thing or two about how to wind a man around her little finger.

Except for Slade Blackwell. His nearness was affecting Lisa's ability to think clearly. There was a latent sensuality in his dark good looks that got to her.

She shivered a little, and crossed her arms over her chest.

"Cold?" he inquired. He gave her a lazy smile. Lisa realized a little too late that she had left her jacket in his car. She shook her head and began to walk down a garden path. Slade walked with her.

"I've had time to think over our conversation—or should I call it confrontation—the other night." There was a decidedly caressing tone to his low voice. His mouth was awfully close to her ear, she realized with a start.

"What about it?" Lisa had to swallow the breathless catch in her voice.

"I've decided that it's mutually counter-productive to declare war on each other."

She looked up at him. His mouth had softened into a smile that was a little too potent in its charm for Lisa to handle. She looked beyond him to a dark shape that she realized was a cannon, probably a Civil War relic permanently mounted in the garden, though she couldn't read the plaque on its base. Its barrel pointed across the bay waters to the distant fortress of Fort Sumter.

"What are you suggesting?" There. That was a better approach. Lisa sighed inwardly. She sounded much more in control of herself when she issued that question.

"That we compromise."

"What kind of compromise do you mean?" She darted a sharp look at him, barely able to see his features what with her tinted glasses and the gathering dusk.

"The kind that lets us join forces."

"No, Slade. That's impossible. We're never going to see eye to eye."

"Well, no. Not if you're always going to wear sunglasses, even when it's dark."

She walked a little faster, not wanting to field any questions about her eyewear. "I need them. Spare me the snotty comments, okay?"

Lisa heard his impatient sigh but ignored it. She strolled around the mounted cannon, like a good little tourist. At least it would be something to report to her aunt. She heard his measured footsteps following.

"Why is a compromise impossible?" he argued smoothly. "Why should we keep fighting each other? We'll both end up losing."

He still seemed to believe that she was intervening because she wanted Mitzi's money, which was totally weird. That was what he wanted and he obviously believed it was the only thing she was interested in. Lisa hesitated. Perhaps this was another way to get the proof against him that she needed.

Slade noticed her hesitation and came a little closer. "It makes sense, doesn't it?"

"Perhaps," Lisa conceded, at least temporarily until she could think his suggestion through.

"Are we going to walk around the cannon again?" he said. "We could go in circles like this all night."

She had to smile as she stepped back onto the path. "I'd rather not."

He reached out a hand to her when she stumbled a little over a cobblestone and let it rest on her back when she straightened quickly.

His fingers were warm against the lower curve of her spine. The smooth material of her champagne-colored pantsuit made his touch seem all the more sensuous against her skin.

She was much too aware of the man at her side, aware of him as a man. A tall, muscular, sexy man. But underneath that well-groomed, compellingly handsome exterior was a predatory lawyer who was up to no good, she reminded herself.

If she had needed any confirmation, she had received it a moment ago when he had suggested they work together to obtain Mitzi's money. She almost had to agree to go along with it so she could prove to Mitzi what Slade was really all about.

Her attention shifted to the body of water glistening ahead of her in the twilight. The White Point Garden was located almost on the tip of the peninsula of Old Charleston. Lisa's steps faltered, slowing almost to a stop as she stared at the water.

The surface was smooth and reflecting, giving no idea of the current flowing underneath. It reminded her of Slade. She had no idea what was going on in his mind.

"That's the Ashley River," Slade said quietly. "This is where the Ashley and the Cooper rivers flow together to form the Atlantic Ocean."

Lisa had read that whimsical claim of the Charlestonians in a guidebook. From here, it looked like it could be true. But she had to harden herself to Slade's easy charm.

"I'm not interested in a geography lesson," she said impatiently. She turned to face him, tipping her head back to see his features. "How do I know I can trust you?"

"How do I know I can trust you?"

"That's not an answer, Slade."

He shrugged. "The answer is we would have to trust each other."

"Honor among thieves, huh?" Lisa shook her

head. "You don't know the meaning of the word honor."

"Do you?"

"You have the most annoying habit of asking me the same questions I ask you. Why?"

"No real reason. Except perhaps to demonstrate that we think alike."

She paced along a path that wound closer to the water. He kept up with long strides, taking one for every two of hers.

"No, we don't, Slade. And don't expect me to forget that fight."

"Mitzi called it a squabble."

Lisa waved a dismissing hand. "Mitzi came in after the shouting was over."

"And the slapping," he reminded her. "I didn't tell your aunt about that."

"Why would you?" Lisa said.

"You were the one who started the hostilities, Lisa."

He was calmly and deliberately baiting her again and, fool that she was, she was rising to snap at it. She breathed in deeply. She would not let him make her lose her temper. She would not let him distract her with a kiss, either.

"Okay, Slade. You didn't tell on me. I guess I'm supposed to be grateful."

He looked as if he didn't care. "Listen to me, Lisa. With each of us trying to prove to Mitzi that the other is no good, we're going to end up making her doubt both of us."

"And a third party could end up with all the money." Lisa followed the thought to its logical conclusion.

"Unless we come to an agreement," he said.

"Tell me more." The least she could do was lead him around by the nose. Or down the garden path. She increased her pace and he followed but he didn't seem about to satisfy her curiosity concerning the agreement he was so hot to make. They didn't talk and it wasn't long before they were back where they started. She could see the car.

"We'll discuss it after dinner." Slade smiled and touched his hand to her back again to guide her to the car. "I booked a table for seven-thirty. We're late but I'm sure they'll hold it for us. In the meantime, let's call a truce."

"A truce?" Lisa laughed in disbelief. "Are you serious?"

"Of course." They went around a tall magnolia. "You need time to get used to the idea of trusting me."

"I doubt if I ever will," Lisa said and meant it.

"You've made progress," he commented.

"Why?"

"Because you said 'doubt,' and didn't issue a flat statement to the effect that you would never trust me." He seemed satisfied with that lawyerly pronouncement.

"A technicality," Lisa said.

"Remember?" He arched a dark brow in wry amusement. "My profession deals in technicalities."

"Well, I don't," she said sharply—more sharply than she had intended. "I deal with what's real."

Slade glanced at her as he reached to open the passenger door of the luxurious car. He didn't say anything, but she saw a faint smile touch the edge of his mouth.

CHAPTER SIX

Contented, Lisa decided—that was the only word to describe the way she felt. The restaurant was sumptuously elegant yet relaxing at the same time, two qualities that seldom went together.

The food had been excellent and her head was a bit fuzzy from the wine, but it was a pleasurable kind of fuzziness. She took another sip of the dry white wine in the stemmed glass. Soft music played in the background, gently romantic, setting the mood.

The table was small, intimately so, with Slade sitting directly across from her. Lisa studied him openly, the intensity of her green gaze masked by the tinted lenses of her glasses. His thick mane of hair had a raven sheen to it; his black-diamond eyes glittered with an inner fire.

His tanned features could have been chiseled in stone, yet they were so very male and so very compelling. But maybe she was using the wrong word— no stone could ever possess the vitality that Slade had.

That vitality and charm had been working its

magic on Lisa all evening. Slade's particular brand of charm was more potent than others she had known because it was so subtle. He didn't use an ounce of flattery, yet he made Lisa feel so good inside. It made him dangerous, but at the moment she was in the mood to flirt with danger.

It was crazy the way her mind was capable of dividing itself. One part of it was thinking about him, analyzing the things about him that set him apart from ordinary men. Another part of her mind was registering every word he said so she could make the appropriate responses when they were required.

The third part was noting other things about him. She liked the low pitch of his voice, smooth and rich like velvet. And she liked the way the corners of his mouth deepened when he thought something was amusing but didn't openly smile.

He said something dryly funny and Lisa laughed. "I was beginning to think you'd drifted away somewhere. You should laugh like that more often." A slow smile spread across his mouth, making an impact on her pulse.

"And you should smile like that more often," she replied, aware of the husky tremor in her voice but not caring.

"We're beginning to sound like a mutual admiration society," Slade pointed out, amused with the turn the conversation was taking.

"Mitzi would be astounded," Lisa declared with a laugh.

"I doubt it. Knowing Mitzi and her penchant for happy endings, she would find a romantically logical reason." Instantly something flashed across his face—a look of irritation or impatience, Lisa couldn't be sure which. "Mildred mentioned that

you'd barely returned to the house when I arrived.
You were out sightseeing with your friends, I take
it." The subject was deftly changed.

Lisa wondered why. Surely Slade didn't think
she was becoming romantically attracted to him.
Well, wasn't she, a small voice said. Wasn't she just
a little bit curious to find out what it would be like
if he made love to her? She was afraid any answer
that came to mind would be self-incriminating and
she tried to ignore the little voice.

"I was out with Peg and Susan for part of the
day," she lied. "I browsed through the shops in the
morning and the three of us went sightseeing in
the afternoon."

"Where did you go?"

She hesitated for only a fraction of a second before she thought of that guidebook again. "Brookgreen Gardens. The statuary there is breathtaking.
Unfortunately, we got caught in rush-hour traffic
on the way back—that's why I was so late."

"There are some very fine American sculptors
represented there," Slade agreed. "Which was your
favorite?"

Was he testing her? Lisa wondered, then decided he wasn't. "They were all so beautiful, it's impossible to pick one," she hedged.

"True. Brookgreen Gardens is very impressive,
especially with its avenue of live oaks."

"Yes, isn't it?" Lisa smiled.

"Shall we go?" Slade asked unexpectedly. "I believe the restaurant is closing."

"What?" Lisa glanced around, surprised to see
only two other tables occupied in the dining room.
"Yes, of course."

As she reached for her purse, Slade moved to
the back of her chair. She just adored his Southern

good manners, she had to admit it. "It was a delicious meal. Thank you," she offered, rising as he held the chair out.

"My pleasure." But there was something distant in his reply.

The car was parked nearly a block away. Slade insisted that Lisa wait outside the restaurant for him to bring it around. As his long, smooth strides carried him away, she shivered slightly, feeling she had been abandoned to the cool of the evening.

Reflections from the flaming torches mounted on the building front flickered over the brick walls and the arched windows. Lisa shifted nearer to their light just as Slade's gorgeous car drove up to the curb in front of the restaurant.

There was no indication of the chilling aloofness she thought she had detected in Slade moments earlier. She decided it must have been her imagination that made her think he had suddenly withdrawn. There was nothing cool about his attitude as he helped her into the passenger seat. In fact, his smile was quite disarming when he turned to her after sliding back behind the wheel.

"Would you like to go back to Mitzi's or do you want to take a driving tour of Old Charleston by night?" Slade asked.

It was late and she would have to get up early to go to the office. The wisest choice would be to go directly to Mitzi's but she heard herself opt for his second suggestion.

"The driving tour."

She was crazy, she thought, settling back in her seat and smiling at herself. She basically distrusted Slade yet she was strongly attracted to him. She should feel wary instead of so contented.

"Why the smile?" He slowed the car as he turned a corner onto a rough, cobblestoned street.

"Must be the afterglow of good wine," Lisa sighed, confused by the change in her emotions without really caring.

"I noticed it mellowed your temper."

"Yours too," she countered, and glanced out the window.

The street they were on ran along the waterfront. On the opposite side of the docks were brightly painted old houses abutting each other. "Cool. Look." She pointed them out to Slade. "Each one is painted a different color."

He gave her a curious look. "That's Rainbow Row. I thought you'd been touring Charleston these past few days. How did you miss Rainbow Row?"

"Oh . . ." Lisa breathed in nervously, running the tip of her tongue over her lips. "I haven't toured Old Charleston yet. Mostly we've been taking other tours, like out to Fort Sumter and the military academy."

"The Citadel?"

"Yes. I've been saving Old Charleston to see with Mitzi. She's used it and the Low Country of South Carolina as backdrops for her romances. I'm sure she would know all sorts of unique things about it. But tell me about Rainbow Row," she urged, wanting to get away from a detailed discussion of how she'd spent her time the past few days.

"The oldest house here dates from the 1740s. They're private residences, very much in demand. In the eighteenth century, this was the waterfront district. The different colors are meant to set each one apart."

Passing the row of colorful houses, he turned at the corner. Lisa had the sensation of slipping into the past. With the buildings and houses shadowed by the night and few cars on the narrow streets, the modern touches seemed to be hidden from view, steeping the night in history.

Making another turn, Slade directed her attention to the house on the left. "The Heyward-Washington house, one of the places entitled to claim that 'George Washington slept here.' Thomas Heyward Jr. was one of the signers of the Declaration of Independence."

Lisa had barely focused on the shadowy exterior when he pointed at something else. "Does that look familiar to you?"

"Vaguely," she admitted, wishing now they weren't taking the tour in semidarkness. In the daylight she might know why it seemed familiar. Instead she had to ask, "Where have I seen it?"

"*Porgy and Bess*, the operetta. Cabbage Row inspired the setting for it. There used to be vegetable stands along the sidewalk, hence the name."

They drove down more streets, past more historic points of interest. It was a tour Lisa would definitely have to make by day. There was too much to see, but she was glad the first time had been by night. It made the antique charm of the city come to life, its pearly glory more than just imagination.

She gazed silently out the window as Slade made another turn. She recognized the street, having walked it every day to his office. Her aunt's house was just off this street. Her gaze settled on a white mansion set well back, protected by lace grillwork and overhung by massive guardian oaks draped with Spanish moss.

"Of all the mansions in Old Charleston, I think that one is the loveliest," she told Slade.

"Which one?"

"The one there," she pointed. "We're just approaching it."

"Want to get closer?" A half smile touched his mouth as he gave her a questioning look.

"Sure," Lisa agreed, thinking he meant that he would drive closer to the curb so she could have a better look at the mansion by night. Instead he turned the car in through the grillwork gates. "What are you doing?"

"You said you wanted to get closer."

"Yes, but I didn't mean this close. Hey, I walk by it every day—"

"You walk by it?" His quiet voice immediately seized on her statement.

Lisa silently blamed her careless remark on too much wine. She had been lulled into a false sense of security. She had to remember that Slade was still her adversary.

"Yes," she added with what had to be her millionth lie. "On my way to meet Susan and Peg. They usually pick me up at the corner." Even though his lean features were slightly shadowed, she could still see the twist of skepticism about his mouth. "We can't stop here," she protested as he parked the car near the front entrance of the large white house.

"I know the owners very well," Slade insisted. "They won't mind if you have a look inside."

"There's no one home." The windows were dark but that didn't seem to bother Slade as he climbed out of the car and walked to Lisa's door.

"They're away but they left the key with me," he explained, helping a confused Lisa from the car.

"One of your clients, huh?"

"More or less. I handle their legal matters from time to time. I've known them for years." He guided her up the three steps to the door. Taking a key from his pocket, he inserted it into the lock and opened the door, switching on a light just inside it before stepping back to let Lisa walk in first. "The house is closed up until fall, so the furniture has all been covered. But you can get an idea of the layout."

The oak floor of the foyer was polished to a high sheen. Ornate plaster moldings rimmed the ceiling. Light gleamed from the delicate crystal sconces on walls lined with fine paintings.

Still feeling like a trespasser, Lisa tentatively moved closer to inspect them. Her eyes widened at the first, a portrait of a man with raven hair and dark eyes, dressed in the height of fashion, fifty years ago. Slade was just behind her and she pivoted to face him.

"The owners must be relatives of yours," she said wonderingly.

"My parents," he smiled.

"Why didn't you tell me instead of letting me think that—" Lisa didn't voice the rest of her question. She knew exactly how she would have ended it: something to the effect that the owners had to be more people whose money he was, quote unquote, managing. Obviously, that wasn't even remotely true and she didn't want to introduce that subject to their conversation. He was right, the wine had mellowed her somehow. She just didn't want to argue with him tonight.

"Were you thinking the worst?" he mocked.

"Never mind. It doesn't matter." Lisa turned away, forcing the irritation she didn't understand from her voice. "Would you show me around?"

Despite the white dropcloths covering the furniture, there was a warmth to the house. Their footsteps echoed hollowly on the wood floors as they toured the rooms of the lower story and followed the freestanding spiral staircase to the second. Yet the house didn't really seem empty.

"Don't your parents spend much time here?"

"Not any more. Not since my father bought the farm," Slade said. "They spend all but the late autumn and early winter months there."

"He moved to the farm with your mother shortly after you became a partner in the law firm, didn't he?"

"Yes." Slade paused, looking at her curiously. "How did you know?"

"Mitzi mentioned it to me, I guess." She shrugged, covering her slip with a lie. "Did you live here?"

"All my life." Slade started walking again, his hand at her back bringing her with him.

"Why don't you live here now?" She glanced up at him. "I mean," she laughed self-consciously, "it seems like a shame for this beautiful house to be empty for even a day."

"It's too big for one man."

"Yes, it's a family house," Lisa agreed, thinking of the numerous bedrooms meant for a brood of dark-haired, dark-eyed children. "Where do you live?"

"In the old carriage house," he told her. "We remodeled it for me when I was in college."

"Oh, a bachelor pad. How very cool. I suppose the next thing you'll do is invite me there." Lisa said it jokingly.

There was a gleam in his eye when he replied. "Sure. Come on up and see my world-renowned collection of naked-lady paintings and my titanium martini shaker and the hot tub in the living room and all those other things bachelors are supposed to have."

"Do you have them?"

"No," he laughed. "But it's a nice place."

"I'd like to see it," Lisa said. "Some other time, though. Mitzi will worry if I get in too late." She had a feeling she was becoming too friendly with Slade, the wrong kind of friendly. If she was going to be nice to him, it should be with the intention of getting information from him and not just to make small talk. He was making her lose sight of her goal.

"You have one advantage over me," Slade commented as they walked through the foyer to the front door. "You're on vacation and can sleep late in the morning. I have to be in the office first thing, which means getting up early."

"So do I." Lisa realized what she'd said and rushed to cover it. "Not to be in an office, of course, but meeting Peg and Susan first thing in the morning."

"Again? I thought you were here to visit Mitzi."

"I am, but she just seems so preoccupied with the book she's working on. It's silly for me to hang around the house every day waiting for her to finish." She sounded more defensive than she wanted to, but it couldn't be helped. "It is my vacation. Besides, I have the weekend to spend with Mitzi."

"Then you can act the dutiful and devoted niece, is that it?"

Her mouth opened to protest the tinge of sarcasm in his voice, but she caught herself in time. "I think I can play the role as effectively as you play Slade Blackwell, the loyal attorney."

The last light was switched off, throwing the mansion into darkness. Lisa waited at the steps while Slade locked the door. When he joined her, she started to descend the steps to the car, but his hand caught at her arm to stop her.

"I'm almost sorry the truce is over." He seemed to make the admission reluctantly.

Lisa agreed but she wouldn't admit it. "You started it."

"Sooner or later, one of us is going to have to grow up and stop saying infantile things like that."

"I assume you mean me," she said heatedly. "You did start it, though."

"Okay, I'll concede that point," he said. "I started it. Maybe we both need to grow up. If I count to three, could we begin simultaneously? So it would be perfectly fair, unlike real life?"

"Oh, shut up, Slade."

"We can't keep insulting each other if we're going to be partners."

"Who said we were going to be?" Lisa retorted. "I'm not convinced that I need you."

"Yes, you are. It just sticks in your craw to admit it." There was no mistaking the complacency in his tone. He was utterly sure of himself—and her.

"Maybe it's the other way around." She stubbornly resisted making the admission even though she knew she would eventually. Once Slade believed that she was on his side, he would confide exactly how he was siphoning off Mitzi's money. "Maybe you need me more than I need you and *you* don't want to admit it."

"But I already have—when I made the proposal that we should work together," he reminded her. "What do you say? Are we partners?"

"I'd like to think about it." Now why had she said that, Lisa wondered. Maybe she subconsciously wanted to make him sweat a little.

"What is there to think about? You know you've already made up your mind." He seemed to find her resistance funny.

"Maybe I have." Lisa threw him a haughty look and added a toss of her silver blond hair just for the effect. "Maybe I've decided the answer is no. Did you think of that?"

He drew back, and she could see his slight frown. "If your answer was an outright no, you wouldn't have come with me tonight. You would've told me to get lost at the gardens, But you didn't. That means the answer is yes."

Lisa glanced away. "You're awfully sure of yourself," she said with annoyance.

"No." His thumb and forefinger captured her chin and turned her back to face him. "I'm sure of you and the way your mind works."

His comment riled her but it was the shiver of feeling evoked by his touch that got her attention. It rippled down her spine in tiny, highly pleasurable waves.

Damn the wine, she thought. It had been a while since she'd polished off her last glass but it was still making her light-headed. The ground seemed unsteady beneath her feet. Slade stood tall before her and she wanted to sway against his solidness and regain her equilibrium. It was the craziest sensation because she knew she was imagining all of it.

His gaze focused on her face, his dark brows drawing together. His eyes seemed to touch every one of her features until he stopped at her lips, softened with tender vulnerability. Slade bent his head toward her, then stopped as if waiting for a protest from Lisa.

She felt a fevered awareness that he was going to kiss her again, even though she had vowed not to let that happen. Yet she had to face a shocking fact: she wanted him to. This ambivalence toward him was insane, but she made not the slightest move to stop him or say no. His dark head moved down, closing the distance until there was none.

The brush of his sensual mouth against hers drew a gasp, as her nerves tingled with sweet shock. Lightly he explored the lips he had tasted once before, then deepened the kiss with a lover's passionate skill, as if there were no greater thrill on earth than kissing her again.

She opened her eyes only when he raised his head. The kiss had been that good.

"This is crazy," she murmured, voicing the bewilderment she felt.

"Yes," Slade agreed, not needing to ask what she meant.

"I don't even like you," she added.

"I know."

His hand left her chin and ran through the silken strands of her hair, tilting her head up to his again. Her lips parted instinctively on contact, a storm of sensations racing through her body at his possession. There was no holding back in this kiss, and she felt the shuddering response she made to his demand.

Abruptly Slade drew away, frowning as he looked down at her. There was a hardness to the line of his jaw, a checked anger in his expression. Shaken by her reaction, Lisa turned away, trying to control her runaway senses.

"We'd better leave," he said tightly.

"Yes." Lisa had to agree. She had to stay away from him.

He was still frowning when he helped her into the car and walked around to the driver's side. He reversed the car out of the driveway without saying a word and got out one more time to shut the gates. It was only a few minutes' drive to Mitzi's house, but the heavy silence made it seem much longer.

When he stopped the car near the portico, Lisa didn't wait for him to play the perfect gentleman. She darted out, saying a soft good night that was lost in the slam of the car door.

Slade didn't follow. Before she went into the house, she glanced back at the car. He was watching to make sure she got in safely, a thoughtful frown still darkening his face.

As Lisa opened the door and entered, her aunt walked out of the study. Lisa struggled to appear composed, running a hand quickly through her hair and taking off her sunglasses. Mitzi glanced at the watch on her wrist, her expression registering astonishment.

"Is it that late already?" she said.

Lisa immediately seized on the remark to keep the questions at bay. "Have you been working all this time, Mitzi?"

"I guess I have," she said with a little laugh. "I got so wrapped up with that manuscript that I lost track of the hour. I hope you didn't think I was waiting up for you."

"You know, for a minute it did seem like I was living at home again, with Mom mysteriously appearing when I came in the front door after a date." Lisa smiled nervously, remembering how astute her mother was at reading her mind. She hoped Mitzi didn't possess the same ability.

"How was your evening? Did Slade take you someplace nice for dinner?"

"It was very nice." Lisa named the restaurant and Mitzi nodded her approval.

"I do apologize for backing out like that at the last minute."

Her tone was sincere, and Lisa was convinced that her aunt's reason was quite genuine and not a sneaky attempt to get her and Slade together.

"Slade explained why you couldn't come. I hope you managed to rescue your heroine."

"Oh, I did. I mean, I figured out a way for the gallant hero to do it. He was off in another part of the plot and it took me the longest time to cut him loose."

Lisa smiled. Her aunt tended to talk about her characters as if they were real people she couldn't always control. She supposed it was what made Mitzi's books so popular, even if she hadn't hit the big bestseller lists yet.

They yawned at exactly the same time, and then laughed. "We're both exhausted," Mitzi said. "Come on, let's go up to bed. No—wait a minute. I want a cup of real cocoa. With a big ol' marshmallow melting on top."

"None for me, thanks," Lisa said quickly.

Mitzi nodded. "Mildred is going to kill me for messing up her clean kitchen. I'll have to scrub out the pot and cup."

"Use the instant cocoa and the microwave."

"It's just not the same, honey. Now get to bed."

Lisa heard the clank of cookware as she went up the stairs, glad to have dodged any questions about Slade.

Once behind the closed door of her room, Lisa changed into her nightclothes and crawled into bed. She didn't switch off the light right away as she stared up at the swirling cream satin of the canopy. Everything seemed suddenly very complicated. It was because of that kiss and the way she had responded to it. But more and more, it was because of Slade. She turned off the light and tried to sleep.

* * *

The next day it was difficult to face him as Ann Eldridge. Lisa tried to be coolly professional around him and failed miserably. It was a good thing that Slade was too busy to notice or he would have seen how nervous his temporary secretary was in his presence.

He was bent over her desk signing some correspondence she had typed that he wanted to go out that day. Lisa found herself studying the way the overhead light gave a blue-black sheen to his hair.

Her gaze slid to his profile, to the hard male line of his mouth. Only it hadn't been hard and unyielding when it covered hers. There was a persuasive mastery to his kiss that had melted her.

What was more important, she had let herself respond fully. She only wished she hadn't liked it. But she'd loved it. It was so much easier to hate him than to be caught by conflicting emotions.

She glanced into the dark black of his eyes and he returned her look with a puzzled one of his own. Immediately, Lisa looked down, trying to cover the sudden confusion that brought a warmth to her cheeks.

"Something wrong, Ann?" he asked.

"No, nothing."

"Was there something you wanted to ask me?"

"No."

He shrugged and handed her the letters. Slade had been in a brooding mood all day and his sudden interest in her made Lisa apprehensive.

Perhaps he was perceiving Ann Eldridge as a person instead of just glancing in the general direction of a here-today-gone-tomorrow temp he didn't have to remember. The thought was unnerving.

Lisa looked down at her desk, reminding herself that men didn't notice wigs in the same way

that women did, of course—just look at the rugs
some of them sported. But maybe he had figured
out that her red hair was fake.

"If it's about your wages—"

"The agency pays me directly and will bill you
later," she said, looking at him over the top of the
letters she held in such a way as to cover her
mouth. "Was there anything else you wanted me to
do?"

"Yes. Call Miriam Talmadge for me."

Lisa went pale.

"Find out what time she expects her niece home
this afternoon."

"Her niece?" Lisa repeated weakly, her face becoming even whiter.

"Yes, that's what I said."

"If—if Mrs. Talmadge asks why you want to
know, what should I tell her?" Her heart was
pounding.

"Tell her it's none of her business," he said
cheerfully.

"I can't say that."

"Hey, I was kidding. Just tell her that I'll be over
this evening to see Lisa—and her," he added as a
definite afterthought.

"All right," Lisa breathed, glad to have advance
notice of his visit for once.

Pushing back the sleeve of his jacket, Slade
glanced at his gold watch. "If you happen to reach
Lisa, put the call through to me. I'll be in Drew's
office. But make sure to tell me what Mrs. Talmadge
says if you don't."

"Right."

Slade was already walking away. After he had left
her office, she toyed with the idea of speaking to
him as Lisa Talmadge, pretending to be at her
aunt's home. But there was that little problem of

caller ID—he would see at once that the call was coming from her extension.

Lisa was losing her mind. She was sure of it.

Disguising her voice, she called Mitzi as he'd asked, and got Mildred instead. She told the house-keeper to expect Slade that evening, and then buzzed Drew's office phone to tell Slade that Lisa was expected home around six.

The knowledge that she would be seeing Slade that evening didn't make the day go faster. Instead it worked in reverse, every minute dragging as she tried to guess his reason. Not knowing what to anticipate made her skittish.

She picked at her dinner when she got home, much to Mildred's annoyance. Every sound that came from outside the house made her pulse sky-rocket, thinking it was Slade arriving.

"I don't know why Mildred didn't think to invite Slade to dinner." Mitzi sighed as she poured out the coffee later and handed a cup to Lisa. "There was certainly enough food to go around, especially since you ate so little."

"I wasn't very hungry."

The cup was clattering in its saucer and Lisa realized that her hands were shaking. She quickly set the coffee on the table in front of the couch, clasping her hands together in her lap.

"I had a big lunch." The truth was she hadn't eaten anything. As a result, she felt weak, but the thought of nibbling even one of the small cakes on the coffee table was not appealing.

"You haven't told me how you and Slade got along last night. We were both so tired when you finally came in, but now I want to hear all about it." Mitzi settled back in her chair, her own coffee cup held steadily in her hands, a bright gleam in her brown eyes.

"Okay, I guess." Lisa tried to shrug away the question but her aunt couldn't be so easily put off.

Mitzi tsk-tsked. "Now what kind of an answer is that? Something interesting must have happened."

"Not really," Lisa said. "We went out to eat—I told you about that. We talked, drove around for a while, and he brought me home."

"Sounds like an awfully quiet little evening."

"It was." Lisa rubbed her temples with her fingertips. She was getting a headache, as if she wasn't miserable enough at the moment.

"Guess that quarrel you two had wasn't all that serious," her aunt said with a knowing grin.

"Mmm." Lisa couldn't think of anything to say that Mitzi wouldn't jump on. A monosyllable would have to do.

"You two looked so cross when I walked in that night."

"Did we?" Lisa slumped down into the sofa. The doorbell rang. She didn't budge. She even closed her eyes.

"Aren't you just a ball of fire," her aunt said, laughing. "I'll get it. Must be Slade." She rose and went to the door.

Lisa got up from the couch and walked to a window, lifting aside the curtain to look outside. Without turning, she knew the instant Slade entered the room. She felt the force of his gaze and tensed.

"Hello, Lisa." The greeting seemed to be forced from him, his tone clipped and taut.

"Hello, Slade." An artificial smile curved her mouth as she glanced over her shoulder. Lisa felt all the more confused about why he had come and wished she knew why her heart was beating so wildly.

"We were just having coffee. You'll join us, won't

you, Slade?" Mitzi said, already reaching for the third cup sitting on the coffee tray.

"Yes." The answer was given automatically, without much interest.

"Something the matter?" Mitzi asked.

His dark gaze flicked to Lisa. "It was a rough day at the office. I guess I brought some of it with me."

That wasn't true. It actually had been fairly quiet. Lisa wondered why he'd said that. She stared at him, sensing his restlessness. Although he wasn't moving, she had the sensation of him prowling the room.

"Here you go, Slade." Mitzi handed him a cup of coffee. "Lisa, yours is getting cold." She looked from one to the other of them with lively interest.

"How was your day, Mitzi?" Slade asked. "Got that plot figured out?"

"Goodness, yes," she said. "It's coming along nicely."

"You know, I never did get a chance to read that review."

"You mean that clipping I sent Lisa for? I put it somewhere safe. On my desk, I think. Or maybe the floor underneath it. No, no, I'll go look," she concluded when Lisa started getting up. "You two stay right here and chat."

When Mitzi set down her coffee and bounced out of the room, Lisa and Slade exchanged a wary look.

CHAPTER SEVEN

Lisa didn't exactly feel like chatting, unfortunately. She watched Slade set down his coffee, knowing that he'd accepted a cup just to be polite to Mitzi.

"You know," he began, "it occurred to me that I was taking your agreement to our arrangement for granted. You really didn't give me a direct answer last night." He sounded calm and controlled, yet there was an undeniable electricity in the air.

"Oh. I thought I had." Lisa shrugged, not quite meeting his gaze.

"Come on, Lisa. Don't play games."

He clearly wasn't going to be put off. "Of course I agree," she said in an offhand voice. "Like you said, it's counterproductive for us not to work together."

He shot her a doubtful look. Maybe her attempt to sound casual didn't convince him.

"Is that direct enough for you, Slade, or do you want me to sign a binding document with a lot of 'whereases' and 'hereinafters'?"

"Skip the sarcasm," he said in the same calm tone.

"You seem to bring it out in me."

"You managed to be civil last night," Slade reminded her.

"I had too much wine last night."

"Was it the wine?" he asked softly. "I've been wondering that all day myself."

His admission caught her by surprise. *She* had been on his mind all day long? *She* was the reason for his moody preoccupation at the office? Interesting, she thought. So he had been going over what had happened last night just as she had. It must have been an unsettling experience for him as well.

Suddenly, in one long stride, Slade was at her side, his hands spanning her waist. His touch sparked a sensual flame that raced through her. And it was a very dangerous flame, considering that they weren't alone in the house.

"I haven't had any wine today. Have you?" he asked. The undercurrent of sexual tension in his voice belied the rhetorical question.

She shook her head. He slowly pulled her toward him. Her face was tipped upward, her lips parting before he even touched them. The heady urgency he was arousing was more deeply intoxicating than any wine. Almost of their own accord, her hands slipped inside his jacket, sliding around the solidness of his waist.

Instantly his arms circled her, shaping her full curves to the hard muscularity of his body. The caress of his hands on her hips sent the flame he'd sparked leaping high, consuming her with the scorching heat of desire.

Every other man who had ever held her was erased from her memory in that one instant. None had ever come close to Slade's strength and mastery—the very things she resented about him. But she knew in her soul that she had to have both. She couldn't help a shiver of physical regret when he dragged his mouth from hers.

"Mmm. You've got the magic—very sexy magic, Lisa. You put a spell on me."

"I wish," she said softly. If she could do that, Lisa wasn't sure whether she would want to make him disappear or keep him by her side forever. It was hard to resist kisses this good. He could easily seduce her right now—if not right here—and she wouldn't be able to stop.

He kissed her again and took his sweet time about it. *Damn him,* Lisa thought, when he finally stopped to take a breath. Slade was the one who possessed the magic, trapping her inside the charmed circle of his arms with such sensual skill that she didn't even want to struggle free.

"Take off those damned glasses," Slade growled.

It was the slap back to reality that Lisa needed. She twisted out of his arms at last, turning her back on him and taking a trembling step away. Her heart was knocking against her ribs, her breath coming in shaky gasps. She clasped her arms around herself, bereft of his embrace and overcome by her emotions.

"I don't want to become involved with you, Slade, emotionally or physically," she declared but much too weakly. "I want this to be a purely business arrangement." Eventually she would have to expose him and she wanted to be able to do it without pain or regret.

"Do you think I don't?" His low voice had a husky tremor.

"I don't know," she sighed.

His hands touched the sides of her waist, then

slid up higher to cup her breasts. Lisa shook with need, trying to move away from the hard pressure of his thighs and lower body.

"I didn't intend for this to happen. In fact, it's the last thing I want."

Even as he made the desperate statement, he was burying his mouth in the silky hair at the curve of her neck.

"Me too." But delicious shivers were racing down her spine from his rough caress.

Her hands were clutching his muscled forearms, as if she could control what he touched and when. She didn't really want to. She simply held onto him, inviting his intimate caress by not denying it. A wave of longing swept through her—powerful, inescapable, and dangerous.

"It's happened, so what are we going to do about it?" Slade breathed raggedly against the sensitive skin of her neck.

"Stop it."

"Can you?" he laughed cynically.

"I don't know." Lisa closed her eyes against the temptation of looking into his.

Tightening his hold, he molded her more fully to his male length. "I want you, Lisa." His hand slid over her hip once more.

"I know." How could she ignore the pressing force of his desire, any more than she could ignore her own?

Suddenly Slade let her go, leaving her to sway unsteadily without the support of his body. Long, impatient strides carried him away from her until nearly the width of the room separated them. Lisa stared hungrily after him, not able to deny her desire even when he was no longer holding her in his arms.

"What do you expect from me, Lisa?" he demanded, gritting his teeth in an effort to regain some self-control. "Besides a guaranteed share of your aunt's money, that is."

"Nothing." Hot tears scorched her eyes, still hidden by the tinted glasses. "You know something, Slade? I wish I'd never met you," she added in a choked whisper.

He seemed about to answer but turned instead to stride swiftly to the door before Lisa could comprehend his intention.

"Where are you going?" she breathed in confusion.

"I'm leaving. Say something to Mitzi, okay? Whatever excuse you come up with will have to do. I'm sure it won't make me look good!" He slammed the door as he left. The bang echoed in the room, followed by another, somewhat muffled one as he slammed the front door behind him too.

Lisa flinched at each sound. She hadn't had the slightest clue that she could make him that angry. Slade was the kind of man who prided himself on his control of every situation, but he'd really lost it this time.

So had she. In a very different way. But there was no time to dwell on the humiliating aspects of her passionate response to him. Mitzi entered the room.

"Goodness! Slade was really in a temper when he left," she declared. "I can't leave the two of you alone for five minutes. What happened?"

"We—argued," Lisa answered tightly, trying to sound natural.

"About what?" Mitzi inquired.

"Does it matter?"

"I suppose not," Mitzi sighed in reluctant agreement. "Mercy me, I bet you don't see this much drama at the television station, Lisa."

Lisa shook her head without replying right away, her arms folded across her chest. Her job—her life—in Baltimore seemed long ago and far away. She felt like a totally different person somehow and yet she had only been in Charleston for a few short days. Slade's doing, she thought unhappily.

"We produce a news show, Mitzi. Not a drama."

"Of course," her aunt said absentmindedly. "I know that, dear. But I wish you and Slade could get along. You're two of my favorite people, you know."

Lisa nodded.

"But you can't seem to," Mitzi continued. "What a pity. After last night, I'd hoped that—"

"Last night was a mistake." In more ways than one, Lisa could have told her. A fiery tear slipped from her lashes and she wiped it away with the back of her hand.

"Lisa, you're crying!" Mitzi was plainly astonished by the discovery.

"I always cry when I'm angry." Or hurt or confused or frightened, she thought.

"I'm going to have a talk with Slade," Mitzi said firmly.

"Don't bother. He'd only laugh."

"But honey—"

"You don't know Slade!" Lisa interrupted, releasing the pent-up frustrations of her emotions. "You don't know what he's really like! Arrogant—demanding—sexy—" Oh, God, Lisa thought wildly. Had she really said that last word? She turned red with shame.

"Well, no"—Mitzi tried to hide the laughter in her voice—"I don't think I do know that side of him very well."

Lisa hadn't felt so mortified in years, not since being a teenager and reeling from one crush to another. She mumbled some unintelligible excuse and rushed from the room.

Once inside, she locked the door, but no one came to invade her privacy. She wept all alone for several miserable minutes, wondering what the hell had happened to her usually unshakable confidence, her great sense of humor, her ability to roll with the punches, and a few other fabulous qualities she'd been born with. Slade seemed to be able to make her forget all about everything but him when she was in his arms.

She gave one last prodigiously emotional sniff and wiped away her tears, telling herself sternly to stop it. She had to think this through.

Lisa flung herself on the perfectly made bed and pulled out a pillow, punching a comfortable hollow for her weary head to lie in. She could not shake the troubling feeling that she had found something precious—and couldn't keep it.

But she didn't want to admit, not even to herself, what that something precious was. With her head pounding and her body aching, she finally fell into an exhausted sleep some time after midnight.

The next morning, Lisa awoke with a start, She was late for work. Then her head sank back onto the pillow. It was Saturday and Slade's office was closed. Relief trembled through her. She wasn't up to turning herself into Ann Eldridge, the temp he never noticed.

She rolled out of bed anyway. A glance in the mirror made her wince. Her green eyes were bloodshot from her crying jag and there were dark smudges under them. She would need those sunglasses to hide it all.

She pulled on jeans and a white tank top, applying a pale pink lipstick that wasn't pale enough. Her own pallor made it look way too gaudy. She rubbed it off with a tissue and ran a comb indifferently through her silver blond hair.

Once downstairs, she managed a smile at Mildred, but the housekeeper only sighed. "Mitzi is in the study working. Today is the day I polish the furniture, so if you'll be wantin' breakfast, you'll have to wait a while."

"Juice and coffee is fine. And I can fix my own." Lisa had no appetite.

"Okay." Mildred moved toward the living room in no great hurry, a bottle of citrus-smelling oil in one hand and a clean rag in the other.

In the end, Lisa had only a paper cup of orange juice, not wanting to leave a mess for the housekeeper, before she wandered out the back door into the garden. She meandered under the large oaks, brushing away an occasional long strand of hanging moss from her hair.

The moss seemed more dismal than romantic to her today, but it went with her dismal mood.

Last night she had even considered packing her bags and leaving—anything to escape Slade Blackwell. But that would mean that Mitzi would still think of him as her gallant protector, rescuing her from malfunctioning stoves and muttering housekeepers while she scribbled happily in her study. And he helped himself to her money, Lisa thought grimly.

It occurred to her that she ought to go to the police with her suspicions but she dismissed the thought. Working in local news had brought her into the gritty offices of the Baltimore Police Department more than once, and she knew that a lot of cops tended to treat women with something less than respect. Lisa still had not obtained hard evidence of any kind.

But if she stayed . . . she would be at his mercy, so to speak. His sensual, skillful caresses made her just plain stupid, she thought ruefully. And it wasn't like she was inexperienced. She should be capable of warding off unwanted attention from a man. The problem was that she wanted him to do . . . whatever he wanted. All Slade had to do was touch her and she melted like a scoop of ice cream in July.

Never, not once, had she imagined that she might fall in love with a man she didn't trust. Well, maybe she hadn't fallen in love with him yet, she thought. Could be just lust.

But if she did fall in love with him, would she be as conscientious about protecting Mitzi? Lisa still didn't understand how an intelligent, mature woman could be such an airhead when it came to money.

Of course, they hadn't discussed the subject in depth. Was there something Lisa didn't know?

She walked and thought, and thought and walked. Maybe her aunt wasn't quite as flighty as she seemed to be. And maybe her aunt was perfectly happy with the situation. It was possible that Mitzi and Slade had an arrangement of their own, and that now and then Slade took a little here and a little there as a tax-free reward for his services.

Okay, stop it, she told herself. She had obviously seen too many white-collar crooks get caught. The local news liked to feature them but those guys never seemed to hang their heads like other criminals and always claimed it was an unfortunate misunderstanding.

Slade would not have offered to share the take with Lisa if he and Mitzi had an arrangement like that.

Nothing seemed as simple as it had when she'd arrived. An oak twig brushed her cheek and she snapped it off in irritation, twirling the tiny, green-leafed stick between her fingers.

She had no idea what to do next.

Sighing, Lisa looked up into the massive branches of the tree above her. She could just see a crude but sturdy platform built into the vee of two thick limbs. There had to be a way up. The trunk was too straight to climb. She circled it and found slats of wood nailed securely to the other side, meant to be used as a ladder.

A tree house was exactly what she needed. She could sit there for a while and escape the wicked world, far above all her problems.

The slats offered easy hand- and footholds, and up she went. She scrambled onto the platform, happy to have made it. Settling into a comfortable, cross-legged position, Lisa felt a whole lot better. There was something uplifting about getting back to nature, even if it was only in her aunt's yard.

She heard the crunch of footsteps in the grav-eled driveway and looked down. She tensed, a sixth sense warning her that Slade had returned. The minute he came into her sight, he stopped, glancing upward to the tree house where she sat. His hard features were expressionless as he gazed directly at her.

"Go away," was all she said.

"I want to talk to you, Lisa," he said evenly.

"Well, I don't want to talk to you."

"Don't be childish."

She fought the temptation to stick out her tongue and throw acorns at him.

"Lisa," he said almost sternly. "Come down from that tree."

She ignored his order. "How did you know I was here?"

"Mildred told me that she saw you wander outside. I've found Mitzi so many times in that tree that I guess I automatically looked there first."

"Mitzi? Up here?" Lisa repeated, finding it difficult to imagine her fifty-two-year-old aunt climbing trees.

"Yes," Slade said dryly, "your aunt is remarkable in more ways than one. If you don't come down, I'll come up. You'll find that platform is a little cramped with two people on it."

He would climb up, Lisa knew it, and she glared at him angrily. He took a step toward the trunk and the crude ladder.

"I'll be right down," she muttered, and scooted along the platform to reach the slats, being careful not to get splinters in her hands.

A few feet from the ground, Slade took hold of her waist, ignoring her gasp of protest, and lifted her the rest of the way down. Lisa twisted free of his hold the instant her feet touched the ground. Her pulse was still racing even after Slade had let her go.

"What do you want?" she said coldly. But inside she was feverishly aware of him.

Slade stared at her for a long moment. "Mitzi told me you'd been crying."

His hands reached for her sunglasses and Lisa knocked it away, instinctively defending her identity. "She had no right to tell you that!" But she couldn't deny it. Not even the tinted sunglasses could conceal all the traces of her pity party for one.

"Mitzi hasn't had many chances in her life to

play mother hen. You can't blame her for springing to the defense of the little chick living in her house." He looked at her thoughtfully. "Hmm, I can understand why she gave me a lecture. You do look like you need protection."

"You're wrong," Lisa said. "You and Mitzi both are wrong. I can take care of myself."

"Can you?" Slade's tone was skeptical. "How much of your aunt's money will you need?"

"Shut *up.*"

He gave her a wry smile. "That's a mature thing to say. You look like a hurt little girl right now, do you know that?"

"Will you get out of here?" she demanded hoarsely. "I don't want pity. Especially not yours."

"I'm not offering any."

Lisa turned away in agitation. "What are you doing here? Who invited you anyway?"

"I invited myself. I wanted to see you."

"Why?" she said bitterly. "Were you afraid after last night that I'd renege on our deal?"

"You know, that didn't occur to me," Slade said grimly. "Maybe it should have."

"Yes. Maybe so."

His hands fastened onto her upper arms, pulling her around to face him. Lisa turned her face away, unable to meet his compelling gaze.

"Let me go," she snapped. "I'm not going to go back on our agreement."

He drew her closer. Lisa raised her hands to wedge herself away from his chest, but one hand accidentally came in contact with bare skin where his unbuttoned shirt opened at the neck. His body warmth melted her resistance and the dark hair on his chest tickled her sensitive fingertips.

"Last night—" Slade began.

"I'm trying to forget about last night," Lisa interrupted. "Nothing happened. You didn't kiss me."

"Right." He took a deep breath. "Whatever you say. Am I allowed to apologize?"

She shook her head. "No. Like I said, we should just forget about it."

Slade didn't let her go. "I can't. It isn't possible." His warm breath was fanning the top of her hair.

Lisa nestled instinctively against his neck, feeling the pulse beating wildly there, in tempo with her own racing heart. She shouldn't stay in his arms, she knew that. Why was it that she seemed to say one thing and do another when he was around?

"I don't want to become involved with you." Her protest was almost issued in a moan of surrender. "It would complicate everything."

"Do you think I don't know that?" Slade said softly.

"Then leave me alone."

He offered the opposite. "Spend the day with me, Lisa. Mitzi's going to be working and she's already told me you aren't seeing your friends today."

"No." She shook her head. "I can't. I won't."

"We won't talk about Mitzi or her money," Slade vowed. "It'll be just you and me. Together."

The temptation to just say yes was nearly irresistible. To have one day with Slade, simply being happy, might . . . make her change her mind about a lot of things.

"No." Her refusal was vehement.

"You make me crazy, you know that?" He held her a little away from him. "I mean, here you are in my arms, practically undoing my buttons, and you're saying no. I don't get it."

She stiffened. "You don't have to get it. Just accept it. And your buttons were already undone."

Slade gave her an exasperated look. "Hey, I plead guilty to wanting to breathe. It's Saturday. I don't have to wear a suit and a tie. All I wanted was to spend some time with you. Talk to you."

Lisa walked a few steps away and turned around again to face him. "What did you want to say?"

"Only one thing but it's a big thing." He put his hands on his hips and faced her just as squarely. "I'm falling in love with you and I don't know what the hell to do about it."

She breathed in sharply. "You can't mean it."

His mouth twisted. "Do you think it was easy for me to admit or accept?"

"I don't know." She wavered. "You can't love me."

"That's what I've been telling myself ever since I left the house last night," Slade admitted with a rueful smile. "But I know the worst about you, Lisa. Today I'd like to find out the best."

His assumption made her wince. She had played her part a little too well, if only for a little while, and convinced him that she was up to no good, just like him. They made a great couple, no doubt about it.

Yet she knew that he really *was* dishonest and had undoubtedly helped himself to money that didn't belong to him. Why didn't that change the way she felt about him?

"Mmm . . ." she wavered. She couldn't bring herself to accept his invitation. "It wouldn't change anything."

"We won't know unless we try." He lifted an expressive brow. "And if we argue, well, so what? I might get bored if we didn't."

Lisa held her breath for an instant, then released it in a long sigh. "No, I can't go."

"Why?" Slade demanded.

"It's—it's too risky."

"Why?" he said again. "Because you might find out that you're in love with me? Is there a chance of that?"

Moistening her lips nervously, Lisa finally admitted, "Yes."

The smoldering light that leaped into his dark eyes took her breath away. "If there's a chance of that," he said tightly, "we can find out right here and now."

Her lips parted to protest but his mouth opened over hers to silence her voice, devouring her lips with masculine hunger. Lisa surrendered instantly to the sensation of his kiss. Her hands slid around his neck inside his shirt collar, feeling the flexing of his muscles as he crushed her against him.

The erotic excitement she felt drove out all doubt about the wisdom of loving him. There was only the here and now, just as he'd said. The sensual pressure of his lips as they explored hers had her quivering in eager response, needing to know him as intimately as he was discovering her.

His weight pressed her backward until the rough bark of the oak tree they still stood under was rasping her back, exposed by the sleeveless tank top. His muscular leg slid between hers as Slade pinned her arching body against the trunk.

His hands slipped under the hem of her top, finding the heat of her bare skin and evoking a pleasure that aroused her even more.

Her breast seemed to swell in delight when his hand curved over the lacy cup of her bra. Lisa yearned to feel the nakedness of his hard flesh beneath her fingers. Lacking his expertise, her fingers fumbled with the remaining buttons of his shirt. In her awkward attempt, she scraped her elbow against the rough bark and gasped at the sharp pain shooting up her arms.

Slade immediately straightened, pulling her away from the tree. "This is a hell of a place to make love to you," he laughed raggedly near her ear, nuzzling its lobe before dragging his mouth away.

Weakly Lisa rested her head against his chest, still not quite back on earth. Without knowing it, she whispered his name.

"Love?" Slade roughly demanded an answer.

"Yes." She closed her eyes at that startling truth.

"And you'll spend the day with me?"

Lisa trembled. "Yes."

His arms tightened around her. "Do you have any idea how much I want you?"

"I think so." She rested against his chest, her fingers spreading across it in a sneaky caress. She knew how much she wanted him.

"So soon . . . are you sure?" Slade's whispered question was filled with agitation. Lisa could hear the frown in his voice. "Maybe there never is a perfect time and a perfect place."

"I doubt it."

He captured her chin and lifted her head so he could study her face, his eyes shadowed by seriousness. "Lisa, I want to spend the afternoon getting to know you and I don't mean physically. We'll have time for that. I want to know about your family and friends, what you like and don't like. Everything that makes you . . . you."

"Yes." She seemed to be agreeing with everything he said but that wouldn't last forever. Maybe that was why she was clinging so tenaciously to those few moments they would share.

He gave her a hard, swift kiss. "Wow. It's not going to be easy to keep my hands off you when you look so delectable, but I'll try," he promised. "As long as you don't get me too excited." Clasping her wrists, he held her away from him. "Run into the house and let Mildred know you're coming with me. I'll have you back in time for dinner tonight."

"Should I change?" Lisa glanced down at her rumpled tank top and snug jeans.

"You're fine as you are," he assured her.

"All right," she nodded. "Just give me five minutes to comb my hair and put on some lipstick."

"No." His grip tightened when she would have pulled free of his light hold to go to the house. Lisa looked up into his intent gaze. "I want you looking just the way you are—as if you'd just been kissed hard. By me."

"Slade, what will people think?" She was faintly embarrassed yet thrilled by the possessive ring in his voice.

"They'll think we're in love," he informed her with more than a trace of arrogant satisfaction. "And maybe even that I've made mad, passionate love to you. I haven't, but I will."

"Oh, really?" Lisa had to challenge him. She had given in to everything else too easily.

"Yes, really." For an instant, he drew her against his chest as if to establish his mastery over her. "And if you don't hurry into the house with that message, I'll change the order in which I want to get to know you better." He finally let her go.

"Hey, Slade," she said softly, standing motionless, loving him and not trusting him simultaneously. "The first thing you should learn about me is that I don't like being told what to do."

"Okay." Amusement deepened the corners of his mouth. "I won't tell you what to do anymore. I'll show you."

Taking her by the shoulders, he turned her

around to face the house. With a slight shove and a playful slap on her rump, he sent her on her way.

Entering the house through the back door, Lisa went in search of Mitzi. In the foyer, she heard the clicking of a computer keyboard coming from the study. Hesitating, Lisa decided not to disturb her aunt and began looking for the housekeeper.

After going through all the rooms but the study on the ground floor, Lisa continued her search upstairs. She found Mildred in her bedroom, polishing the chest of drawers.

"Here you are." Lisa was slightly out of breath. "I was looking for you."

"I always polish the furniture upstairs first," Mildred informed her. "I don't know why I bother. Nobody hardly ever comes up here. I'm just wasting my time." She pulled out a drawer and ran a cloth around the edges and sides. "But it has to be done. So I do it first. That way I leave the downstairs until last and I have to do that. I can't put it off because somebody is always running in and out."

Lisa wasn't really interested in hearing Mildred's psychological methods of keeping house. "Slade is here and—"

"Yes, I know. I answered the door when he rang the bell. As if I haven't got anything better to do than run up and down stairs seeing who's at the door."

"Right. Well, I came to tell you that he's asked me to spend the day with him." Not even the housekeeper's grouchiness could diminish the happiness Lisa felt at the prospect of spending an entire day with Slade. "I'll be back in time for dinner tonight."

"And I've got a casserole in the oven for lunch," Mildred grumped and opened another drawer. In alarm, she backed away with uncharacteristic speed. "What is that thing in there?" she demanded. "It looks like some furry animal."

Lisa realized which drawer Mildred had opened and went white. "It isn't an animal," she started to explain but Mildred was already reaching a tentative hand into the drawer.

"It's hair!" she exclaimed, touching it.

"It's a wig."

"A wig?" The housekeeper took it out of the drawer to examine it more closely. "You didn't have a wig when I unpacked your things. What would you want with a wig? And a red one at that?"

The woman's attitude made Lisa feel as guilty as if she'd stolen it. "I . . . I bought it to play a joke on somebody." It was difficult to look the housekeeper in the eye and lie. "And I guess I always wondered what I'd look like in red hair."

"Waste of money, if you ask me." Mildred sniffed in disapproval as she stuffed the wig back in the drawer.

Lisa inched toward the door. She didn't want to think about posing as Ann Eldridge, or anything at all about the reasons she'd come to Charleston, not today.

"You'll tell Mitzi where I've gone?"

"I'll tell her." The woman reached for the bottle of furniture polish, but it was empty. "Now I've got to make another trip downstairs. This just isn't my day," she complained.

"Slade is waiting for me. I have to go." Lisa turned to leave the room and Mildred was right behind her.

At the bottom of the stairs, Mildred spoke up. "I still don't understand why you'd want to buy a red wig when you have such beautiful hair."

"I told you I just did it for the fun of it," Lisa replied with a trace of impatience, anxious to drop the subject.

At that moment, Slade rounded the corner, his dark gaze lighting on Lisa. "Your five minutes are up. Are you coming?"

"Yes." She almost dashed past Mildred to reach him and get him out of the house before the woman said any more about what she'd found in Lisa's drawer.

If Slade had appeared just a little earlier, he would have discovered her ruse. Lisa dreaded the moment when he would find out more than ever. Not because she hadn't obtained the evidence she wanted, but now because of what it would mean personally.

Outside, Slade opened the car door on her side. "I almost wish you'd said no."

"Why?" She held her breath.

"Because then I could have persuaded you to change your mind all over again." He grinned at her in a very male way.

Lisa released her breath in silent relief as he closed her door and walked around to the driver's side. A little voice inside her head said she was being a fool, but she ignored it.

CHAPTER EIGHT

The rest of the morning and afternoon was spent driving. As Slade put it, if he had to concentrate on the road, he would be less tempted to take back his statement that they would just talk.

They traversed the whole Low Country area around Charleston, stopping at noon to lunch in a crowded restaurant and again in midafternoon for a cold drink.

Lisa didn't remember the last time she had told anyone so much about herself. But then they'd both talked a great deal. The subjects had ranged from their childhood, their family and friends, to their work and hobbies, the kind of music they liked, and the books they read. Yet they both carefully avoided the subject of Mitzi Talmadge.

Myrtle Beach and the Golden Strand were far behind them now. Each rotation of the tires was taking them closer to Charleston. It was inevitable that the afternoon had to end. Staring at the Highway 17 sign at the side of the road, Lisa realized it and wished they were sixty miles from Charleston instead of six. She sighed with regret.

"What's wrong?" Slade let his gaze move to her for a second, then looked back at the highway.

"Nothing," Lisa insisted, but she knew he would persist if she didn't distract his attention. "There must be a boom in baskets. I've never seen so many stands along the road selling them. Just look at them all!"

"You must have seen the stands before," he said.

"No, I haven't."

"But you had to come this way to get to Brookgreen Gardens." He eyed her curiously.

"Oh," she laughed self-consciously. "I guess we were talking so much we never noticed any roadstands. You know how it is when it's just girls. Peg and Sue and I like to talk."

Slade nodded and Lisa hoped she had covered the tale she'd told before about going to Brookgreen.

"Okay, next stop on the guided tour." He slowed down and pulled over by one of the stands. "A traditional craft. Low Country baskets."

"Tell me all about it," Lisa smiled.

"These are coil baskets. The technique of making them was brought to America from Africa by slaves. The skill and designs were passed down from one generation to the next, sometimes with new designs and new artists being introduced along the way. Come on and we'll take a look. Can't neglect your education," he mocked gently.

With Slade at her side, Lisa inspected the roadside display. The baskets came in all shapes and sizes, some intricate in their designs, some plain, some with lids, and some open.

An elderly black woman sat in a chair to one side of the stand, a sweater around her shoulders. Her nimble fingers were busy creating the coiled base of another basket, but not too busy that she was unaware of Slade and Lisa looking over her display.

"Generally women make the show baskets," Slade explained, "and men make the sturdier baskets that were used on the farms and plantations."

He pointed to a large, very shallow one. "That's a fanner basket, used for winnowing rice. Big crop in the Low Country once upon a time, because of the high water table."

Lisa picked up a smaller basket to study it more closely. "The craftsmanship is amazing," she murmured more to herself than to Slade. "How do they make them? What do they use?"

"The show baskets use sweet grass sewn together with a split leaf of palmetto. The dark stripes in some of the baskets are decorative, made by long needles of pine straw." He showed her the stitches of the palmetto leaf radiating out in a straight line from the center of the coil basket. "The work baskets use bulrushes and split white oak or split palmetto butt for more strength. All from around here, probably." He waved at the landscape.

"I think I saw some palmetto palms along the way."

Slade nodded. "The materials are getting harder to find. A lot of the land where palmettos and sweet grass grew has been developed." He glanced at the basket in her hand. "Would you like to have that?"

"Yes, it's beautiful, but—" Lisa started to point out that she had no money with her.

"My first gift to you." Slade didn't let her finish as he gently took the basket from her and walked over to the elderly artist to pay for it.

A few minutes later they were on the road head-ing toward Charleston. Lisa held the small coil basket in her lap. Her first gift from Slade. He had said it would be the first of many.

But whose money would pay for them? His or Mitzi's? She stared out of the window, wishing she hadn't thought of that. It spoiled her pleasure in the gift and, somehow, the day.

Neither of them spoke in the last few miles to Mitzi's house. Lisa gazed absently out the window, lost in her melancholy thoughts, and Slade had to concentrate on the traffic that got heavier as they entered the city limits of Charleston.

The scrolled wrought-iron gates were open to admit them to the driveway of Mitzi's house. Slade stopped the car in front of the portico and switched off the motor. Without a word, he climbed out of the car and walked around to Lisa's door.

"We're here," he announced as he opened.

"Yes." Her reply was as bland as his comment.

They both seemed caught in the web of tension between them. Walking to the carved entrance doors of the house, Lisa attempted to lighten the mood.

"Did I bore you this afternoon?" She tried to sound teasing but there was an anxious note in the question.

"I don't know when I've been so—bored with a woman in my life," Slade mocked.

Lisa glanced away, feeling more than a little hurt. "Don't make jokes, Slade."

"Then don't ask stupid questions."

At the door she turned, her hand poised on the knob, wishing she didn't feel as if she was leaving him for good.

"Want to come in for a few minutes?"

"No." Slade leaned an arm against the jamb, effectively blocking her from entering the house immediately.

His dark head bent toward her and Lisa moved forward to meet him. The passion she sensed in the first touch of his lips told her how much restraint he'd exercised that day. But his desire seemed about to take over.

"I've been wanting to do that all day," he said, dragging his hard mouth from her lips to nuzzle her earlobe. "That and more."

Her one free hand was exploring the rough texture of his face while the other still crazily held on to the basket. Lisa pressed herself closer to his length. She trembled with longing as he explored the base of her neck and the hollow of her throat, finding her pleasure points with seductive ease.

"Slade, I don't want you to ever let me go." The plea came from her without thought, soft and heartfelt.

His mouth broke off the burning contact with her bare skin as he held her close to him. She felt the inner shudder of longing he tried to conceal.

"Come over to my place tonight," he ordered, in a voice that was husky and raw.

"I—can't," Lisa said, not wanting to deny him.

"Yes, you can." His arms tightened around her. "After dinner. Mitzi won't really care—she just wants to work on that book. Or come after she's gone to bed, I don't care."

"No!" She shook her head, wanting desperately to agree.

"Damn it, Lisa," Slade began, his need for her surpassing his patience.

"Slade, I just can't."

He let her go. "Okay. No means no. I hear you." He paused for a moment, but he didn't seem to want to give up. "What about tomorrow?"

"I have to devote a day to Mitzi," she insisted. "It's only polite. I can't go running off again or she'll think I came here just for free room and board during my vacation."

"Right. We don't want to hurt her feelings. There's a lot at stake."

Here we go again, Lisa thought unhappily. What was at stake was Mitzi's money, of course. What did love have to do with that?

Slade seemed about to argue, then changed his mind. "Okay, I'll see you Monday. We'll have dinner." A tight smile quirked his mouth. "And then we'll see what happens."

"Yes," Lisa agreed with a strained smile, a sense of depression settling over her. "I'd better be going in." She turned toward the door and he didn't try to stop her. "Good night, Slade," she murmured, aware that he hadn't moved.

"Lisa." It was a husky demand to come back to his arms.

At the feathery brush of his fingers against her hair, Lisa opened the door and bolted inside. Closing the door, she leaned against it, knowing that she loved him and wishing more than anything that she didn't. Seconds later she heard the slamming of the car door and the starting growl of the engine.

The rest of the weekend dragged by. By Monday morning, the strain of being perky for Mitzi's benefit was beginning to show on Lisa's face. While Lisa was walking to Slade's office, she debated the wisdom of carrying out her masquerade as Ann Eldridge for another day.

She had to, she decided. There was no way to prove her suspicions otherwise. The thought made her utterly miserable. She understood why she had unthinkingly turned her reversible green-and-black plaid jacket to the all-black side today—it matched her grim mood.

Drew followed her into the office when she arrived. "A redhead in basic black. Wow. Wow."

Down, you dog, she thought and gave him a scowl.

"How about lunch today?" he asked hopefully.

Dream on, Drew. But all she said was "No."

She was much too tense to make small talk over a sandwich, even if her lunch break was three hours away. And her nervousness was unlikely to go away.

"I don't think you're ever going to say yes," Drew sighed.

The outer office door swung open and Slade came striding in. Energy radiated from him with the blinding force of direct sunlight, and Lisa was glad she was sitting in her chair. The sight of him made her weak, especially when he walked directly to her desk and flashed her one of his devastating smiles.

"Good morning, Ann, Drew." He picked up the morning mail sitting in the in-box on her desk and began glancing through it, a trace of the smile still on his mouth.

"Good morning, Mr. Blackwell." Lisa had to lower her gaze to keep from devouring him with her eyes.

Drew whistled softly. "Introduce me to her, Slade."

"What are you talking about?"

"I want to meet the girl who made your weekend so bright that it carried over to Monday morning. She must be something," Drew declared, so intent on Slade that he missed Lisa's blush. "So introduce me."

"Not a chance." A rich, throaty laugh came from Slade, sending delicious shivers over Lisa's skin. "She's all mine and I intend to keep it that way."

When Slade disappeared into his office, Drew turned to Lisa, his eyes wide. "I get the feeling Cupid has struck. I swear I saw a whole bunch of little arrows sticking out of his back. I don't know who's luckier, Slade or the girl."

A warm glow brightened the green of her eyes. "Both, I hope." It was almost a silent prayer that it could be so.

"Slade's in love and you've turned me down for lunch." Drew shook his head. "I couldn't feel more left out if I was locked in a tower with the key thrown away."

"Your turn will come," Lisa offered.

"Yeah?" he asked glumly. "When?" He picked up what little mail there was for him, and left.

Slade came back in, carrying a stack of papers and folders that he dumped on her desk.

"You can file these this morning, Ann," he said.

"What about those contracts you said last Friday had to be typed first thing this morning?" Lisa reminded him.

He paused at his office door, a recklessly indifferent look on his handsome face. "Forget it," he shrugged. "Do them later. Or tomorrow. The day is too beautiful for drudgery."

Her mouth opened in disbelief, but Slade was already closing his door. Maybe he didn't realize how uncharacteristic his reply had been, but it left Lisa little doubt that their weekend time together had changed him. For the good. And maybe, just maybe, he really did love her, just as he'd said.

If love had the power to change everything, *absolutely* everything, they might be in luck. Maybe there would even be a happy ending to the mutual deception they had entered into regarding Mitzi. It might not be a rational ending, but . . . With an irrationally happy smile, she turned toward the stack of filing to be done.

She blinked. Black letters seemed to leap from the tab of one of the folders and her heart stopped beating for a split second.

Talmadge, Miriam.

With shaking fingers, Lisa pulled the folder out of the stack, staring at it almost in dread. It was what she had been waiting for—to have Mitzi's file in her possession. She closed her eyes for a second, wishing that it hadn't happened.

The telephone rang shrilly. Lisa hesitated, then quickly slipped the folder in a desk drawer and answered it. When she transferred the call to Slade, she ignored the closed desk drawer. Picking up the stack of papers and folders, she carried them to the metal cabinets, setting it all on top of one, and systematically began filing everything in the proper place.

Not that the files had magically straightened themselves out in the short time she had been working in the office. She still had to rely on the guess and search approach. As a consequence, one-third of the stack remained to be filed when Slade emerged from his office.

"I'll be gone for about twenty minutes if anyone's looking for me," he told her, still with that contented look burning in his dark eyes.

"Yes, Mr. Blackwell," she nodded.

When the outer door closed behind him, she walked back to her desk, sat down in her chair, and stared at the desk drawer. She clenched her hands tightly in her lap, then pulled them apart to reach for the telephone, finding a reason to stall the inevitable for a few more minutes.

When she'd left the house that morning, she hadn't said where she was going or how long she would be gone because she hadn't been that sure she would come to the office. She dialed Mitzi's number, fabricating another story in her mind as to why she wouldn't be home until early evening.

"Talmadge residence." The call was answered on the second ring.

"Mildred, this is—" she began.

"Lisa, is that you?" Mitzi picked up the extension and the housekeeper hung up the kitchen phone.

"Yes, it is," Lisa said nervously. "I was call—"

"I'm so glad you did!" Mitzi interrupted her. "Exactly sixteen minutes ago I typed those six magic letters."

"What?" she asked blankly.

Mitzi laughed. "The End. I've finished my new novel!"

"That's wonderful," Lisa agreed with forced enthusiasm.

"More than wonderful! It's fabulous!" her aunt gushed. "And it calls for an immediate celebration. Where are you? Let's meet for lunch at a swanky restaurant."

Her heart sank. "Well, actually, Mitzi, I'm—"

"Oh, no, don't tell me you can't make it." Mitzi sounded genuinely crushed. "If you're with your two friends, bring them along. We'll make a party of it."

"No, no, they can't make it." Lisa rubbed her hand across her forehead, feeling a headache start to pound in her temples. She just couldn't disappoint her aunt. "But I can meet you at noon. Where would you like to celebrate?"

Mitzi suggested a restaurant that, thank God,

was within walking distance of the office, and Lisa agreed. Her aunt sounded jubilant when Lisa hung up while she sighed dispiritedly. She opened the desk drawer to take out Mitzi's folder and Drew walked in. She closed the drawer with guilty swiftness.

"Aha! I caught you doing your fingernails, didn't I?" he said with mock anger. "If you don't have lunch with me, I'll tell Slade."

"You're out of luck. He isn't here," Lisa said.

"Where did he go?"

"He didn't say. All he told me was that he would be back in twenty minutes." She shrugged, and rose from the desk to return to the filing.

"Hmm." Drew stood there, his hands shoved in his pockets. "I guess I'll keep you company until he comes back." He wandered over to the cabinets where Lisa worked. "What are you doing?"

"Filing. Want to help?" she offered.

"No, thanks," he smiled and eyed her lazily. "So you won't give in and have lunch with me?"

"Nope."

"Just as well. Considering the benevolent mood Slade is in, he'd probably send you out for a manicure if I told him I'd caught you doing your nails. Not that they need doing." He caught one of her hands and refused to let it go. "Beautiful nails. No wonder you can't type."

"Now you know my darkest secret." Lisa firmly pulled her hand from Drew's grasp just as Slade returned.

"No holding hands during office hours, you two," he chided them. But he was smiling. "Don't forget the mighty Burt. What if he showed up here, Drew?"

The telephone rang, interrupting Drew's reply.

Lisa started toward her desk but Slade waved her away. "I'll answer it." He picked up the receiver and Drew gave Lisa a disbelieving look.

"Slade Blackwell," he said briskly. Lisa turned back to the cabinet, resisting the desire to gaze at him. "Hello, Mitzi, how are you?"

Lisa froze, the folder in her hand poised above the open file cabinet drawer, her fingers tightening as they gripped the stiff paper.

"It goes here," Drew whispered, indicating a spot between the folders already in the drawer. She shoved the folder between them.

"You did?" Slade was speaking again. "Congratulations . . . lunch today?"

He seemed to hesitate and Lisa pivoted quickly toward him. "You have an appointment for lunch, Mr. Blackwell," she reminded him, hoping she didn't sound as panicked as she felt.

Slade glanced at her briefly, then smiled suddenly at the mouthpiece. "She's meeting you at noon? Of course I'll be there, Mitzi."

"What about your appointment?" Lisa said nervously when he hung up.

"Who was it with?" He glanced at the day's calendar with remarkable unconcern. "Art Jones? Call him up and change it to another day."

"So *she* is going to be there." Drew gave a suggestive stress to the feminine pronoun.

Slade flashed him a look, his dark eyes shining with an inner brilliance. "I'm not inviting you, Drew. It's bad enough that her aunt is going to be there."

"Nobody wants to eat lunch with me," Drew said with a trace of exasperation.

"Too bad," Slade chuckled quietly. "Did you want to see me about something, Drew, or are you hanging around in here just to bother Ann?"

"No, there's something I want to discuss with

you. That is, if you think you can concentrate on business for five minutes and forget the mystery goddess," was the reply.

"Don't think I can." Slade grinned.

"Mr. Blackwell?" Lisa heard herself asking for his attention.

He turned, absently curious. "Yes?"

"I have a dentist's appointment during my lunch hour," she lied. "Would it be all right if I left a little early?"

"No problem."

A few minutes past the arranged time, Lisa walked into the restaurant. her silver-blond hair fell soft and loose about her shoulders; the red wig was tucked safely away in her bag. Her jacket was reversed to the green-and-black plaid side, which didn't go too well with the smoke-blue sunglasses perched once again on her nose.

A movement at a far table caught her eye. Having seen Lisa enter the restaurant, Slade was rising to meet her. Lisa's steps faltered as he moved toward her. She wasn't attempting to feign surprise at seeing him there. Her momentary uncertainty was caused by the panic racing through her. She managed to force it back and smile as they approached each other.

It wasn't too difficult to smile warmly, not with his heart-stopping look fanning the fires of her love. Slade halted, letting her cover the last few feet that would bring her to his side. Tall and darkly male, he stood before her, commanding all of her senses.

Not seeming to care that they were in a very public place, he bent his head toward hers, stealing Lisa's breath away with a hard kiss that was frustratingly brief for both of them. When he straightened, she swayed toward him and his arm curved around her shoulders to guide her to the table.

"Hello." His low greeting was caressing. "You didn't expect to see me here, did you?"

"No, Mitzi didn't mention that you'd be joining us," Lisa could say truthfully.

The smoldering light in his eyes seemed to physically and lovingly touch each of her features, making her want to melt under the fiery glow. The possessive curve of his arm added to the boneless sensation.

"Sunday was the longest day of my life," Slade whispered.

"For me, too," Lisa admitted softly. They were nearly at the table where Mitzi waited, and Lisa had to tear her gaze from Slade's ruggedly handsome face. "Hello, Mitzi." But her voice still echoed the velvet quality induced by the magic of Slade's nearness. "Sorry I'm a little late."

"I didn't mind waiting, although I think Slade did." There was a knowing and pleased gleam in her aunt's eyes as she studied the two of them together.

Lisa flushed warmly as she sat in the chair Slade held out for her. Bending forward, Slade pushed her chair to the table, his face relatively close to her hair.

"Do you know something?" He took the chair to her left, a slight smile on his face. "You wear the same fragrance that my temp secretary does. Or maybe it's the same shampoo."

"Really." She kept her tone absolutely neutral and reached for a roll. She had no intention of eating it but maybe tearing it into tiny little pieces would keep her hands from shaking.

"Jealous?" he said laughingly, not seeming to care how much of their new relationship he was revealing to Mitzi. "You don't have to be. Could be my imagination, you know. Just goes to show how you haunt my every waking moment."

"I see." The roll was in large crumbs by this point. Mitzi looked at the little heap on Lisa's bread-and-butter plate with a fractional frown.

"You look beautiful, by the way," Slade went on. "Green is your color. Everything is your color."

"Thank you," Lisa responded nervously.

"Of course green is her color," her aunt spoke up. "Why shouldn't it be, with those—" The waiter appeared, opportunely for Lisa, with glasses and a chilled bottle of champagne.

"Champagne!" Lisa was delighted to interrupt Mitzi and keep her from remarking on the green of her eyes. "We really are going to celebrate!"

Minutes later the three of them were clinking glasses as Slade made the toast. "To your newest book. May it be the most successful one yet. Congratulations."

For a time the talk centered on Mitzi's latest, its plot and characters, and Lisa was able to relax. When Slade refilled the glasses, Lisa automatically reached for hers to take another sip, but he stopped her.

"Wait." His hand moved to the inside pocket of his suit jacket. "I don't mean to steal your thunder, Mitzi, but we have something else to celebrate."

Puzzled, Lisa didn't understand what he meant until she saw the velvet ring box in his hand. She breathed in softly when he snapped it open to reveal the rainbow brilliance of a diamond solitaire.

"I didn't intend to give you this until tonight," he said huskily. "But when I found out we'd be having lunch together, I couldn't wait. Give me your hand, Lisa."

She was too overcome to speak or move. The

moment seemed surreal. Yet a crazy happiness radiated from the shimmering tears in her eyes as she gazed at him. There was an equal depth of feeling in the depths of his.

"I know this is very soon," he began, "but I couldn't see any reason to wait. Even though I know there's someone else."

"There is?" Mitzi looked wonderingly at Lisa. "Mercy me! Who?"

"I'm not going to mention his name," Slade said. "And I have a feeling he doesn't mean all that much to you, Lisa."

She felt sick to her stomach.

"Am I right?"

She didn't answer.

Mitzi clapped her hands twice and hooted. "Get on with the proposal! This is great!"

"Please, Mitzi," Slade said, looking worriedly at Lisa. Heads had turned at the sound of her voice and Mitzi shut up. But the older woman leaned forward in her seat, watching both of them with rapt attention.

"Lisa, just listen. Our relationship is just beginning. But I want it to last. And I want you to know that I'm totally serious."

Lisa nodded, still unable to speak.

"Will you wear this ring? Do you understand what it means?"

She drew in a long, shuddering breath and heard herself reply, very simply, "Yes."

He nodded, giving her a look of such warm passion that she felt herself melt inside.

Mitzi wiped a tear from her cheek with her napkin and waved it in triumph. "She said yes!"

A few of the other restaurant patrons lifted their glasses and murmured congratulations. Lisa was thrilled, mortified, and scared to death. Next would come the explanations. He would probably take the ring back to the jeweler's that very day.

But her own desire to love him, to be loved by him, was just too strong. She extended her hand to him so that he could slip it on. Slade fumbled with the little box and took out the ring.

He held her left hand, slipping it past the first knuckle of her fourth finger. It stopped.

"Damn," he swore under his breath. "Well, I did have to guess the size."

"It's beautiful, Slade," she whispered.

"I'll take it to the jeweler's for you and have it made larger," Slade offered, watching her closely.

"That isn't necessary," Lisa refused, and hurriedly slipped the gold ring into her jacket pocket, "I can do it."

"Put the ring on her finger, Slade," Mitzi urged. "I want to see it."

Her hand was shaking badly as he slipped the diamond ring on another finger. It never occurred to her to refuse it. When Slade smiled at her, Lisa knew that she loved him no matter what.

"Do you like it?" he asked.

"It's beautiful." She smiled radiantly.

"Stunning is the word," Mitzi exclaimed, reaching for Lisa's hand to examine the ring more closely. "I just hope you two know how happy you've made me. I should've guessed something like this would happen. There were sparks from the instant you met."

"Didn't I tell you that's what she would say?" Slade mocked.

"So when is the wedding?" Mitzi wanted to know, still admiring the ring.

"Soon," Slade promised with typical self-assurance. "As soon as Lisa wants to, I mean."

Mitzi proposed a toast, followed by more talk,

before they gave their orders to the waiter. But all the while Lisa was uneasy.

There was nothing in Slade's attitude to make her feel that way. She still basked in the warmth of his gaze and the touch of his hand. The problem seemed to be solely her own: a guilty conscience.

After the meal was served and the dishes taken away, neither Mitzi nor Slade seemed inclined to leave. Lisa was intensely conscious of the passing time, knowing how close it was to 1:30. And Ann Eldridge was supposed to take only an hour for lunch.

Twice she tried to make excuses to leave, but each time Slade used his persuasive charm to see that she didn't. Being newly engaged, Lisa couldn't exactly claim that she had, oh, a few errands to run and just skip out the door. She was stuck at the table until either Mitzi or Slade made a move.

More seconds ticked away before he glanced at his watch. "Oh, hell. It's nearly two o'clock. I have to get back to the office." He kissed Lisa on the cheek and Mitzi beamed. "Much as I hate to leave you ladies, there is work to do."

"I understand," Lisa assured him, smiling with relief.

Rising from his chair, he rested a hand on her shoulder, saying good-bye to Mitzi first before glancing down at Lisa. "I'll see you at seven tonight, if not before."

"Yes," she agreed, lifting her head to receive a brushing kiss from his mouth.

There was no hope of beating him back to the office, not when she had to change into Ann Eldridge somewhere along the way. So she lingered for several more minutes with Mitzi before resorting to the much-used pretext of good old Peg and Sue as the reason she couldn't come back home.

"Run along," her aunt said, not raising a single objection. "I know you're just dying to show off that engagement ring."

"Thanks, Mitzi," Lisa said. She pushed her chair back and gathered up her things. "I knew you'd understand."

CHAPTER NINE

Lisa walked into the office and quailed under a piercing look from Slade.

"Do you realize it's past two o'clock?"

"I'm sorry. I know I'm late but I didn't realize how late." She launched into the speech she had been rehearsing since leaving the restaurant. "I was at the dentist. But just as I got in the chair, there was an emergency—a little boy had a permanent front tooth knocked out."

No. Cancel that part. She didn't know enough about that subject to sound plausible and decided to stop while she was ahead. If she was ahead. "So I waited for a while and then came running back," she said breathily. "I can stay later to make up for it."

"No need for that," he said gruffly. He seemed to relent but he didn't take his eyes off her for a second. He had never looked at her quite this closely as Ann Eldridge, Lisa realized. Nervously, she walked around him and scurried in back of her desk, keeping her bewigged head down as she always did in the office.

"Thanks for being cool about it," she said. "I mean, when you gave me permission to leave early, I thought I'd be back on time."

"No big deal," he responded smoothly. "I came back only a few minutes ago myself."

Lisa felt the tension mounting to a screaming pitch. "Did you?" The brightness of her reply was forced. "Guess we both took a long lunch."

"Right," Slade said. "And I did something I thought I'd never do."

"Really? What was that?"

"I asked someone to marry me."

"Congratulations. That's amazing." It really was. She had been totally amazed. And he would be too when this crazy game of charades came to an end. Really, really amazed—and really, really angry.

Lisa knew she had to find the right moment and the right words to explain everything. If only he would go into his inner office and get busy so she could think.

But Slade continued to stand by her desk.

"Was there anything else, Mr. Blackwell?" She tried to prod him into leaving. "Will you be taking the rest of the afternoon off? Or did you want something?"

"There is one thing . . ." Slade paused. "I'd like to buy my fiancée an engagement present. I wondered if you would have a suggestion."

"Oh, umm, no. I've never met her. I really wouldn't know what to suggest." She could hear the agitation in her voice and wondered if he did too.

"What did your guy—Burt—buy you for an engagement present?"

Lisa swallowed hard. "He . . . he didn't have enough money for one. Not after he bought the ring." She hated all these lies. They were tearing at her soul. And she didn't think she'd said they were engaged—or had she?

"Didn't you say he was in construction? Those guys make pretty good money."

"He was laid off." Her reply was flat. At least it served to conceal her uneasiness.

"That's too bad."

"Happens," she murmured and began moving papers around on her desk to give her trembling hands something to do.

"What company did he work for? I know most of the ones in and around Charleston," Slade said.

Lisa wouldn't have been surprised if he knew every single one—which made it impossible for her to make up a fictitious company.

She decided to plead ignorance. "Oh, gosh, what was the name of the firm? I forget."

"Really?" His gaze narrowed. "But if there had been an emergency, what would you have done?"

"He has a cell phone."

"How can you explain forgetting the name of your fiancé's company?"

She tried to make her reply sound nonchalant. "Am I on trial here? I feel like I'm in the witness box."

"No." He stuck his hands in his pockets and paced the room. "I was just hoping you would tell the truth without being forced to."

"What do you mean?" She absolutely would not look up at him. She traced a finger along the edge of her desk. The grained wood was a little scarred from years of use. She noted every scratch and speck while Slade continued to pace.

"Explain," he said at last.

"Explain what?"

"For starters . . ." He strode over to her desk, reached down and opened the drawer, revealing

Mitzi's folder lying on top of the other papers. "What is this doing in your drawer?"

"Oh. That." Her throat was dry and her heart pumped wildly with fear. "It was in the stack of stuff you gave me to file. I didn't finish before noon, so I put it in my drawer rather than leave it lying out."

"I see," he murmured. "But it got me to thinking—I really haven't been paying enough attention to what goes on around here."

"I'll, uh, do it now," Lisa said. Her hand was shaking as she picked up the folder and walked to the filing cabinets.

Slade watched her as if he had nothing better to do, but his continued presence in the room was scraping her nerves raw. She didn't know how much more she could stand.

"Did you have time to eat anything for lunch?" he asked unexpectedly as she went through the file drawer to find the proper place for Mitzi's folder.

"No, I didn't," Lisa lied. "I don't like to eat before I go to the dentist. If I have food in my teeth I get the brush-and-floss lecture. Like I can do that in the office."

"But he must be a good dentist. You have a beautiful smile," Slade said.

"Thanks." She jammed the folder in the wrong place without looking at it or him.

"And beautiful green eyes," he added.

"Whoa," she murmured. "You're starting to sound like Drew."

Slade moved across the room to stand beside her. She stepped back from the filing cabinet. He closed the open drawer with a swift, silent motion.

"And you can really file. I like that in a woman."

"Huh?"

Slade took her by the shoulders. "What kind of fool do you think I am, Lisa?"

"Slade, let me explain." Her heart was hammering in her chest and she could scarcely breathe.

"Okay. Let's get back to the explanations. Just because I was a little too preoccupied to look at a temp secretary in the beginning—"

"Why was that, Slade?"

"Maybe because I was a little too pissed off by your ineptitude. And your attitude. And—"

"Any other 'tudes you didn't like, Mr. Blackwell?" She put her hands on her hips and glared at him. He looked down at the lining of her jacket before she realized it was showing. The plaid lining of her reversible jacket.

"You have a smart mouth, Lisa." He got a little closer. "Mind if I kiss it?" He didn't wait for a reply but claimed her lips in the hottest, longest smooch she'd ever had. She came up gasping for air. But she was still not sure if this was a fight or what. Slade had let her tell a few more lies, acted like he'd believed them, then pounced like a panther. She was completely at his mercy—or lack of it.

Lisa flattened herself against the filing cabinet, the metal cool to the hands she spread against its surface. But he grabbed the left one.

"Where's my ring?"

She kept her voice down, suddenly realizing that the receptionist might hear and come running. "In my pocket. And it's my ring, not yours. You gave it to me, remember?"

He nodded and let go of her hand. "Yeah. What a moment. I looked into your eyes . . . but it didn't hit me until I got back here. So when did you plan to tell me just what this was all about?"

"Soon. Very soon."

The door to the reception area opened and Drew sauntered in to Lisa's office. He came to an abrupt halt at the sight of them so close together, obviously in the middle of an argument, and he gaped for a speechless second. "Slade, what the hell are you doing?" A disbelieving look widened his eyes. "Ann, are you all right?"

"Her name isn't Ann." Slade ran his fingers through the hair of Lisa's short red wig and suddenly tightened them. He pulled it off.

She hadn't had time to pin back her real hair and her silver-blond locks tumbled freely over her shoulders.

"Holy cow!" Drew yelped.

Slade tossed the wig to him. "You like redheads. Here's a trophy. You can have it stuffed and mounted for your den."

"I don't have a den," the other man began to say, utterly confused.

"Get out of here, Drew."

The shorter man stood his ground. "Not until Ann tells me she's all right."

Lisa nodded. "Thanks, Drew. Everything is fine."

"Really?"

"Really. You just happened to walk in when things got weird. Slade and I were—discussing things." She didn't want to say "fighting."

"Things, huh? Like what kind of things?" Drew asked.

"True love," Slade said sarcastically. "Ain't it grand?"

"I wouldn't know," Drew said. "I've never been in love."

"Then you have nothing to contribute to the discussion," Slade said, lowering his voice. He glanced meaningfully at the door and then at his friend.

"Okay, okay. I'll go. But I want a full report on my desk in the morning."

"I'll have Lisa type it up," Slade said.

"Your name is Lisa?" Drew looked at her curiously.

She nodded.

"What about Burt? How does he fit into this?"

"There is no Burt," Slade said. "There never was a Burt. There never will be a Burt. Lisa is going to marry me."

Drew gaped at both of them. "Let me know when you two get it all figured out, okay?"

Slade gritted his teeth. "Later, Drew."

"Later." He left.

Lisa and Slade stood only inches apart for a few seconds more. Then he drew her into the circle of his arms, while her own hands spread over his muscled shoulders. Just when she ran out of breath, he broke off the kiss.

"No matter what you think of me, just know that I love you, Slade."

He didn't reply right away but stepped back and looked into her eyes. She couldn't look away. Not anymore.

"How do I know you're not lying about that too? You haven't said one true thing to me since the day we met."

"I wanted to—to protect Mitzi. I didn't know you at all. And you seemed to have so much influence over her. She was always talking about you."

He made a wry face. "Mitzi's a little lonely."

Lisa nodded. "I know. And she's very impractical. So I had my suspicions. And one thing led to another. When you took me for a temp, I just jumped in. I didn't think too much about what would happen next. I thought I could get the information I needed from your files and get the hell out in a big fat hurry."

He looked ruefully at the filing cabinets. "Our so-called system is too screwed up to find anything in a hurry."

"Well, it's not like that was your fault." She ran a hand through her tangled hair, smoothing it as best she could. "I don't really have a better explanation. Stuff kept happening. The stories got out of control. Nothing made sense."

Slade sighed. "Sounds like a first draft of one of Mitzi's mysteries. Before she figures out the plot, makes the hero and heroine fall in love, and ties it all up with a big red bow."

"Right."

"Now we have to explain this to her."

"She'll love it, believe me," Lisa assured him, letting him take her in his arms again. "Mitzi can dine out on a story like this for years."

Slade kissed the top of her head. "Did you really think I was after her money?"

"I didn't know," Lisa answered. "But you weren't very forthcoming."

"Have you ever heard of lawyer-client confidentiality? I'm not supposed to tell the whole damn world everything I know."

"Okay, okay. You have a point. Let's not argue about all that right now."

"I agree." He kissed her again. "We can argue about it later."

"Slade . . . at some point we're going to have to straighten all this out."

"I have all the time in the world," he said, nuzzling her neck.

"Obviously, we're going to have problems trusting each other."

"Obviously." His hands glided over her hips and pulled her close.

"If you would stop that, I could think."

Slade stroked her back and her hair. He looked into her eyes again. "Are you sure you want to think? Seems to get you in a hell of a lot of trouble. You have Mitzi's knack for dreaming up crazy plots."

"Maybe I do," she said. "But we have to think this through if it's going to work. I want to be sure . . . about us."

He set her away from him but held onto her hand. "First things first. Let's go talk to Mitzi."

She nodded and walked beside him, letting him open the door to the reception area. Drew was there, talking to Ellen Tyler in a low voice. He straightened when he saw them come out. Lisa smiled nervously at the older woman, who stared at her silver-blond hair for a second and then put on a polite smile.

"Hi, Slade," the shorter man said. "And hello, Lisa. Hey, you never did tell me your last name. Guess it isn't Eldridge."

It was an awkward moment.

"It's Talmadge," she informed him.

Drew and the receptionist exchanged a look. "Talmadge?" Drew said at last.

"You heard the lady," Slade said. He left with Lisa on his arm.

CHAPTER TEN

Lisa twisted her hands nervously and stopped pacing as Mitzi entered the comfortably furnished living room. She hoped and prayed that her aunt would not be angry.

Any ordinary person would be. Fortunately, Mitzi's eccentricity might mean that she would only find the comedy of errors amusing and not appalling.

Lisa made a mental list of her transgressions: she had not consulted her aunt in the first place; had undertaken an amateur investigation that seemed just plain nuts in retrospect, even if she had meant well; and had taken advantage of her aunt's hospitality to fall head-over-heels in love in about a week. Mitzi wasn't the only person who would want to hear the whole story, of course.

Lisa sighed. She was never going to be able to explain any of it when she got back to Baltimore. Lisa planned to convene her girlfriends, and give them the condensed version. Minus her unfounded suspicions. Leaving out the really bad wig.

She figured that if she waved that sparkly diamond around enough and showed them a picture of Slade, they might not ask too many questions.

But Mitzi was another matter.

Slade had insisted that Lisa tell her aunt exactly what had happened—and why. There seemed to be no way out of it. She looked up at the door into the living room as her aunt entered.

"Hello, honey. You said you wanted to see me?"

"Yes."

Mitzi took her usual chair and settled back, looking at Lisa expectantly. "Is it about Slade's proposal?"

"Yes—and no."

"Please don't tell me that you've changed your mind. I've been on the phone and spreading the news. About time he came to his senses and realized what a wonderful girl you are. Oh, I'm so happy that you're his one and only, Lisa—"

"That's the problem," Lisa broke in. "There was more than one of me. And he just found out."

"Whatever are you trying to say?" Mitzi leaned forward and looked worriedly at Lisa.

"I, ah, pretended to be someone else while I was here."

"You did? Who? Why?"

Lisa could see that she had aroused Mitzi's curiosity. And Slade had been right on target when he said the situation was a lot like one of Mitzi's plots.

"Um, Slade's temporary assistant. I worked in his office."

Mitzi's eyes went wide. "So that's where you went every day. I thought there was something a little fishy about those invisible college friends of yours. I'm not stupid, honey."

"No, I didn't think you were, Aunt Mitzi," Lisa said hastily.

"I just thought you were meeting Slade on the sly and didn't want me to know about it. And I was right," she finished triumphantly.

"Well, he didn't know it was me. I wore a wig . . . and I didn't look at him."

Mitzi regarded her with astonishment. "Mercy me! Why did you do that?"

"I—I wanted to get into his files. I was sure he was stealing from you. So I tried to get your file to investigate, but I wasn't any too successful. And then when I—"

Her aunt shook her head. "I can't believe I'm hearing this. You should have come to me right away if that's what you thought."

"Well, I didn't. And I regret it. But I thought if I could find proof, you would be more likely to believe me. And then he said some things that seemed to corroborate my suspicions. And some things that I said made him think that I was up to no good."

"This just doesn't make a whole lot of sense," Mitzi declared. "Now I know I can be an awful flibbertigibbet when it comes to money, but Slade has never given me the slightest cause to doubt his honesty. He helped me through a very difficult time, out of the kindness of his heart. I truly think that he's one of the last Southern gentlemen, just like his daddy."

Lisa gulped.

"For heaven's sake, you must know that. You accepted his proposal and his ring."

"I guess I did. I mean, I know I did. But I wasn't expecting him to do anything like that. He took me totally by surprise. By the time I got back to the office, he'd put two and two together and discovered my disguise."

"I wish I could have been a fly on the wall for that scene," Mitzi laughed. "Do you mind if I use it in my next book?"

Lisa threw up her hands. "Go ahead. We had it out then and there. And we left the office after I, um, explained as best I could and we talked some more—" She looked up at the sound of the doorbell. "That's him."

Mitzi didn't get up right away. "Tell me one thing, Lisa. Do you love him? Do you want to marry him?"

"Yes," Lisa whispered. "Yes. And he still wants to marry me."

"And do you understand that you made a huge mistake?"

"Yes."

"And did he forgive you?" The older woman ignored the second, more insistent ringing of the bell.

"Sort of. I think so. Shouldn't we get the door?"

Mitzi laughed. "Do you two know how silly you are? I never heard of anything like this. Come to think of it, I won't be able to use it in my next book, because no one will believe it."

The doorbell rang a third time and Lisa got up.

"I'll let you do the honors, darlin'."

Lisa headed for the door in a hurry, going past her aunt, but banging her shin against the marble-topped table and stopping to rub it. Mitzi caught her arm.

"Here's my advice. Kiss him senseless before you start arguing again. You two have a whole life ahead of you to do that. But if you're smart, you won't."

"Thanks, Aunt Mitzi."

Lisa went past her and flung open the door. Slade had his hand in midair, ready to press the doorbell again. She took it and pulled him to her—and she followed Mitzi's advice.

Don't miss this romantic excerpt
from Janet Dailey's
LONE CALDER STAR,
available now from Kensington . . .

There is something about Saturday night that has always drawn a cowboy to the lights of town, and Quint was no exception. While drinking and carousing had never been part of his nature, a cold beer, a good meal, and a change of surroundings held a definite appeal for him.

Fort Worth with its array of nightspots sat northeast of the Cee Bar with other towns of varying sizes lying in between. Quint left the ranch with no particular destination in mind, but he turned in the direction of Loury. The Corner Café hadn't crossed his mind until he saw the fluorescent glare of its lighted windows. The sight summoned up an immediate image of Dallas with her pale copper hair and unusual light brown eyes.

Quint found himself wondering whether she was working tonight. At almost the same moment, he remembered all the times in the past when he had been a stranger in a strange town and experienced the loneliness that could be found in a crowd. A familiar face suddenly had more appeal than a beer and a good meal. In the blink of an eye, the decision was made and he swung the pickup into an empty parking slot in front of the café.

Dallas saw him when he walked through the door. One glimpse of his high cheekbones, the slight bronze cast of his skin, and the black gleam of his hair when he slipped off his hat, and she identified him instantly. Oddly, her spirits lifted. The night suddenly didn't seem to be as dull and ordinary to her as it had before he arrived.

The touch of his gaze was almost a tangible thing when he saw her crossing to a booth, a heavily laden serving tray balanced on one arm.

She nodded to the table he had occupied on his previous visit. "You can sit at your old table if you like," she told him.

"Thanks." His eyes smiled at her.

There was a warmth in their gray depths that Dallas didn't recall noticing before. Considering some of the things her grandfather had told her about him, she had a feeling she might have been too quick to dismiss him as an ordinary cowboy.

After she finished distributing the food orders on her tray, Dallas collected a glass of ice water and a cup of hot coffee from the counter and carried them to his table.

"I didn't expect to see you in here tonight." She set the water and coffee before him.

His eyes gleamed with amusement. "You didn't really think I'd leave town just because you told me I should."

"It was good advice." Dallas still believed that. "Or have you found that out? I heard you went to the Slash R."

"News travels fast," he replied, neither confirming nor denying.

Dallas realized that he had seldom given her a

direct answer. "It's a small town. And anything to do with the Rutledges spreads like crazy. And the news that you bought hay from them went through this town like a category-four tornado."

"They were just doing the neighborly thing." He reached for the menu and flipped it open.

Dallas liked the way he played down the purchase. "Maybe, but the Slash R has never been known for making neighborly gestures."

"Maybe no one's given them a chance," he suggested, tongue-in-cheek.

Dallas reacted with a crooked smile that grooved a dimple in one cheek. "Yeah, right."

His smile widened into something dazzling and warm that snatched at her breath. "For a minute there I thought you were going to accuse me of being a fool again."

The remark was an instant reminder of the futility of one man attempting to stand against the Rutledges. It sobered her. "I don't think you realize how big the odds are against you."

An amused dryness entered his expression. "I imagine the odds were long that I'd get any hay, too." Without giving her a chance to reply, he asked, "Is it safe to order a steak?"

"Yes. It's just the meat loaf you need to avoid," she told him.

"In that case, I'll have a T-bone, medium rare, and a baked potato with all the trimmings."

"What kind of dressing on your salad?" Dallas pulled the order tablet from her apron pocket and flipped to a new sheet.

"Blue cheese, if you have it."

"Coming right up," she promised and moved away.

When she left, that lonely feeling closed around Quint again. Looking at the empty chairs pushed up to his table, he realized that it was her company and conversation he wanted.

There was a glimmer of rare annoyance in the glance he flicked at the scattering of other customers. Their presence forced Quint to put aside any hope he might have entertained of persuading Dallas to join him at the table. The knowledge left him with an edgy, irritated feeling, something that was new to him.

The sensation didn't fade until she returned to his table a few minutes later and placed a salad liberally drizzled with blue cheese dressing before him.

"I thought it would be busier than this on a Saturday night," Quint said to prevent her from walking away.

Her easy smile gave him the impression that she didn't mind being drawn into conversation, perhaps even welcomed it. "The supper crowd always comes early. By now the homebodies are back in front of their televisions and the rest are bending their elbows at Tillie's."

"Tillie's. That must be the local bar," Quint guessed. "Is it here in town? I don't remember driving by one."

"It's a block off the main drag, so it isn't a place that you would happen by," she explained. "Tubby's sister owns it. I keep telling him they should merge the two businesses. He'd have more customers if he sold beer and she'd have more if she sold food. But he just turns a deaf ear to the idea."

"Sounds like a good one to me. We have a place like that back in Montana," he said, thinking of the former roadhouse called Harry's in Blue Moon that had always sold both food and liquor. "Come Saturday night, it's packed to the rafters."

She tipped her head to one side, curiosity entering her expression. "Is that where you're from—Montana?"

"Born and raised there," Quint confirmed with a nod. "How about you? Are you a native Texan?"

"Of course." There was an impish light in her eyes. "Care to guess where I was born?"

Quint laughed softly in response. "Something tells me it might be Dallas."

"It's a little obvious, isn't it?" she agreed.

"I'd say you were lucky the hospital wasn't in Fort Worth."

"True. Although my mother told me that if she had gone to Fort Worth to deliver, she would have named me Gentry. But when I was born in Dallas, she thought it would be more original to name me after the city of my birth. Of course, you have to understand, she had an absolute aversion to commonplace names. Her own was Mary Alice, and she hated it."

Made sensitive by the recent loss of his father, Quint was quick to note her use of the past tense in referring to her mother. "How long has she been gone?"

"It was seven years ago this past spring."

"It's hard losing a parent," he said, speaking as much for himself as for her.

"Yes." But she seemed a little surprised that he understood that. After an instant's hesitation, Dallas glanced down at his untouched salad. "You'd better dig in," she told him. "Your steak will be up soon."

Left alone again, Quint picked up his fork and started on the salad with a renewed appetite, only distantly aware that his conversation with her, brief as it had been, had stimulated a male kind of hunger as well.

During the course of his meal, he had more occasions to talk to her, some exchanges longer than others. On a subconscious level, Quint knew it was all part of an age-old dance between a man and a woman. He had long ago become familiar with the steps to it, the advance and retreat, and the waiting and watching for that signal from the woman indicating her interest, or lack thereof.

With the only other remaining customer at the cash register, Quint let his attention focus on Dallas, recalling the small, personal things he had learned about her tonight and the thousands more he still wanted to know—things like whether her hair felt as smooth as it looked, and the look of her light brown eyes when passion glazed them.

There was a natural grace to the relaxed, yet erect, posture of her body, long and slim and unmistakably feminine in its well-proportioned curves.

His bill paid, the man at the register headed out the door, and Dallas emerged from behind the counter and looked directly at Quint, her eyes bright and alive to him.

"Ready for more coffee?" Her warm smile was an encouragement to agree.

But Quint wasn't really interested in another cup of coffee. "What time do you close?"

And here's a look at
Janet Dailey's
CALDER PROMISE
available from Zebra . . .

Laura stayed against Boone, tipping her head back to look up at him, conscious of his hands clasped around her bare middle, knowing that he was equally aware of it. She laid her hands on his upper arms as if to push away, then left them there to feel the rock-hardness of his biceps.

"I had forgotten how strong you are," she murmured.

"Funny. I hadn't forgotten how beautiful you are." There was a primitive quality to the look of desire in his dark eyes.

Just for an instant, she pressed herself more fully against him to make certain the feel of her body against his would be imprinted in his mind before she drew back. "I was beginning to wonder," Laura said with a touch of coyness, "considering how long it took you to get here."

"Then you did want me to come," Boone stated, a cocky kind of male confidence flaring in his expression. "On the phone you didn't seem all that excited about seeing me again."

"A woman shouldn't sound eager," she told him. "It wouldn't be proper."

"You don't look all that proper." His glance dropped to the bareness of her middle and the navel that was exposed by her low-riding jeans.

She laughed. "That's because I seldom feel proper around you. Besides, being proper can become boring, and I hate being bored." Turning her back to him, Laura unlooped the reins from around the stallion's neck and stepped to his head, then glanced back at Boone. "Want to walk along while I take The King back to his stall and unsaddle him?"

Boone looked at her with a surprised frown. "Can't someone else put him up?"

"On the Triple C, a rider takes care of his or her own horse. Only guests can get away with passing them off to someone else. It's an ironclad rule that can be broken only in the event of a dire emergency." Laura paused to slant him a provocative glance. "Did you think I had led a pampered life?"

"A woman like you deserves to be pampered."

"Careful," Laura warned lightly. "Some women might mistake a remark like that for a proposal."

"What makes you so certain it isn't?" Boone countered, matching strides with her when she struck out for the stallion barn.

She gave him a considering look. "It might be," Laura conceded. "You do seem to be the impulsive type."

"And you aren't?"

"Oh, I'm definitely impulsive, but never rash."

"There's a difference?"

"Definitely." But Laura didn't bother to explain the distinction, choosing to change the subject instead. "So what do you think of the Triple C?"

"It's quite a spread." It wasn't so much his words as his expression that told Laura he was impressed by what little he had seen.

"I'll take you on a tour of it after I get The King settled in his stall," she said. "And I'll show you the horses that will be up for auction. That is, after all, the reason you're here." Her sideways glance invited him to deny that the horse sale was the main attraction for him.

Boone didn't disappoint her. "It's hardly the only reason."

"That's good to know. By the way," Laura said, making another lightning-fast change of subject, "did Tara pass along the invitation for you and Max to join us for dinner tomorrow evening?"

"She did."

From her bedroom window Laura saw the Land Rover pull up in front of The Homestead. Even before Boone stepped out of the vehicle, she felt that little hum of excitement that came with being confronted with a challenge. She had spent much of the last two days constantly in his company, at his side, but never alone with him. It was part of her plan—to be within reach, yet out of reach.

Briefly Laura toyed with the idea of making an entrance, then rejected it as too dramatic. She paused in front of the mirror and absently ran a smoothing hand over the waistline of her teal-colored dress, then gave her blond hair a push to increase its fullness and exited the room to run lightly down the oak staircase.

As she reached its broad landing, her grandfather's voice reached out to her. "There you are. I was just about to holler upstairs and let you know your guests had arrived." He stood outside the double doors to the den, his aging body tilted to one side as he leaned on the support of his cane. "I thought you might want to be on hand to welcome this Crockett fellow in person."

Laura opened her mouth to correct him, then saw the twinkle in his brown eyes. "Honestly, Gramps, you are as bad as Trey," she admonished with affection and crossed the living room to his side.

"You mean that isn't his name?"

"It's Boone, and you know it. Now hold still. Your tie is crooked." She reached up to center it. "And please try to be on your best behavior tonight. I think he might want to marry me."

Unimpressed, Chase Calder responded with a harrumph. "He certainly isn't the first."

"I know." Laura smoothed the lay of his collar. "But he's the first I might consider accepting."

"Really?" He showed his surprise.

"Yes, really. So, be good."

"I thought you just met him when you were in Europe."

Laura didn't bother to recount the number of times she had seen Boone, first in Rome, then in England and on the Triple C. "Now, Gramps," she reasoned instead, "when have you ever known me to be slow at making up my mind about anything? And just imagine the kind of splash a marriage between the Rutledges of Texas and the Calders of Montana would make."

His gaze narrowed, anger flaring in the wells of his eyes. "I knew it was a mistake to let you spend all that time in Europe with Tara. That's the kind of talk you hear from her."

"But if I hadn't gone, I might never have met Boone," Laura responded.

"Do you love him?" The question bordered on a challenge.

Considering how close she had come to falling in love with Sebastian, Laura didn't consider love to be the most trustworthy of emotions. But she had long ago learned that where women were concerned, her grandfather tended to be idealistic rather than pragmatic.

"Any woman could love Boone, including me." She believed that. More importantly, Laura was confident of her ability to manage him. "Wait until you meet him, Gramps." She hooked an arm around his and directed him toward the entry. "He's one of those big, tall Texans with a potent animal magnetism that can make any girl's heart beat faster."

By Best-selling Author
Fern Michaels

Weekend Warriors	0-8217-7589-8	$6.99US/$9.99CAN
Listen to Your Heart	0-8217-7463-8	$6.99US/$9.99CAN
The Future Scrolls	0-8217-7586-3	$6.99US/$9.99CAN
About Face	0-8217-7020-9	$7.99US/$10.99CAN
Kentucky Sunrise	0-8217-7462-X	$7.99US/$10.99CAN
Kentucky Rich	0-8217-7234-1	$7.99US/$10.99CAN
Kentucky Heat	0-8217-7368-2	$7.99US/$10.99CAN
Plain Jane	0-8217-6927-8	$7.99US/$10.99CAN
Wish List	0-8217-7363-1	$7.50US/$10.50CAN
Yesterday	0-8217-6785-2	$7.50US/$10.50CAN
The Guest List	0-8217-6657-0	$7.50US/$10.50CAN
Finders Keepers	0-8217-7364-X	$7.50US/$10.50CAN
Annie's Rainbow	0-8217-7366-6	$7.50US/$10.50CAN
Dear Emily	0-8217-7316-X	$7.50US/$10.50CAN
Sara's Song	0-8217-7480-8	$7.50US/$10.50CAN
Celebration	0-8217-7434-4	$7.50US/$10.50CAN
Vegas Heat	0-8217-7207-4	$7.50US/$10.50CAN
Vegas Rich	0-8217-7206-6	$7.50US/$10.50CAN
Vegas Sunrise	0-8217-7208-2	$7.50US/$10.50CAN
What You Wish For	0-8217-6828-X	$7.99US/$10.99CAN
Charming Lily	0-8217-7019-5	$7.99US/$10.99CAN

Available Wherever Books Are Sold!